The Dragon Bard

by

Mary Gillgannon

Mary Gillgannon

*To Jim Morrison, for believing in the power of
words and music to change the world.*

ChApteR 1

Off the southern coast of Scotland, 541 C.E.

They were going to drown him.

The grim truth struck Bridei ap Maelgwn as he lay shackled in the filthy bottom of the hide and wicker boat and listened to his Irish captors discussing his fate. They probably didn't realize he knew their language, but in his years as a traveling bard he'd picked up many tongues. The skill seemed pretty useless now. Better if he'd trained as a warrior like his brother Rhun. Then he might have had some chance of escaping when the Brigante chieftain's men dragged him out of the guest lodge and marched him to the coast.

He still didn't know what he'd done to anger Dolgar or why the northern chieftain wanted to be rid of him. It was one thing to sell him to the slavers. Quite another to pay these ruthless men to throw him into the sea once they were away from the coast. For that was surely what they intended. Having heard "how far?" and "don't want him to wash ashore", his heart had begun to hammer in his chest. The feel of the metal shackles on his wrists and ankles was horrible enough, reminding him of the last time he'd been enslaved. But now he knew the purpose of the heavy chains was to make sure he ended up on the bottom of the sea.

He imagined the weighty shackles dragging him down. The cold, choking water filling his lungs. The sea creatures feeding upon him until there was nothing but a still-shackled skeleton in the cold, dark depths.

He fought off the sick horror the images aroused, and tried to think of a way out of his predicament. His only hope was to convince these men he had value to them beyond the price they'd been paid to be rid of him.

Perhaps he could suggest that if they took him south to Gwynedd, his father would pay a substantial sum for his freedom. Although Dolgar had once taunted him that his father cared little whether he lived or died, Bridei felt certain Maelgwn wouldn't want him to be at the mercy of the Irish, the bitterest enemies of his people.

But for the same reason, Bridei knew it was unlikely these men would be willing to venture into the territory patrolled by his father's warriors. These men would likely consider ransoming him to his father a very risky venture. He would have to think of something else.

Maybe the fact that he was a bard would sway them. He'd heard the ability with words was greatly prized by the Irish. They called their bards "filidh" and accorded them as much respect as they would a prince. The thought filled him with sudden hope and he raised his head and shouted out in Irish: "I'm a bard! Let me go, or face the wrath of the gods! If you kill me, it will be a much greater evil than killing a warrior. Are you willing to live with such an awful deed weighing upon your spirit?"

He could tell the three men were startled by his outburst. As they stared at him, he met each man's gaze in turn, then continued in a voice that rang with confidence: "Consider this, if you keep me alive and unharmed, you can sell me for gold once we reach your land. In addition to my ability with a harp and my gift for telling tales, I can read and write. I would be of value to some chieftain as a scribe. I don't know what Dolgar paid you to be rid of me, but you can likely get tenfold more if you keep me alive."

As the three men continued to gape at him, Bridei began to wonder if they had any idea what he was saying. They might be so backward and uneducated they didn't even understand the notion of the written word. He started to explain, but the man with bad teeth, who he'd heard the others call Lun, glared at him and shouted, "Silence!"

Bridei clamped his lips together. He'd give them a little time to think about his threat. Let their dread of the spirits and the unknown arouse their fear and anxiety.

His captors returned to their rowing and started to talk among themselves. Bridei listened intently.

"It seems a waste of a sound and healthy man who will fetch us a nice pouch of silver," said the youngest of the slavers, a brawny fellow with dark red hair.

"But what about the bargain we made with Dolgar?" Lun responded.

"He warned us our victim was a clever fellow who would try to talk us out of killing him."

"Who cares about Dolgar? The Brigante will never find out what we've done," the red-haired man asserted. He gestured to Bridei. "If we cut out his tongue, he won't be able to tell anyone who he is. Our betrayal will never get back to Dolgar."

Bridei suppressed a gasp of dismay. Death was almost preferable to losing the ability to speak. Words were his gift, the attribute that compensated for all his other lacks. He might not be as tall or brawny as Rhun but he could talk circles around his brother. He might not be able to inspire men into following him into battle like Arthur, but he could bring them to tears with a sad tale or make them laugh with a merry tune. He'd never desired the life of a warrior, even if most people thought it the only choice for a man of noble blood. Instead, he believed as his mother once told him, that to be a bard was to be blessed with magic, a power much greater than prowess with a sword. Words shaped the future, she said, much more than any battle ever would.

"But if he's a bard, cutting out his tongue would make him next to worthless," put in the third man, whose graying hair marked him as the oldest of the bunch.

Lun made a sound of disgust. "He's no bard. No man his age could have learned all the tales necessary to become a *filidh*. And where's his harp?"

Bridei jerked his head up and shouted, "They wouldn't let me bring it! Give me a harp and release my bonds and I'll show you what I can do!"

Lun squeezed past the other two men. Hunkering down in front of Bridei, he pulled a knife from his belt and held the weapon to Bridei's throat. He smiled, showing brown, rotted teeth, and his stinking breath filled Bridei's nostrils. "You're no bard, but a spoiled, arrogant prince. The son of the great Dragon, Dolgar said you are."

"Aye, I'm Maelgwn the Great's son. All the more reason to let me go. You know my father will pay handsomely for my return."

"Will he now?" the slaver sneered. "And what makes you think I want his gold?"

The knot of fear in Bridei's stomach tightened as the Irishman pressed his knife against his throat. The Irishman barred his ruined teeth like a snarling wolf. "Your father killed my brother. 'Twould be only fitting if I did the same to you."

Bridei could see the irony of his situation—that he should die at the hands of one of his father's enemies. Perhaps he should tell this man that Maelgwn had no love for him and wouldn't be particularly grieved to hear of his death. But he doubted his captor would believe him.

Nay, he must think of some other way to keep the Irishman from cutting his throat. No argument he'd set out so far had convinced the slavers. These were hardened, desperate men, who risked their lives every time they went to sea. What would possibly persuade them?

Bridei gazed into the scarred, weathered face of his captor and beseeched the gods for inspiration. All at once it came to him. He drew back from the blade as much as possible and spoke in his most powerful voice. "If you've heard of my father, you must also have heard of my mother, Queen Rhiannon. She's a sorceress and she has taught me of some of her magic."

"Magic?" Lun sneered. "What sort of magic?"

Bridei made his voice thunderous. "Hear me now. I call upon Taranis the Thunderer to bring a storm that will fill the sky with lightning and make the rain pour down and fill your boat. I call upon the hag Cailleach to send the wind to churn the water into a seething whirlpool. I call upon the god of the sea, who you call Llyr, to send great waves to overwhelm this vessel and send it to the bottom of the ocean. Then, the goddess Rhiannon, the dark lady of death, will gather together your souls and carry them away on her white horse to the twilight realm of the Other Side. Your spirits will dwell there for all eternity, trapped forever between worlds and never able to find peace!"

The Irishman shrank away, his eyes wide with dread. Bridei got to a sitting position, then awkwardly stood. The boat swayed beneath his feet, nearly pitching him over, but at least he'd put a little distance between himself and the knife. He closed his eyes and stretched out his arms in supplication. *Let them believe me*, he thought, sending a silent petition to whatever gods might listen. *Heed my plea. Don't let them kill me.*

As he stood there—the weight of the shackles dragging at his shoulders as he struggled for balance on the pitching boat—he felt a little foolish. Of all the things his mother had taught him, calling down curses wasn't one of them. And the idea that she was a sorceress was only a tale spread by the priests who resented her influence over his father. But these men couldn't know that. The gods willing, he might have at least bought himself a little time. Time to reason with them and make them see it was to their benefit to keep him alive.

Bridei opened his eyes as the sea grew rougher. All three Irishmen were staring at him, their mouths agape. The wind shifted and a gust of cold, damp air struck him from behind. At the same time, a wave caught the boat. The vessel floated upwards, then crashed down. Bridei landed hard in the bottom of the boat, icy sea water splashing over him. When he lifted his head, he saw the slavers lashing themselves to the sides of the vessel. They were muttering what sounded like curses, or maybe they were praying. Bridei raised his head higher and saw the sky had turned an ugly gray-green color. Huge, white-tipped waves swirled around the boat, foaming in angry ferocity. *By the wheel of the heavens, what have I done! I didn't really mean to summon a storm!*

His stomach began to roil and churn like the sea around them. He sank into the bottom of the boat, which reeked of fish, saltwater and leather. The vessel continued to rise and fall in a sickening rhythm. Bridei's stomach convulsed and he struggled not to vomit.

* * *

The storm raged, a tumult of cold, lashing rain, brutal wind and heaving waves. Bridei was aware of little, his consciousness sucked down into the maelstrom of his own misery. But gradually the boat no longer pitched and tossed like a piece of driftwood caught in the rapids of a mountain stream. He willed himself to raise his head. Two of the Irishmen were using hide buckets to bail seawater. Lun—the one who'd threatened Bridei with the knife—scanned the sky, as if trying to determine how far the storm had blown them off course.

Bridei wondered the same thing as he imagined them floating helplessly past Eire and disappearing into the realm of sea monsters and other fateful dangers at edge of the earth. He shivered, half from dread and half from the cold seeping through his rain-soaked tunic. Had he truly summoned the storm gods? It hardly seemed possible.

One of the slavers noticed he'd roused. The man's blue eyes went wide and he made a sign in the air, an ancient symbol against evil. Then he called out to his companions: "Lun. Colla." He pointed to Bridei. As the three men watched him warily, Bridei considered his precarious situation. If the slavers decided his presence in the boat was a bad omen, they might yet throw him overboard. He must encourage them to keep him alive. "If you get me safely to land," he said, "I vow I will call off the curse."

The Irishmen exchanged looks, then returned to bailing out the boat. Bridei slumped down again, pressing his face against the hard timber frame of the vessel. Most of the nausea had passed, but he still felt utterly drained.

* * *

When he woke it was night, and the sky was a dark blue ocean netted with tiny silver stars. The Irishmen had apparently decided what direction their homeland lay and were rowing hard to reach it. Bridei's anxiety had eased, but he couldn't altogether relax. Until he reached solid ground, he wouldn't feel safe.

The men rowed all night, making Bridei marvel at their stamina. He dozed off again and when he woke a greenish land mass was visible in the distance. As the shore drew near, Bridei sat up and gazed at it with curiosity. He'd always heard Eire was a realm of treacherous, rocky coasts and gloomy mists. Instead, he observed softly rounded hills rising above the shoreline. The grass covering the hills was the most vivid green he'd ever seen.

As the boat neared land, Lun and the two other men climbed out. Wading into the surf, they guided the vessel in. The currach came to rest on the beach below an outcrop of rocks. Bridei got shakily to his feet and attempted to climb over the side. With his wrists and ankles shackled, he had to tumble himself over the edge. He landed on the wet sand and struggled to stand. By the time he got to his feet, he sensed something was wrong. The slavers were talking in low, nervous voices. He caught the words "ill luck".

A moment later, he observed the cause of their dismay. Two men were coming down a pathway through the rocks. The men were garbed in green and gold patterned trews, leather jerkins and linen tunics. Long swords hung from their belts and they carried round, wooden shields decorated with bronze strips and bright colors. They moved briskly, with the intensity of men with a purpose.

As the warriors came closer, the slavers began frantically pushing the boat back into the water. Bridei tried to decide what to do. Should he throw in with the slavers, who he knew he could intimidate, or take his chances with the approaching warriors? The fierce expression on their faces alarmed Bridei. What if they thought he was one of the slavers and decided to attack? Then he remembered his shackles. As the men drew near, he raised his manacled wrists and called out in Irish, "May the gods bless you for rescuing me. I was taken captive and brought here against my will."

The two warriors didn't respond, but swept by him with their weapons drawn. They raced down the beach and into the water, shouting insults at the departing slavers. "Thieving dogs!" and "Cowardly wretches!" were some of the words Bridei was able to make out, although the speech of these men was even more heavily accented than Lun and his companions.

When the slavers' boat was only a dark spot among the gray and white swells, the warriors gave up their harassment of the departing men and returned to where Bridei stood. They resheathed their weapons, but continued to regard him with suspicion. He smiled pleasantly and said, "Bless you for rescuing me from those foul, worthless wretches. I feared for my life at their hands."

The men's dour expressions didn't relent. The taller warrior—who had a long auburn mustache and pale blue-green eyes—grabbed Bridei by the arm and shoved him toward the pathway up the rocky slope.

"Where are you taking me?" Bridei asked.

When the man didn't answer, Bridei jerked away and tried to assume a dignified pose. "Despite the chains I wear, I'm not a slave. My father is Maelgwn the Great, king of Gwynedd. I was taken captive by one of his enemies and sold into slavery. If you can find a way to return me to my homeland, you'll be rewarded handsomely."

The auburn-haired man gazed at him with skepticism, and Bridei realized how disheveled and filthy he must appear. He could hardly blame these men for not believing he was a prince. Both of them seemed very young, perhaps less than twenty winters. The smaller man had lighter red hair and fair skin covered with freckles.

The auburn-haired fellow grunted and gave Bridei another shove along the pathway.

Bridei continued to resist. Glaring at the man, he said, "Tell me where you're taking me."

The auburn-haired man looked at his companion and muttered something indecipherable. Bridei began to wonder if they understood him. Among the British tribes there was a great variation in the way words were pronounced. It might be the same here. Speaking in slow, careful tones, he repeated, "I refuse to go any farther until you tell me where you're taking me."

The man unsheathed his sword and jerked his head toward the pathway. The message in his eyes was clear: *If you wish to remain alive, you will obey.*

Bridei reluctantly started up the hillside. Typical warriors. They refused to think for themselves but followed orders blindly. He hoped their chieftain was less bull-headed.

As they reached the top of the cliff and moved inland, Bridei's gaze took in harvested fields bounded by stone walls and jewel green pastures dotted with black cattle and cream-colored sheep. A fertile, prosperous land. No wonder the warriors who guarded it were so aggressive and hostile. They must fear attack at all times.

This thought was confirmed when he saw a fortress in the distance. A large ring fort sat on the crest of a hill, its stonework glinting silvery white. A formidable stronghold, and likely the residence of the chieftain who ruled over this territory. Bridei wondered what sort of man he was. Would he be able to bargain with him and negotiate his freedom?

As he walked, Bridei marveled at the soft kiss of the balmy air and vividness of the vegetation. It was well past the fullness of the harvest moon, yet this place still retained the mellowness of summer. In his homeland, autumn could be dazzling, as the trees and bushes turned red, gold and bronze, the berries ripened and the last stands of flowers gleamed purple, white and gold among the dull bronze of bracken and fern. But all too soon the meadows faded, the forests lost their glorious color and the sullen gray skies brought rain and sleet. It surprised him that Eire, a place of which he had heard such dark, forbidding tales, could appear so welcoming and lovely this late in the year.

His curiosity grew until he couldn't help questioning his closemouthed captors once again. "What tribe are you from?" he asked. "What's the name of your chieftain? At least tell me the name of the man who will decide my fate." When they still didn't answer, Bridei made his voice pleading. "Think how you would feel if you were cast ashore in a strange land and had no idea what was to become of you."

At last, the auburn-haired man stopped and fixed him with a stony gaze. "Our leader isn't a man, but a woman, Queen Dessia."

Bridei was startled. No women wielded such power in Britain, although he'd heard things were different before the Romans came. His next reaction was delight. His mind began to whirl with plans of how he would beguile this Queen Dessia. He'd compose a tale extolling her greatness, her kindness and beauty. Then he would ask her to put him on a boat back to Britain, his passage to be paid when he arrived.

Perhaps fortune had smiled upon him when the slavers' boat was carried off course and landed in this place. He thought again of the storm. Had he caused it? And if he had, did that mean the gods had planned for him to come aground on Eire in the kingdom of Queen Dessia?

A tingle of foreboding moved down his spine. Dolgar had sold him to the slavers so they could murder him, and they would have done so if he hadn't cursed them using the most potent forces he could conjure. Bridei recalled the moment he spoke the names of the gods, the strange sensation he'd experienced, as if some energy moved through him. Was that the power of the deities? It was rather unsettling to think about. Better to attribute his rescue to simple good luck.

For that matter, he still didn't know that everything was going to work out to his satisfaction. Queen Dessia might ignore his protests and make him a slave. The feel of the chains on his wrists and ankles reminded Bridei of how trapped and helpless he was. What if Queen Dessia refused to listen to him? He tried again to question his captors. "What sort of woman is Queen Dessia? Her lands appear very fertile and rich. How does she keep them safe?"

The auburn-haired man stared at him. Then a faint smile formed on his lips beneath the heavy mustache. "The queen is a sorceress. She uses magic to fend off her enemies."

Bridei suppressed a laugh. Perhaps this Queen Dessia possessed some wit and cleverness after all. He wondered how she maintained the ruse, what tricks she used to convince her subjects—and her enemies—of her power. "What sort of magic?" he asked. "Have either of you ever seen her work a spell?"

"Nay," the younger warrior answered. "She does her conjuring alone in her tower."

"Then how do you know her powers are real?"

The young warrior spoke patiently, as if explaining something to a child. "Of course her powers are real. Otherwise, Cahermara would have been overrun by our enemies long ago."

He had a point, Bridei thought as he glanced around at the peaceful landscape of farmsteads, pastures and harvested fields.

A few moments later, Bridei spied the tower the man had mentioned. In the center of the circular fortress, a large stone column rose several dozen cubits above the rest of stronghold. Bridei had seen similar high, round structures in the lands north of the Brigantes, although none of them had been surrounded by fortifications. He saw a small, narrow window in the highest part of the tower. From that vantage point Queen Dessia would be able to survey her kingdom and keep watch for any enemy attack. But these men hadn't spoken of her keeping watch in the tower, but working magic. Was she truly a sorceress?

Bridei considered the witchwomen he knew: His mother, although that was more rumor than truth. Morguese, his cousin and Arthur's half-sister. He could almost believe Morguese was able to see the future and perhaps even do a few things to influence it. But she obviously hadn't possessed the ability to work a spell of protection. Her son, Mordred, had died at the battle of Camboglanna, despite all her efforts to keep him safe.

Thinking of magic, Bridei was again reminded of the storm. He still experienced a sense of awe when he recalled what had happened. Was it possible he had powers he'd never guessed at? What if the tales of his mother's sorcery were more than tales? What if she possessed magical abilities and had passed them on to him?

The thought intrigued him, but he remained wary. All his instincts told him sorcery was dangerous, especially when used by someone completely untrained, as he was. When he returned to Gwynedd, he would have to visit his mother and ask about these things. By the gods, he missed her. It had been near ten years since he'd looked upon her face.

He pushed the thought from his mind and focused on his surroundings. The overgrown earthworks of the fortress had obviously been constructed some seasons ago, but a section of the stone wall remained unfinished. This was a relatively new dun, which made the story of Queen Dessia's "spell of protection" even more interesting.

Bridei glanced up at the tower. Was she watching from that hawk-like vantage point even now? Did she already know of his arrival? Thinking of his disheveled condition, he turned to his captors. "I would like to wash before I meet your queen, as a courtesy to her."

The auburn-haired man grunted his assent.

Chapter 2

They had a visitor. Dessia stared out the window of the tower facing into the hillfort. Keenan had come up a short while ago and made the announcement. The man wore iron shackles, Keenan said, but he didn't look like most of the miserable wretches brought ashore by the slavers. This man held his head high, and was even now washing at the cistern.

She could see the captive now. He'd stripped off his tunic and was dousing his head and upper body with water. He had a long, lean torso, with broad shoulders and well-defined muscles. His shoulder-length hair was as black as raven feathers. Gazing at him, a strange sense came over Dessia. She felt like she knew this man, yet she couldn't imagine where they might have met. Perhaps it had been when she was a child, when her parents were alive and the old Cahermara a bustling fortress. But nay, this man was young. If she were a child, then he would also have been a child.

Dessia chewed her lower lip, wondering why the look of him aroused such a strong feeling of familiarity. He was a foreigner, certainly. The leather trews he wore, the blue tunic he was now rinsing out in the cistern—neither garment looked like something belonging to a man of her people. And Keenan had mentioned the visitor had been brought in wearing heavy shackles. Clearly, his captors had considered him dangerous. Perhaps he was. Observing his graceful movements, she sensed he would wield a sword with strength and quickness.

The thought made Dessia uneasy and she moved away from the window. Perhaps she'd made a mistake when she told Keenan to have Scanlan and Flann remove the man's fetters. But she hated the slavers and was eager to be rid of any sign of them. They raided the coasts of foreign lands, stealing their victims away from their homes and forcing them into cruel servitude. Usually their captives were women and children, helpless to defend themselves.

She moved back to the window. How had this strong, apparently healthy young man been taken by the slavers? She saw no marks of violence upon him. He was still leaning over the cistern, rinsing out his tunic, and she could see that the skin of his back was smooth and unblemished, with fine, sleek muscles beneath.

Once again, she forced herself away from the window. Her wits must be addled. It was absurd for her to regard this man with such keen interest. She would listen to his tale and send him on his way.

A moment later, she was back at the window. Keenan had said something about the visitor claiming to be the son of a British king. She could imagine that possibility. Although the man wore no torc or other ornaments, the slavers would have stolen such things. His tunic was richly colored and no crude warrior or farmer would make such an effort to clean himself. But if he was a prince, how in the world had he ended up in the hands of the slavers?

Dessia chewed her lower lip. What a puzzle this man was. The sense she'd seen him before gnawed at her. Whenever she looked at him, her body seemed to tingle with warning. She'd felt this way only one time previously—the day her mother and father were killed and Cahermara burned to the ground. All these years later, she was convinced it could only be magic that allowed her to survive. There must some sort of force guiding her life. She could feel it. Yet, so far, she'd never been able to control the mystical power that seemed to surround her.

Not that she hadn't tried. She glanced at her scrying bowl, resting on a table littered with copper bowls, manuscripts, stone jars and dried herbs. How often had she stared at the gleaming surface of the oil in the scrying bowl, seeking a vision? How often had she perused the ancient manuscripts, seeking out the ingredients and procedures necessary to work a spell of protection? She'd encountered hints and tidbits of information, but nothing she could really use. As for the scrying bowl, it remained empty and dark. The few times she'd thought she'd caught glimpse of something, it had turned out to be her own wretched face staring back at her. She was a fraud. No charm or spell she evoked had ever done anything. Yet she kept trying. The power she sought seemed so tantalizing near. If only she could find a way to access it. Find the right words to chant, the proper combination of ingredients.

Fortunately, no one guessed at her failure. The tale that she was capable of great sorcery had worked wonderfully to keep her enemies at bay. If not for her reputation, Tiernan O'Bannon would have long ago stormed Cahermara, taken her captive and forced her into marriage so he could claim her lands for his own. Her skin crawled at the thought of her greedy neighbor and her heart felt like a stone dropped into an icy mountain pool when she considered losing her lands, all that remained of the heritage of the once proud Fionnlairaos.

She clenched her hands in anguish at the thought, then deliberately relaxed them. Worrying over these things wouldn't help her. She had to be patient, to keep trying to unlock the secrets of the unseen forces around her. In the meantime, she used more traditional means to guard her lands. Her men constantly patrolled the area around Cahermara, and eventually stout stone walls would encircle all of the rath, creating a formidable barrier.

If only the walls were finished. Their construction seemed to progress with painful slowness. She needed more men to do the work, but she couldn't spare any warriors for the task, and the youth of her people were needed for farming, herding and fishing to ensure they had enough food to eat. But it was so frustrating to wait. So hard to be patient. She wrapped her arms around her body. The feeling of foreboding grew stronger. *Something is happening*, her instincts seemed to say.

Dessia shivered, then returned to the window. She could no longer see the visitor. He must be on his way to the hall. Keenan had said he would bring him shortly.

The thought aroused Dessia to frantic activity. Why had she spent the last few moments contemplating the past instead of preparing for the future?

She strode to the door and called down the stairs for Aife. When the maidservant entered, Dessia was waiting in her shift. "I need you to help me dress and comb out my hair. We have a visitor."

Aife assisted Dessia in putting on a fresh gown and fastening a gold and green enamel belt around her waist. Then Dessia seated herself on a tall stool and the maidservant began combing Dessia's hip-length tresses. "What sort of visitor?" the maidservant asked. "A trader?"

"Nay, not a trader. A foreign man captured by slavers. Keenan and Flann ran the slavers off, then brought the man here."

Aife stopped combing, her slender hands poised over the dark red strands. "You're having me fix your hair so you can meet a slave?"

"Of course he's not a slave." Dessia motioned that Aife should resume combing. "The visitor appears to be well-born. Even if he were not, I have no desire for him to return to his homeland thinking the people of Eire are crude savages."

"Certainly not," Aife responded.

"Besides, as queen, I must always present an image of power and authority. You never know what might get back to my enemies. Any sign of weakness would bring them down upon me like a pack of wolves on an unprotected flock." Dessia wondered if Aife saw through to the truth— that having observed how attractive the visitor was, pure female pride made her want to greet him looking her best.

"You think this man is a spy?" Aife asked.

"He could be. I'll know more after I meet him." The thought hadn't really occurred to her until Aife mentioned it, but now Dessia considered the matter, it was a possibility. What if O'Bannon or some other chieftain had hired this man to discover if her magical abilities were real?

Her heartbeat quickened. She must be very careful of this visitor.

Aife arranged a circlet on Dessia's head and placed the matching gold and emerald torc around her neck. Still feeling nervous, Dessia made her way down the stairs to the feast hall.

The large round chamber was empty except for a serving woman tending the main hearth. Climbing the low platform at the end of the hall, Dessia quickly took a seat in the massive carved oaken chair where her father had once sat. It was one of the few things she'd been able to salvage from the ruins of the original fortress. She smoothed her green linen gown, decorated with red and yellow braiding, and straightened her spine.

A short while later, Keenan entered, the raven-haired man following behind him. At last Dessia could see the visitor's face, and it was as fine and comely as she'd expected. He wore only the hint of a beard, a dusky down outlining the square shape of his jaw. His nose was straight and narrow, his mouth, full and sensual. And his eyes—by the gods, it seemed unfair that a man should possess such amazing violet blue eyes, surrounded by thick black lashes!

Shaking off such thoughts, Dessia forced herself to meet the visitor's gaze. "Who are you?" she asked.

The man bowed low, then straightened, his movement as graceful as a cat's. His dazzling eyes glinted with warmth. "I'm Bridei ap Maelgwn, lately of Britain, although I have lived many places." He paused and a slight smile touched his well-formed lips. Then he continued in his rich, vibrant voice, "I play the harp and musical pipe. I compose poems, sing songs and recite a hundred different tales. I can write Latin and a little Greek, decipher runes and tally accounts. I would be a most useful and entertaining addition to your household, Queen Dessia. In exchange for my services I would ask only that you provide me with a small chamber of my own, food and drink such as you give your warriors, and the freedom to come and go as I please."

As he finished his speech, Bridei felt rather startled by what he'd just said. He'd intended to entreat Queen Dessia to help him return to Britain. But somehow, at the last moment, different words had formed on his tongue. Why had he offered to serve her? Had she put some sort of spell on him? Or was it simply a response to her remarkable beauty? For Queen Dessia was stunning. Masses of dark red hair cloaked her tall, voluptuous form. Her face was a pale, delicate oval, set with gleaming jewel-green eyes and a coral mouth. She was a goddess. As bold and magnificent as Epona, lady of horses. As radiant as Arianrhod, queen of the moon and stars. Merely looking at her made Bridei's loins grow tight.

But he'd encountered beautiful women before and never been so profoundly affected. This woman stirred not only his body, but his spirit. Being in her presence brought all his senses to life, forcing him react with true emotion, instead of the cynical detachment with which he usually regarded the world. It was unsettling. Unnerving. But he had no intention of enduring the situation for long. He would beguile her and make her seek do his will rather than the other way around.

At the same time, he told himself that there really was no reason why he shouldn't remain here over the winter. There was nothing left for him in Britain. Nothing except the darkness and confusion that Arthur's death would have wrought. He was well out of it. Well out.

He repeated the phrase in his mind as he waited for her response.

She shifted her body, then licked her lips, a gesture of stunning eroticism. At last, she said, "You appear far too young to possess the skills you boast of. And you haven't told me how you came to be here. My man, Keenan..." She motioned to the warrior who'd escorted him there, making Bridei feel a sudden surge of jealousy. "He says you were wearing slave chains when he found you. How came you to be captured by those loathsome men? Where is your family? Your clan? Why would you offer your services to a stranger?" Her green eyes narrowed. "You've been brought to Eire against your will. Why would you choose to stay here rather than returning to your homeland?"

Good questions, all of them. Bridei felt a surge of admiration. Queen Dessia's mind was keen as her beauty. She might be young, but she wasn't naïve. Life had tempered this woman, as heat strengthens a sword blade. He remembered the tale the one warrior had told him, of how the rest of the queen's family had been killed when she was a child. All at once, he knew exactly how to win her sympathy.

He made his expression sorrowful. "If you haven't heard, there was a great battle in my homeland last summer. Our brave, valiant leader, Arthur ap Uther, was defeated and killed by the Saxons. Fighting at his side was my older brother Rhun." He hung his head dramatically. "I'm still mourning my loss. While the remainder of my family yet live in the mountain kingdom of Gwynedd, I haven't the heart to visit them. I can't bear to look upon my father's face and tell him that his eldest son is dead."

He slowly raised his gaze and assessed the effect of his words. She looked stricken, as if he had been speaking of her family rather than his own. Pain creased her fair brow and her mouth trembled. He quickly bent his head again, repressing a smile of satisfaction. For a moment, he had been unsettled, but now he was back to usual self. The perfect tale to melt this lady's heart had sprung effortlessly to his lips. Now he had only to move in for the kill.

He waited a moment, then sighed deeply and once more looked into her eyes. "Call me a coward, if you will, but I am weary of the war and fighting that has torn apart my homeland. I seek a place of refuge, and this lovely bit of land, bordered by the wild sea, warmed by a gentle sun and blessed with soft, sweet rain, seems the perfect place to mend my spirits."

He had her, there was no doubt of it. A sheen of tears glazed her green eyes, reminding him of sunlight shining upon a still forest pool. She looked so tender and sweet... and young. He could see the wounded girl she'd been, only partially hidden beneath the trappings of the proud queen. She could still weep over loss and injustice. Her spirit had not formed the tough, impenetrable shell that his had.

He made himself smile, a wan, weary smile. In a moment, she would agree to let him stay in her household. Then he need only offer a few more soulful looks and touching tales and she would eagerly welcome him into her bed.

But even as he considered the splendor of this prize, he couldn't help wondering what he had done—offering up his freedom, his independence, to serve this exquisite young queen. He glanced down at his hands and saw the pale reddish lines marking the place where the iron fetters had encircled his wrists. Those shackles were gone, but it felt as if they had been replaced by other invisible and yet more powerful bonds.

Chapter 3

Oh, this Bridei ap Maelgwn was a clever one. Dessia exhaled deeply and sought to compose herself. He knew exactly what to say to bring to mind her own bone-deep grief. But the very fact he played upon her emotions so skillfully made her suspicious. Why should he come here and seek a place in her household? Was he a spy for Tiernan or one of her other enemies? The thought sent a tremor of foreboding down her spine. Her hold upon her Cahermara was so tenuous.

If he was a spy, it might be wise to keep him close. That way she could control what he saw and heard. For a moment, she contemplated what it would be like to have this man in her household, entertaining them during the long winter nights. That deep, throbbing voice filling the hall. His presence like that of a beautiful wild beast, arousing her fascination. There was no denying a part of her was loath to have him gone.

Which was why he was so dangerous. He was the most compelling man she'd ever encountered. As her resolve wavered, she knew a sense of disquiet. Perhaps she should call together her warriors and ask for their advice. But to do so seemed weak and indecisive. No man would seek out his advisors in this circumstance. A man would send Bridei ap Maelgwn away without hesitation. She should do the same.

But if she sent him away, she would never solve the mystery of why he was here. If he was a spy, she would never learn who he was spying for.

She met his gaze, wondering what secrets those midnight blue eyes concealed. All her life, she'd survived by obeying an inner sense that alerted her to danger. But now that voice was silent. This man made her skin tingle and her heart race, but no sense of alarm or urge to flee came over her.

She raised her gaze to peruse the dark-haired stranger. Was he truly a bard? He looked like no *filidh* she'd ever seen. Or was he some supernatural being, come in disguise? The old tales told of heroes and gods who appeared in the guise of swans, salmon, ravens or deer. If a being could shapeshift into an animal, then perhaps this man could transform himself in more subtle ways.

Indeed, as she looked at him, the room behind him altered and she saw a great, cavernous hall. Hanging on the wall behind him was a crimson banner emblazoned with a gold dragon. A wind blew through the hall and the banner shifted and wavered, making the golden beast seem to spring to life.The image faded and Dessia took a deep, steadying breath. Was it a vision? Her first Seeing? She'd spent countless hours staring into the scrying bowl and discovered nothing. Why would such a thing come to her now?

You must decide. He is waiting.

The sound of hammering pierced her awareness and reminded her of her need for workmen to build the fortress wall. A plan began to form in her mind. She wouldn't send this man away. But neither could she risk having him close by in her household. She would tell him that if he wanted to stay, he must serve her as fitted her purposes. Not as a bard, but a laborer.

She almost winced, imagining his slim fingers clutching a hammer. His long, graceful back bent over a pile of rocks. That smooth skin begrimed with dust. But then she hardened herself against such thoughts. He'd offered to serve her, and she needed workmen. If he found the situation demeaning, he could leave and seek a place elsewhere.

She met his relentless gaze. "I've decided. You're welcome to remain here, but not as bard and entertainer. I've no need of such services. What I lack are men to help rebuild the fortress. If you're willing to swing a hammer and carry heavy stones, I can offer you a place in my household. Otherwise, my men will escort you from my lands."

She saw his eyes widen, then a surge of anger darkened their vivid blue depths. He reminded her of an imperious raven with its feathers ruffled, or a cat hissing when displaced from its cozy spot by the hearth. A heartbeat later, all trace of animosity vanished from his face. His full sensual mouth quirked in a rueful smile. "I can't see I would be much use to you for such purposes. Surely there are bigger and stronger men in your household more suited to that kind of labor."

She smiled back tightly. "Aye, I have such men in my household, but they are occupied in guarding my lands. It was those men who rescued you. Otherwise, you would be on your way to the slave market of Ath Cliath at this very moment."

Bridei struggled to conceal his displeasure. Queen Dessia's last words seemed to carry a warning, reminding him his freedom was dependent on her pleasure. He should refuse her request and bid her farewell. Now that he was free of the slavers, he could go wherever he wished. He could explore the rest of the isle or return to Britain.

But since he possessed no coin or anything else of worth, traveling around this foreign land wouldn't be easy. He might once more fall victim to unscrupulous men. The thought of being forced to wear shackles again made his blood run cold.

Or, he could stay here and pretend to accept the bargain that was offered. Over time, he would find a way to improve his circumstances and get what he wished

He glanced again at the queen, his gaze lingering on her heart-stopping loveliness. Queen Dessia might pretend to be a cool, calculating leader, but underneath that haughty facade was a woman. And it had been a very long time since he'd met a woman he couldn't beguile.

His confidence returned. He would persuade Queen Dessia he could be of use to her in other ways than as a crude laborer. Indeed, there was no reason not to make another attempt now. He took a deep breath and began to sing. The song poured out of him easily. A witty tale. It appeared at first to be a love song, a man lamenting the death of his lady. He describes her beauty, her loyal heart, her sweet nature. Then the tale shifts so it seems as if the object of the song is another warrior. The words extol the valiant heart, bravery and loyalty of the beloved one, the battles the two shared together and numerous times they saved each others' lives. Only at the end, as the refrain praises the loved one's "clear, fine eyes" and "grace and swiftness, like the hind racing through the woods" does it become clear that the song is about a man's favorite hound.

Bridei watched the auburn-haired queen as she listened. He could tell she was impressed with his voice, and caught up in the theme of the tale, grief over the loss of a loved one. At the end, when she laughed as she realized the true subject of the song, he had to struggle not to reveal his sense of triumph.

But his satisfaction was short-lived, for after one quick outburst of mirth, her expression grew grim and determined once more. "You're very skilled," she said, "But that doesn't change the fact that it serves no purpose for you to amuse me if my fortress remains unfinished and my kingdom in peril. My offer remains the same. Serve me as fits my needs, or don't serve me at all."

She crossed her arms for emphasis, tantalizing Bridei with the swelling curve of her full breasts beneath the thin linen gown. Her response both irritated and surprised him. Was she immune to his appeal? Had she cut herself off from her womanly feelings for so long that her heart had grown cold and that magnificent body unresponsive?

Impossible. This woman was too young to live as a crone the rest of her days. Her face and form were sensual in the extreme. Her vibrant hair and brilliant eyes glowed with the fire of a passionate nature.

Perhaps she'd already given her heart to another. Some women weren't susceptible to him because they were already in love with someone else. His brother's woman, Eastra, had been like that. He'd been able to win Eastra's admiration, but never touch her heart. But if Queen Dessia had a lover, where was he? Dead? Had this lovely queen lost her sweetheart? Was that the source of the sadness that haunted her exquisite countenance?

To find out, he would have to spend time with her, and once she set him to work as a laborer, it might be days before he saw her again. He couldn't give up yet. He must try one more time to convince her he had worth beyond her need for workers.

"You haven't heard me play a harp," he said. "If you fetch one, I'll show you what I can do. I vow that with such accompaniment I can near match the goddess Rhiannon's gifts... and she was said to be able to charm the birds out of the trees with her music."

"A harp?" She cocked one auburn brow mockingly. "Where do you propose I get a harp?"

"Surely... somewhere in your kingdom..."

Her mouth quirked bitterly. "Long ago my enemies robbed us of all such luxury items."

"You hardly seem poor." He motioned to the gold circlet binding her hair, the stunning torc at her neck.

Her expression grew taut. "If not for the treasure my father saw fit to bury before our enemies overran us, I would have nothing. But a bard's harp was not among the objects spared. And since our vile attackers killed my family and destroyed my home, bringing music and poetry back into the hall has been the least of my concerns."

He must try another approach, find another way to demonstrate her need for his abilities. Bowing his head, he said, "You've endured a great tragedy. All the more reason you need a bard. I could compose a song paying tribute to your family. With my words I would keep their memory alive and make certain your people never forget what they've endured. I could tell the tale of how you survived." He gazed at her intently. "How you have boldly rebuilt your home and reestablished the rule of your line. There's great power in words. I can give you and your family a kind of immortality. Having heard the tale I will tell of your despair, your defeat and your kingdom's rebirth, no one will ever forget it."

Already the story was taking shape in his thoughts, his mind working away at how he would use the pain of Queen Dessia's past to create to song that would touch all who heard it. Perhaps this was why he had been sent here, borne upon the fierce wind of the storm to this isolated realm. Here he had found a subject worthy of his talents. A beauteous queen, the victim of cruelty and slaughter. But one who rose triumphant from the ruins, like the magical bird called the Phoenix in the tale told by the Greek bard in Narbonne.

Caught up as he was in the glorious potential of the story, he was unprepared for Queen Dessia's response. She rose to her feet, her expression so full of fury, he was startled. "I don't need to be told what I've lost, bard," she said in a low, throaty voice. "Or praised for how hard I've worked and struggled to overcome the blow my enemies dealt me. What I need is strong hands to carry stones to rebuild the walls of Cahermara. It's protection from my enemies I require, not cruel reminders of what they've taken from me!"

She climbed down from the platform where her chair was situated and swept past him. The swiftness of her movements stirred the air of the hall, leaving behind the faint scent of herbs and the provocative odor of her body. He breathed it in, recognizing the sweetness of female skin overlaid with a hint of perspiration. Not the sweat of labor, but emotion. Anger, pain and fear made up the heady brew filling his senses.

He felt stunned, and more intrigued than ever. This woman possessed many mysteries. Mysteries that aroused his mind and loins with equal intensity. He had no intention of leaving now, not until he'd fully explored Queen Dessia's enigmatic thoughts... and the provocative curves of her lush body.

* * *

Dessia lay on her bed and tried to relax. Her heart still pounded, forcing the blood through her veins as fiercely a spring flood surging down a mountain glen to the sea. What was wrong with her? What had this man done to her? It was madness to allow him to remain at Cahermara. By the gods, the effect he had on her was terrifying. She sat up, her muscles taut as iron, her breathing shallow and rapid.

"My lady, are you ill? Can I bring something to soothe you?"

Dessia turned to see Aife watching her with a worried expression in her blue eyes.

"I'm... well enough." Dessia lay down again, thinking of the great crest of emotion that had washed over her when the man offered to compose a tale about her family. His words had brought all the horror of it rushing back, as fresh and bitter as if it had happened yesterday. For a moment, she'd feared she would break down and weep in front of him. Curse him! How had he guessed at the raw wound inside her?

She let out her breath in a sigh. He was a clever man. A bard who used words as a skilled warrior uses his sword. *And you have just offered him a place here.*

The thought made her get up from the bed and go to the window. How could she have been so foolish? Even if Bridei ap Maelgwn remained on the other side of the rath breaking rocks, that was still far too close. She should send someone after him right now and tell him she'd changed her mind. Have her men escort the visitor off her lands and warn him not to return.

But how could she justify banishing him? What tale could she tell her people that would make such a response appear reasonable?

She could always say he'd insulted her or made improper suggestions. Indeed, there had been something almost insolent in his manner. The way he looked at her, as if he were imagining how she would appear naked.

But it was hardly enough of an affront to order the man off her lands. There were certain laws of hospitality that must be respected. She'd already behaved quite rudely. To go beyond that was to risk offending the gods. The legends and tales were full of stories of deities testing leaders to see if they behaved in an honorable fashion. What if this man really was a god in disguise?

The thought made Dessia shiver. Bridei ap Maelgwn was comely enough to be a deity. And his strange offer to serve her also reminded her of the old tales . . .

Stop it, she told herself. *He's as human and mortal as you are.* This was ridiculous—worrying that offending him might bring some sort of curse on her household. "Nonsense. Utter nonsense." She repeated the phrase to herself, trying to quell the tremors of unease in her stomach.

* * *

Bridei sat down near the pile of worked stone and wiped his brow. He could feel the eyes of the other workmen on him, but he didn't care. If they commented on his taking a respite, he would say he'd taken on this task of his own free will and therefore could rest when he wished.

They were probably making wagers on how long he would last. As well they might. This was the first time he'd ever done this sort of physical labor—the tedious and exhausting task of crushing rocks to form the mortar for the rath walls, then mixing it with lime, sand and water and stirring it into a paste. At least it was less wearing than carrying and shaping the stones, the task that occupied most of the other men.

Bridei examined his fellow workers. There was the mason, a stout, balding fellow who did none of the lifting or carrying or mixing, but instead directed others, making certain the mortar was the proper consistency, the stones laid evenly and sealed in securely. Every little while, the mason would climb up on the scaffolding and get out a string with weights and assess whether the work was straight and even. Or, he would walk over to where the workmen were shaping rocks and examine several pieces, sometimes dropping them on the ground to gauge their weight and solidity.

The other workers included a man of middle years with a scraggly brown beard and one eye missing, a massive fellow whose blue eyes had a vacant gaze that suggested his wits were not quite right, and three youths whose ragged, plain-woven garments and uncouth manner suggested they were farmers' sons. Misfits and farmers—those were his companions.

At the thought, Bridei's anger resurfaced. He was no crude laborer Queen Dessia could use as she saw fit! He was descended from a line of kings. He'd been an honored bard and translator for the great warlord Arthur ap Uther. Only a woman would treat him like this, he thought contemptuously. A man would easily see his skills as a poet and musician were much more valuable than the strength of his muscles. A man would place Bridei beside himself in his hall to sing his praises and extol his valor and magnificence as a leader. But Queen Dessia was a woman and so she dismissed him.

Bridei nursed his resentment for awhile, then forced himself to let go of it. He'd learned years before not to let any emotion affect him for long. Men who allowed their feelings to rule their lives usually ended up doing stupid things. He was cleverer than that. He would find a way to get what he wished of Queen Dessia. Someday the proud Queen Dessia would yield, and yield utterly. At the thought, a smile quirked his lips.

But to reach his goal, he must learn more about her. He must press these workmen for information.

The opportunity arose when it began to rain. As the downpour intensified, the workmen sought refuge beneath a shelter made up of several hides stretched over timbers anchored in the ground. Bridei joined them, grateful for the chance to rest and to be able to question his companions. Turning to the big, bald workman, he asked, "How long have you served the queen?"

The man answered in a rough, guttural voice. "All my life."

"What sort of mistress is she? Does she treat you kindly?"

The man shrugged. "She shares what she has with us. Even if she wasn't generous, it wouldn't matter. My father's father's father served her family."

"What of the rest of you?" Bridei's gaze probed each man in turn.

They all answered the same. Their families had served Queen Dessia's family and so they also served her.

Bridei turned back to the bald man and inquired, "How long ago was the queen's family killed?"

The man frowned at him. "Why do you wish to know?"

Clearly, these men were protective of the queen. He would have to earn their trust before he probed deeper. He bowed his head in deference. "Forgive me. I haven't introduced myself. I am Bridei ap Maelgwn of Britain. I was taken captive by a group of slavers and brought to this place."

He motioned to each man in turn and they gave him their names. The balding man was Nally, the one-eyed one, Cori. The slow-witted youth was Eth and the three rough farmers, Birr, Usan and Derry.

Bridei started to ask another question about the queen, but the one-eyed man, Cori, stopped him. "I don't believe you're a slave," he said. "The queen has never used slaves."

Bridei gave Cori a reassuring smile. "You misunderstand me. I said the slavers brought me here. Then Queen Dessia's commander—Keenan, I think his name is—took me to the queen and I chose to serve her."

"Breaking rocks?" Nally snorted.

Bridei smiled. "I'll admit I didn't choose to serve her in this particular way. I'm a bard, a *filidh*. I offered to entertain the queen and fill her hall with laughter and music. She refused." Bridei felt his smile tighten at the thought of the lady's rejection. He shook off the bitterness. These men must not see his resentment. "Since I no longer have a harp nor any possessions of value, I feared it might be dangerous to travel on to the next settlement. Although mixing mortar is not my favored task, at least I know that here I'll be treated decently. It seems Queen Dessia has a care for your comfort and safety." He motioned to the rain, still falling steadily. "Many leaders would insist you work even in foul weather. And they wouldn't think to provide shelter."

The man named Nally nodded. "Aye, the queen has always been concerned for her people, even workers such as us."

Bridei nodded back. "A most considerate and noble woman. And one who has suffered a great deal. Apparently her whole family was killed and her home destroyed?" He looked at the men questioningly.

"That's true." Cori nodded. "Ten years ago, the original fortress was attacked. The rath walls were made of wood back then and the enemy warriors burned the place to the ground. Everyone was killed, except the queen, who was but a girl at the time."

"How did she survive?" Bridei asked.

The workmen seemed to hesitate, then one of the farmers, Usan it was, spoke in a breathless whisper. "She shapeshifted into an animal." He nodded, dark eyes shining. "None can agree on whether it was a raven, a cat or a deer, but there can be no doubt it was some cunning, wary creature. That's how she survived."

Bridei repressed a snort of laughter. While it was intriguing to imagine Queen Dessia—with her jewel-green eyes—as a sleek, elegant cat, he wasn't such a lackwit as to take the story to heart. A tale it was, enhancing her status among her people, a compelling legend to make them hold her in even higher regard. "What happened after that?" he inquired. "How did she wrest her lands from her enemies?"

Another of the gawky youths answered him, Derry this time: "The people sheltered her in the countryside until she was a woman grown. She trained as a warrior all the while, learning the skills of sword, bow and arrow and spear. Then, when the enemy had become lax and unwatchful, she gathered together those warriors left remaining from her father's forces and took back her lands, including this place."

"How long ago was that?"

"Three turns of the seasons," Nally answered. "She decreed the rath must be rebuilt in stone, so it could not be burned. But it's a long, hard task." He gazed wearily at the piles of undressed rocks lying nearby.

"And she can spare few men for the doing. Those who know how to wield weapons are needed to guard her lands. Nor will she take men away from tilling the soil and looking after the herds, lest we all go hungry."

Cori spoke again. "When winter comes, she asks for younger sons to come to the rath and put in a turn at the work. In a few weeks, I expect more to join us. But even with a score of workers, it's slow labor. We can only hope we're able to finish these walls before our enemies fall upon us once again."

"Who are your enemies? What tribes do you fear?"

"Mainly the Ruathfia," Nally answered. "Tiernan O'Bannon is their chieftain. 'Twas he and his men who killed the old king and razed the fort. Now he waits for his chance to fall upon us once again."

Bridei was puzzled. "Why doesn't this O'Bannon attack now, while the curtain wall remains unfinished? It seems to me this place is ripe for the taking."

"Oh, aye," the simple-looking man, Eth, answered solemnly. "Many have thought so. But Cahermara is guarded by magic. That's what keeps our enemies at bay."

"Magic?" Bridei quirked a brow. "You believe some sort of spell surrounds the rath?" Despite his skepticism, as he said the words, Bridei felt a strange sensation, like a cold finger tracing the length of his spine.

The men all nodded gravely. Eth said, "The queen is a powerful sorceress, and she's worked great magic to keep Cahermara safe."

This was the same story that the two warriors had told him. He supposed Queen Dessia did look the part of a sorceress, with her fiery beauty and impressive bearing. And perhaps men here were more easily awed than those of his homeland. The priests swarming over Britain had done much to discredit the old tales, to make magic and sorcery things that educated men didn't admit to believing in.

A part of Bridei couldn't help wondering if there wasn't something to the stories of the protective spell. Since he'd called down a storm using a power he didn't know he possessed, his skepticism in such matters had weakened considerably.

Still, he couldn't quite accept that Queen Dessia had magical abilities. It was more likely a clever way to intimidate her enemies. Even he, who was no warrior, could see how vulnerable Cahermara was. With the defenses unfinished and a good share of her men scattered over the countryside rather than patrolling the area immediately around the fortress, the dun— or rath as the Irish called it—would not be difficult to take with a strong, determined force. Not that he wished for something like that to happen to Queen Dessia or her people.

That thought reminded him to ask, "What's your tribe called?"

"We're known as the Fionnlairaos," Nally answered. "It means people of the white mare."

Again, Bridei experienced a sense of premonition. In his country the white mare was the symbol of the goddess Rhiannon, who rode a pure white animal as she collected the souls of the dead and bore them back to the underworld. Everywhere he looked there seemed to be reminders of gods and magic. It made him uncomfortable. He thought of the storm and of how he'd summoned the powerful forces of the sea and the sky. It was those forces that had brought him to this place. Why? And what price would he have to pay for calling on their aid?

ChAPTER 4

She huddled in the near darkness of the root cellar. From above came the sounds of fighting ... and dying. Screams and cries. Dessia crouched low and put her fingers in her ears, trying to block out the terrible noises. A few moments later, some instinct jerked her to alertness, and she removed her fingers from her ears and listened intently. Footsteps above her. Very near. She glanced up at the wicker covering over the entrance to the cellar. A shaft of light pierced the gloom and she knew she'd been found.

She looked around the crowded chamber for something to use as a weapon. Spying a basket of cabbages, she pulled it near. She grabbed one of the cabbages and prepared to fling it. A dark form filled the opening, blocking out the light. The next moment the man was in the cellar. His huge sword gleamed in the torchlight filtering in from above as he moved towards her. Dessia let out a scream of rage and terror and flung the cabbage at his head

* * *

Dessia sat up with jerk. She was shocked to find herself lying on her bed in the tower room. The dream had seemed so real, so incredibly, appalling *real*.

She took gulps of air as she tried to calm herself. Perspiration glazed her skin and her throat felt raw, as if she really had screamed. Fierce emotions broke upon her consciousness, grief and horror to realize how much of the dream was true. Her family had died that day. They were gone forever. She wondered why the dream had come to her now. What did it mean? Was it a warning? Or a chastisement?

The gods might be angry with her because she hadn't avenged her family's death. Surely that was the reason she'd been spared. The gods had sent the phantom cat that guided her to safety. She'd been allowed to live because the gods meant for it to be so. The dream was a reminder of their claim upon her.

Anguish forced her from the bed. Wrapping her arms around herself, she began to pace about the small chamber. Tears of frustration stung her eyelids. She was doing the best she could. How could the gods reproach her? A child had no chance of wreaking vengeance. She'd had to grow up first, and learn to defend herself. As soon as she was able, she'd returned to the crumbling ruins of her father's once proud fortress. It had taken nearly a year to build a settlement there and raise the walls in timber. Then she'd realized such defenses were not enough. The rath must be rebuilt in stone. She'd told herself she dare not take revenge on O'Bannon until she and her forces had a safe place to retreat to, but perhaps that belief was false. Perhaps the gods wanted her to attack now, this winter. The dream might be a sign.

She went to the window and threw open the shutters. Cool, damp air assaulted her face and chilled her sweaty skin beneath her fur-lined bedrobe. In the east, she could see a faint thinning of the gray curtain of night. Almost dawn. She would never sleep now. Her body seemed to pulse with wild energy.

She dressed quickly, not bothering to wake Aife. Rather than putting on a gown, she donned a warm woolen tunic and trews. From one of the clothing chests, she removed a broad leather swordbelt and secured it around her hips.

She slipped out the door and ventured down the dark stairway, moving stealthily. The realization that she was sneaking out of her own home made her smile, then the weight of her responsibilities again descended. She could escape the rath, but she couldn't escape her duty. The awareness seemed to crush her, making her feel as she had that night in the cellar, overwhelmed and helpless. She shoved away the gnawing self-pity. Life was hard and brutal, a struggle for all creatures. She should not bemoan her lot. To do so was to risk angering the gods.

Down in the hall, one of the maidservants was tending the hearth fire. Dessia nodded to the woman, then moved behind her father's chair and took down her shield and sword from the wall above. As she sheathed the sword on her belt, she considered that no one who saw her make this early morning journey would be alarmed. By now the people of Cahermara were used to her going off alone. They imagined her "powers' would protect her. The thought brought another smile to her lips.

Outside the hall, she headed for the gate. The guard there bid her good morning, then climbed down from the watchtower to undo the latch. As soon as the man had opened the gate the width of her body, Dessia slipped through.

She made her way down the hillside, and at the bottom, found the pathway leading to the ancient oakwoods. It occurred to her that she was following the same route the phantom cat had taken on the night of the attack. She could still remember the terror of that journey, her awareness that although she might be escaping death, it was possible she was headed toward a fate even more horrifying. Children were warned against going into the Forest of Mist, taught to fear not only the wild beasts lurking there, but also the magical beings who ruled the enchanted realms, the space between this world and the Other Side.

But she'd never encountered anything fearful there, not that night nor anytime since. Over time it became a refuge, a place where she could escape the burdens of her life. Seeing the dark mass of trees in the distance, Dessia quickened her pace.

* * *

Where was she going—alone and armed like a warrior? Bridei stared at the gate the queen had just passed through. Something had woken him a short while before, and he'd left the barracks where the workmen slept and went out into the near dawn. There was just enough light to make out a tall, slim figure, armed with sword and shield, moving through the settlement. Curious, Bridei had followed. It was only when the mysterious person halted and called up to the guard that Bridei realized it was the queen. He'd grinned in appreciation of the way the male attire showed off her feminine form, emphasizing rather than concealing her delicious curves. Then he crept nearer and watched as she vanished through the gate.

Now he contemplated how he could follow her. What tale could he tell the guard to convince the man to let him pass? He puzzled on the matter, then decided to try another approach. Turning, he headed to the other side of the rath, to the place where he'd been working earlier that day. Passing the piles of rocks, he climbed the scaffolding to the top of the half-finished stone wall. His hand found a purchase on the timber fortification outside the wall and he scrambled up. Crouching on the edge of the wooden palisade, he warily regarded the ten-foot drop to the ground, then made the leap. He relaxed his body as he fell and rolled as he landed, a trick he'd learned as a youth. In seconds, he was on his feet, his clothing damp with dew, but his body uninjured.

He wasted no time in hurrying around the perimeter of the rath. But when he arrived on the other side of the fort, he saw no sign of the queen. It was too dark to see very far. He would have to guess which way she'd gone. The sea lay to the east. Would she have traveled that direction? Nay, he didn't think so. She was too shrewd to venture out into the open along the coast, especially since she knew the slavers were about. A lone woman would have no chance against a group of men, even if she were armed.

Which was another puzzle. Why was she carrying a sword and shield? Was the weapon for protection? But protection from what? If she feared attack, she would have taken an escort.

Perhaps she wearied of being confined in the rath. He could well understand such a feeling. After only three days behind the fortress's walls, he was also growing restless. It was a comfortable enough settlement, but small and crowded nonetheless. Nothing like the vast walled towns of Gaul, or even the old Roman colonae of Britain.

But if the queen sought fresh air and freedom, where was she headed? Bridei tried to recall the landscape around the rath. He'd had a good look at the area when he'd been up on the scaffolding the day before. Rolling hills all around, except for a dark swathe of oakwoods extending deep inland. His mother loved the forest, he recalled. She'd told him she never felt more content than when she was among the trees with their spirits all around her. Did Queen Dessia have a similar affinity for the wildwood?

Bridei started walking. It was only a hunch, but better than nothing. If he were wrong, he'd at least see another part of the Fionnlairaos' territory. Again, he puzzled on the name of the queen's tribe. He'd seen no horses since arriving in Eire and certainly no white ones. Did the name hail from a time in the past when Dessia's ancestors possessed horses? Or was it an allusion to a supernatural animal?

This Irish queen and her world intrigued him. Ireland reminded him of the wild hills of his homeland, yet this realm was subtly different. There was less darkness here, as if the ancient forces of land and sea and sky were not quite so harsh and primeval. This seemed to be a place of more sunshine and less shadow than Gwynedd.

He entered the woods, thinking his quest was probably hopeless. In this wild tangle of old oak, elm and hazel, it would be next to impossible to find her. Unless she'd kept to the pathway. For there was a trackway here, very narrow but clearly visible among the undergrowth of the autumn woods.

Along the path, bryony and rowan bushes glistened with red berries, while overhead great, ancient oaks spread their boughs, their dull gold leaves half fallen. There was still plenty of greenery here, the yellow green of hazel, darker hues of the ivy and vivid mosses, as well as a few late flowers—yellow agrimony and purple loosestrife. He heard birdsong; chaffs and warblers staying late in the season. The Blood Moon was waxing. In his homeland, the excess stock would soon be butchered in preparation for winter. But the grass here was still green, so perhaps they didn't have to cull their herds.

As he progressed deeper into the woods, he encountered pigs rooting among the acorn mast, calling to mind the rich pork in the stew he'd eaten the evening before. Like his people, the Irish appeared to eat more meat and cheese than bread. Although he'd seen some fields of barley and wheat, they were relatively small compared to the rich pastureland where cows and sheep grazed.

The path grew even narrower, then disappeared altogether. Bridei peered into the dense, nearly impenetrable foliage. Why would the trackway simply end? It was almost as if the woods were urging him to turn back. Then he heard the sound of water, a little runlet trickling over the ground. He decided to find the stream and follow it.

The ground sloped downward as he set out through the underbrush, and he had to struggle over many fallen branches. It was dark here, as if the sky overhead had grown overcast even as dawn broke. He glanced upwards, wondering if it would rain. When he returned his gaze to the pathway, the ground had disappeared beneath a layer of mist. In a few moments, he was completely surrounded by whiteness. He could still see, but not well enough to be certain of his footing. A prickle of fear crept along his spine and he turned around, contemplating heading back. But he couldn't do that either. The mist was even thicker that direction.

His sense of unease increased. It was as if the forest conspired to make him lose his way. Ridiculous. A patch of woodland couldn't reason or plan. Holding out his hands, he started forward, determined not to give in to his growing sense of alarm. His progress was painfully slow. He must first determine the size and location of the trees and bushes ahead of him, then climb over them or go around. It was terrifying to feel like a blind man. His heart beat faster and faster and his skin grew clammy with sweat. Where would he be when he finally reached the end of the mist?

His body trembled with the strain of moving so slowly. By the gods, what was happening? He'd never feared magic or sorcery. He had memories of his mother telling him about the old gods, the powerful ancient forces that governed the land, but he'd dismissed them as he had all the other deities he'd heard of in his travels. Now he wondered if there was not more to her tales than he'd guessed.

He could feel some sort of power here, an almost palpable force. It felt as if he were at the whim at that force, as helpless as if he were in slave shackles with armed guards surrounding him. Was this spirit of the woods merely toying with him or did it have a purpose? So far, all he could be certain of was that he was hopelessly lost.

Anger surged through him and he moved forward. He refused to cower before this unseen presence. If it struck him down, so be it!

The ground sloped steadily downward. He must reach the bottom eventually. Unless he'd entered some other realm. Again, he experienced a sense of foreboding. Did the bewitchery of this place have anything to do with Queen Dessia? A ruler and their land were often connected. Bridei had heard of rituals where a king symbolically mated with the earth goddess to ensure his land's fertility. And darker rites where a king was sacrificed to rid the land of a curse.

Despite himself, Bridei shivered. For all his exertions, he felt cold. What was this place? He struggled forward, not knowing what else to do. At last, he reached level ground. A few steps further and the mist began to thin. He was in a kind of valley, and through the autumn woods he could see a lake. It glistened in the soft morning light like a vast moonstone.

He walked toward the lake, feeling both relieved and awed. If sorcery had brought him here, then it must be a benevolent force, to guide him to such a beautiful place. As he approached the lake, he saw something that reinforced his sense of good fortune. There, in an open area near the edge of the water, was his quarry—the lovely Queen Dessia.

Chapter 5

At first he couldn't make out what the queen was doing, with her sword drawn and her shield at the ready. Then he decided she must be training herself in weaponry. She parried and lunged, as if engaging an invisible opponent. The intensity of her efforts amazed him. Her face was flushed and her expression and movements bespoke desperate concentration, as if she fought for her very life. He wondered if she did battle against some terrifying but invisible enemy. If she were in danger, how could he aid her? He had no weapon. Even if he did, he could hardly engage a foe he couldn't see.

But perhaps she didn't need his help. Her movements were rapid and precise and she wielded the heavy weapon with remarkable strength. Who would have guessed a woman could appear so formidable? And yet for all her ferocity she remained the essence of grace and femininity, the lines of her body as elegant as the curving patterns on a brooch fashioned by a master craftsman.

She seemed to be driving her opponent back. Back and back. Her enemy appeared to surrender. She held out her sword as if the tip touched her unseen opponent's throat, forcing them to beg for mercy. Bridei was filled with satisfaction at the sight of her evident triumph. Although he was certain by now that her adversary was imaginary, it still pleased him to see her prevail. He clapped his hands in approval. "Well done, lady."

At the sound of his voice, Queen Dessia whirled around. Her green eyes met his, brilliant with shock. Then her expression grew hard. "What are you doing here? How dare you..." Her voice trailed off and she glanced around in obvious dismay.

"I saw you leave the rath and followed."

"But the forest..." She shook her head in confusion. Clearly, she hadn't expected the forces guarding the woods to allow him to pass. Encouraged, he drew nearer. The men's clothing she wore emphasized her femininity, accentuating the narrowness of her waist, the delicacy of her wrists and hands, the slenderness of her neck. She was garbed as a warrior, but all he could see was her womanliness, her vulnerability.

As he drew nearer, she raised her sword in a threatening gesture and sprang into a fighting stance. "You'll come no closer."

"I'm not your servant to command."

He could tell his response infuriated her. But beneath the anger was fear. He gestured, feigning amazement. "You would use your weapon on an unarmed opponent? That would hardly be honorable."

She let out a hiss of rage. "Come no closer."

He moved slowly, deliberately, nearer. Her expression grew furious, then desperate. For all her ruthlessness in mock combat, he wondered if she'd ever engaged in real battle, ever injured or killed anyone. He paused a few paces away and held her gaze. The strain was beginning to wear on her. Her hand holding the sword had begun to tremble. Observing that sign of weakness, he moved into action, sweeping past her right side before she could bring the sword around. She tried to turn but he was already behind her. He grabbed her around the waist and pinned her arms against her body.

She writhed and twisted, struggling to get away. But she was untrained in this sort of close combat and not as strong as he was. When she paused for breath, he grabbed her right wrist and twisted until she dropped the sword.

She let out a scream of outrage and flailed and fought some more. But trapped as she was, her body tight against his, she was unable reach his face or strike a blow. After a time, she stopped struggling and Bridei allowed himself to enjoy the intimacy of their position. Her firm buttocks pressed against his groin. The soft swell of her breasts pressed into his forearm. A violent wave of lust surged through him and he thought she must surely feel his erection hard against her bottom.

But mixed with his arousal was a touch of pity. How defeated and helpless she must feel at being trapped in his arms. She was breathing heavily, her chest rising and falling in rapid rhythm. Clearly, she was furious with herself for letting this happen. She hadn't truly believed he would lay hands on her. Otherwise, she would have fought much harder.

That was his advantage, and he had pressed it. Even now, he didn't think she wished to be away from him. While her mind told her to fight, her body was perfectly willing to surrender. He had the knowledge and the skill to tip the balance so she would yield. But he also knew that even subtle coercion was risky. If he took advantage of her vulnerability, this haughty queen could end up hating him. He might ease his lust, but it would be at the cost of the ultimate prize.Knowing this, he allowed himself one last moment to savor the feel of her against him. To inhale her scent, so tantalizing and provocative. Then he released her and stepped back. "Never underestimate your opponent," he said. "You thought because I was unarmed, you could easily best me. But in very close combat, weapons aren't as important as cunning and speed."

She didn't move, but remained facing away from him. Bridei wondered if she would retrieve her sword and attack him. If she were really angry, she could certainly do some damage. At last she turned around. Her green gaze met his, flaring with anger and despair. "Teach me," she said. "Teach me how to do what you did."

Bridei couldn't help smiling. "There's nothing to teach. Having experienced the maneuver once, I'm certain you won't allow it to happen again. And if I'd been a real threat, you wouldn't have left yourself open in the first place. I had the advantage because you didn't truly see me as the enemy. I'm certain you would do much better if your life were at stake. But you knew I wasn't a man to fear."

Her eyes widened, then she frowned in dismay. Her expression said clearly, *Oh, but I do fear you, more than you know.*

Struggling not to reveal his triumph, Bridei said, "I'll give you a bit of advice. If a man should ever grab you from behind and hold you as I did, there are things you can do to get away, instead of flailing about like a hare in a trap."

The comparison made her flush with anger. Oh, this woman was proud, almost desperately so.

"Here. I'll show you." He drew near and pulled her into his arms once more. This time she didn't struggle, partly because she was expecting it, but also, he thought, because the feel of him holding her didn't displease her. This way she could yield to her body's urgings without being humiliated.

"There are several things you can do," he said. "You could stomp on my foot, hard on the instep. Or you could jerk your head back and hit me in the face with your skull. Both moves would cause me significant pain, enough that I might release you. But you can't hold back. You must do as much damage as you can, as quickly as possible." He released her again. This approach might prove to be quite effective. Get her used to the sensation of having him close, then withdraw. Her body would come to yearn for the feel of his.

"Now if a man grabs you from the front, there are other strategies." He turned her around to face him and held her tightly by the arms. "When positioned like this, you can try to stomp on my foot, but it's probably easier for you to bring your knee into my groin and hurt me that way." He held her gaze at he said this. Let her think about his groin, what that meant in another connotation. "But again, you can't make the assault half-hearted, or think to spare your opponent serious injury. If you hurt your attacker this way, yet fail to disable him, he's likely to fly into a rage and kill you."

He let go of her arms and stepped back. "Women are easy to kill. A powerful blow to a female's fragile skull and she is finished. Or, a man can snap her neck as a panther kills a deer. He doesn't have to be bigger than the woman, only stronger. And most men are stronger than most females. You're not a small woman. Nor I a particularly large man. Yet, on pure strength alone, I would prevail."

"Unless I had a weapon," she said.

He smiled. "As long as you managed to keep hold of that weapon. And as long as your opponent wasn't more skilled than you are." He gestured. "You come here, thinking to train on your own, but if you truly wish to learn the art of swordplay, you should engage with a real opponent, not an imaginary one."

"That's not why I come here," she said coldly. "I do train on the practice ground with my men, and I've taught them not to hold back when they fight me."

"Have you ever seen real combat?"

"Of course!" Her eyes flashed with affront. "How do you think I regained my lands?"

"Most women don't fight their own battles, queen or no. I'm impressed you risk your own life for your cause."

"It's been a few years since I've done so," she admitted. "My men have handled the skirmishes and raids since I've regained Cahermara."

Bridei thought he saw a shadow cross her face. "Why do you come here if it isn't to train for battle?" He looked around, taking in the mystical beauty of the lake. "Do you seek out this place to practice your magic?

For a time she didn't answer, then she spoke abruptly. "Why did *you* come here? Why follow me?" Her tone was aggressive, accusatory. She was back to her role of a queen addressing her disobedient subject.

"I don't think that's the real question—is it?" He cocked his head in bemusement. "I think the real question is how I managed to breach the barrier of enchantment you've set upon this place."

"I've set up no barrier, conjured no spell..."

"Nay?" He raised his brows. "Can you tell me honestly that there isn't some force guarding this place? That the mist that rose up and surrounded me was a normal one?"

Dessia struggled to form a response. Should she take credit for something that was not her doing? Would telling him she'd worked a spell make this man have a little more respect for her? She doubted it. It seemed nothing discouraged Bridei ap Maelgwn. What an insolent, aggravating man. To think he'd dared to lay hands on her. Held her against his body, tight as a lover's embrace. She'd clearly felt his arousal, and she couldn't seem to push the memory away.

"Perhaps the forces here don't answer to your command," he said, "but have their own purpose. If that's so, then you must consider that whatever bewitchment surrounds this place allowed me to pass. Clearly, we were meant to meet here." He smiled again, that mocking, bedeviling smile. "Perhaps this is a warning to you. A reminder that your defenses *can* be breached."

She couldn't keep the irritation from her voice. "You haven't told me why you chose to come here. Why follow me? I thought things were settled between us. I told you my terms and you agreed. I need workmen to build the walls of Cahermara. That is the only capacity in which I'll allow you to remain on my lands."

"So you said. But that was before I followed you to this place. Before you realized I'm no ordinary man, to be set to breaking rocks all day. I didn't speak of this before, in the hall where anyone might be listening, but I, too, know a little of sorcery." His blue eyes glinted like those of a small boy sharing a secret. "Indeed, that's the real reason I survived my entanglement with the slavers. One of them was going to kill me, but I called down a curse on him and his companions. A great storm arose, the high waves and fierce winds nearly swamping the boat."

Dessia sniffed in disbelief. "If you called down a storm, how did you know the wind and waves wouldn't send you to the bottom of the sea along with your captors?"

He smiled ruefully. "I had no way of being certain I would survive, but it seemed I had a better chance with the weather than with the slavers, who intended to slit my throat and throw me overboard. And as violent as it was, the storm didn't last long. Only long enough to carry the vessel off course. Which is why I'm here. The sea gods brought me to the shores of your lands. Surely that means the deities wished for us to meet, that there's some great purpose the two of us share."

The conceit of this man! To imply he knew the will of the gods! Yet despite her resentment, Dessia couldn't altogether suppress the shocking awareness that she'd begun to think the same thing. She recalled her reaction when she first saw Bridei, the sense she knew him somehow. Then there was the strange vision she'd had while talking to him in the hall. Even more unsettling was the fact that he'd surprised her here, in a place where she'd been so certain she would be left alone.

No one else had ever followed her to the lake. The people of her lands might enter the very edges of the woods for hunting, to gather firewood and to allow their livestock to forage, but as far as she knew, they never dared venture this deep into the Forest of Mist. This place was said to belong to the Ancient Ones, the fairy folk, and few were willing to risk an encounter with beings from the Otherworld.

Of course, this man didn't know the old tales, which was why he wasn't afraid to come here. But still, *how had he gotten past the mist?* She was used to it by now, and only experienced a brief moment of apprehension when the pale, formless vapor enveloped her. But for someone who'd never experienced the sensation of fumbling blindly in an unknown, sheet-white realm, it should have been terrifying enough to send him fleeing for his life.

But little seemed to trouble this man. He was so sure of himself, so maddening cool-headed and smug. Even now he watched her with that lazy smile, as if he didn't care what she thought. Nothing seemed to affect him. Nothing reached him. Was it because he knew he could always call upon his own magical abilities for protection?

The idea intrigued her. Did this man possess the secrets she sought, the means of defeating her enemies once and for all? To find out, she must risk that he would discover what a fraud she was. Without her reputation for magic, she was desperately vulnerable. If her enemies ever learned she wasn't truly a sorceress, the Fionnlairaos were doomed.

A terrible risk, and yet ... if this man could really call down a storm, then she very much needed him on her side. If she ordered him back to the menial labor of breaking and carrying rocks, he might decide to move on and end up offering up his services to one of her enemies. She couldn't allow that to happen. From the first, it seemed as if fate had brought this man to her household. As much as she feared him, she dare not risk sending him away.

"It's agreed," she said. "I'll share my secrets with you, if you will share yours with me. I would like to learn how to call down a storm, to curse my enemies by the forces of sea and sky."

"And what, in turn, will you offer me?" he asked. "What magic do you know?"

She took a deep breath. "I've worked a spell of protection around Cahermara. As long as it remains intact, the rath can't be taken."

"And you will tell me how you did this?"

What could she say? She must make him think her powers were real. She nodded. "I'll show you the spell." She could come up with some pretense of magic. But if he were truly a sorcerer, he might realize it was all a bluff.

"What now?" he asked. "Shall we go back to the rath? Or do you want to stay here? It's certainly a beautiful place." He glanced at the lake, a vague smile touching his lips. "A pity we didn't bring any food. This would be a lovely spot in which to break our morning fast. Next time we come, we should bring some provisions."

What was he talking about? One moment they were discussing magic; the next, he behaved as if they were children frolicking in the woods. Was all of life a game to him?

Resentment stabbed her. "I haven't time for such foolishness," she snapped. "I have responsibilities. A duty to my people and to my family, dead these ten years. I must put all my efforts into protecting my kingdom and avenging the great wrong that was done to me. If you wish to exchange knowledge of the magical realm, that is one thing. But I'll have no part of your other witless plans."

"Ah," he said, approaching her. "So you're telling me you have no time for pleasure, for laughter and gaiety? But what if that's what the gods demand? What if they favor those who make merry and enjoy life to the fullest?"

"They don't," she said bluntly, "Or, at least the ones I know of do not." That was an untruth. There were plenty of tales of the deities being playful and full of pranks.

"A pity," Bridei answered. "If I thought the gods were grim, cheerless beings, I would refuse to honor them." He took another step nearer. "Life can't be all duty. There must also be joy and laughter, music and poetry. Those things are like the dawn, breaking through the dark night sky as morning comes. For as much as there is darkness, there is light. And as much as there is sadness, there must also be celebration. Everything in life is a balance of opposing forces. For every aspect of a god or goddess that is cruel and harsh, there is a side that is bountiful and generous."

He was so close now. In another moment, he would reach out and touch her. And if he did, she very much feared she would weaken totally. His words aroused such an aching longing inside her, a yearning for the dreams and joys that had perished the night Cahermara was destroyed.

She took a deep steadying breath, praying he didn't guess her distress. "I thought we were going to share information about spells and enchantments," she told him curtly. "I seek knowledge and power, not fanciful explanations of the gods' benevolence."

"But doesn't all magic come from the gods? They shape the patterns of our lives. If we wish to change our destiny, we must access their power."

"I don't know what you mean. I've never considered such things." As soon as she spoke, Dessia knew a sense of chagrin. Now he would guess how unskilled and ignorant she really was.

He shrugged. "In truth, I haven't considered these matters much myself. All my knowledge of enchantments and spells comes from my mother, who I haven't seen in many years. Yet when I speak of these things, it's almost as if her voice is inside my head, whispering things I thought I'd forgotten."

There was something wistful in his face as he spoke. She pounced upon it. "Why haven't you seen your mother for so long?"

The breach in his defenses seemed to open even wider. She observed genuine grief in his expression, a kind of desolation.

"Is she dead?" she pressed.

His smile was quick. "Nay, the Lady Rhiannon is not dead. I'm certain she remains young and beautiful, like her namesake, the goddess of dreams and enchantments."

"Then why don't you visit her?"

Bridei's expression grew bitter. "Because she lives with my father, and I have no desire to see *him*."

"Why? Did you quarrel over something?" To her—who would give nearly anything to see her family again—his attitude was baffling.

His blue eyes glittered like cold, hard jewels. "One does not 'quarrel' with the Dragon. When the Dragon gives an order, it is obeyed."

"The Dragon—is that what they call your father?" She remembered what had happened in the hall—how the emblem of a golden dragon had appeared behind Bridei.

He nodded. "The Dragon of the Island, the fiercest warlord in all of Britain."

"And you are his heir?"

He gave a harsh laugh. "Not likely. I have an older brother who my father dotes on. Rhun can do no wrong, and is brave and noble beyond belief. Of course... " His expression darkened. ". . . he was killed in battle this past sunseason, so I suppose some would think me next in line for the kingship. Not that I would even consider such a thing." He gave a dramatic shudder. "I have no desire to be a king. It sounds like a very disagreeable life. And my father would never name me as his successor, even if I were the last of his line. He'd rather have his favorite hound rule after him than his cursed, evil-tainted second son."

"Cursed?"

His countenance grew even grimmer. "It's a long tale, and one I don't choose to bore you with." He gestured impatiently. "Since you refuse to allow yourself to enjoy the beauty of this place, we might as well return to Cahermara." He executed a low bow. "After you, milady."

Dessia retrieved her sword and sheathed it, then started toward the thick woods. This man's moods seemed to change as swiftly as the clouds in the winter sky, making conversing with him was as exhausting as physical combat. He constantly left her feeling off-balance and wary. At any moment she feared to make a fatal misstep and find herself with blade of his wit at her throat.

The sound of his voice from behind her made her jump. "And as we make our way back, will the mist rise again?"

"Nay. The mist doesn't guard the way back, only the way here."

He was right behind her. So close he could reach out and touch her. The thought affected her profoundly. She thought of him watching her. His gaze taking in the shape of her body, clearly revealed by her attire. A bolt of anger pierced her. Never before had she concerned herself with how she looked in trews and tunic. It was a functional way to dress, and with most men it made her feel powerful and in control, knowing that if she drew her sword, she was more than a match for them. But with this man, everything was different. He never seemed to forget she was a woman. And because of his continued sexual regard, she couldn't seem to forget it either. It put her at a disadvantage. Though she might outrank him as queen and be at least his equal as a warrior, as a man facing a woman, he had all the advantages.

He'd made that clear already. She thought with a sense of embarrassment of the shameful way he'd overpowered her and made her drop her sword. Clever tricks, and yet she'd succumbed easily. It was partly, as he said, because she hadn't seen him as a serious threat. A mistake, a very grave one. How could she have been so foolish? If she ever did anything so stupid when confronted with a real enemy, she would surely die.

Her earlier worry suddenly returned, making her shudder. What if this man were allied with O'Bannon or some other chieftain who coveted her lands? He might have made up the tale of being the son of a British warlord. Yet there were many details that rang true, and it didn't feel like he was lying when he talked about his past. That was real, she was certain.

She also couldn't see him allying himself with someone like O'Bannon. Or any man. This Bridei ap Maelgwn was too proud and self-sufficient. He called himself a prince and behaved like one.

He spoke again. "Have you ever considered that if you marked the pathway on the way back, you might be able to find it more easily when coming from the rath?"

She shook her head. "The mist would still rise, obscuring whatever signs were used to indicate the way. Besides, the forest is enchanted. It would be foolish to try to control things in this place."

"I suppose you're right," he said. "But it's unsettling to travel blind through a mist. To trust you won't end up lost forever."

"Ah, trust, is that not the way of all magic?" She turned halfway around so she could catch sight of him. As always, she was stunned by the perfection of his face. His graceful features. Those white even teeth and impossibly blue eyes.

"Tell me," he said. "How long have you been going to the lake? When did you discover it?"

She turned away, concentrating once again on the pathway. "I was a child when I first went to the lake." The memories came rushing back. The horror of fleeing her burning home. The terror that sent her into the woods.

"You must have been a very bold child," he said. "Few adults would dare to venture near such a place, let along a young girl."

She thought of the cat leading her to safety. In all the years since, she hadn't seen the creature.

"Why did you go there?" he asked. "Was it simple curiosity... or something else?"

The peaceful clearing around the lake had been her refuge. She'd survived there on berries and nuts, staying for nearly half of a cycle of the moon. It was a deer that finally led her out of the woods, a beautiful hind that came down to the lake to drink. As she had with the cat, she knew she was meant to follow the creature. The deer led her to the other side of the forest, where there was a small farm, with small plots of oat and barley sprouting through the dark earth. She approached a boy tending a flock of sheep, and he took her back to his home, where his father recognized her as the chieftain's daughter. She lived there for a time, helping as much as they would allow her. Then she moved on to another farm. And another. For nearly six years, the people who honored her father as king had sheltered her and hidden her, allowing her time to grow to womanhood.

But she would not tell this man those things.

She didn't respond, but instead, quickened her pace. A few more steps and the forest ended. In the distance, Cahermara rose upon the hill, its pale stonework gleaming in the early morning light. From this direction she could see the unfinished part of the wall, reminding her of all the work left to do. If she could learn magic from this man, perhaps the construction process could be hastened. For that matter, if she discovered a *real* spell of protection, the security of the rath wouldn't have to depend upon stout stone walls.

Almost as if he knew her thoughts, Bridei said, "I'm confused, lady. If you've worked a spell to repel your enemies, why bother with stone fortifications?"

Dessia focused her gaze straight ahead. She couldn't let him guess the truth. If he were a spy, he would alert her enemies to her vulnerability. And if he were a sorcerer, he would never agree to share his knowledge if he realized she had nothing to offer in exchange.

"I'm building the wall as a deterrent for invaders from the sea," she answered, "men who might not have heard of my reputation."

"But if there's a spell in place, wouldn't it repel them as well as your other enemies? Why bother with all this work?"

She struggled to come up with a response that would satisfy him. Finally, she said, "Spells can be broken. If my enemies should find some way through my magical defenses, I want to have something else in place to keep them from overrunning Cahermara."

"What could break a spell?" Bridei asked. "Perhaps another spell, one evoked by a magician whose powers are even greater than yours?"

There seemed to be a threat behind his words, the implication he doubted the strength of her magic. Her muscles grew taut. She should never have agreed to this exchange of knowledge. Sooner or later he would realize she was bluffing. When he did, what would he do?

Bridei suppressed a smile, feeling quite pleased with himself. Now that he had the advantage, he meant to press it. "I'm eager to discuss these things further," he said. "To share information about magic. But clearly, we can't do it in the hall. We must meet somewhere private."

She turned again to look at him, her expression glowering. Grudgingly, she nodded. "I'll meet with you in the tower, which serves as my work area. But first, I would like to refresh myself."

"Of course." He smiled at her. She was inviting him into the place where she slept. Once there, things would fall naturally into place. He cared little about spells and sorcery. What he wished to discover was what her supple, womanly body would feel like beneath his and whether she was as fiery and passionate as her vivid coloring suggested. He'd never had a woman like this one. A queen. A warrior-woman. A sorceress. The very thought fired his blood with such intensity that he had to remind himself the chase was part of the fun.

Patience. Let it unfold as it will. Like a long and complex tale that lasts well into the night.

ChapteR 6

When they reached the rath, Bridei went to the cistern to wash, then made his way to the hall and the stairway leading up to the queen's tower. He climbed the stairs, his muscles taut with anticipation. Near the top, he paused and inhaled the scent wafting down from the chamber above. The sharp, slightly astringent odor reminded him a little of his mother's workroom when she was mixing dyes for her weaving and embroidery. "Dessia?" he called out softly.

"Aye. You may come up," she answered.

He took the last few stairs and entered the chamber at the top. Dessia stood with her back to him, gazing out one of the small, narrow windows. He quickly surveyed the furnishings of the chamber: A bed draped with curtains and piled with furs and blankets. A large work table cluttered with manuscripts, jars, bowls, half-burned candles and bundles of herbs. Storage chests and baskets on the floor.

When she didn't speak or turn around, Bridei went to the table. He picked up a nearby manuscript and scrutinized the document. It was written in Greek rather than Latin and was obviously very old, the parchment yellowed and stiff. She must have paid dearly for such an ancient piece. He unrolled the manuscript and started to translate. "By the light of the new moon, take the caul of a newborn babe and the bones of a nightingale—"

"What are you doing?" Crossing the room in three brisk strides, she tore the parchment from his hand.

He smiled at her. "I thought you were going to share your lore with me."

She let out a gasp, her green eyes shimmering with emotion. "First, you must prove to me that you possess knowledge of magic yourself."

He shrugged and let his gaze stray to her heaving bosom. She'd bathed and refreshed herself since he'd left her. He could smell the fragrance of the herbs used in her bath. They merged with the natural odors of her skin to create an intoxicating brew. As Bridei inhaled the heady aroma, he decided he'd never desired a woman as much as this one.

The plain russet gown she wore hung loosely on her body, unadorned with belt or brooch. Her hair had been combed out and arranged with bronze pins that held it away from her face. The drab gown emphasized the feminine contours beneath, while the simplicity of her hair refined the elegant perfection of her features. He wanted to take her in his arms and kiss her senseless.

She stepped back and spoke sharply: "I'm waiting. Prove to me that you aren't wasting my time, that you truly know magic."

With effort, Bridei focused on her words. "What do you want me to do? What sort of test of my abilities did you have in mind?"

She took another step back and crossed her arms. "You said you could call down a storm."

He shook his head. "I can't call upon the gods to perform a trick simply to please you. The powerful forces that are the source of my magic aren't to be used for trivial things."

"But you must show me something. How else can I believe your claim?"

"Perhaps you'll have to take it on faith... just as I must accept that you have power. It could be that you're lying. Perhaps all of this..." He gestured to the jumble of objects on the table. ". . . is an elaborate deception to make your enemies believe you're a sorceress."

"Of course my powers are real!" Her eyes went wild, and her whole body seemed to thrum with tension.

Why should she be so defensive? Bridei thought. *Unless his accusation struck too close to the truth?* "Prove it," he said. "Prove you know magic."

Her nostrils flared. "You, first."

Bridei smiled at her challenge, then glanced around the room, wondering what he should try. He was bluffing as much as she was. Fortunately, he was used to pretending to be something other than what he was. Every time he told a story, he took on the attributes of the people he described: The noble, valiant warrior going into battle. The maid weeping for her lost love. The king who has lost his kingdom. He could transform himself into any one of them. This was no different. He was trying to prove to Dessia that he was sorcerer. What he needed to do was think like one. His gaze fell upon a bronze bowl on the table and he pointed to it. "Do you seek out the future in that?"

"Aye. Sometimes."

Looking at her, he could tell she was lying. He approached the bowl, observing the oily surface. It would be easy to pretend to see something. But what? He stared down into the glistening orb of oil, waiting for inspiration. Something glowed in the depths of the bowl. It must be a reflection of something, perhaps the light from the window. The glow intensified until he could see clearly that it was flames. Bright, intense flames. They danced wildly around a timber wall. There was a figure by the wall. A girl. She had long red hair. Her face was streaked with dirt. She turned to look behind her, her eyes wild with fear.

Bridei swallowed. He could feel the girl's terror. It filled his body. She wanted to scream, but if she did, they would find her. She moved closer to the wall and saw something near the ground. A cat. Tawny colored, like the flames. She began to follow the cat as it moved stealthily along the wall. All at once, the cat disappeared.

Bridei could feel the girl's desperation. Her panic. He saw her hesitate, wondering if she should follow the cat. She looked around. He couldn't tell her thoughts, but he could feel her emotions clearly: grief and despair. She took a choking breath, like a sob, then ducked down and crawled through the hole in the wall. Reaching the other side, she got to her feet. For a few heartbeats, she paused. Then she saw the cat and followed it into the darkness.

The vision in the scrying bowl vanished, the surface turning flat and opaque. Bridei raised his gaze and stared at Dessia. "That was you, wasn't it? That's how you escaped Cahermara the night your enemies burned the old hillfort. It was the cat. It led you to safety."

She looked back at him, her green eyes wide with shock. "What?" she asked in a choked voice.

Bridei looked back at the scrying bowl and a chill went down his body. What was happening to him? First, he conjured a storm. Then he saw a vision. He didn't want to know magic. Such things carried with them too much power, too much responsibility. He longed to go back to being who he'd always been, the carefree bard who took his pleasure where he could.

Dessia drew near to him. "Teach me," she whispered, her voice fervent. "Teach me how to do that."

With her so close, he recalled why he'd come here. He intended to bed this beautiful woman, and there was like no time like the present to begin his seduction. Pulling her into his arms, he lowered his mouth to hers.

He'd fully expected her to struggle. To draw back and perhaps even strike him. But she did none of those things. Instead, she stood frozen in his embrace, as if she were too overcome to react. To his surprise, the feel of her in his arms seemed to scatter his own wits. As his mouth tasted hers and his nostrils inhaled her scent, he felt himself lose control. A wave of passion crested over him, drowning him in urgent need.

When she began to respond, he barely retained enough conscious thought to grapple with her clothing and try to bare more of her exquisite flesh. Struggling with her heavy wool gown, he finally succeeded in exposing one of her breasts. With a groan, he pressed his face against the silken mound and sucked her nipple into his mouth. She reacted with a desperate moan of her own.

Her spine arched. Her supple body shuddered in his embrace. He felt as if she were graceful harp and with each delicate touch upon her body he made music. As he licked and suckled, the music surrounding them soared. Triumphant. Magical. He switched to her other breast and was overcome by the taste and feel of her. The need to be closer, to sheathe his flesh in hers grew more intense. He tried to maneuver her to the bed, but as he did so, his foot became entangled in a nearby basket. He lost his balance and they both went down.

The impact seemed to jar him from his daze of passion, and he realized how utterly overcome he was. Warning sounded in his mind. Control was something he sought to maintain at all costs. To allow all restraint to slip away was dangerous. Very dangerous.

He struggled to remember the rules of this game he'd played so many times. *Get off of her. Help her up. Be the gracious, courtly bard. You can always begin again later.* "Milady, my pardon. I've hurt you." He stood and reached out a hand to help her to her feet.

She gazed at him almost unseeingly, as if she was still trapped in the web of their lust. With her fair skin flushed a lovely rose hue and her green eyes wide and dilated, she looked so enticing he wanted to pounce on her again, to make love to her right on the floor. But his fear of her effect on him held him back. Always before, he'd been the seducer, never the one seduced. What this woman did to him was frightening.

She seemed to become aware of what had happened... or almost happened. Realizing the neckline of her gown was pulled down, exposing one of her breasts, her face flooded with heat. She gave a gasp of embarrassment and sought to cover herself. Ignoring his outstretched hand, she stood and her expression turned furious. "How dare you? How *dare* you?" she demanded, her voice quavering.

He wanted to apologize, to tell her he'd been so overcome he'd lost all restraint. But he couldn't let her know she had that sort of power over him. He hurried to slip the cynical mask back into place. "How dare I... what?" he asked lightly. "Make love to a beautiful passionate woman who desires me?"

"I don't... desire you!" Even as she said the words, he could see she knew they were a lie. Her face turned an even deeper shade of rose. Her mouth worked, then her eyes grew hard and cold. "I should call my men. I should have them flog you for your audacity!"

He smiled. "It's not necessary to whip me to cause me to be completely overcome in your presence. Merely looking at you accomplishes that." He would make a jest of what he felt for her, and she'd never guess the terrible power she held over him.

With a shaking hand, she pointed toward the door. "Leave me. Leave now."

"What about your promise to share magic with me?" He cocked his head and fixed her with a sardonic gaze. "I've upheld my part of the bargain. Now, it's your turn."

"Get out!" she cried, her eyes wild. "Get out!" She looked as if she meant to shove him out the door. Her obvious panic amused him, but not so much he forgot his own situation. She was right. It would be best if he left. If he stayed, he would have her in his arms again in no time. And then there would be no turning back.

"Very well," he said. "I'll leave." He looked at her one more time, savoring the vision she made. Then he took the few paces to the door and went out.

Dessia stared after him. A part of her longed to call him back. To ask him to continue what he'd been doing. But she couldn't do that. It would be utter madness. She'd almost let him . . .

Thinking of it made her swallow hard. What had come over her? For a time she'd been completely under his power. *Power.* All at once she remembered the scrying bowl and the vision he'd seen. Somehow he'd caught a glimpse into the past and knew the secret of how she'd escaped Cahermara that night. He must truly possess magic.

She exhaled a shaky breath. How could that be? How could he know?

She went to the scrying bowl and stared into it. As usual, she saw nothing. Tears filled her eyes. It didn't seem fair that he should succeed where she had failed. But perhaps he hadn't. He might have found out what happened that night from someone close to her. Although she'd never told anyone about the cat, she knew there were rumors she'd turned into an animal and that's how she'd escaped. Perhaps he'd heard the stories and guessed the truth, that she hadn't become an animal, but one had led her out of the hillfort.

It sounded very far-fetched and a part of her didn't believe it. But it was the only possible explanation. Otherwise, she'd have to accept that he knew magic. And if that were true, he must know she was a fraud.

The realization panicked her. She wanted to call him back and pretend to work some sort of spell. But that was ridiculous. If he were a truly a sorcerer, he would know she was only pretending.

Her thoughts whirled in circles and she wrung her hands with helplessness. Perhaps she should send Bridei away, banish him from her lands. But if he were a spy, that was the worst thing she could do. He already had enough knowledge to ruin her.

But she couldn't believe he was a spy. He was a prince and a talented bard. Although he had no wealth now, he could easily acquire it by other means than spying for the chieftain of a small territory in Ireland.

Worst of all was the thought that she didn't really want to send him away. A part of her was beguiled by him, deeply, dangerously beguiled.

Whirling, Dessia began to pace. After a time, she paused at her scrying bowl and stared hard at the oily surface. "Help me," she whispered. "Show me what I should do."

Nothing happened. The gleaming surface remained blank and empty.

CHAPTER 7

Bridei straightened and rubbed his aching back. He could scarce believe he was still spending his days breaking rocks. It was mind-numbing, exhausting work. The last few nights he'd fallen asleep almost the moment he lay down on his pallet in the workers' barracks. There was no reason for him not to seek a more satisfying position elsewhere. But somehow he couldn't bear to leave.

He glanced up at the tower and remembered kissing Dessia. The feel of her body against his. The incredible taste of her lips. The heady, intoxicating scent of her skin. He couldn't get those few moments out his mind.

Picking up the heavy hammer, he swung hard at the rock on the flat stone he used as an anvil. He reminded himself that he had nowhere to go, nor any means of starting a new life. Of course, that hadn't hindered him in the past. He'd often traveled with nothing except his harp. As he raised the hammer again, a pang of longing went through at the thought of the beautiful instrument he'd left behind in north Britain. If he'd arrived with his harp and had a chance to play for Queen Dessia, he felt certain she wouldn't be treating him like this. She'd have recognized his artistry and understood his worth.

Another blow and the rock finally shattered. He smashed the big pieces into smaller ones, then use a shovel to load them in the bucket. Lifting the bucket, he carried it over to where the other men were mixing mortar.

Nally nodded at him. "You're getting faster. Might end up being worth something after all." The dour workman's blue eyes lit with uncharacteristic humor.

Bridei only grunted in response. He supposed there might be some value in enduring this harsh labor. At least it was making him strong, and wielding the hammer kept his hands from getting soft. If he ever had access to a harp again, he wouldn't have to work so hard to build up the calluses on his fingertips.

The thought aroused another wave of regret. He yearned for his harp like some men might yearn for a woman. Music had been a part of his life for so long, it seemed it was a part of his very being. The melancholy he felt brought to mind an old ballad, and as he returned to where he'd left his hammer, he began to sing. He noted that the other men were watching him, but since he was singing in his native tongue, they wouldn't be able to understand the words. That pleased him. He wasn't singing for an audience, but for himself.

It was a sad song, vibrant with longing for what might have been. As he sang, he allowed himself to dwell upon the few regrets he had. He thought about how much he missed his mother. Would he ever see her again? He missed his homeland as well. The wild hills and dense forests. The broad, open coast where as a child he'd watched the sun set like a burning ember being quenched the Irish Sea. The same sea that crashed and foamed against the high cliffs that bordered Queen Dessia's lands. He was so close... and yet so far away.

He took a few blows at the rock to show the men he could work while he sang. But as he reached the last lingering notes of the melody, he paused and put all his heart into the music.

As soon as he finished, he went back to his task. After breaking several more rocks, he had enough to fill the bucket. When he carried it over to where the other men were working, they all stared at him. It was simple-minded Eth who finally spoke, "You're a good singer. The best I've ever heard. But that song was so sad. It brought tears to my eyes, even though I didn't understand the words."

"It's supposed to be sad," Bridei answered, feeling irritated.

"Don't you know any happy songs?" Eth asked.

"Aye. I know dozens. I just wasn't in the mood for them." Bridei paused and gestured. "My current circumstances don't exactly inspire mirth."

Eth frowned at him, his broad face creased with puzzlement. Cori said, "Bridei means he's not happy here, so why should he sing cheerful songs."

"Why don't you like it here?" Eth asked. "We get plenty to eat and a warm, dry place to sleep. At first Bridei felt exasperation. But then he realized Eth's point. For many men, having food and a secure roof over their heads meant a great deal. But since he'd had those things most of his life, they weren't enough to satisfy him. He glanced at the other men and considered how to answer. In this instance, it seemed the truth would serve well enough. "I'm sad because I no longer have a harp. I've played the instrument since I was a very young man, until it's become almost a part of me. I miss my harp like some men might miss a family member or a lover."

"A harp." Eth's face creased in thought. "I wonder where we might get you one. I would like to hear you play."

"Don't be foolish," said Cori. "Harps are very expensive, the sort of thing you have to pay for in gold."

"How difficult are they to make?" asked Eth.

"It depends on the harp," Bridei answered. "The kind of harp I'm used to playing takes years to make." He thought of his beloved instrument, with its elegant triangular shape and intricately-carved frame of lime and ashwood. "Such an instrument is beyond the skill of anyone but a master craftsman. But I've also used a much less complex kind of harp called a lyre. It only has six strings and is made of one kind of hardwood. Then you would need bronze or iron for the pins and gut or bronze for the strings."

Eth nodded. "I might be able to find a piece of wood and shape it. But you'd need a smith to make the pins."

"I'm certain Niall would be willing to make them," suggested Cori. "At least if he knew what it was for. The few times we've had a *filidh* come to visit, he's enjoyed their performances as much as anyone."

"And next time a steer or pig is butchered, you could have Cook save back the entrails," Eth added.

"That might mean she would make fewer sausages," said Cori, grinning.

"I'd willingly give up a few sausages to hear Bridei play the harp," Eth responded.

Bridei couldn't help smiling at the farmboy's serious expression. Although he'd brought up the idea of making a harp half derisively, the men's obvious enthusiasm for the project made him consider that it might truly be possible to make some sort of simple instrument. Even a primitive harp would be better than none at all. Besides, all this focus on his musical ability might force Queen Dessia to relent and let him perform, instead of breaking rocks.

"The frame's the main thing," he said. "You need a good-sized piece of hardwood. Ash preferably. I can show you the size and shape to cut it. You'll need two pieces glued together..."

* * *

Dessia gazed out the tower window. From this vantage point, she could just barely make out the four men who were supposed to be building the stone wall guarding Cahermara. Instead of working, they were gathered around Bridei ap Maelgwn. She could see him gesturing, while the rest of the men watched with rapt attention. She gritted her teeth, then muttered, "I thought at least my workmen would be safe from his charm. But, nay, they've fallen under his spell the same as everyone else."

"Milady, did you say something?" Aife asked from behind her.

"'Twas nothing," Dessia responded.

"Did you hear Bridei singing?" asked Aife. "He has a wonderful voice, doesn't he?"

"Aye," Dessia admitted grudgingly.

"Perhaps you could have him could sing in the hall some evening. After he's finished his other duties."

The serving maid's wistful tone sparked a pang of regret in Dessia's chest. It seemed very harsh to refuse Aife's request. Especially since her main reason for refusing to let Bridei perform was that she feared being in the same room with him. Against her will, her mind strayed to the memory of him kissing and fondling her. Merely the thought of that passionate embrace made her knees grow weak. It had been as if they were made for each other... their bodies fitting together like two halves of a whole.

As if to remind her of his compelling charm, Bridei began singing again. Dessia looked out the window and saw he was working as he sang, swinging the hammer in rhythm to the song. This was a much simpler song than the first, but his voice was still compelling. Listening to him, she started to weaken.

Such talent was a gift, and it seemed unfair to deny her people the benefit of it. For a few moments she wavered, then another thought came to her. What if her people were so charmed by Bridei that they grew complacent? If they became less vigilant, it might be exactly the opening her enemies needed. Indeed, rather than spying, that might be Bridei's purpose here. He might have been sent by her enemies to distract her from her goals.

The thought horrified her, especially when she considered how close she'd come to giving in. The one kiss they'd shared had weakened her to the point where she'd nearly lost control. She must never let Bridei get that close again. To have him around, even as a laborer, was too risky. She must find a way to be rid of him.

The chief obstacle to sending him away was the fear he would go to her enemies and betray her secrets. But what if she found some other means of being rid of him? There should be a least one more trading party coming to visit before winter set in. Maybe she could pay them to take Bridei far away from Ireland. It would require gold she was loath to part with, but it might be worth it. Even if Bridei eventually made his way back to Ireland and had contact with her enemies, it wouldn't be until next spring. By then, the stone wall would be finished—she hoped—and they would be in a better position to fend off attack.

She had only to wait until the traders came... and keep her resolve from wavering in the meantime. It seemed wrong to force Bridei to go with the traders. But she had no choice. She had to be rid of him somehow. Of course, there was the possibility he wasn't a spy. If that were true, then she'd be doing him a grave injustice. Her actions would be almost as loathsome as the slavers who'd brought him to this place. But she couldn't think about that. She had to be strong and consider what was best for her people.

She turned away from the window. Let Bridei ap Maelgwn sing his heart out. And let her people enjoy it. But he would have to do so while he worked. She wouldn't relent and let him perform in the hall. That would imply she'd accepted him as part of her household, and then her plan to send him away against his will would seem even more despicable.

* * *

The next day when he went out to the work area, Bridei found the other men gathered around Eth. Eth held out a flat piece of wood. "Will this do for making a harp?"

Bridei stared at him. He hadn't thought they would take him seriously, nor act so quickly. "Aye, it will work," he said after examining the wood.

Eth beamed. "We'll start tonight." When Bridei raised his brows in surprise, Eth added, "We can't work on it during the day because we're busy building the wall for the queen."

"What about going home to help your family?" Bridei asked. Unlike the other workmen, Eth didn't sleep in the barracks but returned to his father's farm every night.

"I've talked to them, and they've agreed this is more important."

Bridei raised his brows again. For a poor farmer to consider building a harp more important than having his son help with the chores was rather amazing.

Bridei resumed his task of breaking rocks. After a moment he cast a glance up at the tower. Queen Dessia had sought to keep him from plying his trade as a bard. Wouldn't she be surprised when he gave his first performance using a harp her people had made? Of course, there was much to do before that happened. Despite what he'd said, he wasn't entirely convinced Eth and the other men could build a decent-sounding harp. But for them to even attempt it was a contradiction of Dessia's wishes.

Bridei wondered what she'd do when she found out what was going on. Would she take the harp away? Or would she give in gracefully and accept his natural role as a performer? He'd decided he would tell her he was willing to keep working on the stone wall during the day and perform in the hall in the evenings. That way she couldn't say he wasn't useful to her.

A sigh escaped his lips. He was behaving like fool. Staying here when there were so many other opportunities out there. Households where he'd be treated like a prince and have a dozen women vying to warm his bed. But try as he might, he couldn't convince himself to leave.

He paused in breaking rocks and surveyed the hillfort with its partially finished defenses and the rich lands surrounding it. Part of the reason he stayed was the sense the gods had sent him here for a purpose. There did seem to be an aura of destiny surrounding Cahermara. The eerily beautiful lake and the enchanted forest that seemed to guard it. And even Queen Dessia herself. The miraculous way she'd survived when the rest of her family perished. Recalling the vision he'd seen of her as a girl, he felt a sense of foreboding. His first Seeing... and it had been of Dessia.

"Bridei?"

He looked up to see Nally watching him with a bemused expression.

"I vow, you're acting more witless than Eth today. Don't tell me some wench has caught your fancy. That's what that blank, sheep-eyed look usually means. I wouldn't think a man like you would succumb to such nonsense."

Bridei forced himself to laugh heartily. "In a way, you're right about me being a lovelorn fool. I was thinking about the harp the men are making. I can hardly wait to get my hands on the sweet beauty. I've been without the pleasure for so long."

"Well, you can drool over your paramour at night while they're working on her. For now, you need to keep to the task at hand. The weather's been mostly clear for a fortnight, but that won't last. In the meantime, we have to get as much done as possible."

"Understood," Bridei answered as he took his place at the mixing cauldron and began stirring the sand, lime and water that formed the mortar.

* * *

Aife entered the tower chamber and came to stand in front of Dessia. "Milady. You asked to speak to me."

Dessia struggled with how to phrase what she was asking of her maidservant. It was embarrassing to request that Aife spy on Dessia's own people. But she knew no other way to find out what was going on with Bridei and the other workmen. "I would like you to go to the barracks where the workmen sleep," Dessia said. "Tonight after they've eaten their evening meal. I want you to find out what they're up to."

"But why? What do you suspect them of doing?"

"I don't know. That's why I'm sending you to find out."

Aife's expression was puzzled, then her gaze snapped back to Dessia's. "It's the visitor, isn't it? The man named Bridei. You want me to find out if he's a spy."

"Even if he is, I doubt he would be so foolish as to reveal himself. Nay, what I want to know is how he and the other men spend their evenings."

"Why?" Aife looked even more perplexed.

"I've seen them gathered together on the work site, deep in conversation. I want to know what they're talking about. I don't really think they're planning anything evil or treacherous, I'm just curious as to what they're up to."

"But how shall I explain what I'm doing there?"

Dessia wanted to roll her eyes but didn't. Part of the reason she liked Aife was that she was so guileless and sweet. But in this instance, her forthright innocence was a disadvantage.

Dessia searched her mind for a plausible reason for sending Aife to the barracks. "Tell them that Cook has made a special treat for them. Say she prepared it on my orders... because I've been so impressed with their progress." Not true. She was certain they would have made much greater progress if Bridei hadn't distracted them with whatever scheme he'd involved them in.

Dessia motioned to Aife. "Go to the kitchen and ask Doona to make some honey cakes. Then tonight, when the cakes are finished, take them to the workmen. Linger while they eat and report back to me, both on what they were doing when you entered the barracks and their conversation while they ate."

"Honey cakes will make them thirsty," Aife pointed out. "Perhaps I should take them something to drink as well."

"And excellent idea," Dessia responded. She needed to loosen the men's tongues and make them relax. Water wouldn't fit the purpose, while mead might be too strong—she didn't want them to wake up the next day with aching heads. There was a bit of wine left over from last summer. She usually saved it for visitors, but at this time of the year the only people likely to travel to Cahermara were traders from across the sea, and she could purchase more wine from them.

"There's some wine in the root cellar," she told Aife. "Have one of the kitchen boys bring it up. But the men shouldn't have too much. A cup apiece should suffice."

"That's a lot to carry," Aife said.

"Aye, it is," Dessia agreed. For a moment she entertained the idea of helping Aife transport the food and drink. It was tantalizing to contemplate seeing Bridei up close again. But that would defeat the purpose of her plan. If she were around, the men wouldn't talk freely.

"Have one of the kitchen boys carry the wine in a ewer while you carry the cups and honey cakes in a basket." Dessia gazed at Aife, waiting for her to broach the next problem.

"Could the honey cakes be made with nuts?" Aife asked.

"I don't see why not. Now go. We don't want to wait until the last minute to tell Cook."

As Aife left, Dessia mused that she'd never realized Aife fancied nuts. Indeed, there was probably much she didn't know about the serving girl, or the other people of Cahermara either. They served her eagerly, but saw her as apart and above them. It made life quite lonely sometimes. It would be nice to have a companion of her own status, someone to share her thoughts with. The traitorous idea crept into her mind that Bridei ap Maelgwn would be more than willing to serve as her confidante and "friend". She gritted her teeth at the thought.

* * *

Dessia paced in the tower room, her body taut with tension. It seemed like hours since she'd watched Aife and the auburn-haired kitchen boy crossing the yard on their way to the workmen's barracks. She envisioned the men sitting around eating honey cakes and drinking wine. Bridei's blue eyes would sparkle and he would make jests and flirt with Aife, then laugh in that rich, musical voice of his.

Stop it! This is ridiculous! You can't be jealous of a serving girl!

She went back to the window and peered down into the deepening twilight. A moment later, she heard the door open. Aife burst in, her face flushed and her eyes gleaming with excitement. "I know what they're doing! They're making Bridei a harp!"

"What?" Dessia exclaimed. "What do you mean they're building him a harp?"

"You should see it! They've gotten a lot done already. Eth has cut the frame and is working on the part called the tail. Niall is making pins to hold the strings in place, and Cook has saved back some gut that when dried will make the strings. Bridei says the instrument will have limited range, in that it only has six strings. But 'twill be better than nothing." The sparkle faded from Aife's eyes. "You look angry. What's wrong?"

"I was very clear with Bridei ap Maelgwn. I told him soon after he arrived that I didn't need, nor want, a bard in my household. The man not only ignored my wishes but cajoled and manipulated the other workmen into subverting my will."

"But why don't you want him to perform for us? He could do it in the evening, when it's too dark for the men to work on the wall. What would it hurt to have him sing a few songs?"

Dessia turned away from the maidservant. There was no way she could tell Aife that she feared if she listened to Bridei perform, she would fall utterly under his spell. But she had to give some sort of explanation. Perhaps a partial truth would suffice.

She turned back to face Aife. "I've accomplished a great deal these past ten years. I've fought off my enemies, reclaimed my family's lands and rebuilt my home. I've done those things by being single-minded and determined, and letting nothing distract me from my goal. Bridei ap Maelgwn threatens all of that. I worry he will entice us with his tales and cause us forget our ultimate goal, which is to make Cahermara so strong and formidable it can never be attacked."

"I don't think any of us are so foolish or weak-witted that we will suddenly shirk our responsibilities if we have a little entertainment and pleasure in our lives," said Aife. "Indeed, I think it would make most people work all the harder during the day, knowing they have something to look forward to in the evenings." Aife's voice grew pleading. "Please. At least give him a chance. Let him perform at least one time when the harp is finished."

Dessia sighed. "I can't fight all of you. When the harp is finished, he may perform."

Chapter 8

This was absurd, Dessia thought as she walked toward the workmen's barracks. The whole fortress was her domain. She had the right to access any part of it. Yet her heart was fluttering in her chest as if she were a young girl spying on her elders. She paused just outside the door and sought to regain her composure. Then she entered the long, low building.

The men, including Bridei, were all seated around Eth. On his lap, Eth cradled an oblong piece of wood. With one big beefy hand he was doing something to the top of the object. The men were all watching him, their attention so firmly fixed on him that no one noticed her entrance.

Dessia cleared her throat and all the men looked at her. They got to their feet, their expressions startled and slightly shamefaced. All except Bridei. He stood with maddening slowness, like a cat languidly stretching.

"Milady. We didn't expect this pleasure." Bridei's violet blue eyes bored into her, making her feel breathless.

"I wanted to see how the harp was coming," she said, trying to sound crisp and matter-of-fact.

Eth stepped forward, holding out the wooden object with reverence. "See, Milady."

"It looks like no harp I've ever seen," she said.

Bridei moved closer to her. The sheer impact of his physical presence affected her so strongly she almost pulled back. "It's a lyre harp," he answered in his rich, well-modulated voice. "They're common in Gaul and among the Saxon tribes." He took the harp from Eth and gestured as he spoke. "The strings, once they're ready, will be attached to these pins, and to this small tailpiece below. The musician strums across them like this, and the sound resonates down through the frame, which is hollow inside."

"And you showed them how to make this?"

"Aye. It's a bit crude compared to the instruments I'm used to." He flashed a reassuring smile at Eth. "But I think it will have a decent sound. We have to wait for the gut for the strings to cure, and then we'll know."

"How long will that take?" Despite herself, Dessia was fascinated. It seemed almost magical that a piece of wood, metal pins and some pieces of cowgut could be made into a musical instrument.

Bridei shrugged. "A week or two."

"That will give Niall time to finish the adornment," said Eth, taking the half-made harp back from Bridei.

"Adornment?" asked Dessia.

"Aye. He's making some metal decorations for the harp. The bits of metal will go here and here." With his big fingers, Eth gestured to the top of the harp and to a place below where the strings would be attached.

"And where is the metal for these decorations coming from?" Dessia gave Bridei a searching look. "I assumed the slavers had seized all your possessions."

"I had nothing but the clothes on my back when they dragged me onto their boat."

"So, where is this precious metal coming from?" she persisted.

"You'll have to ask Niall."

His manner was cool, almost disdainful. Dessia felt a surge of anger. "Aye, I'll do that." Straightening her shoulders, she left the barracks.

The whole experience unnerved her. She felt as if Bridei had somehow taken over her household. He was the one they listened to, rather than her. He was the one who made decisions about what her people would do and how they would spend their time. If it had been anyone else involved but simple Eth, she'd have put a stop to all of it. But it seemed cruel to take away the young man's dream. How his eyes had glowed as he spoke of the harp, transforming his broad, plain face. And the other men were clearly keen on the project as well. Even level-headed, solid Nally seemed enthused about the harp.

The thought aroused a new sense of irritation in Dessia. Her only hope was Niall. She'd explain to the smith that she couldn't afford for him to spend his time on something so frivolous. She needed him to make tools and weapons, not decorations for a harp. And then there was a matter of the metal involved. Metal was too precious to squander on ornamentation. She'd make herself clear. There was probably nothing she could do about the harp itself, since it was nearly finished. But she would be very plain about this bit of nonsense. The smith was one of the few individuals who had their own dwelling inside the fortress walls. As she approached, she saw it was dark. The smith and his wife must have gone to bed. She turned away with a sigh. The conversation would have to wait until the morrow.

* * *

That night she dreamed again of her escape from the burning fortress of Cahermara. But this time it wasn't a cat that led her to safety but Bridei. When he appeared he was carrying a harp over his shoulder. He smiled and beckoned. She followed after him. The next thing she knew they were on a hillside, and Bridei was seated on the ground. He settled the harp in front of himself, set his fingers to the strings and began to sing.

She woke feeling chilled and uneasy, wondering if there was a message in the dream. If it meant she was supposed to trust Bridei and let him stay. But the thought didn't sway her from her plan of talking to the smith. As soon as she was dressed and Aife had fixed her hair, she set out for Niall's workshop.

Entering, she saw the smith was making a sword, vigorously pounding the heated metal of the blade. The sight relieved her. The smith hadn't abandoned his duties. But there was still the matter of the metal he was using for the harp.

Niall looked up and saw her. He nodded, then said, "Let me finish this. It takes a long time to get the metal to the right temperature."

She waited while he worked the blade with swift, skillful blows of the hammer. He wore no tunic and the muscles in his massive shoulders and arms rippled and flexed as he worked. She admired the power exhibited by his body and at the same time thought of Bridei and how he'd looked without his tunic. He was much more finely made than the smith, his muscles much less massive. But he was still strong. She recalled the implacable feel of his arms as he pinned her against his body while they were at the lake. She also recalled the feel of his manhood pressing against her buttocks. The memory caused a shiver of desire to course through her.

She jerked her attention back to the smith. After a few moments, he held up the sword blade with his tongs. The tip was sleek and pointed, the edges, thin, sharp and deadly. She murmured her approval, then watched as he plunged the sword blade into a tub of water to cool it.

"Is it finished?" she asked.

"Nay. It must be reheated several more times until it's hard and strong enough to tolerate use in battle."

"I'm glad to see you're working on a sword," she said. "We can always use more weapons."

He didn't respond, merely cocked a sandy brow, clearly wondering why she was there.

She said, "The men are making a harp for the man the slavers left. They told me you were fashioning some metal pieces to adorn it."

"That's true," he answered.

"Where did you get the metal?" She hated the accusing sound of her voice. But metal was something that had to be purchased from the traders. By rights all the raw material Niall used in his work belonged to her.

The smith shrugged. "I had a few odds and ends lying around."

Why did everyone act as if the harp was none of her business? It was very aggravating. "Have you gotten very far on the decoration?"

Niall shrugged again. "A fair piece."

Dessia took a deep breath, striving for calm. "May I see what you've done?"

Niall went to the back of the shop, then came back a moment later and held out his hand.

"That's not bronze! That's gold!" she exclaimed. "I can't believe this! How dare you use up our small store of costly metal for this! You're going to have to melt it down. I won't allow *my* gold to be used for such a purpose!"

"It's not your gold," said Niall.

"Where did it come from? Nay, don't bother answering!" she snapped, jerking her head towards the workmen's barracks. "I'm certain I know where it came from. That lying wretch Bridei had it. Well, perhaps you should consider how *he* came by it." She pointed to the delicate piece of metalwork. "The gold in that undoubtedly represents payment from one of our enemies. Can't you see what's going on? They've hired Bridei to spy on us. And you've all fallen right into their trap." She let out a hiss of exasperation.

Niall answered slowly, "The gold didn't come from him. It came from several people. Including my own wife. She had a pair of earbobs from her mother, who served your parents, as you may recall. Ona has never worn them. When would she ever have reason? So, when she heard about this plan to make the bard a harp, she gave them to me. The rest of the metal came from Beatha and Sorcha. They also had jewelry that I melted down."

Dessia's anger turned to embarrassment. She'd all but accused Niall of stealing from her. "Can I hold it?" she asked.

He handed her the piece of metalwork. It was nearly as thin as parchment. The design on the front was exquisite, with the swirling lines of gold making a spiral. "It's beautiful," she said. "I had no idea you could make anything like this."

Niall shrugged. "When would I have the chance? I spend my days making swords and knives and plowshares."

"But how did you learn to do this?"

"My father taught me. He used to make fine metalwork for your father. In fact, he probably made Ona's earrings that I melted down. I regretted destroying his work, but I couldn't miss this opportunity to see what I could do on my own." He looked at her, his greenish blue eyes gleaming like polished stones. "I've also studied some of the pieces the traders have for sale. You never let them show you jewelry, but usually if I offer to sharpen a knife for them or some other favor, they'll take out their finer wares. Some of the pieces have colors on them using a technique called enamel. I'd like to learn how to do that. But of course..." He shrugged again.

Dessia was amazed. She could see how intent he was, how much this project meant to him. Although she'd never thought of Niall as an artist, he was, in as much as Bridei was one also.

The thought of Bridei reawakened her irritation. "I understand your desire to develop your skills. But I wish you'd come to me when the matter first arose. If you want to spend your extra time making jewelry or other fine ornaments, I have no problem with that. But this harp..." She trailed off, uncertain how to explain her objections. Starting again, she said, "The problem is not the metalwork or even the harp itself. The problem is this man Bridei. I don't trust him, yet I'm afraid to send him away for fear he will go straight to my enemies and tell them how weak our defenses really are."

"What about the spell of protection?" Niall asked.

"I... I don't know how long I can maintain it. The magic involved is... it's not permanent. It has to be renewed periodically and I worry that someday it will weaken or fail altogether." As much as she hated admitting how vulnerable they really were, she didn't feel she had a choice. She had to make *someone* understand the threat Bridei represented.

"But why are you so concerned that Bridei is a spy? He seems harmless enough to me."

That's because you're not a woman, Dessia thought. But she said, "Something about him makes me uneasy. Ever since he arrived, I've had these strange dreams. I feel as if the gods were warning me of something." Niall nodded solemnly, looking concerned. "It may be nothing," she said, "but I can't afford to take any chances."

"Of course not," Niall agreed. "But despite your doubts of him, this man Bridei is clearly a skilled bard. I see no reason why you shouldn't allow him to perform. Nor do I understand why this matter of the harp concerns you. All the work on the harp is being done after our other duties are finished. I worked on the metalwork decorations until very late last night, yet I still fired up the forge this morning at the same time as always."

"Very well. As long as it's not interfering with your other responsibilities." She knew she was defeated. There was no objection she could make that would satisfy him, or anyone else at Cahermara. She'd lost this battle, and Bridei—curse his handsome face—had won.

But the war wasn't over, she assured herself as she left the smithy. Thinking about Bridei's smug, mocking expression the night before aroused her ire to fever pitch. She couldn't bear to let him think he'd had his way completely.

Instead of heading for the hall and her own chamber, she strode out the gate and around the side to where the workmen were laboring on the wall. Observing Bridei mixing mortar, she gestured for him to approach her. She was pleased to see that his hands were caked with lime and dust, and the rest of him none to clean either. He wouldn't dare think of laying hands on her in this condition.

"Milady." He inclined his head in an elegant gesture.

"I'm willing to let you and the men continue to make the harp, and even to let you perform in the hall when the instrument is finished. But I'm not doing this to gratify you, but because my people work hard for me and I want to reward their loyalty and devotion. If they're keen to hear you play a harp and sing, I will allow it. But that doesn't mean I've accepted you as a part of my household or that your position here is secure. I might decide at any time to send you away."

"I wouldn't presume to think I'd swayed you or charmed you in any way. Nay, not you, mighty queen and powerful sorceress that you are."

"Don't be insolent," she snapped.

"Why not? You treat me with contempt and have no regard for my abilities. Why should I accept such treatment from you? I could leave at any time and go to another household. I don't doubt that even at the most meager farm in Ireland I would be greeted with more graciousness than what you've offered."

"Then why don't you leave?" Dessia demanded, losing control. "I've never stopped you."

He cocked his head, looking thoughtful. "Perhaps I will go elsewhere, but not until the harp is finished and I've played for your subjects. They deserve that much at least."

"Aye, they do. They've worked hard to build this harp."

His expression changed, the scornful mask falling away. "Do you know why the harp means so much to your people? Do you understand why they've gone to so much trouble? I'll tell you," he went on before she could answer. "It's because they're starved for music and pleasure in their lives. You speak of the harshness of *your* life, but you don't realize how it's been for them. Working every day for you and at the same time trying ensure their own survival. They've had no respite, no chance to make merry and celebrate and take joy in being alive. You're a cruel ruler, to deprive them so. What would it have cost you to have a feast now and then, to let them get drunk on mead and have some traveling entertainer perform for them? But nay, you've decided to dedicate your life to grimness and duty, so they must live the same way."

Dessia gasped. "That's not true! We've had feasts. In late summer when my clients bring me the tribute they owe me we always butcher a steer and have a grand meal."

"Once a year?" Bridei's voice was contemptuous. "And did you have any entertainment at the feast? Or was it a dutiful, cheerless affair, mirroring the rest of your habits?"

"We've had bards come. I think there was one here last spring... or was it the year before..."

"See? It's been so long you can't even remember. And what about celebrating the traditional rites marking the turn of the seasons? I thought when I came here that perhaps people in Ireland had different beliefs, different gods. But I've found out that many of the gods here are the same as those of Britain. So why don't you celebrate Beltaine, the festival honoring the sun god Belenos's return to the sky? Or perform rites at Imbolc in honor of the goddess of fertility, who my people know as Rhiannon and yours as Brighid?

"People honor the gods to let them know they value their gifts," he continued. "If you're so concerned for the welfare your people, you might want to consider how you've turned away from the powerful forces that protect them. And even if you don't celebrate the traditional festivals, you should have a feast just for the sheer pleasure of it. Your people are starved for music and laughter. Just because you're willing to let yourself shrivel up and grow old before your time doesn't mean your people have to follow the same—"

"Stop!" Dessia cried. She felt tears come to her eyes, and she turned away and fought them back with all her will. He was right... about all of it. She had been very lax in observing the traditional rites due the gods. When she first regained Cahermara, there'd been too much to do and she hadn't felt they had the resources to waste on such things. Later, when it would have been possible to observe the turning of the seasons, she'd been too bitter to make the effort. She'd blamed the gods for her family's misfortune. They'd turned away from her, so why should she honor them?

But of course that wasn't true. She might well have died the night the rest of her family had been killed. Should have died, in fact. But she hadn't. The gods had saved her. And yet, for almost ten years now, she'd ignored them. The realization stunned her. The next moment she was furious that Bridei was the one who pointed these things out to her.

Whirling around, she snarled at him, "I suppose you're a devout, dutiful servant of the gods and that's why they've favored you."

He laughed. "Hardly. Most of my life I haven't even thought about them, let alone concerned myself with how they might influence my life. Of course, you could argue the things that have happened to me recently may be their way of punishing me for failing to heed them. I may be favored in some ways, but that doesn't change the fact that I'm stuck in a foreign land with no possessions of my own other than my now-tattered clothing." He gestured to the ragged garment he wore. "I'm also at the mercy of a capricious and often spiteful queen who threatens to banish me every time I turn around."

"Capricious! Spiteful!" Dessia's arm drew back of its own accord, and she was on the verge of striking him when she realized that doing so would prove his words true. She lowered her arm and swallowed, feeling once again as if she might weep. What was it about this man that brought out the worst in her?

His voice dropped in pitch, becoming that rich, vibrant instrument he used when he sang. "Of course, the queen whose favor I depend upon is also beautiful and proud and absolutely magnificent, and I count it as no great hardship to stay in her household. Though she may be stubborn and foolish, I know that she has a warm and tender heart and cares for her people much more than most rulers. She is also bold and brave, and like the rest of her subjects, I am honored to serve her."

The sound of his voice throbbed through her, filling her with longing and hunger. She wanted to move close to him and have him hold her in his arms. If they hadn't been near the work site, in plain view of the other men, she probably would have done so. Instead, she drew a shaky breath. "What pretty words you speak. But I must remember how skilled you are at flattery. It's the thing you do to earn your livelihood. I'm sure you don't have to stop and think what to say. You know all the compliments by heart, are well aware of what every woman wants to hear."

His expression grew fierce and passionate. "But you're not *any* woman. You're a queen, and that makes my admiration for you all the more keen. Do you think I tell every woman she's magnificent? That I comment on what a fine ruler she is? The truth is, I admire you not only for your beauty, but also for your bravery and determination, your selfless devotion to your people and your cause. My criticisms are only meant to remind you that there is more to life than duty and struggle. I want to see you smile and laugh... and dance. If you will let me perform not only for your people, but for you alone, I vow I can give you those gifts."

Bridei drew near, so close she could see the dusky shadow of whiskers on his jaw. Dessia shivered, remembering the hunger with which their lips had met, as if they were starving people at a feast. The boundaries between their bodies blurring until she hadn't known where her own self ended and his flesh began.

"Nay!" She backed away. "I'll allow you to perform for my people in the hall, but I won't give you a chance to use your ruthless charm on me in private." Whirling, she stalked off.

* * *

Bridei went back to breaking rocks. His hands holding the hammer trembled. Thank the gods she'd walked away. Maybe her pride would keep her from ever allowing him to get close to her. But was that what he wanted? If it was, then why didn't he leave? Why stay here and torture both of them?

He couldn't understand what was happening to him. Never before had he felt this way. It was if the ground beneath his feet had turn to marsh mud. He wanted her with a passion he'd never experienced before. And yet, he was afraid of her.

He didn't know what to do. Reason told him to leave. But he couldn't quite make himself do it. And now there was the matter of the harp to consider. He had to stay to see the thing through. It would be nearly a fortnight before the strings were properly dried and seasoned. Then they would have a feast and he would play.

And then, the gods willing, he would leave.

Chapter 9

Dessia gazed out at the gray sheets of rain. Shivering, she closed the shutters and stepped away from the window. She was trapped inside for another day, and so was everyone else in the hillfort. Since they couldn't work and their barracks were so cold, Nally had asked if the workmen could gather in the hall where the roaring fire in the hearth provided plenty of heat. He'd given them tasks to keep them busy—making arrow shafts, scraping hides, polishing weapons and tools. But these were all things that required little concentration, and after a while, someone—probably Eth—had suggested that Bridei could tell them stories to pass the time. Now, Bridei was down in her hall, entertaining and charming her people. The thought of it made Dessia want to scream.

As she paced in the small chamber, Aife entered. The serving girl set the tray containing bread and cheese for Dessia's morning meal on the table, and said, "You should go down, milady. There's no sense you staying up here where it's so drafty and cold."

"I have work to do." Dessia gestured to a parchment lying on the table.

"Begging your pardon, milady, but you've been working on those manuscripts for months now. Taking one day off won't change anything."

"I have no desire to listen to Bridei tell a bunch of silly tales."

"Oh, but he's not telling tales now."

Dessia stopped pacing and looked at the serving girl. "Has he run out of stories? Or have the workmen grown tired of listening to him?"

"Nay. I vow they would be happy to listen to him for another fortnight. But he said it wasn't fair for him to entertain the people in hall and ignore the others who had tasks in the kitchen or other areas. So, instead of telling tales, he's switched to talking about places he's been and things he's seen. Of course, that's almost as interesting as any tale. Yesterday he told about a place called Narbonne, across the sea on the other side of Britain. There's a huge market there where they sell all sorts of things—slaves and horses, silks and spices. It sounds like an amazing place. Then, he described the conflict between his people and the Saxons. He told about this warrior king named Arthur, who tried to drive the Saxons out of Britain, but who ended up being defeated and killed by his own son who'd allied himself with the enemy."

A thought came to Dessia. Maybe this was her chance to learn more about Bridei's background. She would ask Aife to question him. If she could get him to talk freely, she might be able discover if the story he told about being captured by slavers was really true.

"I want you to do something for me," she said to Aife, "I want you to go down to the hall and ask Bridei questions about his homeland and his family. Don't let him tell you that such things aren't interesting or avoid the subject. Be coaxing and sweet and let him think you're so enamored of him that you desire to know every detail of his life. Ask him how he ended up with the slavers. Where they captured him and why the slavers didn't worry that someone would come after them."

Aife nodded. "You're trying to find out if the story he gave us is true."

"Aye. That's exactly what I'm doing. He won't be suspicious or threatened by you, so he's more likely to tell you the truth, or at least let something slip. I'm going to be there listening, although he won't know it."

"How will you manage that?"

"I'll be in disguise." Dessia grew excited as the plan began to take shape in her mind. She would dress up as one of the serving women and remain on the edges of those gathered around the fire. If she appeared old and bent and slow, Bridei would never notice her, especially while he was flirting with Aife.

"Very well, milady. I'll do it. But I'm not certain your plan will work. Bridei strikes me as a man who's very careful about what he says."

"But his tongue might loosen if questioned by you, a pretty maid who acts besotted with him."

"I'm not certain he'll believe I have any interest in him. I think he knows how I feel about Keenan."

"Keenan?" Dessia was stunned. She'd had no idea her serving maid had any interest in her man-of-arms.

Aife blushed and ducked her head. "I... I am fond of him, milady."

Dessia didn't know what to say. She felt vaguely resentful. Keenan was the person whose loyalty she depended upon most. She didn't need a rival in her own serving maid. Of course, Keenan's responsibility to her was a much different matter than his personal affections. And he might not feel the same way as the Aife did.

"Does Keenan return your affections?"

Aife blushed a deeper hue of rose. "I think so, milady."

Dessia nodded stiffly. She knew her reaction was unfair and unkind. There was no reason her maid shouldn't have a paramour. No reason Keenan couldn't have an interest in another woman besides her. But somehow, this knowledge hurt her... and made her feel deeply alone.

It was also aggravating that Bridei—who barely knew either of these young people—should be aware of their fondness for each other while she'd been oblivious.

"Milady, do you want me to go down and start asking Bridei questions now?"

Dessia's thoughts snapped back to the present. "First, I need to have you help me create a disguise. I'll need some old clothing and a basket of sewing or something else I can be working on."

* * *

Dessia waited until midmorning to creep down the stairs. She wanted as many people as possible to be in the hall, so it would be less likely Bridei would notice her. As she'd hoped, the hall was crowded. Everyone from the workmen to the warriors to the women of the fortress and their children had come to the hall to escape the weather and also—she felt certain—to hear Bridei. They'd all brought tasks of some sort. The women had their spinning, sewing and weaving. There was a large loom that was set up near the hearth, and Sorcha was working on a piece of a blue and red plaid fabric. Meanwhile, the men busied themselves polishing and oiling weapons and tools and carving implement handles and other things made of wood. The children played quietly in one corner. In the center of the gathering, near the hearth, was Bridei. He was using a cloth to polish the wood frame of the harp and appeared quite involved in the task.

Dessia pulled the grimy, raw wool shawl lower over her face. Hunching her shoulders and keeping her knees bent to make herself appear shorter, she shuffled forward, moving to the side of the hall where most of the women were. A few of them glanced at her curiously, but didn't say anything. She hoped they'd think she was Glenna, an elderly widow who lived not far from Cahermara and who sometimes came to the fortress to sell honey or baskets. While it would be unusual for Glenna to be out in this weather, it wasn't impossible.

A woman named Finola gave up her stool so Dessia could sit down. Still keeping her head bowed, Dessia nodded and murmured her thanks. She was very grateful to be able to sit, as standing hunched over was becoming a strain. From the cloth bundle she carried, she took out a half-finished basket and positioned it on her lap. As she pretended to be weaving it, the long sleeves of the ragged tunic she wore fell back, revealing her fingers with their smooth skin and manicured nails. She quickly adjusted the fabric, hoping no one had noticed.

Her heart began to race as she considered how foolish she'd look if anyone recognized her. How would she explain why she'd come to her own hall in disguise? Her tension grew until at last she saw Aife enter carrying a basket of embroidery. Instead of joining the other women, Aife made her way through the men to where Bridei sat near the hearth. Aife sank down on the worn hide at his feet. Bridei immediately leaned down and said something to her, likely offering her a seat on the bench next to him. Dessia saw Aife shake her head and then, getting to her knees so her face was close to Bridei's, Aife continued her coaxing. Smiling, Bridei shook his head. Aife persisted. Although Dessia couldn't see her maid's face, she could imagine her pleading expression, her dainty dimples and small white teeth. Her blue eyes would sparkle and her voice would be soft and cajoling. How could Bridei resist?

Dessia watched as Aife turned and gestured to everyone gathered in the hall. It was clear she was trying to convince Bridei that the rest of the people would enjoy hearing him tell of his life as much as she would.

Bridei responded, and Dessia held her breath. It would be very aggravating if he refused Aife's request. She would have gone to all this trouble for nothing. All at once he straightened, and smiling broadly, announced to the room, "Aife has asked me to tell you about my homeland and my family. Although it's a rather dull tale, she assures me that after being stuck inside for two days, you're all eager for any sort of diversion."

Dessia smiled faintly. How clever Aife was, to appeal to Bridei's yearning for an audience. Although he strove to appear modest, his natural arrogance had won out.

"I was born in north Gwynedd," Bridei began, "on the western edge of Britain. Gwynedd is a rugged land of steep mountains and heavily forested hills, but it also has verdant green valleys and beautiful beaches. Most of my people—who call themselves the Cymry—are not farmers, but herders, as much of the land isn't suitable for raising crops. We have sheep and some cattle, but not as many as you seem to have here in Eire. I grew up along the coast, at my father's chief fortress of Deganwy. It's a stronghold similar to Cahermara, although Deganwy is situated on a hill right above the coast, enabling us to keep watch for raiders from the sea."

"Is that how you were captured and brought here? By raiders?" asked one of the men.

Bridei shook his head. "In the years before I was born, boats from Ireland used to land on our beaches and steal away women and children to enslave. But my father and his warriors put a stop to that. They killed enough of the slavers that word spread that Gwynedd wasn't a good place to raid."

"If you weren't captured by slavers in your homeland, where did it happen?" asked Aife.

Dessia watched as a bitter expression crossed Bridei's face. The next moment, it was gone. "It was in the north, at a place known as Catraith. And I wasn't captured by slavers, but given to them by the local chieftain. You see, I'd angered him, and he decided to get rid of me by giving me to the slavers."

"What an awful betrayal," one of the men said. "You must have been very angry."

Bridei smiled wryly. "Of course, I may have deserved such treatment. After all, I did bed the chieftain's daughter. She was willing, but still..." He gestured casually and continued to smile.

There was laughter among the crowd, but there was an uneasy edge to it. Those men who had daughters weren't much amused, and some of the women had to be thinking sympathetically of the young princess.

Dessia first reaction was anger and the thought that the wretch deserved exactly what he'd gotten. But then she considered the story more carefully and realized something sounded false. Bridei might be unscrupulous enough to bed a chieftain's daughter, but he wasn't foolish, and that's how this story made him sound. There was also the look on his face right before he answered Aife's question. The obvious bitterness Dessia had seen didn't jibe with the carelessness with which he told the tale. *He's lying*, she thought. *But why?*

As Bridei returned to describing Gwynedd and recounting amusing incidents from his childhood, Dessia's suspicions grew. Bridei had dismissed the matter of his enslavement very abruptly. Perhaps the reason he didn't give more details was because it had never happened. How was she going to find out more? Perhaps she could have Aife seek him out later and press him for details. But if she did that, she would have to rely on Aife to interpret his answers. Frustration built in her. She'd been so certain this ruse would allow her to see the real Bridei. Instead, she'd discovered more layers of lies and deception.

But she wouldn't give up. The day was early yet. She listened as Bridei talked about his father, Maelgwn the Great: "They call him that because he's very tall. Taller than any man at Cahermara. My eldest brother inherited his height, but I did not. We have different mothers, and my mother, the lady Rhiannon, is a tiny thing, as dainty and fine to look upon as one of the fey folk, who your people call fairies. I have my smaller stature from her, and because I was not a huge monster of a man, I chose not to become a warrior." The look of bitterness crossed his face again. "It was a matter of great contention between my father and myself. He never believed there was any other worthwhile life for one of his sons. Odd in a way, considering that he spent nearly five years in a house of holy men."

Several people gasped in surprise. It was Eth who asked what they were all thinking. "Your father became a holy brother? But why, if he was a warrior and a great king?"

"It's a strange tale, and a sad one," Bridei answered. "You see, my father's first wife, a Roman British woman named Aurora, died in childbirth. The babe died as well, and my father was very distraught. Although the match had been made for political reasons, my father loved this woman. When he lost her, it broke his heart. He cared for nothing and almost lost his will to live."

Dessia could almost hear a sigh of sadness fill the hall. Who among them had not lost someone they loved and been so bereaved they could scarce go on? She herself had dealt with that crushing grief for many years after her family was killed.

Bridei continued, "I think in some way my father blamed himself for Aurora's death. A senseless idea, and yet many people react that way. He also had many regrets, for although he came to love this woman deeply, the early days of their marriage had been stormy and wrought with strife. He couldn't stop thinking of all the time he'd lost. And then there was the babe that perished with her. His son, the promise of his line.

"He didn't know it then, but he had another son. My eldest brother was conceived before my father was married. Rhun's mother kept his birth a secret, for reasons of her own. And so, after Aurora died, my father was beyond caring for anything. He went to a nearby priory and told them he wanted to give it all up—his kingdom, his power, his wealth. He became a brother and lived a modest and holy life of prayer and contemplation for nearly ten years."

"What happened then?" Eth asked. "Why did he leave the priory?"

A faint smile quirked Bridei's mouth. "The story he tells is that one of his former warriors came to him and told him his kingdom was falling apart and the people of Gwynedd desperately needed him. He says he returned to being king because it seemed to be his duty, what God wanted him to do. For myself, I think he must have become heartily bored in the priory after all those years and was more than ready to leave."

There was laughter at this, and Bridei joined in. "At any rate," he continued, "he came back, fought to regain the lands that had been lost, married my mother—which is another tale altogether—and once again reigned as the powerful warlord they call the Dragon of the Island."

As she had the first time she heard Bridei call his father by this name, Dessia felt a chill down her spine. Her vision didn't waver and she didn't see a crimson banner with a gold dragon on the wall, but she vividly recalled the image and the way it had appeared, and wondered again what the gods were trying to tell her about this man.

Bridei continued to regale his audience with stories about his father's rise to power and his prowess in battle. Dessia grew impatient. This was all very interesting, especially the part about his father's first marriage and his decision to enter a priory, but it brought her no nearer to finding out Bridei's true motives. She wondered if Aife was ever going to coax Bridei to turn the subject back to himself. Her back ached from being hunched over and the awful cloak she wore was scratching her skin.

At last, Aife said, "You've told us a great deal about your family and homeland, but I can't help wondering why you haven't returned to visit for so many years."

Dessia watched as Bridei's eyes narrowed. "Ah. You're thinking that if my father is such a great man, why do I want nothing to do with him? Yet it was he who sent me away. We had a falling out when I was very young, only barely grown, and we've never repaired the rift."

"What was the falling out over?" Aife asked, her voice so gentle that Dessia could barely hear her words.

"It hardly matters now," Bridei answered brusquely. "I was only fourteen winters when he banished me from his household. I was resourceful, but fourteen is a very young age to be on one's own." He paused and looked around the room, making eye contact with his listeners. As he glanced her direction, Dessia swiftly ducked her head.

It wasn't until he began speaking again that Dessia dared raise her gaze. Bridei seemed to be looking far off into the distance and his voice had grown contemplative. "When I left Gwynedd, I was yet a boy in many ways. But somehow I survived. I found my way to the eastern coast of Britain and hired on with a ship's crew. It wasn't a pleasant life, but it enabled me to eat. I traveled many places. North to the land of the Saxons and Frisians, west to Less Britain, where the people speak a tongue very close to that of my homeland, then south and down through the narrow straits of the Pillars of Hercules. Passing through there, we reached an inland sea and followed the coast of the land of the Iberians until we reached Gaul and its chief port, Narbonne. I've told you about the market there, but I haven't told what happened to me the first time I went there. I made the mistake of getting separated from my shipmates. Some men seized me and took me to the slave market and sold me."

A wave of shock seemed to pass through those gathered in the hall. Dessia herself knew a surge of sympathy for Bridei, or at least the boy he'd been. It must have been terrifying, to be enslaved at a mere fourteen winters of age, so far away from home and all hope of rescue.

"What happened then?" Aife asked breathlessly.

Bridei's smile was tight. "Most of what you'd expect. I won't go into the brutal details, but suffice to say I didn't like being a slave. But one good thing did come of it. While I was a captive I learned to play the harp. I also found out I had a pleasant singing voice and a way with words. When I finally escaped, I had the means to earn my keep. I was also much better able to fend for myself in other ways. It's not only the British and Irish races that honor musicians and poets. Most civilized peoples have respect for bards and accord them a place of honor in their households. Your queen, being the exception, of course."

Dessia suppressed a gasp. The audacity of the man—to imply she was some sort of uncouth barbarian because she'd hadn't asked him to serve as her bard! She must have made a sound, for Finola turned and looked at her. Dessia froze in dread, wondering if she would be exposed. There could hardly be a worse moment for it, just after Bridei had ridiculed her for her treatment of him.

But everyone else seemed to be too caught up in Bridei's tale to notice her. "How long were you a slave?" Eth asked. "How did you escape?"

"I was a slave for nearly two years. As for how I escaped, it was simple. I killed my master." Another murmur of shock and surprise rippled through the hall. Bridei went on: "My master wasn't well-liked, and once he was dead, no one in his household saw fit to detain me. By the time the authorities arrived, I was long gone. The difficult part was making my way back to Narbonne. The man who'd purchased me lived in a land far to the east, and I had to get passage back across the great sea. But I managed to do it, and even kept the harp I'd stolen. It was an incredible instrument. My master was a merchant and had a house full of rare and beautiful things. Furniture of fine wood, gilded with gold and cushioned with brilliant-hued silk fabrics, gaming pieces carved of ivory and set with jewels. He ate from plates of gold and drank from pearl-encrusted goblets. And the food we dined upon was also splendid—rare fruits, spiced meats, and the most delicious wines."

Dessia could feel her mouth watering and realized she hadn't eaten that morning. But it wasn't simply hunger his words aroused, but a yearning of all her senses, as he painted a picture of a world of exotic, provocative delights.

"And your harp?" Eth asked. "Was it also decorated with gems and gold?"

"Nay, it had no adornments. Its value came from its exquisite tone. With twelve strings, it could capture every sound from the whisper of the wind through the leaves to the boom of thunder, yet it was small enough to fit into a pack. I carried it with me for nearly ten years, until I was forced to leave it behind when the Catraith chieftain gave me to the slavers."

"But now we're making you another harp," Eth said, gesturing to the half-finished instrument on Bridei's lap. "Soon you can play it, and make all those sounds you told us about."

"I'll try," answered Bridei.

One of the women approached Bridei with a pottery cup and handed it to him. Bridei thanked her and tilting back his head, took a deep swallow. Watching the grace of his movements, Dessia was struck by the sheer beauty of the man. She had a strong suspicion why the foreign merchant had purchased him. At fourteen years old, Bridei would still have been a boy, and a strikingly attractive one at that. Dessia had heard of bedslaves, and the taste of some men for young males. The thought of it horrified her and aroused her intense sympathy for Bridei. She couldn't imagine being used in such a way. To endure such treatment at such a tender age—how could anyone ever get over it?

But was the story true? Perhaps these things had actually happened to someone else, someone Bridei had known in his travels. Yet the cold rage she'd seen on his face as he talked of killing his master—that was surely real. What a puzzle Bridei ap Maelgwn was.

* * *

Had Queen Dessia discovered what she wanted to know? Bridei sipped the hot cider Beatha had brought him. His gaze strayed to where the queen sat, dressed in her ridiculous disguise. He'd known it was her as soon as she entered the hall. For all her efforts to hunch over and shuffle as she walked, she was too tall to be the withered crone she sought to portray. He was surprised no one else had taken note of her. But these people were comfortable here, while he was a stranger and must always be on his guard.

He'd let down his defenses in other ways, having told the people of Cahermara more about his life and his background than he'd ever told anyone. He wasn't certain why he'd revealed so much. Perhaps it was because he'd known Dessia was listening, and he wanted her to realize he'd suffered in his life, that she wasn't the only one who'd endured terrible things.

But the part about the chieftain's daughter in Catraith, that had been a mistake. Implying that he'd seduced a young noblewoman hadn't earned him much sympathy. He'd only told them that because he feared the truth wasn't convincing. There really was no good reason for Dolgar to have sold him into slavery. Although the Brigante chieftain might have disliked him, it was out of character for Dolgar to plot murder. Someone must have paid him to do it. That awareness had gnawed on Bridei ever since the slavers put shackles on him.

But he really didn't have time to puzzle on that now. There were much more interesting matters to pursue here. He wanted Dessia to feel sorry for him. To convince her that he'd been wronged in his life as much as she had in hers. This strange business of telling about his life instead of made-up stories might well accomplish that.

He glanced at Aife, wondering what she would ask next. It was obvious Dessia had ordered her maidservant to probe into his background. Aife would never have done so on her own. She was far too absorbed with grim, dutiful Keenan to have an interest in any other man.

Almost as if she could read his thoughts, Aife gave him an uncertain smile and said, "Given what happened to you when you were young, it must have been very distressing for you to be taken captive by slavers a second time. And then cast ashore in a strange land where you knew no one. I'm sure you were very relieved when Keenan rescued you."

"Aye, my heart lifted as soon as I saw him," Bridei responded. "I could tell he was a man of character and wouldn't abuse me. Then when he told me about Queen Dessia, my hopes lifted even higher. He swore she was a most generous and just ruler and I had nothing to fear from her." As he said this, Bridei looked directly at Dessia. She bowed her head instantly, and he knew an intense satisfaction. How delightful to have this opportunity to make her regret how she'd treated him.

Bridei looked at Aife expectantly, wondering what she would ask of him next. But it was Beatha who spoke. "Have you ever been back to your homeland since your father sent you away? Ever told him what happened to you?"

Bridei felt his stomach tighten. It was one thing to talk about his father as a bard would, describing him from a distance. But relating the story of the animosity and conflict between them cut very close to the bone.

He shrugged, trying to loosen his shoulders. "I don't see the point of telling him what I endured. Although I'm certain my father didn't intend for me to endure slavery and abuse, it happened and there's no unmaking it."

"So, you've never made up your differences?" It was Aife who spoke this time, her voice tinged with regret.

He felt himself becoming angry, and had to fight to keep his voice calm. "Nay, we never did."

"A pity," Aife said. "Your father sounds like a good man, and one who is capable of learning from his mistakes. Perhaps if you went back there and spoke to him..."

Bridei gritted his teeth and tried to control his temper. He wouldn't let these people, and Dessia especially, see the resentment and anger he still felt towards his father. "Perhaps," he answered in a tight voice. "But I'm unlikely to have an opportunity to return to my homeland anyway."

"Why is that?" Nally asked.

Bridei shrugged. "How would I get there? I have no wealth to purchase passage back to Britain, and I'd rather not travel there the way I came here, on a slaver's boat."

"But now that you have a harp, you'll be able to earn a living again." Eth's broad face lit up. The next moment his pleased expression faded. "Not that we want you to leave. We'd like you to stay here forever.

Wouldn't we?" He gestured to those gathered around.

They responded with a chorus of enthusiastic "ayes". Everyone seemed to be smiling and gazing at him fondly, and Bridei was touched by their obvious regard for him. Although he'd played for halls full of chieftains and kings and been greeted with rousing approval, it had seldom felt as gratifying as this. As he'd told Dessia, these people had suffered and strived for ten long years and were so starved for music and entertainment it was heartbreaking. They needed him. Even more surprising was the realization he wanted to stay, and not only because he had unfinished business with Queen Dessia. There was something about this place that made him feel whole and content. For a man who'd been a restless traveler for nearly his whole adult life, it was an astonishing discovery.

But he dare not let anyone see how he felt. If there was one thing he'd learned in life, it was that caring for anything too intensely inevitably led to suffering and loss. He cast a quick look at Dessia, wondering what she was thinking. Had he won her over? Did she feel sorry for him instead of distrusting him? He should continue talking, and force her to endure her unpleasant disguise for a while longer. But he was suddenly anxious to get out of the hall.

Rising, he bowed to the gathering. "If you could excuse me for a time. I need to stretch my legs."

Aife got hastily to her feet. "If you're going out, you must take your cloak."

"Aye," "Aye", and "Of course he must," murmured other people around him.

Bridei put on the roughly-woven, stained garment he'd been wearing as he worked on the wall, and started for the door. He'd barely reached it when he saw Beatha approaching. She held out a cloak of thick wool in a brilliant plaid of green and red. "Here, wear this."

"Nay, I couldn't," he responded. "It's too fine."

"Not any finer than the stories you tell. Please. It's my gift to you." Beatha was a plain woman, with weathered skin and rather pinched features, but at this moment her face was made lovely by the warm smile she bestowed on him. Bridei tried to recall what he knew about her. He seemed to remember she was widowed. She'd probably made this cloak for her husband. A lump formed in his throat as he took the cloak and put it on. He turned and hurried out of the hall.

Chapter 10

Outside, the rain was coming down steadily. He pulled up the hood of the cloak, bent his head and trudged forward. His plan had been to go to the midden and relieve himself. But now that he was away from the hall—and already getting soaking wet—he realized he wanted to leave the hillfort altogether.

He made his way across the yard toward the gate, trying to avoid the largest puddles. No wonder he'd always told tales to his audiences. Revealing the real story of his life was far too distressing. In doing so, he'd reawakened memories buried for years. Feelings he hadn't experienced in nearly a decade choked his throat and made his stomach clench. Images of the past that he usually glimpsed from a distance suddenly loomed large and threatening, like ominous shadows cast upon a wall. He was a boy again, feeling the helplessness and despair.

He paused at the gate, trembling with remembered turmoil. Fists clenched and breathing hard, he sought to make the memories go away. To shrink them back to insignificance.

"Bridei? What are you doing out here?"

He jerked around to see Keenan. The warrior wore an oiled leather cape over his tunic, but despite the protection, he appeared soaked to the skin.

"I'm leaving the hillfort," Bridei said.

Keenan frowned at him. "I'm not sure the queen would approve."

Bridei fought back the fury that leapt inside him. It would be foolish to get into a confrontation with someone who wore both a dagger and a sword. He sought to speak appeasingly. "Don't worry. I'll come back. If I were going to run off, I'd choose better weather for it."

Keenan hesitated, clearly uncertain what his duty was. Bridei waited, his muscles as tight as bowstrings. If he had to fight Keenan, he would do so. The mood he was in, he thought he might even prevail.

Keenan motioned with his head toward the gate. "Go. If you don't come back, I'll consider it good riddance."

Bridei's anger notched higher. He longed to tell smug Keenan that he'd just spent the last few hours in the dry, warm hall with the lovely Aife at his feet, and that she'd listened to his every word with rapt attention. But his urge to leave this place was much greater than any satisfaction he could obtain by taunting Keenan. He met the man's cold expression with a frigid look of his own, then went to the gate, and grasping the opening winch, jerked it to the side. The gate creaked open, and Bridei slipped through.

He called himself a dozen sorts of fool as he made his way down the hillside. The trackway was muddy and slick and with every step he struggled to keep his balance. But if he walked in the grass instead, his leather shoes would end up a sodden mess. Of course, that was inevitable anyway. He was going to get soaked to the bone and probably die of a chill. But it didn't matter. He had to get away before the walls of the hillfort closed in on him. Somehow he had to clear his head and regain his composure.

The rational part of him didn't understand what had happened. The things he'd spoken of had happened long ago. Why had talking about what he endured brought it back with such intensity? It was as if he could still feel the shackles on his wrists. See Galacius's face, the lust and eagerness shadowing his dark eyes. His thick fingers stroking . . .

Bridei inhaled sharply and willed his thoughts away from the sickening memories. He had to forget. If he didn't, he would go mad. He increased his pace, stumbling forward blindly. All at once, he realized he was near the forest where'd he pursued Dessia. Although he was wary of the place, today it seemed like the perfect escape. Perhaps he could enter the enchanted woodland and never return.

Most of the trees were bare now but the forest still seemed dense and dark. When he'd been here before the landscape had possessed some of the last richness and fecundity of fall. Now he felt as if death surrounded him. Most of the vegetation was dead or dormant. There were a few bits of green still visible—mosses that grew all year long, a few patches of grass where on fine days the sunlight shone. But everything else seemed to have turned gray or brown. It reminded him of when he'd once walked through a forest in Gaul that had burned in a fire. There was the same atmosphere, as if he entered a wasteland, a place where no life could survive.

He reminded himself that it would turn green and verdant again in the spring. Wood violets, primroses and snowdrops would peek through the dried brown leaf cover. The barren branches of the oaks and hazel bushes would be transformed by greening buds and fuzzy catkins. Vines would curl in wild tendrils around now stark tree trunks. Mosses and ferns would carpet the ground.

Even as he had the thought, it seemed to happen. Ahead, the woodland appeared cloaked in green. He hurried forward, unable to believe his eyes. The trees were fully leafed. The ground covered with vegetation. He halted and turned around, expecting to see the winter-bare trees he'd walked through a moment before. What he saw astonished him. It was as if he'd traveled two seasons into the future. This was no desolate late autumn woodland, but a wonderland of green.

He glanced up at the sky, wondering if he'd stumbled through an invisible doorway into the realm of the fey. The hairs on the nape of his neck stood up as he recalled what had happened to him the first time he'd come here. How the dense mist had risen, surrounding him in blinding whiteness. This experience was even stranger. For a moment he stood frozen, afraid to go forward or back. Then a breeze rustled through the leaves of the trees and he seemed to hear a voice calling, "This way. This way. You must go this way."

Mouth dry, he began to walk in the direction the whispering voice told him to. He thought he was headed down the pathway to the lake. Yet how could he be certain of anything when his surroundings altered before his eyes?

A little farther and the ground sloped downwards and he heard the sparkling melody of the stream in the distance. He remembered the first time he'd come here and his sense of being tested, as if he must prove to the forest guardians he was worthy to enter their realm. Now there was no mist to obscure his way, and he could see the path clearly. He felt like a piece of iron being drawn to a lodestone. What would he discover when he reached the lake? After all he'd experienced, nothing would surprise him.

A thought flashed into his mind that he would find his mother and father standing by the still, pearly waters. He could almost see them in his mind: his mother small and delicate, her pale, freckled skin faintly lined and her russet hair threaded with silver. His father, his massive broad-shouldered form slightly diminished, his face carved into deep planes and shadows and his hair and beard frosted with white. With a shock, Bridei realized he was imagining much older versions of his parents. Was this what they looked like now? Were they even alive, or was he seeing their wraiths? Dread filled him. What if their spirits had called him here to say goodbye?

But then he reached the lake and there was no one there. He glanced around, half-panicked. Was he too late? Had they already left him behind? Tears filled his eyes. He felt like a small child, lost and abandoned in the woods. With effort, he calmed himself. It wasn't real. None of this was. He was having some sort of waking dream. Going to the edge of the water, he bent down, wondering if the lake itself was enchanted. He dipped his hands in and splashed his face. The water was icy cold, very wet and very real.

* * *

The hall was filled with activity. With Bridei gone, people were taking this opportunity to step out to the midden, grab a drink of cider from the big pot Beatha had set near the hearth or to discuss the things he'd told them. Dessia was torn. On one hand, she was reluctant to leave. If Bridei came back and began talking again, she might learn even more about him. But her body was cramped and aching, and she worried someone would speak to her and she wouldn't be able to carry off the disguise.

Reluctantly, she got to her feet, and maintaining her hunched-over position, made her way around the edge of the hall. She reached the stairway leading up to the tower, and turned to survey the hall. If she were seen going up the stairs to the queen's chamber, people would think it odd. Seeing Sorcha coming towards her, she started to panic, but fortunately, Aife had seen what was happening and hurried over. "The queen has asked to see Glynna," she told Sorcha.

Although Dessia had quickly turned away and bowed her head so Sorcha couldn't see her face, she heard the puzzlement in the woman's voice as she said, "The queen? What does she want with Glynna?"

"I don't know for certain," Aife answered. "Perhaps it's about some herb or plant she needs for her spells."

"Oh, aye," Sorcha responded. "Glynna does know a lot about plants. That's actually what I wanted to talk to her about. Nuala the Healer told me that coltsfoot might help my son's cough, but she hasn't been able to find any. I thought Glynna might have seen some in the woods on her way here."

"You can talk with her after the queen does," Aife said in authoritative tones. She grasped Dessia's arm and guided her to the stairs. "Here now, I'll help you, Glynna. The stairs are steep and we don't want you to fall."

As soon as they climbed the steps and reached the tower room, Dessia unfastened the scratchy, smelly cloak and tossed it to the floor. She stretched out her arms and rolled her shoulders, trying to get the kinks out of her stiff muscles. "What misery. I began to think my body would freeze in that cramped position and I'd never be able to straighten up. And that cloak—how does anyone tolerate wearing such rough, scratchy garments?"

"It might be uncomfortable to wear, but if you were outside in the rain, you would find unwashed wool sheds water very well. Not everyone has access to oiled leather garments to fend off the weather. Nor do they have the luxury of staying in their homes when it's foul out."

"I hadn't thought of it that way," Dessia responded, feeling chastened. The next moment, they heard footsteps on the stairs. "Who could that be?" asked Dessia. "You don't suppose Sorcha decided to follow after Glynna."

"Nay, she would not," Aife assured her. "Besides, it sounds like Keenan."

Dessia raised her brows at this, then smoothed her hair and the plain gown she'd worn under the scratchy cloak. Keenan called up a moment later, and Dessia bid him come up.

Keenan came up the stairs, his cape and other garments wet and dripping. He shot a quick glance at Aife, then bowed to Dessia and said, "I'm sorry to intrude, milady, but I wanted to let you know that Bridei ap Maelgwn has left the hillfort."

"In this weather?" Dessia exclaimed. "Why? Did he say where he was going?"

"Nay, but I watched from the gatetower and saw him heading west."

"How peculiar," said Dessia.

"And dangerous." Aife looked at Keenan. "You should go after him."

"Why?" Keenan's expression was glowering. "If he falls into the marsh or the forest swallows him up, I say good riddance."

"That's unkind," Aife retorted sharply. "Although you may dislike the man, he's given the rest of us a great deal of enjoyment. Everyone's eagerly awaiting the day when the harp is finished, so he can play for us.

If something happens to him now, it would be dreadful." She clutched Keenan's arm. "The stories he told of his early life were heart-breaking. His father sent him away when he wasn't yet a man and he ended up being sold into slavery. Yet he survived and was able to free himself through cleverness."

Keenan snorted. "Or deceit and cunning, as some might say." He looked at Dessia. "What say you, milady? Do you think I should go after him?" Keenan's gaze met Dessia's. It was clear from the disgust in his blue-green eyes he thought it ridiculous he even had to ask question.

Dessia frowned as she puzzled on the matter. Where was Bridei going? And why now, in the middle of a rainstorm, with half the day gone? He couldn't hope to get far before dark.

Her attention turned back to Keenan. While she would have liked to have her man-of-arms follow Bridei and see where he went, it seemed unreasonable to ask such a thing. Even if Bridei were spying for her enemies—which she'd begun to doubt more and more—it was unlikely he would meet up with them on a day like this.

She said, "I'm certain he'll be back soon. The weather is too miserable for him to go far."

"The very reason someone should go after him," said Aife, her expression pleading. "Before he gets lost and freezes to death."

Keenan snorted again. "He's a grown man. If he gets lost, then he's a fool who's not worth saving. Besides, when I saw him, he was wearing a rather fine cloak. It won't keep him dry for long in this, but he's not likely to perish with that kind of protection either."

"Oh, aye, Beatha gave him a new cloak before he left," Dessia recalled. "It's a good quality garment. A very extravagant gift, I thought. Beatha could offer that to the traders when they come, and get a fair measure of goods in return."

"Perhaps she thought he'd earned it by entertaining us," Aife responded in cold tones.

Dessia gave the maidservant a look. Could it be that Aife was more taken with Bridei than she'd let on?

Aife seemed to sense her thoughts, or perhaps she was aware her words might have angered Keenan, for she said, "It can't have been easy for Bridei to speak of some of the things that happened to him. His honesty surprised me, and makes me think that his true nature might be much different than the cheerful image he shows the world. I can't help but feel sorry for him. He's had a hard life."

Aife's words aroused a spark of guilt in Dessia's mind. She'd been on her guard with Bridei from the very beginning and always thought the worst of him. She'd assumed his handsome face and natural grace implied a shallow and self-serving nature. But perhaps it was unfair to make that assumption. He might be a much different sort of person than she'd thought. Perhaps, like her, he hid his true feelings behind a mask.

The idea unsettled her, and she began to wonder if someone should go after Bridei after all. The only reason she could think of for him to run off like that was because he was distressed. It was exactly the sort of thing she did when her thoughts were in turmoil. When everything became overwhelming and she didn't know what to do next, she would go to the Forest of Mist. Passing through the mist forced her to concentrate and when she reached the lake, the magical peace of the place always soothed her. Would Bridei do something similar? She looked at Keenan. "What direction he was heading when you saw him?"

"He appeared to be walking northwest, which I thought odd. That means he'll have to circle around the forest to reach the main trackway. It would be much easier for him to head south, especially if he were planning to meet up with someone coming from outside your territory."

Unless he decided to go to the Forest of Mist, Dessia thought. The idea bothered her. That had always been her special place, where no one else dared to go. When she went to the lake, she had a sense of the Ancient Ones watching over her. She felt safe there, and also powerful in her own right. That was why she often practiced swordplay on the lakeshore. She believed that she—and her weapon—might absorb some of the magical essence of the realm. It was also a good place to be alone, to think and untangle her thoughts. Which was the very reason Bridei might also be drawn there.

Her emotions roiled. She felt angry, as if Bridei had stolen something from her. Yet, she also felt a vague worry for him. When the forest had let him pass, he'd been following after her. If he went there by himself, the spirits might turn upon him. If he stubbornly kept going when the mists came, he might end up falling and hurting himself. Or, he might simply get lost and end up traveling in circles. If he were very wet and cold when night fell, he might indeed perish of exposure.

Dessia sighed, then said, "I suppose I'll have to go after him."

"*You*, Milady?" Aife exclaimed. "But why? Wouldn't it be better to send Keenan?"

"Aye," Keenan agreed. "If you deem it necessary, I'll go after him."

He turned to leave.

Aife grabbed his arm. "You must eat and drink something warm before you go. Shouldn't he?" Aife looked at Dessia with pleading eyes.

Dessia motioned. "Go to the hall and eat and drink. Then, when you've warmed a little, return to the gatetower. Despite the weather, I don't want the rath unguarded. In the meantime, I'll garb myself in my warmest clothing and set out after Bridei." She looked at each of them. "This is something I must do myself. He's a visitor under my roof, and I'm responsible for what happens to him."

Keenan and Aife stared at her, clearly baffled. "At least have one of the men accompany you," Keenan said. "It's not safe for you to go alone."

"I've left the fortress alone many times before and always returned safe and whole."

"Begging your pardon, milady," Keenan said, "Your powers may indeed protect you from attack or similar threats, but they won't shield you from foul weather."

"I don't fear the natural elements. Is it not from them that I possess my abilities?"

Keenan and Aife still appeared dubious. But compliant Aife said, "Let me help you dress, milady." She went to the heavy wooden chest under the window. "You must take your fur-lined cloak. And wear two gowns for warmth, at least."

"I think it would be much more practical for me to dress in my trews and a tunic, as I do when I practice with arms," Dessia responded.

"I suppose that's true," said Aife. "Then you wouldn't have your skirts dragging in the mud and getting wet."

Seeing that the decision had been made, Keenan bowed and left.

Dessia stripped off the plain gown and began to dress in the garments Aife fetched from the chest.

* * *

Although she'd hoped the weather would let up before she set out, it was not to be. The rain still poured down, soaking her oiled leather cape. She'd finally convinced Aife that the serviceable garment—borrowed from one of the men—provided better protection than her heavy, fur-lined cloak.

Her gait was brisk and purposeful as she headed toward the Forest of Mist. She couldn't say why she felt so certain Bridei had gone there. Perhaps it was because there was no other reasonable destination. If he'd decided to leave Cahermara permanently, he'd have traveled west or south and taken the main trackway. There was always the possibility he was meeting up with someone. But it seemed unlikely he would set out for an assignation in the middle of the day. If he was a spy and wanted to report his findings, there would certainly be better opportunities than this.

Besides, she no longer really believed he was a spy sent by her enemies. Her early conviction had melted away as she listened to him tell about his life and began to understand that what he valued most was his freedom. Being a spy would entail giving up some of his independence, and she didn't think he would obligate himself in that way.

She'd also discovered that beneath his glib manner and facile charm was another Bridei: a boy who'd been enslaved and brutalized, but who had fought back, survived and even thrived. There was something admirable about the tale he told. He had courage and resolve and—she wanted to believe—a kind of integrity. His parents appeared to be good and decent people, and although he was estranged from them, she couldn't help but think he must also possess those traits.

"You fool,' she said aloud. "In a month, you've gone from contempt to admiration for this man. But you must never forget how skilled he is with words. It could all be a clever tale meant to gain sympathy." She chastised herself with this thought, but her heart and head didn't really believe it.

She reached the Forest of Mist and took the familiar pathway. As always when she entered these woods, she was reminded she was in realm beyond the mortal one. There was a timelessness here, as if the past and future were connected, or perhaps had become same thing. Her senses quickened and her skin prickled, not with warning but heightened sensitivity. There was sudden shift in her surroundings, and she thought how everything was more extreme here. The stark harshness of winter seemed to have arrived already, and the forest was barren and lifeless. Although it had stopped raining, the sky was dark, with no hint that the sun would ever shine again. Instead of the verdant green she was used to, this was a world in shades of gray, with only color visible the deep red of dried berries clinging to the dead and desolate-appearing vines and bushes.

A sense of loss and grief gripped her, and she suddenly felt an urgent need to find Bridei. She tried to hurry, but a light mist rose, obscuring her vision, and she had to move cautiously through the veil of moisture. Although she knew the way, the journey seemed to take longer than it ever had before. By the time she could see the silver gleam of the lake through the trees, her skin was clammy with sweat and she was breathing hard.

Her heart seemed gripped with dread for Bridei. She must find him before it was too late.

At last she pushed her way through the clumps of winter-bare bushes and saw Bridei near the edge of the lake. He had taken off his cloak and tunic and was kneeling at the very edge of the water, leaning forward and gazing intently into the depths of the lake. The panicked dread that had haunted her all the way to the lake rose to fever pitch. She rushed forward calling, "Nay! Don't do it! Don't!"

He didn't move as she reached him. Then, slowly, with great reluctance, he tore his gaze away from the lake and turned to look at her. "Don't do what?" he asked.

Dessia swallowed, feeling very foolish. "I... I thought... that is..." How could she explain her ridiculous conviction he'd been about to throw himself into the water? "I was afraid you were going to fall in," she said.

His brow furrowed as he perused her face. "You were afraid for me?"

Dessia stiffened, her fear and embarrassment turning to anger. "Of course not," she snapped.

He stood, still studying her. "You were."

"Well, perhaps," she admitted. "But only because you're here, in this place." She glanced around at their surroundings, and another wave of shock swept her as she realized the bleak winter landscape had vanished. The waters of the lake reflected a world of green, and the surrounding forest seemed bursting with the ripeness of summer.

Bridei apparently guessed her thoughts, for he said, "Aye, it's amazing, isn't it. After half-freezing on the way here, I found myself actually growing hot. That's why I took off my clothing. But I wasn't going to jump into the lake. The water's cold as ice."

"But what *were* you doing?"

Bridei motioned. "Come closer and look."

She knelt down beside him and gazed into the water. There was reflection of the sky and the trees around them, but nothing else. Bridei let out a sigh. "It's gone now. I should have known it wouldn't last."

"What did you see?"

"The past, I think... or maybe it was the future. I don't know."

"But *what* did you see?"

"Blurry images. I recognized some of them. I saw my parents. I also saw myself when I was young. I didn't want to relive what happened to me, but now that I have, I feel better somehow. As if by remembering, I can finally let go."

"Let go of what?"

He looked up at her and distant expression on his face altered, as if he remembered whom he was talking to. "The pain... and the anger."

"Who were you angry at?"

He grimaced. "The man who enslaved me, obviously. But even more than that, my father."

She nodded. It was reasonable he would resent being sent away so young.

"I'm certain now that my father didn't mean for those things to happen to me," he said. "I don't think anyone guessed I would travel so far from home, or encounter such danger."

"Of course not," she answered. It had struck her as she listened to the description of his father, a man who had loved his first wife enough to grieve for her for years, would never have sent his son away if he'd had any idea he would be enslaved and brutalized.

Bridei shrugged his shoulders, as if shaking off the mood. His gaze focused and his impossibly blue eyes bored into her. "Perhaps you should look into the water and see what secrets the lake holds for you."

For some reason, she felt compelled to tell him the truth. She was tired of pretending to know magic, when in fact she'd never done anything magical in her life. "I won't see anything. I never do. All these years I've chanted spells over the scrying bowl and searched its depths for hours and I've never seen a thing."

"But you haven't looked into the lake."

His words aroused a sliver of hope. Perhaps she'd been looking in the wrong place all along. She moved closer to the water and peered in. All she could see was her own reflection, surrounded by the familiar landscape of the lakeshore. She concentrated, trying not to think how foolish she must look, garbed in the oversize rain cape.

Her eyes began to water with the strain of staring so intently. There was movement in the water beside her and another image formed. She knew a twinge of irritation. Why couldn't Bridei leave her alone? She didn't need his interference. But then she looked at the image of Bridei in the water and realized he was wearing a blue tunic banded with gold and green embroidery, a garment she'd never seen before. The next moment, she looked back at her own image and froze. The gown she was wearing was also unfamiliar. Around her neck was a gold torc that had been her father's, and her hair was unbound, flowing over her shoulders. As she continued to stare in awe, the image wavered and then vanished, leaving only the reflection of herself in men's clothing.

She stepped back from the water, her heart pounding.

Bridei came up beside her. "What is it? What did you see?"

"I saw myself," she whispered. "And it must have been the future... but..." She shook her head, unable to accept what the image conveyed. What she'd seen was herself garbed as a queen. And at her side, as her consort, was Bridei ap Maelgwn.

Bridei watched as Dessia's jaw tightened and her eyes narrowed. Whatever she'd seen had upset her a great deal. "You didn't like it," he said, "whatever it is you saw. I must admit, I didn't like what the lake revealed to me either, at least at first."

"Maybe the things it shows are false," she said. "Maybe it's some kind of trickery."

"Do you really believe that? This place is full of magic. Why should the powerful forces that dwell here have any reason to lie?"

"I don't know."

The sulky tone of her voice amused him. "It's you who's lying. You're lying to yourself. It's just like earlier, when you denied you were worried for me. It seems to me you lie to yourself all the time. If something doesn't fit the rigid plan you have in your mind, you reject it."

"What do you know of me?" she demanded.

He decided it was time to confront her. What he'd experienced in this place had stripped him bare of many of the things he'd believed about his life. It was time for her to face some hard truths of her own. "What are you afraid of?" he asked.

"You," she said. Her green eyes glinted with anger. "I'm afraid of you."

"Is that why you dressed up like a hunched-up old crone and came to the hall to listen to me? Why you ordered sweet young Aife to question me about my life?"

"I have to protect my people," she said defensively. "I need to know who you are and whether you represent a threat to us."

Bridei felt a burst of irritation. "And did you find out what you wanted to know? Am I a threat?"

She seemed to consider this very carefully. Finally, she said, "Perhaps not in the way I thought. But nevertheless... my instincts tell me I should fear you."

She looked so young and vulnerable as she said this. So bleak and near despairing. He felt sorry for her. She tried so hard, seemed so careful never to give her heart, lest she end up having it broken. They were two of a kind, he thought. He used his mask of charm and carelessness to hide his feelings, while she used duty and responsibility to shield herself from the world.

At one time, he would have taken advantage of her defenselessness. Like the wolf that pounces on the weakest animal of the herd, he'd have seized this moment to get what he wished from her. She was as ripe for seduction as she'd ever be. But now that the opportunity was before him, he couldn't do it. What he desired at this moment was to comfort her, to let her know she didn't have to do everything on her own, to carry the whole world on her shoulders.

He reached out and touched her cheek. "You're a fine queen. You do your best for your people and they love you."

She raised her gaze to his, her green eyes shimmering with unshed tears. "But will it be enough? What if it's not enough?"

"We can never know that," he said. "My brother sacrificed everything for Arthur's cause, and in the end, the Saxons prevailed. But that doesn't mean he failed. In the years while they were fighting the Saxons, the enemy built their homes and raised their children in our lands. Over time, they started to become like us. They stopped being the brutal raiders who swept in on the eastern shore and plundered and murdered. Once they settled on the land and began to have ties to it, they became men rather than savages. Farmers instead of warriors."

He sounded exactly like Rhun, Bridei thought with a shock. When he had turned into his brother, the dreamer who believed that good would prevail over evil in the end? It was a foolish, absurd way to look at life. He knew that, and yet, he was starting to hope that his usual cynical outlook was wrong.

He was jarred from his uncomfortable musings when he saw Dessia glaring at him. "Don't you dare say such things!" she cried.

"What? What did I say?"

"You think I'll fail, just as Arthur did. You're trying to prepare me for the day when I have to submit to O'Bannon, or some other chieftain! You think because I'm a woman, I can't prevail! That I can't be a strong leader!"

"I think nothing of the sort. I wasn't trying to compare your situation to the one in Britain at all. I was trying to reassure you, to tell you that I've almost come to believe that it's worthwhile to have dreams, to care so deeply about something that you'll give up everything for it."

"And what is that you care about? What is *your* dream?" She spoke with such scathing sarcasm that Bridei went tense with anger. He'd been on verge of saying how much he admired her devotion to her people and that he was inspired to do whatever he could to help her. But now the folly of such a confession became clear to him. She would never accept his help. She loathed him and thought he was a threat to all she cared about.

The realization hurt, and much more than he could have imagined. The voice in his head reminded him what a lackwit he'd been, to ever let his guard down, to ever care. Smiling his mocking smile, he said, "My dream is to bed you, of course. To feel your lush, lovely body beneath mine. To make you submit."

His words got the reaction he'd intended. Her beautiful green eyes flashed with fury and for a moment, he thought she would strike him. Then she recovered herself and turned and stalked away, disdain and rage visible in every step. "Find your own way back, Bridei ap Maelgwn," she called out. "If you can."

Dessia could feel the tears streaming down her cheeks. Her breath came in choking sobs. Her stomach churned with an excruciating mix of emotions. He'd hurt her. And he'd done it deliberately, which it made even worse. But that wasn't all of it. She had a nagging sense he'd done it because she'd hurt *him*. He'd been speaking with her honestly and she'd responded with sarcasm and scorn. Why had she done that? Was it because she couldn't bear to think he might truly care about her?

She trudged on miserably. The forest had turned dark and gloomy. The rain poured down.

Chapter 11

Bridei was working on his usual task of breaking rocks when he saw Eth and Usan had quit their work and were watching three men approach the hillfort. Two of the men wore heavy packs while the third pushed a hand cart. Since they were arriving from the east, the direction of the sea, Bridei could easily guess they were traders. His presumption was confirmed when Eth grinned broadly and said, "The traders are here. Now we can have a celebration and you can play the harp!"

"I'm not certain it's ready," Bridei said. Seeing Eth's face fall, he added, "Perhaps I should go and look at it."

By the time Bridei had gathered up his tools and washed in the cistern, there was no sign of the traders in yard. The guard at the gate must have taken them into the hall as soon as they arrived. Although curious to meet the traders, Bridei decided to fulfill his promise to Eth and check on the harp.

When he arrived at the smithy, Niall was pounding a knife blade into shape on the anvil. He nodded when he saw Bridei, then continued to work the glowing blade. Bridei went to the workbench and picked up the harp. He ran his fingers over the strings. They weren't as taut as he would have hoped. Ideally, they should cure another sennight.

Niall, having finished shaping the blade, dumped it into the water trough to cool, then came over. "What do you think?"

Bridei was on the verge of saying the strings were still too green when he realized the smith was asking about something else. "Whatever its sound, this harp is a thing of beauty," he said, touching one of the embossed decorations. "Your work is very fine, Niall. As good as anything I've seen, outside the markets of Gaul, of course."

"I'm very pleased with the design," Niall said. "I would have liked to use more gold, but that was all I had." He gestured to the metal piece affixed below the strings. The center of the swirling pattern glinted with small nodules of gold.

"It's actually prettier this way," said Bridei. "The contrast between the silver and the gold makes the design more subtle. More like what the finer metalsmiths make."

Niall nodded again, looking satisfied. "What I'd really like to learn to do is enamelwork. Then I could add color to the pattern. Perhaps when the traders come, they'll have a piece done in that fashion and I can show you what I mean."

Bridei looked up. "In fact, some traders are here. I saw them arriving when I was working on the wall. That's why I came to look at the harp. I presume the queen will have some sort of feast in their honor, and I'd like to play the harp for the gathering. But I'm not certain it's ready." He picked up the instrument again and strummed the strings.

"It sounds good to me."

Bridei shrugged. "It's a little flat in tone, but I'll have to make do. I can't disappoint Eth. I don't think he can bear to wait much longer. And knowing the queen, she'd think it a waste to have people gather in the hall a week from now, after hosting the traders so recently."

"If the traders are here, I should finish up and go meet them," said Niall. "I'm eager to see what they've brought. My store of copper isn't used up, but I need tin and iron badly."

"What usually happens when traders arrive?" asked Bridei. "Will Dessia—the queen—will she have some sort of feast or celebration?"

"Aye. That will be tomorrow night, to give the people who live away from the rath time to get the news and bring whatever goods they have to trade."

Niall went to bank down the fire in the forge. Bridei followed him. "Is it always the same traders who come?"

"Not always. They all use different routes and stop different places before arriving here, so the goods they bring vary quite a bit. The ones coming from the north usually have the better selection, as they haven't yet been to Ath Cliath and Craimor. If they come from the south, we often have to make do with whatever's left after they've visited the main trading settlements on this side of the isle."

"If their coloring has anything to do with it, these men may well hail from the north. Two of them looked almost Saxon, they were so fair-haired, and tall as well."

That information seemed to spur Niall on, for he shoveled up the glowing ashes with more speed than Bridei had ever seen him exhibit. As soon as the fire was safely banked, Niall motioned to the door. "I need to wash and change my clothes. I don't want to meet the traders covered in soot."

"I should do the same," Bridei agreed.

* * *

Dessia sat near the hearth with the traders, all of them drinking wine. To her right was Penrick, a tall, lean man whose skin was so weathered it contrasted startlingly with his hair, which was bleached by the sun until strands of it were almost white. She vaguely remembered him from a few years before, and wondered why he hadn't been back until now.

Next to him was Rinc. He had skin more like her people's, which meant it freckled instead of tanned, though his freckles were so numerous he appeared almost as dark as Penrick. The third man was huge and foreign looking, with a bald head, lightly tanned skin and dark eyes. Because of his size, Dessia wondered if he were a servant brought along to protect his master's goods. Penrick hadn't introduced him, and the man appeared to have little interest in what was being said. Instead he concentrated on his wine, of which he'd already drunk an alarming amount.

Turning her attention back to Penrick, Dessia realized he was talking about the British leader Arthur, telling much the same story Bridei had. "Some people thought Arthur's defeat would be the end of Britain," he said. "But it hasn't really made that much difference, at least in the west and north. The Saxons have made peace with the chieftains there and things continue on much as they have. The tribes in the south and east have lost their lands, of course, but that was happening ten years ago. The holymen hate the Saxons and call them heathen savages, but it hasn't been as bad as people feared. The Saxons are different than the British in some ways, but they purchase parchment and ink, so some of them are literate. And they enjoy music and song, although perhaps not as much as the Irish." he smiled at her ingratiatingly.

"Aye, my people are very fond of music," she said.

"Indeed, we are," put in Aife, who'd arrived with a tray of cheese and bread, as well as more wine. "In fact, we're fortunate to a have skilled bard living at Cahermara," she added as she set down the tray.

"A bard? Where does he hail from?"

"As a boy, he called Gwynedd in north Britain his home," Aife said as she poured more wine into the third trader's cup, "but he's lived many other places since then."

"Gwynedd?" Penrick raised his nearly silver brows. He glanced at Rinc. "It couldn't be Talisen. He's dead. And Aneirin's far too old to travel this far. It must be Bridei ap Maelgwn." Rinc grunted in response. Penrick continued, "Last I heard he was in Arthur's train, but I suppose after Camboglanna, he had to find another patron. Still, I'm surprised he came here."

"You know Bridei?" asked Aife, her voice full of excitement.

"In truth, I've never met the man," said Penrick. He gave Aife an assessing look. "But I've heard tell of him. ... and his effect on young maidens."

Aife flushed, then darted a swift look around the hall, as if looking for Keenan.

Dessia knew a stab of irritation. Penrick seemed to think Bridei captured the heart of every woman he met. Well, he hadn't captured hers.

Even as she had the thought, Bridei entered the hall. His appearance should have irritated her. Instead, she felt the same searing attraction she experienced the first time she saw him. Only now it was even more intense, as every aspect of his appearance aroused a memory: His violet blue eyes gazing at her with tenderness. The feel of his well-shaped, sensual mouth on hers. The strength of his lean, muscular body as he held her...

"It appears even you have succumbed to the young bard's charms," Penrick said, leaning near.

Dessia gave the trader her most withering look.

Penrick shrugged, smiling. "I meant no offense. He's a fine-looking man. If my inclinations ran that way, I'd be intrigued by him myself."

Dessia gritted her teeth. Then she lowered her voice and said very quietly, "The truth is, I can't wait to be rid of the man."

Penrick drew back in surprise. But before he could respond, Bridei reached them. He bowed. "Milady," he said in his musical voice. He nodded to the traders. "My name is Bridei ap Maelgwn."

Penrick motioned to himself and the other men. "I'm Penrick and this is Rinc and Sarlic. We'd already guessed who you were. What takes you so far from Britain?"

"After Arthur's defeat, I wanted to get away," Bridei responded.

Dessia was surprised by his answer. Why hadn't he mentioned the slavers who'd brought him here against his will?

Bridei had seated himself on the bench on other side of the traders. He accepted the goblet Aife offered him and took a swallow. "You'll find that Queen Dessia is a most gracious host. And her people are very generous as well. Indeed, they've done me the great honor of making me a new harp. It's nearly finished." He nodded to the traders. "If you stay another day, you'll be able to judge the results of their work yourself."

"The harp is finished?" Dessia asked.

Bridei glanced at her. "Nearly so. I want to give the strings another day to cure. But then I'll be pleased to play for you and your people, and your guests, of course."

Dessia was torn. On one hand, she was glad her people would be able to enjoy the harp they'd labored on so long. On the other hand, she had a strong sense that once she heard him play, all her lingering resistance to Bridei's charms would vanish.

* * *

"Were you pleased with how the trading went?" Aife asked as Dessia was bathing before the feast.

"Aye," Dessia answered as she sat in the big wooden tub soaping herself. "Their boat was well-stocked and had most of the things we needed. I purchased a good supply of iron and tin for Niall, salt and spices for Doona, and several casks of wine to replace my stores, much of which was depleted by the traders themselves, especially Sarlic. I'm saving the rest of it for the Yule celebration. For tonight's meal, everyone will have to make do with mead or cider."

"I'm certain no one but the traders will care," said Aife.

"And Bridei. He drank a fair amount of wine himself last night."

"To me, he seemed distracted. As if he had much on his mind. Did you think so?"

"Bridei's moods are of no concern to me. And if they were, I'd simply ask *your* opinion of what he's thinking or feeling." As soon as the words were out, Dessia regretted them. There was no reason for her to be short with her maid.

Aife sighed. "You're right. I shouldn't pay so much attention to Bridei. I know it makes Keenan furious. But I can't seem to help myself. He's so good-looking, and when he smiles—" She sighed again.

"Just remember he's worked years to cultivate his charm. It's what he does to earn his livelihood."

"I disagree," Aife said. "Bridei's kind to everyone, not just people he wants to impress or get something from. Consider the way he treats Eth. Why should he go out of his way to talk to a dull-witted farmboy?"

"Over the years, he's probably found that the people who can be of most use to him aren't necessarily those who appear most important. After all, it was Eth's idea to build him a harp, and Eth's enthusiasm is the reason everyone else got involved. So, now Bridei gets a harp and all he had to do was spend a bit of time cosseting Eth."

"Couldn't it be that he felt sorry for Eth and was touched by his interest in music?"

"Really, Aife," Dessia said as she stood and reached for the towel the maidservant held out. "Sometimes you're so foolish."

"I'd rather be foolish than too stubborn to face the truth. I think you're in love with Bridei, but you're terrified he'll break your heart."

Dessia froze, her fingers clutching the towel. Her first thought was to reprimand Aife for her insolence. Her second was to deny the horrifying words. She finally fought through the waves of anger and outrage and said weakly, "I suppose I am a bit infatuated. Is it so obvious? Do you think everyone knows?"

Aife smiled and her blue eyes softened. "I doubt anyone else guesses, and your secret's safe with me. But I do think you must stop denying the truth to yourself. What's so terrible about being in love?"

"I don't want to be vulnerable. I *can't*. I'm responsible for too many people to take such a chance."

"What chance?"

Dessia looked at Aife, her insides tight and aching. "What if my worst fears about Bridei are true? What if he's a threat to all I've worked so hard for?"

"What if he *isn't?* You always think the worst of Bridei, but I think you're wrong to be so suspicious. I think he's a good and decent person who's been forced by life to view the world cynically. Maybe if you gave him a chance, you'd find out he cares for you as much as you do him."

As Dessia finished drying off and allowed Aife to help her into her shift, she considered the maidservant's words. If Bridei were in love with her, that was almost worse. For then she'd have no reason *not* to give into her feelings. And she didn't want to care that much for anyone. Because if she did and something happened to them, she'd have to endure that agony all over again. She thought of how despairing she'd been after her family was killed. Even now, thinking of it filled her with a terrible sense of loss and reminded her of how dangerous it was to love.

"You're afraid," Aife said softly, as if reading her thoughts. "I understand that. It's frightening to feel so much for another person. To know that if they died, you would want to die as well. But it can also be glorious. The best thing you've ever known." Aife's face grew radiant, and Dessia decided that Keenan had nothing to worry about. Bridei might charm Aife, but it was Keenan who held her heart. As Bridei—for better or worse—appeared to hold hers.

* * *

Bridei stood by the worktable in the smith's shop and stared at the harp. He'd heard the expression "having butterflies in your stomach", but never known what it meant. It was strange how nervous he was. Well, not nervous exactly, but filled with a sense of expectation so intense it made him breathless. He'd scarcely touched the harp, wanting to give the strings as much time as possible to cure. Playing it tonight would be like going to bed with a woman he'd never met before that moment, entering her darkened bedchamber and reaching out for her unknown body. He'd have to hope the familiar landmarks would be enough to guide him, and he'd be able to guess what would please her from her response.

The idea of lovemaking immediately brought to mind Dessia, and his apprehension grew even more intense. He thought of the song he'd composed for her. Would she be flattered or angry? Anyone listening would know it was composed with her in mind. They would also know that the man who wrote it was in love with her.

He took a deep, shaky breath. He felt like a man wagering everything he owned on one roll of the dice, and it was terrifying and exhilarating.

Not a good state of mind for a performer to be in. Somehow he had to calm himself. He glanced down at his clothing. After Beatha had given him the fine cloak, the other women—not wanting to be outdone—had gifted him with various other garments: a red and blue checked tunic, a fine linen leine to wear underneath it and a new pair of woolen trews. Nally had jested that he would be finest dressed man in the hall, and Bridei knew it might well be true.

But a part of him felt as if he were walking into the hall naked. For the first time in his adult life, he was going to reveal a part of himself he'd always kept hidden. For a brief moment, as he sang that song, he would take off the mask of nonchalance and let them see the uncertain, yearning boy beneath.

The thought made him so uneasy that his hands shook as he picked up the harp. For a moment, he cradled it against his chest, admiring the workmanship. Regardless of what it sounded like, it was a handsome instrument. The wood had been polished to a shining gloss and the silver and gold decorations glinted brightly.

He stroked his fingers along the strings, then paused, surprised by the sweetness of the sound. It was as if all the love and care that had gone into the making of the harp had infused it with a warm and vibrant tone. He strummed it again, then plucked each string individually, adjusting the pins, tuning it as he went. The fear and anxiety seemed to drain out of him as he played. *This he knew. This was a part of him.*

* * *

It seemed half of Ireland was coming to Cahermara, Dessia thought as she stared out the tower window. A steady stream of people filed up the trackway leading to the gate, more than she could ever recall since her parents' day. She felt a vague stab of anxiety, wondering if there would be enough food. They would have to serve the wine she'd purchased after all; she didn't want to deplete their entire stock of mead, and she couldn't expect the adults to drink cider. And where was everyone going to sit? They'd probably have to eat in shifts, then remove the tables and let everyone crowd in to hear Bridei.

She sought to identify the people she saw. Some of the adults looked familiar, but she didn't recognize any of the children. How long had it been since these families came to Cahermara? How had she failed to stay in contact with so many of her people? She should go out and visit them, as her father had. But she'd always thought it too dangerous to travel far from the rath, and it was difficult without horses. A pang of longing went through her. For generations, her family had been known for the beautiful horses they bred, and now she didn't possess a single one. There was no reason not to have horses now, except she'd have to go to Ath Cliath to purchase them, and then worry about them being stolen as she brought them back to Cahermara. While her enemies might believe the rath was protected by a magical spell, once she was away from it, she feared they would pounce.

The thought made her sigh. She might as well be a prisoner. The only time she felt truly safe outside the rath was when she went to the Forest of Mist. It was a lonely, suffocating existence, although she'd never thought of it that way until Bridei came. When she considered all the places he'd been and the things he'd seen, she knew a pang of envy.

Did everything about that man have to upset her? He made her want things that she'd long ago decided were impossible. Forced her see her life for what it was—stark and lonely. If only she could make things go back to the way they had been. She hadn't been happy, but she hadn't been discontent either. And what Bridei had done to her people was much the same. Having experienced some pleasure and beauty and enjoyed themselves, how would they ever be able to go back to their grim, dutiful existence?

She sighed again, then turned as Aife entered. "You look lovely," she said to her maid. "Is that a new gown?"

"Nay. I merely trimmed an old one with some braid I purchased from the traders."

"It's very becoming. The blue sets off your eyes."

"Thank you," Aife said shyly.

Dessia turned back to the window. Even her maid wasn't the same. After all this excitement, the rest of the winter was going to dull and miserable for her, too.

"What's wrong, milady?" Aife asked. "You seem so melancholy."

"I'm just thinking how hard it's going to be to go back to our usual lives after this feast is over and the traders leave."

"But if Bridei's still here, it won't be so bad, will it?"

"Aye, *if* he's here."

"Has he told you he's leaving?" Aife asked.

"Nay, but he will someday. What's to keep him here?"

"I suppose you're right. From what he's said, he's never stayed in one place long before. Then again, perhaps no one's ever given him a reason to stay."

Dessia turned to Aife, frowning. "And what would that be? I have scant wealth to pay him, and serving as my bard offers little status, especially to a man who has played for the high king of Britain and other important leaders."

"But maybe that's not what Bridei's looking for. Maybe what is he seeks is a place to belong."

"You think he belongs here? But he's not even Irish."

"Aye, I think he belongs here. Even the land accepts him. Keenan told me the day Bridei left the hall in the rainstorm he went to the Forest of Mist. Other than you, no one I know has ever been allowed into that realm."

"How does Keenan know Bridei went there?"

"Because he followed when you left the rath, then waited near the edge of the forest until you came out. Bridei appeared only moments after you did."

"I told Keenan to stay at the hillfort and guard it. How dare he defy my orders!"

"Keenan sought only to protect you. He doesn't trust Bridei. I guess he was afraid if you were alone with Bridei, something might happen."

Something had happened, Dessia thought uneasily. She'd looked into the depths of the lake and seen Bridei standing beside her, looking as if he belonged there. She asked Aife, "Doesn't it concern you that Keenan mistrusts Bridei so much?"

Aife shrugged. "Keenan is just like that. He tends to make up his mind and then never change it. Besides, Bridei is so different from him, I think it makes him uneasy."

"But what if his assessment of Bridei is correct?" Dessia pressed.

"Quit worrying, milady," Aife answered, smiling. "It's time for you to dress for the feast."

* * *

Bridei observed the packed hall from a spot near the stairs to the tower. By now, almost everyone had had something to eat and drink. Except for him. He'd found he was too nervous to consume anything—not an ideal circumstance since he was drinking mead. Perhaps he should switch to cider.

He fingered the harp through the rough cloth he'd wrapped it in, since he didn't want his audience to see the instrument until he played, and told himself to relax. No performer had ever had a more receptive audience. Everywhere he looked people were smiling and talking, their faces were flushed, their eyes bright. Their stomachs were full of beef, pork, cabbage and spiced apples. It was probably the best meal some of them had had in years, at least since the days of Dessia's father. The only sign of discontent were a few small children, who, overexcited by all the activity, had begun to fuss. Bridei wasn't concerned for them. Once he started to play, they would settle down and listen, then fall asleep. He was utterly confident of his craft, so why was he nervous?

Ah, there *she* was, the reason for the vague queasiness in his belly. He watched Dessia move through the hall, speaking to her people, admiring children and babies. She wore a gown of deep red wool, set off by a golden belt and a simple gold neckpiece at her neck. Her hair was unbound and it flowed down from the gold circlet around her temple like the waves of a wine-colored sea. Rosy color suffused her fair skin and her verdant eyes shone like jewels. Taller than most of her subjects, even the men, she looked every inch the proud, glorious queen.

Seeing her, his heart filled with lust and an aching longing he'd never experienced before. Despite her bold, impressive appearance, he was struck by an urge to protect Dessia, to keep her safe. The feeling was utterly new to him. Never before had he responded to a woman this way—or perhaps anyone.

His mood shocked him and increased his unease. He must start playing soon. If he waited much longer, he would be undone.

He started to make his way to the hearth. People moved aside to let him pass and as he heard their murmurs of excitement and expectation, some of his tension began to ease. He'd done this dozen of times before. Nay, hundreds. By the time he took a seat on a stool near the hearth, he was feeling much better.

He waited until the people on the very edges of the hall had quieted, then pulled off the cloth to reveal the harp. A sigh of satisfaction and delight seemed to sweep through the crowd as they saw the instrument. Bridei delicately strummed the strings, then set about tuning them again. As he did so, he heard murmurs and whispers as a description of how the harp had been made passed from person to person. For Niall, and Eth and the other workmen, this was their moment of glory, and he meant to make the most of it.

As soon as he was done tuning, he held up the harp and said, "I know you're all eager to hear me play, but first, I must thank the people who made this beautiful instrument. First of all, I laud Eth. It was his idea that the harp should be made, and his persistence and dedication that inspired everyone else. Many people were involved. Eth found the wood. It was shaped and smoothed and put together by Nally and Cori. The cook, Doona, supplied the gut for the strings." He paused and smiled. "Which means that some of the rest of you gave up some sausages that might have been made instead."

Laughter rippled through the crowd. Bridei continued, "With their patience and craftsmanship, they built this fine instrument. "Then Niall..." he gestured to the burly smith. "He made the harp a work of art." Bridei held up the instrument again, then turned around so that those behind him could see. "I've traveled as far away as Narbonne on the great eastern sea and never seen metalwork that could surpass this."

He let them see the bright ornaments sparkling in the torchlight, then glanced at Niall, savoring the flush of pleasure on his face. "It was Niall's art that imbued this instrument with beauty. Eth and other the workmen's industry and generosity blessed it with grace and warmth. But the magic of the music you will hear this night comes from all of you, from this place, this land, and most of all, from your extraordinary queen."

At last, Bridei allowed himself to seek out Dessia. He'd been vaguely aware of where she was standing, but feared that if he looked at her, he might lose his composure. Now he dared to meet her gaze, to risk his soul in the depths of her green eyes. He cleared his throat and sought to slow his thudding heart, then said, "For it was Queen Dessia's tragic past and her triumphant defiance of her enemies that has inspired me to write this song. Her love of the land and her people that made me understand how truly fortunate I was to have found this place. Her beauty that has captured my heart."

Dessia stared at him, looking so stricken that his mouth went dry. Was she offended? Had he been too bold? If he had, there was no hope for it now. What was done, was done. He resumed his place on the stool and lightly strummed the harp strings. The sweetness of the sound calmed him. He played a chord, and then another, and began to sing.

Dessia couldn't move. Indeed, she could barely breathe. Bridei had said he was singing this song for her, that she had inspired him. Nay, she must not believe it, for if she did, she would want to weep. The melody was crystalline and pure. It made her think of the stream that ran through the Forest of Mist, trickling down to the still, gleaming lake. His voice rose above it, rich and vibrant, as keen as the wind through the trees. And the words were about her. They told her story, revealed her essence: Her grief and despair. Her defiance and resolve. Her dedication to restoring her home, her lands, her legacy.

Then it changed and became a love song. He described her beauty, her proud bearing, her passion. Heated blood crept to her face. From the way he sang, everyone would think he'd bedded her. And then the song changed again, and her embarrassment turned to awe. He'd made her into a magical being, a goddess. She who brings the bounty of the summer, the rich plenty of autumn, the fierceness of winter, the joyous warm of spring. And then he was singing about the land itself. Rich gleaming meadows. Glistening lakes and streams. Wild forests teeming with life. The sky, a dream of light and rainbow colors. Soft, sweet rain. And the restless energy of the sea that washed the shores of the land.

"And the great waves will wash her tears away,
The deep thunder of the surf soothe her aching heart.
Someday, borne on the fierce wind of the untamed sea
Will come a man to love her and stand beside her."

As the last notes died away like the last sparkling drops of a cresting wave falling into the surf, Dessia stood rooted in place. She was afraid to move, almost to breathe. Bridei had sung a song that bared his heart, offering her his admiration, his loyalty, his love, his being. Offering himself. It was a gift so amazing, so unexpected, so... terrifying. She had no idea how to respond. What to do or say.

She was grateful when he began to sing another song, a lively melody. The mood in the hall shifted from utter stillness to a more normal atmosphere of celebration and gaiety. People began to tap their feet and sway to the music, and Dessia immediately thought it was a pity the hall was too crowded for them to be able to dance properly.

But at least the spell was broken, and she didn't feel as if Bridei held her heart in his hands and each movement of his fingers on the harp was like a caress of her soul. She drew a deep breath and licked her dry lips and composed herself to smile at the people around her, and say, "He's very talented. I've never heard the like."

She thought the looks they gave her were searching and curious, but their responses of "Aye" and "Indeed" gave no indication if they thought it odd that she should react to Bridei's passionate performance with such banal remarks. She silently thanked them for their discretion, and focused her gaze on Bridei. While he'd sung the first song, she'd been too embarrassed to look at him. Instead, she'd closed her eyes and concentrated on the words and the melody. But now she let herself feast her eyes upon the audacious bard.

In the dazzle of the firelight, he seemed to glow. The sleek dark sweep of his long hair shone like a raven's wing in sunlight and there was a faint sheen of sweat on his tanned skin, giving it a silvery aura. His features and movements were so graceful that she could almost imagine him as some sort of fairy king, a magical being so fine to look upon that the very sight could steal a human's soul and make them forget everything else. The comparison seemed very apt, for fairies were said to ensorcel their victims with beautiful music.

The first song was over, and now Bridei sang a ballad, sad and keening. She could almost hear the sighs around the hall as he told a tale of two lovers that fate kept apart. His skill was amazing. He had the ability to reach inside his listeners and touch their emotions as deftly as he plucked the strings of the harp.

Thinking of this made her wonder about her earlier reaction. She felt as if he'd declared his love for her. As if he held out his beating, vulnerable heart as an offering. But he was so gifted. It might have all been a performance. How could she ever be certain what he really felt?

The thought made her panic, and she knew she had to get away. The hall was crowded with people deeply under Bridei's spell. In their eyes, he could do no wrong. But as queen, she dare not give so easily. She had to be canny and cautious. She had to imagine every threat. Anticipate every danger.

Half frantic, she started toward the door. People moved aside for her, their faces clearly registering puzzlement. Why was she leaving now? their expressions seemed to ask. By the time she made her way outside, she was breathing hard. She walked swiftly across the yard and tried to decide where to go. When she was a little girl and she was distressed, she would go to see the horses. Stroking the nose of one the animals, she would pour out her tale of unhappiness. Something about being close to the beautiful beasts soothed her and made her feel better.

And if it wasn't the horses she sought out, it was one of her father's hounds or the cats that lived near the storage shed and waited to pounce on the mice the grain attracted. Somewhere along the way she'd lost the intense connection to the animals she'd once had. She'd been too busy being queen to indulge in such simple pursuits. With dismay, she realized that Bridei was right. She'd given up many things to be Queen Dessia, ruler of the Fionnlairaos.

Conflicting emotions warred inside her. She was proud of what she accomplished, but she never felt secure... nor happy either. Was that simply the way life was? Dare she reach out and take what was in front of her? Bridei's vibrant voice and stirring music promised her passion and love. But was that enough to risk everything she'd worked for? What if she allowed herself to be a woman for one night and to indulge in the satisfactions most women knew, and ended up destroying her whole life's legacy?

It was cold outside, and the wind was chill and damp, seeping through her gown. She would have to go back soon; she would have to decide.

Chapter 12

Although Bridei kept playing, he was simply going through the motions, singing a song he'd sung dozens of times before. As soon as he saw Dessia leave the hall, his heart was no longer engaged in what he was doing. Nay, his heart had left with her, and he felt the loss of it as a deep ache in his chest. What did her departure mean? Was she offended? Angry? Had he been too bold? Choked with anxiety, he struggled to keep singing. At last he finished the song. He forced a smile to his face and said, "I'm afraid I need a drink."

Immediately, a half dozen people appeared holding out full cups. He took one from a plain young woman with a shy smile, and found it contained mead. Aye, he needed mead, but more than a cup. He needed enough to bring oblivion. Again, he thought of Dessia and wondered where she'd gone and what it meant. He drank slowly, aware that everyone expected him to continue performing. In the past he would have done so. In the past he would also have shrugged off having a woman walk away from him. But this wasn't any woman, this was Dessia. She made him feel things no one else ever had. But he couldn't go after her. Couldn't disappoint all these people waiting to hear more songs.

He asked for another drink, and drained a second cup of mead. The potent liquid seemed to clear his head, and as it burned deep in his belly, he knew what he must do. He began another ballad and poured all his own despair and longing into it. This one was even sadder than the first, for in the end, when the young man finally returns to claim his love, he finds her dead. Stricken, the man plunges his knife into his chest.

As Bridei sang the final verse, he saw some of the women weeping openly. Aye, weep for me, he thought. *Weep for me. For if Dessia loves me not, then I, too, will want to die.* The next moment, he saw her, near the doorway. The torchlights caught the fiery brightness of her hair and cast her tall silhouette upon the wall. His heart sang with joy. She'd come back.

He celebrated with another song, this one a light, rousing tune meant for dancing. To keep the rhythm, Bridei tapped his fingers on the body of the harp. Soon people began to clap, and the whole hall seemed to vibrate. When the song was finished, he didn't pause but immediately began another one, this one a marching song that kept them clapping. As he started the refrain, he saw two little girls making their way through the crowd. They finally reached him and stood watching with wide eyes. When he smiled at them, they grabbed each other, giggling wildly. They were both redheads, one with ruddy gold curls and the other with straight auburn hair. Looking at them, he thought of Dessia and wondered if they had a child together, if the babe would resemble one of these sweet little lasses.

Oh, my, you are far gone, aren't you? thought the old, cynical part of him that had always kept the world at a distance.

He finished the song, and everyone stopped clapping. For a few heartbeats, the hall was amazingly still. Then it erupted in wild cheers. Bridei stood, and with fingers that trembled slightly, placed the harp on the bench. He felt the warmth and adoration of the people wash over him. It felt good, yet different than usual. Along with pride of accomplishment, he experienced a deep sense of gratification that he'd been able to give them so much pleasure, and repay them for what they'd done for him.

As people came up to speak to him, he answered questions, showed off the harp and nodded graciously to their praises. He was aware of Dessia moving through the hall, mingling with her subjects. Now that the entertainment was over, people began to gather up their belongings and collect their children in preparation for going to bed. Bridei couldn't help wondering where everyone was going to sleep. On a normal night, two dozen or so people slept in the hall. Tonight it would have to accommodate many more, with the rest bedding down in the stables, the barracks and what other shelters they could find.

Out of the corner of his eye, Bridei saw Penrick and Sarlic. He'd been meaning to speak with them ever since they arrived, but not under these circumstances. What he wanted to ask them must be done in private. They approached and talked with him briefly, Penrick commented on the design of his harp, which he said looked much like what Saxon performers used. Bridei managed to respond genially, despite his growing tension. He was desperate to speak to Dessia, to gaze into her eyes and see if he had a chance with her. It seemed she was avoiding him, but perhaps that was his imagination. She did have her duty as hostess. The other question looming in his mind was how they would ever manage to be alone. Would they have to find a secluded place outside the hillfort?

Finally, too restless to remain still any longer, he excused himself from the two traders and made his way through the press of people. Although he could see that many of them longed to talk to him, he kept moving, telling those few who persisted that he needed to use the midden. Once outside, he headed there quickly. As soon as he'd finished, he circled around to the cistern by the gate, moving stealthily in the darkness. He washed his hands and face, then removed his tunic and leine and splashed water on his upper body. Despite the chill of the air, he was sweating from nervousness.

He toweled off with the linen leine, then put it and his tunic back on again. After pacing the perimeter of the fortress for what seemed like an endless while, he started back to the hall.

* * *

Where was Bridei? The question haunted Dessia's brain as she alternately paced in the tiny open area of her bedchamber, went to the window to look out at the darkness, then paced some more. It seemed a very long time since she'd seen him depart the hall. Had he left the hillfort, vanishing into the winter's night? It almost seemed so. But where would he go? To the lake?

She wondered if she should go after him, then realized she couldn't. Cahermara was crammed with people who were her guests. Unlike Bridei, she had responsibilities. She couldn't go wandering off as the mood took her. The thought aroused a stab of resentment, but it was quickly replaced by fear. *Where was he? Was he ever coming back?*

Recalling his magical performance, she had the desperate thought that maybe he *was* some sort of supernatural being, and having set his spell on her, he'd vanished like a will o' the wisp—here one moment, gone the next.

She clutched her hands together in dismay and let out a sigh. Clearly, she was tired and overwrought, or she wouldn't entertain such a fanciful notion. The thing to do was undress and go to bed. There were a dozen things she must see to in the morning. It was witless to stay up and worry about Bridei. He was a grown man, and he'd survived a great deal already. And there was absolutely no reason to think he was one of the Fair Folk... no reason to think that such beings even existed.

With such stern, sensible thoughts in mind, she took off her shoes, then her jewelry, leaving it on the table for Aife to put away. She unfastened the lacing on her gown and pulled it over her head. Now that she wore only her shift, she realized how cold it was in the room and went to close the shutters. Returning to the table, she sat down on the stool and began to unplait the small braids around her face.

* * *

As he'd hoped, the torches had been quenched and only a faint glow from the hearth lit the interior as Bridei entered the hall. The mead and wine had done their work, and most people appeared to be asleep. He struggled to avoid stepping on anyone as he tiptoed around the edge of the hall to the stairs leading up to Dessia's tower room. Reaching the stairs, he started up them, pausing to try to compose himself halfway up.

On the last few steps, he paused again. His heart drummed in his chest and his mouth was dry. What would he find when he reached her bedchamber? The answer to his dreams? Or bitter rejection?

* * *

The process of undoing her braids was tedious, and Dessia had begun to wish she'd asked Aife to stay and help her. But she'd shooed the maidservant off this night, telling her to enjoy herself with Keenan. She imagined them off in some private nook, cuddling and kissing. A terrible sense of emptiness came over her. Bridei was right. She'd given up everything for her grand goal of rebuilding Cahermara and holding on to her family's lands, casting aside any chance for joy or pleasure in her life.

She glanced down at her hands, imagining them shrunken and spotted with age. Her hair, white. Her smooth skin, wrinkled and sagging. A lump formed in her throat as she contemplated herself many years hence. Proud, powerful Queen Dessia, now a dried-up, lonely old crone.

There was a sound on the stairs, and she stood, startled out of her reverie. Before she could even move, Bridei was there.

She looks so young and vulnerable, Bridei thought as he stared at her. Perhaps it was because her hair was unbound and small strands curled softly around her face. Or because she wore only her shift, and the thin garment revealed the womanly contours of her body. Or, perhaps it was her expression. Her eyes appeared dark and haunted and her lips were parted. In surprise? Invitation?

The old Bridei would have entered with assurance, but he felt tentative, uncertain. He bowed. "I'm sorry to disturb you, milady. I wanted to see you alone and could think of no other way."

She nodded.

"The first song I sang, it was ... I wanted to ..." Here he was, a bard, and as tongue-tied as a green boy. "I hope it didn't displease you," he finally finished.

"Displease me? Nay," she responded in a husky voice. "I thought it was beautiful."

Bridei nodded, unsure how to continue. Did she understand what he felt for her? It had all been in the song. He felt his palms begin to sweat, and a part of him, watching from a distance, was incredulous. *Don't just stand there, you fool! Kiss her!*

He took the two short steps that separated them and pulled her into his arms. Although he'd half-feared he wouldn't know what to do next, as soon as their lips met, his doubts and anxieties fell away and he felt—as he had the first time he saw her—that if ever a woman had been made for him, this was her.

She tasted of wine and woman and her scent enveloped him like the most fragrant of flowers. He was consumed by desire, and they kissed and kissed as if they were starving for it. Her body was soft and yielding in his arms, and he thought how different this Dessia was from the fierce warrior queen he'd embraced in the past. He drew away to look at her face, to feast his gaze upon her coral lips and her mesmerizing green eyes. On her delicate nose and strong fine jaw, her elegant cheekbones and haughty brow, and her skin like pale pink dogwood petals. Grasping a strand of her thick wine-dark hair in his fingers, he again brought his mouth to hers, to drown in sweetness.

But drowning wasn't enough. He wanted fire, to burn in her heated flesh. Kissing his way down her neck and shoulder, he cupped one full breast in his fingers and mouthed the nipple through the thin fabric of her shift. As she arched her back and moaned with need, he could barely stand it. He drew back, trying to slow his racing heart and rein in his throbbing arousal. Unless he was very wrong, Dessia was a virgin. To make her first experience one of complete pleasure and delight, he must use all his skill and patience. But he found he could scarcely control himself. He felt like a raw youth, clumsy and brash with desire.

"What is it?" Dessia asked, gazing at him anxiously.

"I..." He smiled what he hoped was a reassuring smile. "I'm afraid I'm going too fast."

She stared at him. "What is it?" she said again. "Don't you want me?"

He laughed weakly. "I want you too much. I'm afraid I won't do it right."

"Right?"

"Aye," he answered, again feeling like a halfwit. "I want to make it good for you. The first time... can be uncomfortable for the woman. I need to make certain you're ready."

"I *am* ready. I feel I will die with it, I am so ready." Her voice was raw and shaking and he saw from her heaving chest and flushed face that she meant her words.

He took her hands gently. "I have to warn you. I won't be able to stop, once we begin."

"And you think *I* will?" Her expression was incredulous.

"I know you think you understand what it's like, but since you haven't yet experienced lovemaking, you can't really know how you'll feel."

"I know this..." she whispered. "I know I will die for certes if you don't kiss me now!"

It was an order, and he felt himself smiling as he pulled her into his arms and leaned down to caress her mouth with his. Aye, she was untried maid, but she was also a queen. Thus commanded, he could do naught but obey.

He'd barely begun to kiss her again, exploring her lips and teaching her the way tongues could touch and caress, when she shoved him away, pulled her shift over her head and jerked it off. The breath seemed to leave his body as he looked at her. She was ravishing. A goddess. Voluptuous, yet lean and strong. Her legs seemed impossibly long. Her breasts, full, rounded and delicious. And the contrast between the delicate pallor of her skin and the fiery color of her maiden hair... Desire scorched him, incinerating the last of his control.

He pulled her near and began kissing her again. His hands caressed her body, exploring the silky skin of her bare shoulders. Down her long, slender back to the firm, plush flesh of her buttocks. He squeezed them with both hands, pressing her pelvis against his erection. She moaned into his mouth and writhed against him, then moved her hands from his shoulders to under his tunic and across his chest. Her fingers stroked him, tantalizing and greedy.

Dessia felt desperate, out of control. She wanted Bridei naked. Wanted to see him as he'd seen her. His kisses inflamed her, making her want more, so much more. To be naked against him. She pulled away, begging, "Please. Take your clothes off. I can wait no longer."

She watched as he took a deep breath, the pupils of his eyes huge, the dark hunger in them swallowing her. He went to the bed and sat down. First, he removed his boots, then his tunic. As he stood and undid his trews, she stared at his naked chest. She hadn't seen him like this since the day he'd arrived and she'd watched him washing himself at the cistern. As she had been then, she was awestruck by his beauty, the graceful lines of his body. Broad, well-muscled shoulders. Lean chest with a sprinkling of dark hair. Narrow waist and flat belly.

He let his trews fall and stepped out of them. Dessia stared some more, her mouth dry. She knew what men looked like naked. Knew also, from seeing livestock, that the male's phallus enlarged before mating. Even so, she was unprepared for the sight of his bold, jutting erection. He looked at her and smiled. "Aye, I am well endowed, milady. All the better to please you."

She nodded, feeling slightly unnerved. He approached her, completely naked, as she was. Pulling her into his arms again, he began to kiss her, and her unease vanished. She knew nothing except the feel of his bare skin against hers. The pressure of his erection against her belly. The inflaming things he did with his mouth and teeth and tongue. All of it combined seemed to drive her to madness. She felt restless and dissatisfied, and she moaned and gasped and ground her body against his. Holding her tight against him, he pulled her toward the bed. The next moment she was lying down upon it and he was on top of her. His kisses moved from her mouth to her neck, then he licked her ear. She felt his hot breath like a jolt of lightning. As he tongued her nipple, she quivered and whimpered her pleasure, clutching him tightly, her fingers twined in his hair. The fire built inside her. A great blaze, ready to consume them both. At last he touched her where she most desired it, his fingers cool against the aching, swollen flesh between her thighs. "Oh, please!" she moaned.

"Aye, soon enough," he whispered back.

If only she knew how tenuous his control was, thought Bridei. How close he was to forgetting everything he'd learned about women and thrusting into her hard and deep. But some lingering remnant of reason kept him in check. She was a maid, and he would not ravish her, no matter how much she begged.

He shifted his body lower, still stroking her, opening her with gentle fingers. She cried out as he bent down and brought his lips to her sweet quim. He held her hips still with his hands as he laved her silken folds with his tongue. His whole body was trembling with his own need and longing, and when she cried out again and her body shook with her release, his restraint shattered. Moving upward, he pushed into her with one quick thrust. She gave a gasping moan and he went still. The feel of her tight flesh around him was near unbearable. He felt as if he stood teetering on the edge of a cliff; one tiny movement and he would go tumbling over. Gasping, he began to move with slow, rhythmic strokes.

Dessia felt waves of pleasure rock her. There was pain, too, but it was so entwined with the other amazing sensations that it didn't matter. She was near mindless with it all. Drowning in a deep, unknown sea. It felt as if he were a part of her, as if his flesh had melded to hers. She breathed his scent and clutched his muscled arms, iron hard as he braced himself over her and moved inside her. Her lower body convulsed and shuddered. She arched her hips and reached to meet him, feeling each thrust like a tingling caress of her soul.

Pressure built inside her. She reached for the rainbow of ecstasy lingering just beyond her grasp and came away with a pulsing, fiery shower of stars. Following the stars down, she reached the earth as her lover collapsed upon her.

Tears filled her eyes. Tears of awe, amazement and tenderness. Although their bodies were no longer joined, their spirits still seemed close. She stroked her fingers through his hair and knew that her life would never be the same again. At the thought, she felt a pang of fear and wondered what she'd done.

Bridei rolled away to lie on his back and waited for the usual sense of contentment to wash over him. It was there, but buried beneath another emotion, something akin to panic. *You won't be able to walk away now,* a voice in his mind warned. He felt very different than he usually did after lovemaking. Not triumphant and self-satisfied, but shaken. Dessia was no ordinary woman, and what they'd shared was far different from his usual experiences. Always before, even at the moment of climax, his mind remained detached. No matter how good it felt, how lovely the woman, a part of him always seemed to be watching from a distance. But with Dessia, *all* of him had made love to her. Flesh, spirit and even the dark, brooding shadow self that followed him everywhere.

Dessia got up and went to the table. Pouring some water into a basin, she began to wash herself. Bridei watched her, trying to think of something light and easy to say. But the sight of her nakedness seemed to render him tongue-tied. She was so beautiful; he could lie here forever and stare at her.

Having finished her ablutions, she went to the other side of the table and poured them each a cup of wine from the ewer there. She carried the cups back to the bed and handed him one. A teasing comment came to mind—that he certainly deserved a drink after all his exertions—but he couldn't seem to get his lips to form the words.

Dessia sat on the side of the bed and drank her wine. After a few moments, she got up, placed the wine cup on the table, and went to retrieve her shift. As she started to put it on, he called out, "Nay!" She looked at him uncertainly.

"If you're cold, come back to bed." He got out of bed and set his wine cup on the table next to hers. Then he returned to the bed and pulled the blankets aside, motioning for her to join him. She slid in next to him and he spread the blankets over them both. For a brief moment, they lay there stiffly. Then he drew her near, cuddling her against his chest. He nuzzled her hair. The faint scent of herbs from the water she washed it with mingled with her own warm, sweet fragrance. He sighed.

"What is it?" she whispered.

"Nothing," he muttered back.

"Is this what you do—*after?*"

Aye. I have to rest, or I won't be able to pleasure you again."

"There's more?" He heard the incredulous note in her voice.

"Aye. There's more." A grin formed on his mouth. How little Dessia knew about what men and women could share.

He tried to relax and sleep but was unable to do so, which surprised him. He was used to taking his pleasure and then going to sleep. Some women found it aggravating, and but it was the way he was. He'd learned when he was a slave how to block out everything and escape into the oblivion of sleep, but now the ability failed him. Perhaps it was because he was so intensely aware of the woman in his arms. Another surprise. Usually, as soon as he bedded a woman, he began to lose interest. But, if anything, he wanted Dessia more than ever.

And it wasn't lust. His body remained satisfied, and his weary muscles longed for rest. It was another part of him that sought to stay awake and savor this moment. Was that what Dessia was doing? For she was surely awake as well. He could sense the tension in her body and her breathing hadn't taken on the deep, even rhythm of slumber.

Even as he had the thought, she pulled away from him and sat up on the edge of the bed. Hearing her sigh, he asked, "What's wrong?"

"I can't sleep."

"Aye. I can't either." He moved to sit next to her.

"What shall we do?"

"We could make love again." Although he wasn't quite ready, he knew if he began to kiss and caress her, he would get in the mood soon enough.

She shook her head and went to get her wine.

He had a sudden uneasy thought. "Didn't you like it? I mean, the first time for a woman isn't always the best. But still..." He found he was holding his breath. Although all his instincts told him she'd reached her peak, he couldn't be certain.

She turned to look at him, her expression almost anguished. "Aye. I liked it. I liked it far too much."

His mood lightened, but he was still uncertain. Why did she look so distraught? "What's wrong?"

She gestured helplessly. "But now... what do we do? And I don't mean the rest of the night. I mean..." He knew the words she didn't say: *What do we do... the rest of our lives?*

The question was familiar to him. Many women had asked him the same thing. He'd always answered in a light tone, suggesting they enjoy this moment and not worry about the future. Then he would pull them into his arms and silence them with kisses. He would make them sigh and moan and forget their worries. Then, as soon as he could, he would leave them. That seemed to him the gentlest way to answer their question, although sometimes they didn't agree. But he couldn't do that with Dessia. She looked so agonized. So vulnerable. Besides, he didn't *want* to leave her.

He also understood why she was asking the question. She wasn't concerned merely for her own wishes and feelings. Because she was a queen, she had to think about how this night would impact her people's future, as well as her own. So, he didn't answer flippantly, didn't pull her into his arms. He simply said, "I don't know."

She nodded at this, as if it was the answer she'd expected, that she'd already come to on her own. That was probably why she was so restless and edgy. For the last ten years, every action she'd taken had been with one goal in mind—to restore her kingdom. Now she'd done something purely for herself, and she didn't know how to reconcile it with her long-held dream.

He not only understood her dilemma, but felt her turmoil echoed in himself. This hadn't been part of his plan either. He'd never meant to come to care for her so much. Having spent his whole adult life seeking never to develop any strong feelings about any person, place or goal, it was shocking to discover himself in these circumstances. What had happened? How had this woman, and this place, these people—how they managed to breach the barriers he'd set up around his heart?

Difficult questions. Far too difficult for him to resolve this night. He told her so. "I don't think either of us is in a condition to find answers right now. Perhaps we should, as they say, 'sleep on it'."

"But that's the dilemma." She sighed again. "Neither of us can sleep."

"I think I have a remedy for that." He moved toward her. While his mind had wrestled with these difficult issues, his body had revived. Looking at her lovely nakedness, he found he was aroused. He pulled her into his arms. "If we can't sleep, perhaps it's because we aren't tired enough."

This is madness, Dessia thought as he kissed her. The more he touched her, the more he loved her, the more confused she became. She felt as if she were drowning, and every time she got her head above water and breathed enough air to clear her head, he pulled her down into the depths again.

Ah, but what a blissful end. She was drowning in pleasure, and the deeper she slipped into the delightful sensations, the more enticing and satisfying they became. His mouth was magic. And the way he touched her, as if he knew her body better than she knew it herself. She would never have imagined it a few moments ago, but her body was already primed and eager for more. Her nipples tightened with arousal and the flesh between her legs no longer throbbed with soreness but with the exquisite ache of desire. When he touched her there, she seemed to melt. Her knees went weak, her body limp against his, and the place between her legs dripped molten wetness.

She lay back helplessly as he slid her legs apart, then closed her eyes as he began to kiss her *there*. The first time he'd done it, she'd felt shock and embarrassment. This time, knowing what pleasure awaited, she gave in easily. She could scarce believe this was happening. That it was her body writhing with passion. Her own voice keening her delight. The tension built and built and then released in wild rush.

The next thing she knew, Bridei was on top of her, whispering. "Try to be a little quieter, my sweetness. If you make too much noise, someone might think I'm hurting you and decide to come to your rescue."

With a sense of horror, she realized she'd been near screaming as she peaked. "By Beli!" she gasped. "What if they're on their way up here now? What will I say? What will we do?"

"Relax. Everyone drank enough wine and mead to keep them snoring for hours. Even if someone did decide to climb the stairs and check on you, they'd call up first"

"But I... what will people think?" She scooted out from under him and got out of bed. "You have to leave! Now, before anyone knows you've been here!"

"Do you really think anyone cares if I bed you? After that song I sang, I imagine most of them expect it."

"Oh, the song!" She collapsed on the bed. "I forgot about the song."

He moved to sit beside her. "It's all right, Dessia. They won't think any less of you for knowing you might wish to take a man to your bed. Indeed, they might like you better for it." He stroked her shoulder. "*Cariad,* you don't have to always be a queen. Sometimes you're allowed to simply be a woman."

Dessia sighed heavily. It was probably too late. After the noise she'd made, at least a few people in the hall had surely woken up. If Bridei left now, they would see him and know the truth. Besides, to send his away, now, after the pleasure he'd given her, it didn't seem right. It was cowardly to even consider it.

She looked at him, at his beautiful violet eyes and his sensual mouth, quirked in a slight smile. Her heart seemed to beat faster, and all her doubts and worries vanished like a mist burning off in the sunlight. "What does *cariad* mean?" she asked.

"Beloved. It means beloved."

Her heart seemed to race faster still. There was such tenderness in his gaze. "What language is it?" she asked.

"Cymry."

She felt something inside her leap with joy. From this man, this charming, clever bard, she might expect endearments to tumble easily from his lips. But somehow she knew he meant this one. He'd spoken in the language of his birth. And the look in his eyes said it was true. He did love her.

Chapter 13

It was still dark when Bridei woke. His body felt wonderfully, deliciously satisfied, and by rights he should still be sleeping. But even in his dreams he seemed aware of the woman sleeping beside him. He turned to look at her, and in the faint light of the guttering candles on the table, feasted his eyes on her delicate features. She looked so soft and female. He felt a strong urge to protect her. It almost made him wish he was a man like Keenan, a trained warrior, tough, brutal and experienced at combat. Perhaps that was the sort of man she needed, one who could defend her and protect her lands and her people. The thought dismayed him. What if he wasn't the right man for her to fall in love with? What if she'd made a mistake? If *he'd* made a mistake in making her care for him?

It was a disturbing thought. Even more disturbing was the realization that he was having it. Never before had he questioned his right to bed a woman. Dessia had changed him, made him a different person. And he wasn't certain he had the skills he needed to survive as the man she'd made him into. He knew how to take care of himself, but he'd never had to worry about anyone else before.

His thoughts were making him restless. If he didn't want to wake Dessia, he must get up. With slow, careful movements, he climbed over her sleeping body, found his clothes and began to dress. With as much stealth as he could manage, he went to the door, unlatched it and slipped out.

He knew a stab of regret as he started down the tower stairs. It would have been delightful to stay until Dessia woke, so they could cuddle and perhaps make love again. But she might sleep hours more. Besides, it was much more discreet for him to leave now. He'd be far less likely to be seen as he exited the stairs. Although he'd meant it when he told Dessia her people probably expected her to take him to her bed, there was no point flaunting their relationship. Tact and subtlety were important in such matters, as he'd learned over the years.

He was in luck. Everyone in the hall appeared to still be soundly asleep, and he was able to reach the door without notice. Once outside, he breathed a sigh of relief, then immediately shivered with cold. Their fine weather had turned. The sky, although lightening with dawn, was overcast, and a raw wind blew in from sea. He doubted the traders would want to set out in this. That served his purposes. There were a few questions he wanted to ask Penrick. The trader seemed to know a lot about what was happening in Britain; perhaps he could come up with some reason for Dolgar's actions.

Although Bridei considered seeking Penrick out, he feared it was too early. The traders had drunk as much as anyone the night before. They might not rise before midday. But as he made his way to the midden, he saw Penrick apparently coming from there.

"By the gods, it's cold out here!" Penrick exclaimed. "I should have brought my cloak."

"Aye, it is," Bridei agreed. "Where are you going?"

"Back to the barracks. That's where the queen put us. I was displeased at first, having found out it's where the workmen stay. But the accommodations aren't too bad. Much better than the crowded hall."

Bridei grinned at him. "You may well be sleeping in my bed. That's where I usually spend my nights."

"But not this one, eh?" Penrick smirked.

"Nay. Not this one." Bridei felt himself bristle. What business was it of this man where he slept?

Penrick smile vanished as quickly as it had appeared. "No offense meant. But I am surprised the queen would house a bard of your skill with her laborers. Or, perhaps, it was your preference. The barracks do afford more privacy."

"Exactly," Bridei answered. He motioned to the other man. "I'll meet you there shortly. There's something I wished to discuss with you."

"I'll be there. Sarlic will stoke up the brazier so we can talk comfortably."

After a quick trip to the midden, Bridei made his way to the barracks.

Sarlic had the brazier glowing, as promised, and Penrick and Rinc were seated on either side. Sarlic sat on the floor by the wall next to the traders' packs. Bridei pulled up a stool next to Penrick. The man fixed his blue eyes on Bridei expectantly.

"I heard you talking about what will happen in Britain now that Arthur's been defeated," Bridei began. "You mentioned the Caledonians. What do you know of them? Are you familiar with their politics?"

Penrick shrugged. "Some. I hear things now and then."

"What about a chieftain named Dolgar?"

"Don't know him."

He'd been afraid of this. Dolgar was a minor chieftain, and probably not important enough that someone like Penrick would have heard of him. Which was what made it all so puzzling. Bridei was very certain Dolgar hadn't acted on his own. So, who else was behind his abduction and the attempt to murder him?

"What's this Dolgar to you?" Penrick asked.

"It's because of him that I ended up in this place. Thanks to Dolgar, I traveled here on a slavers' boat, as part of their cargo."

"Dolgar sold you to the slavers?" Penrick straightened in surprise.

"His plan was to have them throw me overboard. But I was able to talk them out of it. Then we encountered a storm and got blown to this part of Ireland."

"What did you do to anger this Dolgar so much—seduce his wife or daughter?"

"Neither," Bridei answered. "Which makes his actions truly baffling. While I knew the man bore me no affection, I'm surprised he went to so much trouble to be rid of me."

"And so you ended up here, escaped the slavers and joined Queen Dessia's household?" Penrick asked.

Bridei nodded. "The queen has no love of slavers, and as soon as we landed, we encountered some of her men. They didn't give my captors time to bargain, but told them to prepare to do battle or quit these shores. The slavers chose the latter course."

"You must count yourself very fortunate to be alive, and to have found yourself under the protection of such a gracious—and beautiful—ruler." Rinc spoke for the first time.

"Aye, I've been very fortunate," Bridei agreed. "But getting back to the matter of Dolgar, I can't believe he came up with this plot on his own. I'm certain someone else must have put him up to it. Have you heard anything about what's happening in the north that might explain why someone would consider me a threat? I do have some Brigante blood through my mother. I suppose Dolgar might think I sought to contest him as chieftain. But I always made it clear I have little interest in such matters."

Penrick narrowed his eyes in thought. "As a traveling bard, you visit many households and are privy to many secrets. Perhaps you've gained some sort of knowledge that makes you dangerous, at least in the eyes of your enemy."

"If that's the case, then I wish I knew what the secret was."

"That's all I can suggest," said Penrick. "You must admit your way of life gives you every opportunity to be a spy." He gestured with long, tanned fingers. "You visit a royal household and earn the trust of the people there. Then you move on to the household of their enemies and betray their secrets. I've certain there's a great deal of wealth to be made in such endeavors."

"I'm certain there is," Bridei agreed.

Dessia stood inside the door of the barracks, her body wracked with shock and dismay. She hadn't heard all of what Penrick said, but the words "spy" and "betray their secrets" had come to her clearly. Taking a step back, she sought to compose herself. She must have misheard, or perhaps they were talking about something else altogether.

Nay, it can't be true! Bridei wouldn't do that to me!

And why not?

Because he loves me.

Her throat filled with bitter bile. Bridei was the consummate charmer, skilled at winning the admiration and trust of others, especially women. How many women had he called *cariad*—beloved? There were probably dozens. What a fool she'd been. How easily she'd fallen into his clever trap.

But despite her despair and self-castigation, the rational part of her remained unconvinced. She could think of no "secrets" Bridei had learned the night before. Everything he knew that her enemies could use against her, he'd discovered in the first few weeks he'd been at Cahermara. If he were a spy, he should have left to report his findings long ago. There was no reason for him to stay... unless he took perverse pleasure in making his victims care for him. And in her case, making them fall in love.

Such behavior seemed far too callous and cold to fit the man she knew. But *did* she know him? What if there was a part of Bridei hidden away, a dark, sinister aspect she'd never glimpsed? His experience as a youth had been brutal enough to make him capable of murder. Perhaps it had also made him capable of other forms of treachery.

Nay, she couldn't believe that. No one was that good at masking their character. She must be mistaken about what she'd heard. Or, it must mean something else. They must have been talking about another situation altogether.

Moving back to the doorway, she crept forward, trying to hear more. She must have made some sound, for both men looked up. Bridei immediately stood and approached her, a dazzling smile on his face. "Milady, how fare you today? Come and warm yourself at the brazier."

She let him take her arm and guide her to where Penrick and Rinc were seated on stools by a glowing brazier. Bridei motioned to the stool he'd been sitting on. "Sit, milady."

She sat down, her heart pounding, her body rigid. Everything seemed so normal. So relaxed. If they'd really been plotting against her, surely they would appear uncomfortable. There would be some evidence of guilt. She forced herself to speak. "You're all up early."

"As are you, milady. Although as hostess, I suppose you felt the need to check on your guests." Bridei nodded to the two traders. "They seem content to me."

"Aye. I did want to see how you were faring." She glanced at Penrick and Rinc.

"My bed was comfortable," said Penrick. "And the food and entertainment last night were exceptional. We have no complaints."

Dessia looked at Bridei and tried to make her voice light. "And why are you here? Was there some matter you wished to discuss with the traders?"

He shrugged. "Merely catching up on politics in Britain."

Was he lying? She couldn't tell. The gods help her, she couldn't tell at all. His manner was so easy and nonchalant.

"I'm afraid our fine weather is over," said Bridei. "It appears a storm is moving in."

"Aye," said Penrick. "I feel certain we won't be able to sail today."

Good, thought Dessia. That will give me time to figure out what to do. She stood. "Since the weather may prevent many others from traveling, I must go to the kitchen and see what sort of food stores we have left to feed everyone."

"Would you like some assistance, milady?" asked Bridei. His expression so warm, so tender—Dessia felt her heart melt inside her. She forced herself to remember what she'd heard. "Nay. I'm perfectly capable of conducting matters in my own household."

What had gotten into her? Bridei wondered as he sat down again after Dessia had left. She wasn't acting like a woman who'd been well-pleasured the night before. But perhaps that was just her way. She remained as proud and independent as ever.

Penrick apparently also noticed her sharp tone, for said, "The queen seems a bit testy this morning."

"Perhaps she has a headache from too much mead," Bridei responded. "I'm certain she's not the only one who's suffering this morn."

"Aye, that's likely," Penrick agreed.

"There's another thing I wanted to talk to you about," said Bridei. "I'd like to buy a present for Queen Dessia. Unfortunately, I was forced to leave all my wealth behind in Britain. I thought perhaps I could visit some other households in the region and try to earn a little silver or other coin I might use to barter for a gift for her."

"What sort of gift?" Penrick's eyes had brightened, the merchant in him obviously intrigued.

"I'm not certain. Perhaps silk for a new gown. Or a piece of jewelry. Something beautiful and elegant. Something she would never purchase for herself."

Penrick nodded. "Queen Dessia purchases only necessities, and bargains fiercely for those." He motioned to Sarlic and said something to him in a Germanic tongue, a language Bridei didn't know. Sarlic rose, picked up one of the packs and took it to the bed.

"Let me should show you some of the finer things I have to offer," Penrick said, also rising. "I almost didn't bring any jewelry from the boat. But then I remembered that the smith, Niall, is always interested in the finer stuff. He keeps trying to figure out how to reproduce that type of work on his own."

"I recall him saying something to me about that," Bridei agreed. He followed Penrick over to where Sarlic was arranging fabric bundles on the bed.

Penrick selected one of the bundles and unwrapped it. "I showed him some pieces and let him study them. But I doubt it will do him any good. The workshops where they make these things closely guard their secrets about the substances and methods they use to create the various colors. I don't think he is likely to be able to figure out the process on his own."

Penrick held out a round gold brooch with design of elaborately curving lines. Bridei took it and admired it. The whole piece was exquisite, but what made it unusual were the vivid colors of the enamelwork. "Aye, this is stunning."

"You'd have to sing a lot of songs to pay for a piece like this," Penrick said as he put the brooch away. He took out more jewelry and laid it on the bed. Bridei examined the pieces admiringly. "It's all exquisite quality, but I'm not certain it's what I'm looking for. I want it to be something that has special significance for her." He frowned as he struggled to explain. "Something that represents Cahermara, or her heritage in some way."

Penrick nodded. "If you want to have something custom made, you could travel with us to Ath Cliath. There are a number of merchants there who would be eager to have a skilled bard visit their households, and they have the wealth to pay you. Then you could have one of metalsmiths design a piece especially for Queen Dessia."

"A horse," Bridei said suddenly. "The brooch should have a horse on it—to represent the name of the queen's tribe, the Fionnlairaos. That would be the perfect gift."

"The name must be an old one." Rinc said, coming to stand next to them. "I've seen no horses since I've been here."

"Aye. Some years ago, the whole herd was stolen by a man named Tiernan O'Bannon. He also attacked the settlement and killed Dessia's family. Only she escaped."

Penrick's brows rose and he looked at Rinc. "I've never heard this tale. But, then, we've only been trading in Ireland a few years."

"The attack must have happened about ten years ago," said Bridei.

"You say she was the only one of her family left alive?" queried Rinc. "How did she regain her lands?"

"She fought for them," said Bridei. "Gathered together a bunch of men loyal to her father and led them into battle."

"But ten years ago, she would have been a child," Penrick said.

"Several years passed before she was old enough and skilled enough with weaponry to take on O'Bannon. But she did it, nevertheless. Then, having won back her family's lands, she built this rath on the same spot the old fortress stood. Although she made certain this new one was in stone, making it more difficult to attack."

Penrick nodded. "It's a solid structure, or will be when it's finished." He shook his head. "What an amazing tale."

"Indeed it is. That's why I composed a song about it. The long ballad I sang last night told the whole story."

"Aye. I recall it now. I guess I didn't realize you were singing about something that had happened recently." Penrick regarded Bridei assessingly. "It was a very polished song. I assumed someone else had composed it and you were merely altering parts of it to fit the circumstances here."

"Nay," said Bridei, smiling. "The piece was all my own."

It was Rinc who spoke this time: "You're very skilled. If you found the right sort of patron, you could end up a very wealthy man."

"I suppose that's true," Bridei said, "Although I can't promise I would be able to compose pieces the equal of the one last night on a regular basis. I doubt some hoary old chieftain would inspire me the way Queen Dessia has."

Penrick and Rinc both chuckled. Penrick said, "I must say I'm very impressed with what Queen Dessia has accomplished. She clearly has a strong will and the fierce loyalty of her people, but even so ..." He shook his head.

"It must have taken years to build this hillfort," said Rinc. "I'm surprised no one has attacked her in the meantime."

"Apparently her enemies believe Cahermara is protected by a magical spell," said Bridei. "Queen Dessia is rumored to be a sorceress and to use an enchantment to keep her enemies away."

Penrick guffawed loudly, while Rinc gave a snort of derision. "And what do you think, Bridei ap Maelgwn?" asked Penrick. "*Is* Queen Dessia a sorceress?"

"I must admit I've encountered things here at Cahermara that aren't easily explained."

"What sort of things?" asked Penrick.

Bridei shrugged. "There's an ancient forest nearby. I tried to follow the queen there once, but a mist rose up and blocked my way. I've talked to many people here and none of them have ever ventured more than a few paces into that forest. Yet Dessia comes and goes there freely. It's the place she hid when the original fortress was attacked when she was a girl. She also told me there's a lake there and sometimes when she looks into the water, she sees visions of the future."

Even as he said this, Bridei felt a strange sensation, as if a finger of warning moved down his spine. Perhaps he wasn't supposed to speak of these things. His goal was to reinforce Dessia's reputation for magic and help protect her. But even with that worthy intent, talking about the lake and what he'd experienced there might not be right.

"I can see why you—a bard—might be intrigued by such a fanciful tale," said Penrick. "You can probably compose a wonderful song about Queen Dessia and this magical lake. But to me, it sounds like a bunch of superstitious nonsense."

"Think what you like," responded Bridei. "I remain convinced that some force or power watches over Queen Dessia and her lands." Or, at least it had, up until now. What if in speaking of these things, he'd angered the ancient forces and disrupted the magic?

"Perhaps the reason the spell of protection works is because Queen Dessia's enemies believe the tale," said Rinc. "In my experience, the Irish believe all sorts of ridiculous notions. It seems to be their nature, along with being quarrelsome and hot-headed." He scowled in apparent disgust.

Bridei was amused. "You don't appear to have a very high opinion of the Irish."

"They're not the most intelligent of races," said Rinc. "They blame some ancient race they called fairies for many of their misfortunes. And they're always fighting among themselves over next to nothing."

Although he couldn't quite say why, Bridei felt compelled to defend the Irish. He admired their passion and fire. That was why he found Dessia so appealing. "It seems to me that like most people, the Irish fight over land and resources. That's why Tiernan O'Bannon attacked Cahermara all those years ago. He sought to take over Queen Dessia's father's lands."

"Is Tiernan O'Bannon still alive?" asked Penrick.

"Aye. He has lands to the west of here. None of his holdings are on the coast, which limits his access to trade. I'm certain that's at least part of his interest in this territory."

"Under those circumstances, we're unlikely to meet this Tiernan O'Bannon," said Penrick. "We seldom travel inland, and usually only visit larger settlements. We put in here at Cahermara mainly because it's a good stopping place on our way to Ath Cliath. Speaking of which, having you decided to come with us?"

"When are you leaving?" asked Bridei.

"It depends on the weather," said Penrick. "With luck, tomorrow."

"I've like to take you up on your offer," said Bridei thoughtfully. "But I don't want Queen Dessia to know what I'm up to. Perhaps I'll pretend to set off in a different direction and at a different time. Make it look like I'm traveling inland, then double back and meet up with you before you sail."

Penrick nodded. "We'll be waiting for you."

Bridei rose. "On that note, I'll bid you farewell. I have some things to do before tomorrow."

Seeing Bridei get to his feet, Dessia left her spot outside door of the barracks and rushed around to the side of the building. She hid in the corner there until Bridei was well across the yard. Then she left her hiding place and raced toward the gate. She called up to the gatetower and Flann came down. "Where's Keenan?" she demanded.

"Out on patrol," Flann answered.

"As soon as he gets back, have him come and see me," said Dessia.

Flann nodded climbed back up the ladder to the gatetower. Dessia watched him go, her whole body taut with anxiety. "Keenan," she muttered to herself. "I need you. I need you now. You were right about Bridei after all. Curse the lying bard!"

She exhaled sharply, nursing her anger. She had to make herself hate him. But it was so hard.

Her next breath was a sob. She reminded herself of what she'd heard. A lot of words hadn't been clear to her, but she'd made out enough to guess Bridei's plan. His mention of Tiernan O'Bannon was the most damning thing. Then she'd heard him say something about not wanting her to know what he'd up to. At the very end, he appeared to be arranging to meet up with the traders in order to set sail with them. So, he *was* a spy. The only way it could be more obvious was if he'd announced his plan to the whole hall!

At that bitter thought, her anger took over again. Pacing, she outlined her plan, muttering to herself as she did so: "I'll have Keenan follow him when he leaves. Then kill him once he gets a reasonable distance away. Bury his body in the Forest of Mist. No one will ever know. If anyone asks, we'll mention him setting off and the direction he went, then insist we know nothing else."

It was a sound plan, and perfectly justified. She had to do whatever was necessary to protect her lands and her people. She'd killed men in battle. This was no different.

Except it was, a voice in her head reminded her. *You weren't in love with those men!* "By the gods! How can I do this?" she moaned.

She'd never felt so despairing, so conflicted. It reminded her of the night long ago when Cahermara was attacked. Then she'd also felt torn in two. She'd longed to stay and try and help her family, but knew if she did so she would die. She'd feared to enter the Forest of Mist, but also known it was the only place she might be safe.

Once again, she had a wrenching choice to make. Yet it was clear—as it had been that night long ago—she could only make one decision. She had to think of the future, to consider what was best for her people.

But, by the gods, how could she bear to kill Bridei—and in such a cowardly fashion? It was one thing to kill a man in battle. Quite another to kill a man when he was unarmed and helpless. And how would Keenan go about it? Would he run Bridei through with his sword? Cut his throat?

The very idea sickened her. It seemed like such a loathsome, dishonorable thing to do. And even if Keenan was the one who performed the act, she would be the one to blame. And if she were wrong, if Bridei wasn't a spy, if what she'd heard didn't mean what she thought it did, then she would have done something truly evil.

She gave a moan of misery. "What should I do? How do I deal with this?" This was too momentous a thing to decide on her own. But who could she ask for help? Who could guide her? All at once, she knew.

Again, she called up to Flann. When he came down, she said, "I need to borrow your cloak." When he gaped at her, she continued, "I'm leaving the rath, and I don't have time to go up to my chambers and fetch my own."

Flann nodded, still looking puzzled. He took off his cloak and handed it to her. Realizing that he would now be freezing up in the drafty watchtower, she said, "As soon as I'm gone, you have my leave to fetch another cloak." She gestured distractedly. "You can have one of mine if you wish. Tell Aife to give you my old green one."

"Aye, milady." Flann's eyes were round and staring. Dessia was aware her behavior must seem witless, but she didn't care. She must leave before she encountered Bridei. There was no way she could face him.

"Now," she said to Flann. "Open the gate."

Chapter 14

"Where's the queen?" Bridei asked Ona as the serving woman entered the hall carrying a basket of bannocks.

Ona motioned with her head. "Perhaps she's up in the tower."

"I checked there, of course," Bridei said. "I've also been to the kitchen, all the storage sheds, the workmen's barracks, the hall." He ticked off the places on his fingers.

"Have you asked Aife if she's seen her?"

Bridei fought to control his temper. "Aye. She was the first person I asked."

Ona shrugged. "Well, she must be somewhere. Unless she left the dun. Are the traders still here? Could she have gone with them when they returned to their boat?"

"The traders aren't leaving until tomorrow. But you're right. She could have left the rath." Bridei turned and started for the gate. Reaching it, he called up to Flann in the watchtower, "Have you seen the queen?"

Flann came down to answer him. "The queen left the rath a while ago," the guard said. "Most likely heading toward the Forest of Mist. What's wrong with her, do you think?"

"What do you mean?"

"She was behaving very strangely. Had me give her my cloak because she said she didn't have time to fetch her own. Her whole manner was distracted and odd, as if she were upset about something."

Bridei thanked Flann, then turned and walked back toward the hall. Poor Dessia. She must be having second thoughts about what they'd done.

She wouldn't be the first woman to regret losing her maidenhood. Still, her attitude rankled a bit. She'd been more than willing last night, and he'd thought he'd pleased her well. But this was Dessia. Proud, stubborn Dessia. She would find it difficult to admit she'd done something for her own pleasure. Even now she must be agonizing over how what they'd done would affect her plans for her kingdom and her people.

Should he go after her? He imagined finding her by the lake and making love to her in that magical place. It would be amazing, he had no doubt. On the other hand, Dessia had obviously gone there to be alone. She needed to work out her feelings and accept that she had a right to enjoy her own life. As much as he wanted to follow Dessia, consideration demanded he let her return in her own time.

* * *

Dessia walked along the forest pathway, her heart heavy and aching. It was obvious she wasn't going to find answers here. This time there had been no signs of magic at all. No mist had risen as she walked along the pathway. And when she reached the lake, the area around it had been as been as barren and winter-drab as the rest of landscape. She'd gone to the lake and bent down and peered into the water. But the only thing she'd seen was her own face, pale and pinched with tension and distress. In the matter of Bridei, the forces surrounding the lake were silent.

Perhaps that was her answer. The fact that she'd experienced no magic this day might mean her plan to get rid of Bridei was a sound one. Perhaps the forest and the lake were in mourning for what she must do. But that seemed unlikely. If the forces here knew Bridei was a traitor, why had she seen the vision in the lake of him at her side, as if he were meant to be her consort?

Recalling what she'd seen and the sense of destiny she'd felt at that moment, her determination wavered. How could she kill the man who she'd seen in a vision of what surely must be the future? For that matter, how could she kill the man she *loved*? It was unthinkable. There must be some other answer. She had to find it, or she would go mad.

A moment later, she halted on the pathway, relief flooding her. Of course there was another way to protect her kingdom. All she had to do to prevent Bridei from betraying her secrets to O'Bannon was lock him in the souterrain. She started walking again, her mind racing. She was going to have to plan this carefully, and carry out her scheme without anyone except Keenan knowing what was going on. It was especially important the traders didn't guess what she'd done. She'd tell them she had no idea where Bridei had gone, that he must have decided to leave before them. As for her people, she'd suggest that now he had a harp, he'd probably left to find a wealthier household in which to entertain. It sounded plausible. She'd remind everyone that Bridei was traveling bard and had never stayed in one place long before, so why should he linger at Cahermara?

She worried they wouldn't believe her. A few hours ago, she would have also sworn Bridei was content and happy at Cahermara. She'd also have sworn he loved her. But actions speak louder than words, as she'd remind anyone who brought up the matter. Since he'd left, it must mean he'd grown tired of staying in one place. His performance the night before had been a triumph. There was no way he could ever match it. Instead, he'd moved on to somewhere else to dazzle and charm a new audience.

Even as she told herself these things, a part of her screamed in protest that the man she was describing wasn't the Bridei she knew. The man who'd made love to her with such finesse and passion, the man who'd composed a beautiful song for her, that man wasn't capable of any of these things. *He* would never betray her. Never leave her so casually.

Doubts began to eat at her resolve. Perhaps she'd misunderstood the conversation with the traders. Maybe there was some harmless explanation. But how could she take the chance? It wasn't merely her heart that was at stake, it was her kingdom, her people, everything she'd worked so hard for. There was no other choice. She would have to imprison Bridei, at least until she could be certain of his loyalty.

Her mind made up, she walked resolutely toward the hillfort.

* * *

"The queen's back." Aife told Bridei in a low voice. "She's talking to Keenan near the gatehouse."

Bridei was sitting in the hall with the traders. At Aife's words, he rose and motioned to the bowl of pottage a servant had placed before him a moment before. "You can have mine," he told Penrick. "I find I'm not hungry this morning."

Penrick fixed him with an ironic look. "At least not for food."

Bridei didn't respond, but hurried after Aife. His impatience built as he maneuvered through the many people crowded into the hall. He was desperate to see Dessia; he needed to reassure her, and also reassure himself. Never before had he felt this way after bedding a woman. He was elated... but also anxious. What if he hadn't pleased her? What if he'd satisfied her curiosity about lovemaking and now she had no interest in doing it again? What if it didn't mean as much to her as it did to him?

He longed to look at her, to kiss her and hold her in his arms. His yearning for her was like a deep ache inside him, as powerful any urge he'd ever felt. He didn't know how he could bear to leave her for the few weeks it would take for him to accomplish his mission in Ath Cliath. But he needed to accumulate some wealth so he could do something special for her. He'd changed his mind about the gift. Rather than jewelry, he meant to give her something more substantial. Instead of a brooch with the design of a horse, he was going to buy her a real horse, or maybe several.

The idea filled him with such satisfaction he could almost face the prospect of leaving her. And before he said goodbye, he would make love to her once again. He would satisfy her so completely, give her such pleasure that she would never even look at another man. He would win her heart as she'd already won his.

But when he reached the gate, there was no sign of either the queen or Keenan. Bridei knew a moment of consternation as he glanced around the hillfort. It seemed unlikely she'd go to the barracks, since the traders weren't there. What about the kitchen? Perhaps she was making certain that everyone was being fed. But if she was concerned for the welfare of her guests, she'd have gone to the hall, and then he would have seen her. And what was she doing with Keenan? The idea that she might be somewhere alone with the warrior aroused Bridei's jealousy. But that was absurd. Of course, she must discuss matters with her man-of-arms; the security of the hillfort depended on it.

He was mulling over where to look when he saw Dessia walking towards him. His heart seemed to expand with joy at the sight of her. "Milady," he said, smiling. As she drew near, he said "*cariad*," in a softer voice meant only for her. He was startled when she winced instead of smiling. Was she really that uncomfortable with him after what they shared?

"Bridei," she said. "I wanted to ask your opinion on something. Will you come with me?" She motioned.

He nodded, puzzled over her behavior. Dessia didn't seem to want to meet his eyes. What was wrong? He started to ask her, but she turned and walked away before he could. A dozen thoughts went through his mind as he followed her. Finally, he decided she was taking him to someplace where they could be alone. It made sense. She couldn't take him up to her tower room with everyone watching, so she'd sought out somewhere else.

He was instantly aroused and eager. His body throbbed with longing as she led him to one of the storehouses. The door creaked as she opened it. She hesitated a moment before entering. Then she stepped inside. He followed.

"Shut the door," she said. He turned and closed it. It wasn't totally dark inside, but nearly so. He started toward her, intending to pull her into his arms. Something struck the back of the head. He saw swirling lights. Then everything went black.

* * *

"By the gods, you didn't have to hit him!" Dessia cried as she bent down to examine Bridei. Her heart seemed to be in her throat until she found his pulse.

"I had to disable him somehow," responded Keenan. "It seemed the easiest way."

"What if you've hurt him!"

"He'll wake up with an aching head, but recover soon enough. Besides, if what you say is true, the bastard deserves death."

Dessia made an agonized sound. "We don't know for certain that he's really a spy."

"He must be. Why else would he be talking to the traders about such things?"

"I don't know. Maybe I misunderstood. I only caught phrases here and there."

"It would take much less to convince me. Ever since he came here, I suspected he was up to no good. He's so slippery and cunning. Playing up to everyone. What sort of man seeks to charm everyone he meets? I caught him flirting with the cook, Doona, and she's as ugly as the back side of a cow."

"He's an entertainer, a performer!" Dessia exclaimed. "It's his way to try to please people and make them like him."

"Aye, and he's succeeded, hasn't he? Even you've fallen under his spell."

"That's not true. If I'd fallen under his spell I wouldn't be doing this. I'd be..." Abruptly, she remembered whom she was talking to. She couldn't very well admit to her chief man-of-arms that what she longed to be doing at this moment was making love with Bridei.

"Well, I'm glad you came to your senses at last," said Keenan. "I just hope it's not too late. There's no telling what he told the traders. They might go to O'Bannon themselves."

"I don't think so. They have other business to attend to. Besides, even if they're a danger to us, there's nothing we can do. We can't very well imprison or kill them."

"Why not?"

Dessia exhaled in exasperation. "Because it would be a breach of the ancient tradition of hospitality. There's no way to know if the traders are a threat to us. We can't take such drastic action based on vague fears that they might be spies."

"There are ways to make men talk."

"Torture?" Dessia shook her head emphatically. Then she motioned to Bridei. "Shouldn't we get him down in the souterrain before he wakes?"

"You're certain that's what you want to do? It would be much easier to end his life right now."

"I can't," she whispered. "I can't kill him." Even contemplating such a thing made her ache with misery.

"Very well." Keenan bent down and picked Bridei up by the ankles. He began to drag him toward the opening in the floor.

* * *

Dessia paced in the tiny tower chamber. She felt physically ill as she considered what she'd done. *What if he's hurt? What if he doesn't wake up?* She stopped pacing and moaned in despair. Every fiber of her being wanted to go back there, climb down into the souterrain and gather her lover into her arms. It was agony to think of him injured or suffering. But she must be strong. She must remember her duty. She had to protect her heritage, even if it broke her heart.

"Milady, the traders are leaving now."

Dessia turned as Aife called up to her. That was the answer. She must keep busy. So busy she couldn't think about Bridei. She went to the stairs and started down. "I surprised the traders are leaving so soon. I thought they meant to stay another day."

"The storm's blown over, and they're anxious to move on."

Would the traders be looking for Bridei? Dessia wondered with a spasm of dread as they reached the bottom of the stairs. What would she say to them?

She followed Aife through the still-crowded hall and then through the hillfort to where the workshops were located. Penrick and Rinc stood outside the smithy talking to Niall. They nodded to her as she approached. "Where's the bard?" asked Penrick.

"Bridei? I... I thought he was with you."

Penrick raised his brow in surprise. Then he shrugged. "I'm certain he'll turn up soon. Tell him that we had to leave, but that we will... consider the matters we discussed."

"Of course," Dessia answered. Was this Penrick's cryptic way of telling Bridei they would meet up with him after he'd completed his mission? The vagueness of the trader's manner seemed to confirm her worst fears.

Penrick gave a slight bow. "Thank you for your hospitality, milady. And thank your bard, Bridei ap Maelgwn, when you see him. Last night he gave one of the finest performances I've ever experienced. You're very fortunate to have a man of such talent in your household."

Nodding stiffly, Dessia agreed to pass on his words of praise. The traders said farewell to Niall and headed for the gate. They each carried only a small pack, so Dessia surmised that their servant, Sarlic, had already taken the rest of their goods to the ship.

"It's a pity Bridei wasn't here to say goodbye to them," Niall said. "I'm very surprised he isn't around. He spent a great deal of time with them while they were here."

"Aye. As did you." She looked at Niall speculatively. "Did you ever hear them discussing Tiernan O'Bannon or any of the other neighboring chieftains?"

"Nay, milady. Why would they care about our local politics?"

"I thought something might have come up."

"All we talked about was jewelry-making and enamelwork." Niall held out his hand. "Penrick gave me a small brooch to study, to see if I could figure out the technique. He said it was flawed and wouldn't fetch much. As payment, I repaired the clasp on another piece, but I'm certain he made me a bargain."

Dessia glanced at the brooch. It was stunning, the colors of the enamel remarkably bright and vivid. Niall was right. It was very good of Penrick to part with such a fine piece in exchange for a little repair work. Having never before encountered a trader who exhibited such generosity, Dessia was immediately suspicious. Was the brooch a payment for information?

She studied Niall's face. Was he so desperate to advance his skills that he'd betray her? It didn't seem possible. The smith was a solid, straightforward man, devoted to his family and to his work. But it *was* conceivable he'd unknowingly passed on information to the traders. Or to Bridei.

Dessia sighed. It all came back to Bridei. Before he arrived, she'd been confident in her ability to assess people and situations. Then he came along, appearing to be one thing and turning out to be another. Or had he? She'd always been suspicious of him. He seemed too good to be true—too handsome, too charming, too eager to please her. She sighed again.

"Milady, is something wrong?" Niall asked.

She shook her head distractedly. "I'm not certain I trust those traders. They seemed too accommodating, too agreeable."

"Perhaps they were pleased by the quality of our trade goods. Our women are skilled in dying and weaving, and the wool cloth they make is of excellent quality. Our hides are also superior. Besides, Penrick told me that this was a very convenient place for their ship to put in. Much closer than Ath Cliath or Craimor. I also think they were very impressed by Bridei." He paused, then gazed at her searchingly. "Where can he be, milady?"

"I don't know!" As she walked away from Niall, Dessia chewed her lower lip and wished she hadn't been so short with the smith. People were already going to be suspicious when Bridei didn't reappear. If she didn't attempt to behave normally, they might guess she'd done something to him.

But how was she to behave normally when she felt sick with guilt and despair? Although she knew she should mingle with her guests before they left, she didn't see how she could manage it. Everyone would ask about Bridei. And every time she lied and said she didn't know where he was, she would feel the brutal stab of regret. Nay, she would go to her chambers and stay there. Have Aife tell everyone she was ill. It was the truth. She was so heartsick and anguished she thought she would die of it.

* * *

Bridei woke to darkness. From the smell of earth, rot and damp surrounding him, he could guess he was somewhere underground. There was a throbbing pain in the back of his head. Searching his mind for an explanation of his circumstances, he came up with a vague recollection of following Dessia as she made her way among the buildings of the hillfort. She must have brought him here. Then someone—probably Keenan—had hit him on the head. But why? "Why, Dessia?" he asked aloud.

He struggled to come up with a reason for her actions. Perhaps she'd overheard him talking to the traders and knew he was planning to leave Cahermara. She might think he was disappearing for good and this was her clumsy, desperate attempt to keep him near.

He sighed and sat up. When his stomach lurched with nausea, he lay down again. It could be awhile before Dessia worked up the nerve to confront him. In the meantime, he might as well give in to the enticing oblivion reaching out for him.

* * *

Dessia stared out the window of the tower room, waiting for night to fall. As soon as it was dark, she would go to the souterrain and make certain Bridei was all right. She would take him food and water and confront him about what she'd heard. But perhaps that wasn't the best plan. It would be far too easy for Bridei to convince her of his innocence. To explain away what she'd heard with sly, placating words.

Nay. She didn't dare go to him by herself. She'd have to take Keenan. Her man-of-arms wouldn't be so easily convinced. He'd be able to evaluate Bridei's explanations and see if they made sense. If Bridei could make Keenan believe he wasn't a spy, then she'd finally be able to trust her lover. Her lover. That's what he was. But he was also something more. He was her... *cariad,* her beloved. And if it turned out that he truly was a spy, she would never recover. Everything she'd worked for, everything she cared about—none of it would matter. She'd never be the same. Oh, she would go on. She must. Too many people depended upon her. But she would be a shell of what she once was. She would live in a drab, gray, winter-bare world. In her heart, summer would never come.

She sighed for what seemed like the hundredth time that day, and watched the gray twilight seep over the land.

* * *

It seemed like days later when she finally judged it late enough that she dare leave her chambers. She put on her dark green cloak and crept down the stairs and through the hall crowded with sleeping people. Outside the door, she paused and glanced around. The hillfort was quiet. Except for the warrior unfortunate to be on duty in the gatetower this night, everyone must be asleep, including Keenan. She knew a twinge of regret at the thought of waking him. After the last few days, he must be exhausted.

Stealthily, she made her way to the barn. Aife had let it slip that this was where she and Keenan went to be alone. Dessia opened the door, wincing at the creaking sound it made. She started toward the stairs that led to the upper area where hay and straw was stored. Before she got halfway there, she heard a voice call out, "Who's there?"

"Keenan?" she responded in a half-whisper. "Is that you?"

"Milady?"

She could hear the surprise in his voice, and also caught the soft murmur of a woman's voice. As she'd guessed, Aife was with Keenan. Dessia knew a pang of envy as she considered that Aife could enjoy her lover without worrying about his motivations. How fortunate her maidservant was.

Hearing the soft rustle of Keenan dressing, Dessia grimaced with regret at interrupting the two. A few moments later Keenan came down the stairs, fully clothed and wearing his swordbelt. "What's wrong?" he asked in a low voice.

"I going to go see Bridei," she whispered back. "I need you to come with me."

"Now?" Keenan sounded dismayed.

"Aye. I don't dare go there during the day."

"Why not?" Keenan asked, his voice rising. "You're the queen. You can do whatever you think best and no one will question your decisions."

"That's not true," Dessia responded in a whisper. "You know it's not."

She grasped Keenan by the sleeve of his tunic and pulled him toward the door. Once they were outside, she continued, "Everyone loves Bridei. If they find out I've done this, they'll despise me."

"Aye, because they're fools."

"That may be. But it doesn't change the fact that I want to keep Bridei's whereabouts a secret, at least until I can talk to him and try to find out the truth."

"You think you'll get the truth by questioning him?" Keenan's voice dripped with scorn.

"Aye. If you're there. I need you to help me. There must be some way to find out his intentions, what sort of person he really is."

"There is. But you said you disliked the idea of torture."

"Nay. I won't do that. We'll have to find out by other means."

"I suppose we can try," said Keenan wearily.

"I also want to take him some food and water."

"Why? It will be easier to question him if he's weak and uncomfortable."

"I don't care. I want you to go to the kitchen and fetch some food and a ewer of water. I'll wait here for you."

Keenan nodded and left her. Dessia began to pace, partly out of nervousness and partly from cold. And if she were this cold with a cloak on, Bridei must be miserable. A blanket! She must take him a blanket. But where could she get one, without going back to the tower? She wracked her brain, trying to think of some way to obtain a blanket without waking anyone or having them guess what she was up to.

She couldn't come up with anything, so she decided she would give Bridei her cloak instead. It was made of thick wool and lined with fur. It would be warmer than most blankets, although it might not cover him completely. Besides, it was always possible that he would have some explanation for what she'd heard. That he would be able to convince Keenan he was innocent of any sort of treachery. Then they would be able to return to the tower together and keep each other warm that way.

A wonderful, enticing thought, but she must not weaken yet. She had to be *certain* before she released Bridei from his prison. Her thoughts and feelings seemed to be doing battle inside her, and as the conflict raged, her whole being felt ravaged. Where was Keenan? What was taking so long?

More time passed. Dessia started to grow anxious. She started toward the kitchen. All at once, she saw dark shapes moving among the buildings ahead of her. *What was going on?* Someone grabbed her from behind and a hot, sweaty hand clamped over her mouth. Another man held a knife to her throat and whispered that if she made a sound, he would kill her instantly. Her first captor removed his hand from her mouth, then immediately replaced it with a thick cloth. Frozen with shock and fear, Dessia stood rigid as the man secured her wrists.

They marched her, mute and helpless to the gate. Other men waited there, none of them familiar. She was being abducted. The knife blade at her throat made it clear that if she didn't do as they demanded, she would die.

They walked through the open gate. No guard sounded an alert, and Dessia knew a further despair as she realized whoever had been stationed in the gatetower must be dead. As likely Keenan was, too. Deep grief suffused her, then anger. She would make these men pay for what they'd done! But right now her survival depended on her cooperating with them.

They took her a short distance from the hillfort where two other men waited with horses. Dessia decided this was her chance. As the man walking behind her sought to lift her onto one of the horses, she twisted away from him. Another man immediately grabbed her. "Stupid bitch," he muttered. "Don't you know you can't escape *me*."

Although she couldn't see the man's face, his harsh mocking tone made it clear that she was now in the hands of her old enemy, Tiernan O' Bannon. She felt overwhelmed with despair and anguish. She'd worked so hard, struggled so fiercely, and now it was all for naught. *Oh, Bridei*, she thought with almost unbearable bitterness, *how could you do this to me?*

Chapter 15

Bridei floated in a half-conscious state, reluctant to leave the world of dreams. It was so beautiful there. Dessia was beside him and they were making love beside the lake. But then it grew cold, so cold they both were shivering. The lovely images and sensations vanished and he woke to a dark, frigid world of pain.

The change was so wrenching that it took him a few moments to comprehend it. Then he groaned. "By Beli, it can't be true. Oh, Dessia. What have you done?"

He sat up with slow, careful movements and tried to gauge how much time had passed. In this underground chamber, it was impossible to tell. But the extreme dryness of his mouth and the burning ache in his belly suggested it had been quite awhile. Although his stomach was still unsettled, he was hungry.

By now the traders would have left. They'd assume he'd taken off before them, and never guess anything was wrong until he failed to show up for their rendezvous. When he didn't appear then, they'd think he'd changed his mind. In the meantime, Dessia would probably tell everyone at the hillfort that he'd left with the traders. No one would ever realize the truth.

He groaned again; he was utterly at Dessia's mercy. That shouldn't frighten him, but it did. He'd thought he knew her, thought he understood how her mind worked. But this latest incident didn't make sense. If she'd found out he was leaving Cahermara, why didn't she simply confront him and ask him to stay? Why go to all this trouble to imprison him?

The fact that he'd been hit on the head especially troubled him. He couldn't believe Dessia had planned that. She must have asked Keenan to help her get him down in the souterrain, and the warrior got carried away. But if Dessia's plan had been to secure him so he couldn't leave, why hadn't she come to talk to him by now? Why had he been left alone here? How could she desert him like this? Dessia had battle experience. She must know that head injuries were unpredictable and while sometimes the person suffered no ill effects, other times they were ill for days or weeks. In rare cases, they died without ever rousing. Did she care for him so little that she hadn't bothered to check on him?

Or, perhaps she'd come to see him and he'd been unconscious. It was a faint possibility, but he clung to it. He couldn't bear to believe she'd leave him here like this and make no attempt to ascertain he wasn't badly injured. If he thought that, then he'd have to face the terrible possibility she'd left him here to die.

Nay, it couldn't be true. No matter how angry she was, she wouldn't do that. After what they'd shared, it was unthinkable she would do something so cruel.

He consoled himself with that thought and told himself he needed to be patient. Dessia would come soon enough. Or, at the very least, she'd send someone with food and water and he could question them about the queen's motives.

Sighing, he lay down again.

* * *

The gods save me! Dessia thought, *This is a nightmare come to life!*

She was seated on a horse in front of O'Bannon. His arms held her loosely, helping her keep her balance. She could smell him, and the odor of his sweat made her stomach lurch with nausea. Her arms and shoulders ached from her hands being tied behind her body, and she felt cold through and through, not only from the chill of the night air but from the horror building inside her. So far, O'Bannon had only taunted her, but she feared what would happen when they reached his fortress of Dun Cullan.

If he tries to rape me, I'll fight so hard, he'll have to kill me. Although the thought reassured her, a part of her mind knew that it might well be futile. Bound as she was, there might be nothing she could do to prevent being violated. The gorge rose in her throat at the thought, and she knew a panicked regret that she hadn't forced her captors to cut her throat when they first grabbed her.

To keep her mind off the unknown future, she focused on figuring out how this had all come about. How had O'Bannon's men gotten into the hillfort without anyone sounding an alarm? The only explanation was that someone let them in. But who? The traders had left by then, and Bridei was in the souterrain. All at once she realized that no one but her and Keenan knew where Bridei was. Her next thought was that Keenan was undoubtedly dead.

Oh, Keenan! A wave of grief struck her. *I should have listened to you in the beginning! I should have sent Bridei away immediately!*

And yet, that was no solution unless Bridei had been the one to betray her. But he'd never been away from Cahermara for more than a few hours, except the time he went to the Forest of Mist. And if he hadn't met with O'Bannon, how had all of this been planned?

Perhaps it had been the traders. They might be the link with O'Bannon. Maybe they hadn't gone back to their boat after all, but stayed near the fortress and then reentered after nightfall. But that still didn't solve how they'd gotten in. Someone on the inside would have had to open the gate. And it couldn't have been Bridei because he was in the souterrain.

Her thoughts seemed to be going around in circles. As soon as she realized what was happening, she'd blamed Bridei, believing he'd planned her abduction. But the more she thought about it, the more she realized such an explanation didn't make sense. The realization that Bridei couldn't have been part of the plot filled her with dismay. That meant she'd cruelly imprisoned the man she loved and possibly doomed him to death. No one knew where he was. If he were too injured to call out for aid, he would die there. She sucked in her breath at the thought, and O'Bannon muttered, "Not much farther now."

In addition to her dread for herself and Bridei, she felt a growing self-loathing for her stupidity in allowing all of this to happen. If she hadn't been so distracted by Bridei, she might have realized something was amiss. In that way, he was to blame, but no more than herself. Nay, it was her fault. All her fault.

They finally approached O'Bannon's fortress of Dun Cullan. Dessia hadn't been this close to her enemy's stronghold in years. The hillfort was bigger than Cahermara, but built of timber rather than stone, and, therefore, more vulnerable to fire. It suddenly struck her how complacent she'd become after winning back her lands. Instead of living in fear all these years, she should have attacked O'Bannon's hillfort long ago. Should have burned the place to the ground and killed him, just as he'd done to her family.

But by the time she'd regained her heritage, she'd been sick of violence and killing. She also knew that if she launched a full attack on Dun Cullan, many innocent people would die. Women and children. Old men. She hadn't wanted to do something to brutal, and so she'd left O'Bannon alone, hoping they could coexist. It was a foolish hope. A weak and womanly approach. Her father would never have done such a thing. He would have insisted on revenge. Would never have rested until his enemies were lying dead on the ground and Dun Cullan lay in smoking ruins.

Regrets. Regrets. It seemed all she had left. The despair of it made her want to die. To give up and stop caring what happened. But she couldn't do that. She wouldn't add to her failings by being a coward. Somehow she had to go on. She had to endure.

They rode up the trackway and through the open gate of the fortress. O'Bannon reined in the horse and dismounted, then pulled her off and set her down next to him. In the torchlight, she could see the smug expression on his face. If her mouth hadn't been bound, she would have spit at him. But she was trussed and helpless.

Grasping her arm, he propelled her through the hillfort. His men followed, one of them carrying a torch. No one spoke a word.

After walking through a maze of buildings, they reached the far edge of the hillfort. There was a small structure there. One of the other men opened the door and O'Bannon pushed her inside. The man with the torch followed and the small space filled with light. Dessia could see that it was a storage shed, and also see an opening in the wooden floor. Horrified at the thought of being imprisoned underground, Dessia jerked away from O'Bannon. Two of the other men grabbed her, one on each side. She continued to flail and twist. Something struck her on the side of the face. She didn't completely lose consciousness but everything turned hazy and her legs wobbled beneath her.

Vaguely, she was aware they were removing her bonds. The cloth around her mouth was also removed. The next thing she knew, they were lowering her into the opening. They let go of her and she fell the last few feet. Scrambling to stand, she saw she was in a small chamber much like the souterrain at Cahermara. But this one was furnished with a straw pallet, a stool and a table with a lit candle. While her prison wasn't luxurious, it wasn't as grim as she'd feared. The light from the candle helped keep the worst of her suffocating dread away. She took deep breaths, trying calm herself.

All at once, she realized the gag was gone. She immediately cried out, "O'Bannon, you stinking coward! You won't get away with this! I'll set a spell on you and your balls will turn black and rot!"

O'Bannon leaned over the opening. "If you were capable of such things, you would have done so by now. The truth is, the stories about you being a sorceress were all lies. You possess no magic."

She'd dreaded this day for years. Dreaded the time when her secret was revealed. She wanted to ask O'Bannon how he'd discovered the truth. But to do that meant admitting she had no power, and she suspected he was still wary of her. That he wasn't quite certain she didn't have some magical abilities.

"It takes time to make a spell," she called up to him. "Take your chances, if you will. But if you wake up in the next few days and find yourself with withered private parts, you'll know you were wrong. Or, perhaps I'll do something else to you, something even more unpleasant."

O'Bannon laughed, but with a hint of unease. Perhaps she'd bought some time. He might at least wait a few days before raping her.

They placed a piece of wood over the opening and left her. Once more, Dessia gazed around her prison. She wanted to scream, to claw at the walls and try to dig her way out. But the rational part of her knew she'd end up with nothing but torn and bleeding fingers and a raw throat. She must make the best of her circumstances and do what she could to stay alive. The honor of her family demanded it.

* * *

As soon as Bridei woke, the vague dread that had haunted his dreams became real. Maybe Dessia wasn't going to send anyone with food and water. She might intend for him to die here. It seemed more and more likely.

He struggled to think she could be so cold-hearted. It didn't match up with the Dessia he knew. What had happened? What could have caused her to despise him so much? He wracked his brain, trying to come up with a reason for her actions. Even if she'd discovered he planned to leave and meet up with traders, that didn't explain why she would do this. If she were angry at him for abandoning her, she might leave him here for a few days as punishment, but she'd at least provide him with water. To abandon him like this bespoke great hatred and rage. He couldn't think of anything he'd done—or that she might believe he'd done—that would arouse her animosity to that degree.

It was a puzzle, but he couldn't waste his energy trying to solve it. He had to try to do something to free himself while he still had the strength. With effort, he struggled to a standing position. He was weak and dizzy, but at least the nausea had passed. The few apples he'd been able to choke down had helped. But there wasn't that much food left, and he was desperate for water.

He peered up at the hole in the floor above him. The opening was still too far above for him to jump up and climb out. There was no way he could escape without aid. But getting someone to aid him might be possible. Surely in the whole hillfort there was someone who would dare to defy Dessia and help him. All he had to do was let them know he was here.

He took a deep breath and called out, "Help me! It's Bridei! I'm in the souterrain."

* * *

Hearing scuffling sounds overhead, Dessia stopped her pacing and moved directly under the opening above her. "O'Bannon!" she called out. "You miserable coward! Get me out of here! I dare you to face me in combat. I dare you!"

The noises grew louder and she saw someone leaning over the opening. A man, but not O'Bannon. His beard was a grizzled gray rather than black and his face heavily lined. "Milady," he called down. "I've brought you some food. I'm going to lower it down to you."

"Where's O'Bannon? I want to speak to him!"

The man didn't answer but lowered a large wooden bucket. Inside was a cloth bundle and a waterskin. Dessia took the bundle and waterskin and put them on the table. Underneath the bundle was a candle. She grabbed that as well.

The man pulled up the bucket and called down, "Is there anything else you require?"

Dessia laughed bitterly. "Aye. I need a ladder so I can climb out of here. And then I need a sword to kill that wretch O'Bannon!"

The man started to move away. Dessia called out, "Wait! I'm sorry to take out my anger on you. Please stay and talk to me."

"Milady, I cannot. I'm only to see that you're reasonably comfortable and give you the food."

"I'm not asking you to free me. But please tell me what O'Ban... what your lord intends to do with me." Dessia sought to make her voice soft and pleading. It had been a mistake to appear so angry and confrontational.

She needed to play upon this man's sympathies, to remind him that she was a woman.

"I don't know what's going to happen to you," the man answered. "He hasn't said."The man again started to move away from the opening.

"Wait!" she cried. "Tell me your name," she added in softer tones.

The man seemed to hesitate, then said, "I am called Druim."

Dessia drew as close to the opening as she could. Gazing up with what she hoped was a winsome, helpless look, she pleaded, "Druim, I know you can't go against your lord's wishes, but all I want is a little information. Do you know how your lord was able to get into Cahermara? Do you know who betrayed me?"

"Nay, milady. I wasn't privy to any of that. But..." Druim leaned near to the opening. "I don't think he intends to harm you."

"Oh, thank you," Dessia said, inwardly wincing at the timidity she must affect. "I'm relieved to know that."

"I must be going, milady," Druim said.

The man left. Dessia sighed and sat down on the stool. She'd acted like a simpering fool and it hadn't gotten her anywhere. Idly, she opened the bundle. It contained some barley bannocks, cheese and an apple. Simple fare, but it would sustain her. For a moment, she hesitated, then she took a bite of one of the bannocks. She wasn't ready to die yet. Not until she knew who had betrayed her.

* * *

He couldn't keep doing this much longer, Bridei thought. He barely had the strength to sit up, let alone stand under the opening to his prison and shout, and his voice had become a weak croak. At this point, he doubted if anyone could hear him unless they entered the storage shed and bent down to listen.

Resigned, he sank to the earthen floor and closed his eyes. He felt like weeping, but his eyes were so dry that no tears sprang forth. It was no use. He'd tried to summon aid, but either no one had heard him, or no one cared enough for him to defy Dessia. It looked as if he was going to die here, far away from his homeland, alone and unmourned.

Of course, there probably weren't many people who would mourn him in Gwynedd either. His mother would, and perhaps his younger brothers and sisters, if they remembered him. Regrets washed over him. Looking back, his life seemed very empty. He'd entertained a lot of people. Bedded a great number of women. But he'd never allowed any of them close enough to truly care for him. He'd kept everyone at a distance. *Everyone except Dessia.*

He pushed the thought away, telling himself he wouldn't think about her. If he was going to die, he had more important things to consider... such as the way he'd wasted his life. He'd been a fool. Afraid to love, afraid to ever embrace a cause or dream a dream. Although he'd thought he was being careful, it now seemed to him that he managed to condemn himself to a cold, meaningless existence. He felt lost and weary and miserably alone. Things seemed so bleak, so hopeless. He might as well give up and let death take him. It was easy to drift off, easy to succumb to the allure of sleep, blessed, endless sleep.

* * *

"Bridei."

He woke to the sound of his mother's voice. She stood a few feet away, looking exactly as he remembered her. Her hair, a rich warm red. Her skin as pale as moonlight. Tiny as she was, she seemed to radiate a vibrant energy, filling the dark chamber with light. "Bridei," she said again. "What's wrong? Why are you giving up? Don't you understand that if you don't deal with things in this life, you'll only have to face them on the Other Side?"

"But what can I do? How can I change things? I've tried. I've truly tried. But it's no use. I'm going to die here." His voice shook on the last words.

"Oh, Bridei..." She exhaled a deep sigh. "My poor lost son. You still don't understand. Your whole life is waiting for you. All you have to do is reach out and grasp it."

"How? Tell me how." With great effort, he made himself stand and move closer to her. "Please help me," he whispered. "Give me some of your strength. Your magic."

"You don't need it," she said. "You have your own strength." She smiled. "And your own magic."

"That's not true! I'm all alone. No one cares for me. I've ruined everything!"

"Those are the words of a child. But you're a man now. You have to think as a man would. You have to be strong. You can do it. I know you can."

Her form was fading. In another few heartbeats, she would be gone altogether. "Mother," he cried. "Don't leave me!"

"The gods are with you." Her voice sounded in his head. "Ask them to help you."

* * *

He woke later and knew it had been a dream. But what a vivid dream. It almost seemed he could smell the sweet scent of herbs that always clung to his mother's clothing. The fragrance lingered in the air, banishing the dank, moldy odor of his prison. When he was a boy he'd half hated that fragrance. It represented safety and peace, things he'd scorned. Now the smell comforted him, reminding him how his mother used to hold him on her lap when he was little. She always seemed so slender and delicate, yet strong. How he yearned for her strength now. But what had she said—that he had his own strength? She'd also mentioned the gods, and told him to ask them to help him.

It was worth trying. The gods had sent the storm that saved him from the slavers. And it must have been the gods who created the vision he saw in Dessia's scrying bowl and the things he'd seen in the lake. He'd always felt the presence of the Ancient Ones when he was in the Forest of Mist. But it was very hard to imagine them in this place. He glanced around, wondering what god to call out to. Or perhaps it should be a goddess. His mother always said that female deities were more powerful than male ones, because their energy came from the earth.

Ceriddwen represented wisdom, grain and plenty. Arianrhod ruled the moon and destiny, while the great mother goddess Donn was connected to the land. In this place, he couldn't see the moon or the night sky, and he had no magic cauldron as a Ceriddwen did. The great Donn seemed very remote and was seldom evoked in ritual. But there was another great goddess—Rhiannon, the deity his mother had been named for. Rhiannon was associated with death and the underworld, and also horses, which made it very fitting that he should call on her. He was facing death in an underground realm at the hands of a queen of the tribe of the white horse. The goddess Rhiannon was said to ride a white mare as she gathered up the souls of the dead.

But now that he'd decided to ask Rhiannon for aid, how did he do it? When he'd brought the storm, he'd evoked the force of the sea and the might of the weather. How should he reach out to Rhiannon? One of the legends of the goddess was that she was accompanied by three birds who sang so beautifully they were able to bring the dead back to life, or lull the living to sleep. What he needed were some birds that could rouse the living before he ended up dead!

Perhaps, to save himself, he should evoke the magical birds that served the goddess. But how did he do that? Maybe he should try singing. But at this point he was too hoarse and weary to do more than croak. He sighed, then licked his parched lips and called out, "Rhiannon, Great Queen, help me. Give me the strength to sing. Ask your magical birds to join me. Together we will sing a song that will reach the ears of all who are near and draw them to this place to aid me."

Having evoked the goddess, Bridei felt uneasy. Although there was a dark aspect to most of the deities, with Rhiannon it was especially pronounced. She was associated with death and the underworld, which made her a dangerous deity to bargain with. And bargain was what he as doing, although he hadn't offered the goddess anything. Some sort of sacrifice, that was what was needed. In the old days, sacrifices were usually of blood. An animal was killed and its spirit offered up. But he had no living creature to offer. He could give the goddess nothing but himself, offer her nothing except his own life.

The foreboding sense grew stronger. He could feel the goddess's power surrounding him. What if instead of bringing him aid, evoking her brought about his death? But if that happened it would be the goddess's will. He must accept that he might die. "Oh, Great Queen," he intoned. "Give me life. Offer me another chance. If you do so, I vow I will be a different person. I will change and become a new man. One who gives instead of taking. One who loves instead of running away. One who believes in dreams instead of scoffing at them. Send your enchanted birds to sing me back to life and I will join in their song."

He waited, thinking there should be some sort of sign that the goddess had agreed to do his bidding. Nothing happened. Yet the next moment, he remembered his mother's words. *You must be strong. You can do it. I know you can.*

He took a deep breath and began to sing:

Rhiannon, Great Queen,
Send your gilded birds on the wing
Bright music across the orb of time
Their song, sweet and healing
Magic to set me free.

His voice sounded scratchy and weak and the effort hurt his throat, but he knew he had to continue.

Comb moonlight from your long, pale hair
Like dreams falling from the heavens
Enchanted stars to guide me.
Their song, sweet and healing
Magic to set me free.

His voice grew stronger:

Lady Rhiannon
Ride your white mare
Out of the dark shadows of the deathly realm
Gather the souls of your loved ones
Their song, sweet and healing
Magic to set me free.

All at once, he could hear someone else singing along with him. A woman. Her voice was deep and sad, unearthly.

Great mother, divine queen
Bring me water from the enchanted pool
Quench my thirst with memories
Their song, sweet and healing
Magic to set me free.
Carry me on a boat
Across the river of pain and suffering
Sparkling silver coins to pay my way
Their song, sweet and healing
Magic to set me free.

Finishing the chorus, he paused. The mysterious voice paused also. Bridei took a breath and began again. The first time, he had been tentative, singing slowly as the words came to him. Now he sang with his heart, putting his whole being into the song. He forgot that he was weak and thirsty. That he was imprisoned in a dank, dark hole. His strength seemed to return. It was as if the haunting voice that sang in unison with him was filling his body with vitality and power. As he began the song for a third time, his voice rose, as rich and vibrant as it had ever been.

Finishing, he fell silent. Three was a magical number, and Rhiannon was said to be accompanied by three golden birds. He'd evoked Her power. Now all he could do was wait.

* * *

He must have fallen asleep. When he woke, he heard a woman calling: "Bridei? Bridei, where are you?"

He got to his feet, so relieved he was trembling. "Aife? Aife? Is that you?"

"Bridei. Oh, Bridei!" Aife pulled aside the wicker covering the opening above him. "What are you doing down there? Did O'Bannon do this to you?" She sounded strange, as if she'd been weeping.

Bridei couldn't make sense of her question. "O'Bannon? What are you talking about? Dessia put me here."

"The queen? But why would she do that? Was she trying to protect you? Oh, of course she was. She didn't want them to kill you like they... did... Keenan." Aife began to sob.

"Keenan? What happened to Keenan?" Bridei's head was spinning. His wits must be confused by hunger. He couldn't imagine what she was talking about.

It took awhile for Aife to speak. Finally, she answered, her words punctuated by choking sobs. "They... killed Keenan. He was... trying to protect... the... queen... and... they... killed him."

Bridei felt his body go rigid with dread. He could barely draw a breath to ask, "The queen? What happened to the queen?"

Aife gave another heartrending sob. His heart thundered in the chest as he waited for her to answer. "They... took... her!"

He swallowed. Forced himself to take a breath. "Where? Where did they take her?"

Aife sniffed loudly. "I don't know. To Dun Cullan, I suppose."

Bridei felt his insides go cold. Dun Cullan. The stronghold of Tiernan O'Bannon. Dessia had been abducted. She was in the hands of her greatest enemy. The man who'd killed the rest of her family.

"But how?" he whispered. None of it made any sense. He called up to Aife. "What happened? How did O'Bannon get access to the queen?"

"No one knows." Aife's voice was mournful. "It happened at night. Somehow they got in. Killed Keenan. Took the queen."

"Was anyone else was hurt?"

Aife let out another sob, then recovered herself. "Scanlan was also killed. They found his body in the watchtower."

"But if Scanlan was watching the gate, how did they get in?"

"I don't know. I don't know." Aife began weeping again.

Bridei sought for control himself. A few moments before, he'd been concerned for his own life. Now his own situation seemed insignificant. Dessia had been abducted. She was in the hands of her enemy. What might O'Bannon do to her? Bridei told himself he couldn't think about it. If he did, he'd become so crazed with dread he'd be unable to reason.

"Aife," he called up. "You have to get me out of here. I... we... we'll gather together all the warriors and storm Dun Cullan. We'll get Dessia back."

"There are no warriors. They've all left Cahermara."

"Why? Have they gone after the queen?"

"Nay. They ran away. Almost everyone else has left the hillfort."

Bridei was stunned. Dessia's people seemed devoted to her. He couldn't believe they would desert her like this. "But why, Aife? Why would everyone leave?"

She sighed heavily. "They're afraid to stay here. They say that now the spell is broken, it's not safe. They took all the livestock and the foodstores and left. Some of them went back to their families. Some of them are living in the woods."

"But you stayed," Bridei said. "Bless you for your loyalty and your bravery."

"I'm not brave," Aife answered wearily. "I just don't care if die. If O'Bannon's men come back and burn the hillfort, it won't matter to me. My heart is in the grave anyway."

Poor Aife. She'd loved Keenan passionately. Bridei understood her terrible grief all too well. If O'Bannon killed Dessia, he would feel the same. But at least he had some reason to hope. If O'Bannon had meant to kill Dessia, he would have done so already, then taken over the hillfort. The fact that he'd stolen her away instead meant he must have a reason to keep her alive.

"Aife," he said firmly. "Go and fetch a ladder or rope. I must get out of here if I'm going to help the queen."

"But what can you do?" Aife asked in a bleak voice.

"I don't know, but I'll think of something." He must. The Great Goddess Rhiannon had given him another chance at life. She had saved him. Saved him so he could save Dessia.

Chapter 16

Aife came with a ladder and slid it down to Bridei. He climbed up shakily, wishing he wasn't so weak. Although the goddess Rhiannon had given him the strength to sing, she hadn't magically restored him. When he reached the top, he sank down on the wooden floor. "I need water," he said. "And food. Will you help me, Aife?"

She nodded and left. Bridei sat there a moment, then got up slowly. Down in his prison, he'd thought once he got out, all would be well. He'd assumed his greatest challenge would be convincing Dessia she'd made a mistake and somehow winning back her affections. Instead, he faced the daunting task of trying to free her from the clutches of a determined enemy. Even if he had a large and well-equipped army behind him, he wasn't certain it would be possible to force O'Bannon to give up his prize. But he had to do something. Had to try and help Dessia, even if he died in the attempt.

The realization of how much he'd changed shocked him. The old Bridei would have walked away. He'd have grieved for Dessia, but never risked his life for her. Now he felt as if his life had no purpose without her. He'd made a vow to the goddess Rhiannon that he would change, and become a man who cared for others and who lived his life with passion and meaning. But in many ways, that vow wasn't necessary. He'd already changed, and it had been Dessia who'd changed him. She'd inspired him with her determination and her dedication. And she'd made him fall in love with her. He ached to hold her, to be near her; he couldn't imagine going on without her.

The awareness frightened him. He didn't want to end up like poor Aife, lost in grief and despair. But there was no turning back now. Dessia was his soul. Her spirit and his were bound together. He'd seen a vision of them in the lake of the Forest of Mist. Although he'd never told Dessia, after he'd seen the vision of his parents, another image had formed in the dark, still waters of the lake. It was of him and Dessia, standing side-by-side.

The memory heartened him. The gods had sent him a sign they were destined to be together. Their shared destiny might be in the next realm rather than this one, but knowing that made the connection between them no less powerful. As long as he was alive, he must do whatever he could to free Dessia and restore her to her rightful place at Cahermara.

A new sense of determination and resolve filled him, helping to banish the appalling weakness. He left the storehouse above the souterrain and went to a nearby storage shed. Opening the door, he was shocked to see it was empty. The people fleeing Cahermara had taken everything. He knew a surge of anger to think they could be so cowardly. But then he recalled what Aife had told him. Dessia's people had always believed the spell she set upon Cahermara protected them. Now that she was gone, they felt vulnerable and helpless. Some of them probably also remembered what O'Bannon had done when he attacked Cahermara in Dessia's father's day, and they feared the slaughter and destruction would happen again. Still, it was rather foolish of them to abandon the hillfort. It was a stout, formidable fortress. If they all worked together, they could have defended it easily.

Bridei moved on to the next storehouse. There were a few baskets of grain here, but nothing he could readily eat. He began to wonder if despite having escaped his prison, he would still end up starving to death.

Discouraged and hungrier than ever, he started toward the hall. On the way he passed the smithy. The place appeared deserted, and looking inside, Bridei found that the fire in the forge was out and all Niall's tools were gone, as well as the raw metal Dessia had purchased from the traders. Bridei shook his head in consternation. He would have thought at least Niall would stay. On the other hand, maybe everyone thought by leaving the hillfort and taking everything of value from the place, they were doing what Dessia would have wanted. This way, if Dessia could escape, they would be able to come back and help her, having preserved the wealth of Cahermara by hiding it elsewhere.

His hunger and thirst still raged. If he didn't get something to eat and drink soon, he felt as if he would collapse. Then he remembered there was a rainwater cistern behind the smithy, providing Niall with a ready supply of water for cooling metalwork. He went to the large stone basin, knelt down and scooped up handfuls of the icy cold water and began to drink. The water chilled him, but he kept drinking, quenching his terrible thirst.

By the time he'd had his fill, he was shivering. He started walking again, to get warm as much as anything. He went to the hall, hoping to find a fire burning there. It was the same story. The hearth was cold and the vast structure stood empty except for the tables and benches, which had been too cumbersome carry off. Despite his weariness, Bridei crossed the hall and started up the stairway to Dessia's chamber.

Unlike the rest of the hillfort, this room appeared untouched. Dessia's manuscripts on magic lay on the table. The bedcovers were carefully smoothed over the bed. And when Bridei checked the storage chest, he discovered the queen's clothing neatly folded inside.

He took out the garment on top, which was the beautiful red gown she'd worn to the feast. Holding it close to his face, he inhaled deeply. The clothing had been stored away with dried meadowsweet and lavender, but beneath that flowery odor, he detected Dessia's own lovely scent. His throat went tight. For one brief night he'd held her close and felt her heart beating near his. Now he might have lost her forever. Recovering himself, he replaced the gown in the chest and closed the lid. He wouldn't mourn for Dessia yet. There was every reason to believe she still lived. All he had to do was free her.

He went to the table where the scrying bowl lay and gazed into the oily depths. "Rhiannon, Great Goddess, heed my plea. Tell me how to help Dessia. Tell me what I must do." He stared into the bowl until his eyes watered, but saw nothing. It seemed the goddess Rhiannon was much like his mother. She would only give him hints of his purpose. The rest he must figure out on his own. And he would be able to do that much better if he had some food in his belly.

He left the tower chamber and made his way through the empty hall. As he went outside, a marvelous scent drifted to his nostrils. Food. Cooking food. He followed the scent to the kitchen, half-cursing himself for not thinking of going there earlier. Inside, Doona was turning a chicken on a spit. He gaped at her, then grinned. "It's good to see you, Doona. I thought Aife and I might be the only ones left here."

Doona smiled back at him. "It's good to see you as well, my lord. I'm glad Aife heard you singing in the souterrain and got you out of there."

"So, you've spoken to Aife? Where is she now?"

"She went to find more for you to eat." Doona motioned with her head. "There's some pottage over there on the table. Not my best effort, but with what little I had to work with, it's as good as I could do."

"I vow I'm hungry enough to eat sand." Bridei went to the rough board table used for preparing food, grabbed a spoon, sat down on a nearby bench and began to eat voraciously. Doona was too modest, he decided. The mixture of grains, vegetables and broth tasted like ambrosia to him.

"The roasted fowl will be done soon, and with luck Aife will have found some apples or nuts left behind as well," said Doona. "'Tis a blessing you're here, in many respects. Now Aife will have someone to look after, and perhaps she won't waste away and die of a broken heart. Once you've eaten your fill, you must try to get Aife to take some sustenance as well."

"I will, of course," Bridei answered. He finished the last few drops in the bowl. "But tell me, why are *you* still here? Aife said she stayed because she doesn't care if she dies. But I can't see you giving up and waiting for death."

A look of sadness crossed Doona's broad, homely face. "The truth is, I have no where to go. My family were all killed when O'Bannon attacked Cahermara in the days of the queen's father. I suppose I could live out in the woods, as some have done. But I didn't fancy freezing to death. Besides, if O'Bannon does come to torch the fortress, I might have a bit of a surprise for him. I'm pretty handy with a butchering knife." Her dark eyes glinted with a mixture of amusement and malice.

"That's the thing I don't understand," said Bridei. "If everyone stayed put, secured the gates and kept a close watch on the unfinished side of the fortress, Cahermara would be near impossible to take, no matter how many warriors O'Bannon brought. That's why Dessia built the hillfort in stone. She feared this day would come and she wanted to be prepared. But instead of staying and resisting, everyone left. To me, it feels like a betrayal of all Dessia cared about."

Doona shrugged. "If you'd have been around, things might have turned out differently. But once it was discovered Dessia was gone, and Keenan and Scanlan had been killed, panic set in. All these years, everyone believed we were protected by an enchantment the queen had set upon the fortress. But if O'Bannon was able to breach it, then everyone thought something must have gone wrong. The spell must have weakened somehow." Doona gave him an intense look. "There were those who said it was your fault. That you had made the queen fall in love with you and that somehow sapped her magic and weakened the spell."

Bridei didn't know what to say to this. Did he tell Doona that there was no spell, so there was no way anything he'd done could have weakened it? Somehow, that didn't seem right. Better he should take the blame than have people believe Dessia had no magical powers.

He said, "Perhaps rather than the spell failing, O'Bannon simply found a way around it. After all, he didn't attack Cahermara, which was what the spell was meant to prevent. Instead, he found a way in and abducted Dessia. And the reason he got in had nothing to do with the queen's magic failing and everything to do with treachery and betrayal."

Doona stared at him. "You believe someone from the inside let him in?"

"Could it be any clearer? Scanlan was killed so he couldn't sound the alarm. Who could have done that except someone who was already in the hillfort?"

"The traders, perhaps?"

Bridei shook his head. "They'd already left. Besides, they had no reason to betray Dessia. I spoke to them at length and I feel confident they've never met O'Bannon, let alone conspired with him. Nay, it had to be someone who came to Cahermara for the feast, or someone who already lives here."

"Who would do such a thing?" Doona asked, her eyes wide with dismay.

"I don't know. But I do know that no leader can ever be completely certain of the loyalty of all their subjects, including those closest to them. Even the High King Arthur was betrayed by his son." Bridei met Doona's gaze meaningfully. "Can you think of anyone who might have been unhappy with the queen? Anyone who might have felt slighted by her? Or, even someone who might have felt slighted by her father? Oh, aye," he added when Doona frowned. "When people have a grievance, their memories tend to be very long, very long indeed."

"I don't know. I'll have to think on it," said Doona. "It's a chilling notion." She glanced around uneasily. "To imagine a traitor walking among us all this time."

"I doubt it was anyone who lived here at Cahermara. I think it much more likely it was someone who came for the feast, saw an opportunity and somehow contacted O'Bannon to arrange Dessia's abduction."

"What do you think O'Bannon has planned?" Aife asked as she entered the kitchen carrying a basket of apples. "Will he return and lay waste to Cahermara?"

"If he meant to destroy the fortress, he would have done it that night," Bridei answered.

"But why take the queen?" Doona asked. "What does that accomplish?"

Bridei cocked a brow. "A great deal, it seems to me. He's sent everyone fleeing from the safety of the hillfort. Now all he has to do is move in and take control, and Dessia's lands are his."

"But why take the queen prisoner?" Aife asked. "Why not simply kill her and be done with it? That would have demoralized everyone even more effectively."

"That's where you're wrong. If O'Bannon had murdered Dessia, her people might have been outraged enough to fight back. This way, O'Bannon has instilled uncertainty and doubt. Without the clear focus of vengeance, the Fionnlairaos are little threat to him."

"But what's to keep him from killing the queen now that she's his prisoner?" asked Doona.

"Women rulers have a kind of vulnerability that no male could ever have. I wouldn't be surprised if O'Bannon tried to force Dessia to marry him. Then he can claim her lands by right of being her husband."

Doona shook her head and spat on the ground. "That will never happen. Dessia would never agree to marry that wicked pig-faced lout."

"There are ways to persuade people to do things that are abhorrent to them." Even as he said the words, Bridei experienced a shiver of dread. The thought of Dessia being tortured made him want to vomit up the food he'd just eaten. Somehow he had to help her. But how?

Even if he had an army, he had no experience in leading warriors into battle. If Keenan had lived, things might be different. Dessia's man-of-arms had the knowledge and skill to train and mobilize a fighting force. But for a man like him—who knew only enough of warfare to write ballads about the battle afterwards—the idea of attacking O'Bannon was witless. He'd only get himself and his followers killed and accomplish nothing.

Doona pronounced the chicken done. Using cloths, she pulled it off the spit and placed it on the rough board table before him. Bridei motioned to Aife. "Come and join me. And you, too, Doona."

Aife brought the apples over to the table. "Where did you find those?" Bridei asked.

"Doona told me about a hidden food cache under one of the other storerooms. There's some cabbage and beans there as well."

Bridei nodded and they all sat down on the bench and began to eat.

"I don't suppose there's any wine or ale left in that storage cache," Bridei said after a time.

"I didn't see any," Aife responded.

Doona winked at him. "I know where there's another secret store. The queen told no one but me about it." She left the kitchen and returned a short while later lugging a heavy barrel. Removing the lid, she dipped a cup into the contents and handed the cup to Bridei.

"Wine?" he asked, surprised.

"Aye. The queen always kept some hidden in case of visitors."

"At least we won't starve or go thirsty," Bridei said with resignation. "But that doesn't help Dessia."

"But what can we do?" asked Aife. Although she'd eaten a little, she appeared very drawn and pale. Bridei realized he must find a way to help Aife as well as Dessia. But how could he console someone who's lost their reason for living?

As for himself, at least he had a goal to work toward, even if the goal seemed very out of reach. For the first time in his life, he wished he'd become a warrior as his father had wanted. If he were skilled in wielding weapons and planning battle strategy, he might have a chance of freeing Dessia. As it was, he felt utterly helpless, and he hated it.

"I don't know what we can do," he answered. "But we must figure something out."

As he gazed morosely into his wine cup, he realized how foolish he was being. Instead of bemoaning his choices in the past, he must focus on his goal. Although he wasn't a warrior, he had other resources. For years, he'd survived—and prospered—by using his wits. Instead of using brute force and aggression to reach his goals, he'd gotten what he wanted with charm and manipulation. He understood people and what motivated them and was able to use that knowledge to his benefit. There was no reason to abandon this strategy, even as he faced the greatest challenge of his life.

He looked at the two women. "What do you know about O'Bannon's fortress?"

Aife shrugged. "It's called Dun Cullan."

"Is it as large as Cahermara?"

"I don't know. I presume so," answered Aife.

"When was it built? Do you know? Is it older than Cahermara?"

"Probably," interjected Doona. "It was never destroyed as Cahermara was, so there's no reason for it to have ever been rebuilt."

"I wonder if there's a secret entrance into it," mused Bridei. "Many fortresses have a hidden passageway so people can escape if the place is besieged. I presume Cahermara has one?" He looked at Aife and Doona questioningly.

Aife shook her head. "I know of nothing like that here." Then she added, "But there's a cache of treasure buried by the back wall."

"Cache of treasure?" Bridei looked at Aife, then at Doona. The cook appeared as surprised as he was.

"Aye. The queen told me her father buried a chest of valuables somewhere near the rear of the hillfort. I'm not certain exactly where it's buried, but I have an idea."

Bridei stood. "We must find it."

Aife made no move to get up. "But why?" she asked. "What good will it do anyone now?"

"Wealth is always useful," Bridei answered.

Bridei went off to search for a shovel, a plan forming in his mind. If he could get into O'Bannon's fortress, he might be able to use the wealth to bribe Dessia's guards to set her free. But there were problems. He doubted there were enough valuable objects cached away to bribe the whole fortress. And how was he going to get into Dun Cullan to begin with?

He found a shovel behind the smithy, and returned to the kitchen to fetch Aife and Doona. Doona seemed filled with purpose, but Aife walked along listlessly.

"Show me where to dig," Bridei urged Aife when they reached the back portion of the fortress.

"I'll try to remember," she answered. "But it's been a long while since Dessia showed the place to me and Keenan." Her voice caught and she looked as she might start weeping.

Bridei grasped Aife firmly by the arm. "You must try to remember where the cache is buried. Please, Aife. Please try."

Aife sighed. "But what's the point? Why dig it up? Doing so won't bring Keenan back, nor free the queen either."

"That's not true. With the treasure, we might be able to might help the queen," Bridei told her.

"What are you going to do?" asked Doona. "Bribe O'Bannon to let the queen go?"

"I doubt there's enough gold in all of Ireland to sway a man as determined as O'Bannon," responded Bridei. "But I might be able to bribe other people in O'Bannon's fortress and get Dessia out that way."

"But how will you get into Dun Cullan in the first place?" asked Aife.

"I don't know yet," answered Bridei. "The first step is to find the treasure. Please, Aife," he repeated. "Please try to remember where the chest is buried."

Aife shrugged, then pointed an area next to the wall. Bridei and Doona took turns digging and made nearly a dozen holes—grueling work considered how cold and hard the ground was. Finally, they decided to go to bed and resume searching the next day.

After returning to the kitchen to eat some of the leftover chicken and pottage, Bridei went up to Dessia's tower chamber. He took off his clothing and lay down on the bed. Instantly, he was flooded with memories: The feel of Dessia's body beneath his. The vivid spill of her long hair spread out around her. Her fair skin flushed with passion. Her face, so proud and beautiful as she reached her peak. He reached out his arms as if he could crush the memories against his breast and make them real. Then he fell asleep.

* * *

They resumed digging early the next morning after eating some bannocks Doona had made with grain and oil from their small supply. Despite sleeping in a warm bed instead of the hard, cold ground of the souterrain, Bridei felt wearier than ever. A steady rain was falling, and although it helped soften the ground, it also turned the torn-up earth into a morass of mud. It was exhausting, miserable work, and he was near to giving up when his shovel struck something hard.

He flashed a look at Doona, who was huddled against the wall of the hillfort trying to stay warm while she awaited her turn with the shovel. She approached and watched intently as he uncovered a small wooden chest. He dug out the dirt around it and they each took an end and attempted to pull it out. It seemed to be stuck, so Bridei cleared more dirt and they tried again. This time they were able to lift the heavy chest from the earth. The two of them carried it into the storage shed while Aife went to get a torch.

"By the gods, I wonder what's inside," said Bridei. His pulse raced with excitement, banishing his fatigue. The chest seemed incredible heavy. If it truly were full of precious metal objects, it was a huge horde, containing seemingly enough wealth to bribe half the people in Dun Cullan!

Bridei used his eating knife to try to pry open the lid, but the hinges were rusted. "I'll need a more substantial tool to get this open," he told Doona.

She nodded and left. Bridei tried again to open the chest with his eating knife, but got nowhere. Worried that he would break the blade of the knife, he finally sat down on the chest to wait.

Doona rushed back in a few moments later, carrying a large butchering knife. "Will this work?" she asked.

"Let's give it a try," responded Bridei.

It took several attempts, but he was finally able to break the rusted hinges and lift the lid.

Aife had returned with a smoldering torch. She held it as Bridei knelt beside the chest and began to examine the contents. There were numerous objects inside, all wrapped in linen cloth. Bridei picked up the first bundle. As he sought to undo the cloth, it fell to pieces in his hands. "I wonder how long this has been in the ground," he mused.

The cloth had fallen away to reveal a huge gold torc. The design of the piece was very simple—a thick piece of twisted gold. But what astonished him was the size. The torc was several times larger than his neck. "It looks as if it was made for a giant," he said, laughing.

Bridei laid the torc on the ground, and began to unwrap the other bundles. The pieces he uncovered were as amazing as the first one: Enormous crescent shaped neckpieces. Heavy twisted gold bracelets, earrings and clothing fasteners. Beneath the gold objects, he discovered several necklaces, each with amber beads the size of songbird eggs. Bridei held one of the necklaces out to Aife. "Put it on. I'll hold the torch for you."

Aife shook her head. "Nay, I couldn't."

"Please? I want to see what it looks like on."

Aife shook her head again, appearing very ill at ease.

"Doona?" Bridei held the necklace out to the cook.

Doona draped the necklace around her neck. It hung down nearly to her waist. "I don't see how anyone could wear something like this," she said. "It's so heavy it would exhaust you."

Bridei nodded, amazed. Doona wasn't a small woman, yet the necklace appeared far too large for her.

"Take it off!" Aife said suddenly.

"Why?" asked Bridei.

"Because I know who made it. Who made all these things." Aife gestured to the glittering objects on the ground around them. "It could only have been the Firbolgs." She shuddered again.

"Who are the Firbolgs?" asked Bridei.

"A race of giants who inhabited Ireland in ancient times." Aife motioned frantically. "Oh, please! Put the necklace away! Put all of it away!"

"Now that you mention it, I think I've heard the tale," said Bridei. "The Firbolgs were said to be the enemies of the Tuatha de Danaan, who we now know as the fairy folk or Sidhe."

Doona quickly took off the necklace and laid it on the ground next to the other pieces. Straightening, she gazed at Bridei with an anxious expression. "I agree with Aife. We must put the treasure back. If these things belong to the Tuatha de Danaan, they're probably cursed."

"But the Tuatha de Danaan are supposed to be little people. There's no way they could wear these huge pieces," protested Bridei.

"They must have stolen them from the Firbolg," said Aife. "Please." Her voice was pleading. "Put the box back."

"If these objects are cursed, it's likely the curse was set in motion when we opened the box. Putting them back won't make any difference. Besides, we need this treasure to free Dessia." He fixed the two frightened women with a stern look. "We have to help the queen, no matter the risk to ourselves."

Doona nodded slowly, then spoke softly to Aife. "He's right. We owe it to the queen to do whatever we can to free her."

Aife closed her eyes and let out a kind of sob. "It doesn't matter anyway. The queen is imprisoned and Keenan is dead. No curse could be worse than that."

Bridei began to gather up the jewelry, wrapping each piece in the tattered linen. Unlike the two women, he couldn't see this treasure as something to be feared. To him it seemed this cache of valuables must be a gift from the goddess, Rhiannon. She had answered his pleas and sent him the means to free Dessia.

Chapter 17

The goddess Rhiannon must still be aiding him, Bridei decided as he bent down to examine the soft ground. Although it had rained heavily at Cahermara, once he got away from the dun, the hoof prints left by the horses O'Bannon and his men rode were still visible. Straightening, he adjusted the two tunics he wore under his cloak. Sewn into the hem of the one near his skin were a dozen pieces of gold, made by chopping up one of the torcs. Aife had been horrified when she came to Niall's workshop and saw him cutting it up. She was convinced the metalwork had been made by the Tuatha de Danaan and the enchanted race would punish him for damaging the piece. Bridei had ignored her concerns. There was simply no other way to carry the gold. Even the bracelets in the cache were too large to hide easily.

He paused for a moment to survey his surroundings. Although the oak and elm trees were stark and leafless, the grass remained faintly green. He could understand someone falling in love with this part of Ireland. Even in winter it had a seductive beauty. The glistening hills, the shimmering light of the sky, the soft curves of the terrain that were as beguiling as the lush form of a woman. The image made him think of Dessia, and how much she was like this place she held so dear. Both were wild and thrilling, yet could be soft and yielding. Both could seduce you and steal your heart.

His mood darkened as he considered what lay ahead of him. Somehow he must get into Dun Cullan, find out where Dessia was being held and bribe someone to help him free her. He doubted gold alone would be enough to convince anyone in O'Bannon's household to defy their chieftain. In order for them to be willing to help free Dessia, his accomplice—or accomplices—must already hold a deep grudge against O'Bannon. It might take days or even weeks before he found an ally. His first difficulty would be getting into the hillfort. He hoped his scheme to convince O'Bannon to retain him as a bard would work. Dessia had allowed him to remain at Cahermara not because she admired his talents as a bard but because she was attracted to him. He wouldn't have that advantage with O'Bannon. His stomach tightened with anxiety as he realized he was facing the biggest challenge of his life. If he wasn't able to free Dessia, or if O'Bannon had already killed her, he would grieve for her the rest of his life.

It still astonished him that he felt this way. The old Bridei would never have gone to this much trouble, nor taken these sorts of risks. If he were still the man he was before he met Dessia, he would even now be walking toward Ath Cliath, hoping to get passage back to Britain or to find another patron in Ireland.

He felt a vague yearning to return to his old life. It had been so simple, so easy, to care for nothing except himself and his own needs. But there was no going back now. Dessia had a hold upon him that was almost more powerful than his will to live. He adjusted the pack containing his spare clothing, some food and his harp and started walking again.

* * *

Dessia got up from the stool and began to pace. She was wearing a pathway in dirt floor of the cell, but there was nothing else to do, and she had to keep moving or she would go mad. How long had it been since O'Bannon abducted her? It was impossible to tell day from night in her underground prison, but from the number of candles she'd gone through, and the number of times Druim had brought her food and water, she guessed she'd been held there for nearly a sennight.

Seven days, yet it seemed like an eternity. She'd spent every one of them tortured by regrets. It was miserable enough to know she'd lost her kingdom and everything she'd fought for, but the thought of Bridei down in the souterrain, with no food, water or means of keeping warm, weighed upon her even more. She told herself someone would find him. He would cry out for help, and they would hear him and free him from his prison.

But what if Bridei never roused? Or, what if he'd woken and called out, but no one heeded his cries? The whole fortress would be in a state of panic when they discovered she was gone. They wouldn't be looking for Bridei. Or, they might think that since he disappeared at the same time as she did, he was the person who'd betrayed her. Had she not thought the worst of him herself?

She stopped pacing and let out a moan. What a fool she'd been. She'd been unable to trust the man she loved, yet she'd obviously trusted the person who'd betrayed her. How could her instincts have led her so far astray?

Beyond that thought was a more troubling one. Why had the forces that saved her when her family was killed abandoned her now? Had she done something to anger them? Could it be that her inability to trust Bridei and accept his love had turned the spirits of the Forest of Mist against her? She recalled when she'd looked into the dark waters of the lake and seen the vision of herself with Bridei beside her. It seemed a clear sign he was part of her destiny. Yet, fool that she was, she hadn't been willing to believe in him, to trust him.

There could be no doubt that Bridei was special. He'd managed to call down a storm to frighten the slavers. He'd made his way through the Forest of Mist and reached the lake, which no one else but her had ever done. Bitter tears filled her eyes. She'd had many reasons to believe in Bridei, but she'd refused to accept them. Now she'd lost not only her kingdom and her freedom, but the man she loved.

A noise from above jerked her out of her misery, and she swiped the tears from her cheeks. She must not let Druim see her distress; he might tell O'Bannon, and she'd rather die than let her enemy know she was suffering.

The wicker covering was moved away, but when she looked up, it wasn't Druim's grizzled face she saw. Instead, staring down at her, was the sinister countenance of her enemy. "How fare you, milady?" O'Bannon called out in a faintly mocking voice. Dessia clenched her jaw and didn't answer. She couldn't think of a retort sufficient to express her contempt and hatred.

"You seem well enough," O'Bannon continued. "But that could change at any time. Candles are expensive, even tallow ones. Perhaps if you had to spend your days in darkness, it might make you appreciative of your good fortune."

"Good fortune! Ha!" Dessia exclaimed. "The only good fortune I might know is if you fell down through that hole and broke your neck!"

"That isn't going to happen, so perhaps you should consider your choices with more care."

"Choices? I have no choices!" she threw back at him.

"Ah, but you do," O'Bannon answered, his voice silky. "The mistake you've made all these years was fighting me. It's unnatural for a woman to take up arms. Women are supposed to be soft and yielding."

Dessia gave an unfeminine snort. "Some women are like that, I suppose, but not me. I was raised to be brave and bold, to honor my tribe and my heritage. I'll never stop fighting you, O'Bannon. I'll never give in. You might as well kill me now, rather than expect me to yield to you!"

"Kill you?" O'Bannon tsked softly. "That would be a great waste. You're young and healthy and likely to bear fine sons. I'd be a fool to throw away such an opportunity."

Dessia's stomach lurched. She'd rather die than submit sexually to this man. Indeed, she would make certain she did die rather than endure such shame and degradation.

"I see you're thinking the matter over," said O'Bannon. "There's no hurry to make your decision. I can be patient. I've waited a long time for you, Queen Dessia."

Dessia's fury rose to fever pitch. "And you will wait much longer! You can wait until the heavens fall and never will I lie with you!"

O'Bannon's only response was a laugh. The door to her prison was replaced. Dessia stared upwards, her insides churning with frustration and rage.

* * *

So this was Dun Cullan, Bridei thought as he surveyed the hillfort from a distance. The dark timber walls of the palisade stood out starkly against the overcast sky. In a field below the fortress, a herd of horses grazed. A number of them were a misty gray color. Could these be the remnants of the herd the Fionnlairaos were named for?

He turned his gaze to the hillfort and envisioned a small warband creeping up to the fortress at night, setting a fire and forcing their way in when the blaze damaged the timber walls. That was probably the way O'Bannon and his men had gotten into Cahermara all those years ago. It would serve him right if the same brutal methods were used against him.

But there were many problems with this plan. First of all, he didn't have a warband. Even if he could assemble one and convince them to try this thing, there was still the problem of finding Dessia once they got into the hillfort. O'Bannon would keep her some place secure, either close by him or in an underground chamber similar to where Bridei himself had been imprisoned. That was, of course, if she was still alive.

The thought made Bridei's heart sink like a stone in a pool. He told himself that if O'Bannon's goal was murder, he would have ended Dessia's life at Cahermara. Since he'd abducted her, he must have some had other plan in mind. Bridei could well guess what it was. Rape was the ultimate weapon against a woman. By forcing Dessia to marry him, O'Bannon could claim her lands by right of being her husband and Bridei doubted that anyone would dispute the claim. Even in Ireland, where women appeared to have more power and authority than Britain, it would be difficult to argue the matter in such circumstances. If O'Bannon impregnated her, it would be even more futile.

Bridei sought to unclench his hands. The idea that O'Bannon might rape Dessia filled him with a rage so intense he could scarcely breathe, but he couldn't give into his emotions now. He took another deep breath and tried to regain his usual outlook: calm and confident, seldom bothered or distressed about anything. For Dessia's sake, he must become the old Bridei.

With that thought in mind, he started walking toward Dun Cullan. Since it was daytime, the gate to the hillfort was open, but as soon he was within shouting distance, someone hailed him from the gatetower, demanding his name and his reason for being there.

"I'm Bridei ap Maelgwn," he called back. "A traveling bard. I've come to offer my services for a night or two. I've performed for kings and chieftains throughout Britain and Gaul, and I would willingly entertain your lord and his guests for the compensation of a few meals and a place to sleep."

There was no response. Bridei felt a stab of anxiety. What if he were refused entrance? He told himself to pretend it didn't matter. If O'Bannon sent him away, he could always find another place to perform.

It took awhile, but eventually the guard called out, "My lord said to let you come in."

Bridei felt a frisson of warning. Now that he'd gotten his way, he worried it had been too easy. Did O'Bannon guess what he was up to?

He walked swiftly through the gate and was confronted by a well-armed and burly warrior. Although he greeted the man with a pleasant smile, the warrior insisted he hand over his pack. Bridei did so agreeably. "Be careful of my harp. It's the only thing of value I possess." The man examined the contents of his pack, then set it aside. "Now," he said, "remove your cloak."

Bridei quickly complied with the order. Then, guessing that he might be searched for weapons and not wanting the man to feel the gold in his inner tunic, he stripped off both tunics. When he started to undo his trews, the man waved dismissingly. "Don't bother. I've seen enough to be satisfied that you're unarmed."

Bridei put his clothes back on and the man led him into the hillfort. Although he tried to appear casual, Bridei was careful to note the location of every structure he encountered. Dessia might be held in any one of them.

They reached a hall similar in size to the one at Cahermara. Entering, Bridei saw a group of men gathered around the hearth, mending and polishing weapons. In the center was a stocky man of middle years with black hair going gray. The man's shrewd, deep-set eyes focused on Bridei, who reminded himself to remember he was the old Bridei, carefree and easygoing.

When he was a few feet away from the group of men, Bridei bowed, then called out in ringing tones, "Greetings, Tiernan O'Bannon. I am Bridei ap Maelgwn, famed bard of Britain, Gaul and Catraith. I've come to entertain your household. All I ask in return is a meal or two and a place to bed down for the night."

O'Bannon's eyes narrowed further. He responded, "I've heard of you, Bridei ap Maelgwn. Of how you beguiled everyone at Cahermara with your music and your charm, even Lady Dessia herself. If you think you can do likewise here, you are mistaken. This is a warriors' household. We have no use for cunning-faced poets."

Bridei shrugged. "If you think I only know songs and tales pleasing to womenfolk, you're mistaken." He immediately began singing. The song was a stirring, rhythmic tune often sung by King Arthur's men when they were on the march. To mark the beat, Bridei pounded his hand on a nearby table.

He'd once told Dessia that music was his magic, and as he had many times before, he watched as the song cast its spell. He could see the subtle changes on his audience's faces and in their bodies as they anticipated the beat. The driving rhythm was affecting them, making their hearts beat faster and the blood rush through their bodies. Soon they would be ready to fight... or at least to dance.

Bridei glanced at O'Bannon and saw that the chieftain seemed to be clenching his jaw, as if willing himself to resist the music's pulsing lure. As his enemy's his face flushed, Bridei felt a twinge of unease. It was possible his strategy would backfire. Instead of pleasing O'Bannon, the song would end up goading him to violence. But he pushed his doubts aside and continued singing. He must trust the music. Trust the goddess Rhiannon to make certain the song did as he intended.

He repeated the chorus of the song and finished. O'Bannon met his gaze with a hard look. "You're skilled," he said. "But it doesn't change the fact that I have no use for a bard."

"If you rather I didn't perform, I won't. But I would still presume upon the tradition of hospitality and ask that you allow me to spend the night. I've traveled quite far already and I doubt there's another settlement near enough to reach before nightfall." He deliberately mentioned Irish hospitality, hoping to make O'Bannon feel he no choice but to allow him stay the night. If O'Bannon still appeared reluctant, he would point out that Queen Dessia had hosted him for several weeks.

"Very well. You can stay for one night." O'Bannon's expression bespoke reluctance and suspicion. Bridei bowed again and pretended to be well pleased. O'Bannon motioned to the warrior who had led Bridei there. The man approached O'Bannon and the chieftain spoke to him in low tones. The warrior nodded and returned to where Bridei waited, motioning that he should come with him. Bridei followed the man out of the hall.

"What's your name?" Bridei asked his escort.

"Dermot."

"I'm Bridei, but of course you know that."

The man grunted and continued walking.

As Bridei scanned the area for possible places where Dessia might be held, Dermot turned and glared at him. Bridei hurried to catch up. The warrior led him to a roundhouse set off from the rest of the buildings and motioned that Bridei should enter.

The dwelling was decently furnished with two beds, a small low table and woven mats upon the floor. Bridei put his pack on one of the beds, then went out again. Dermot was standing by the door. Bridei said, "I'm certain I will rest there most comfortably. But I wonder if I might have candle or lamp for light and possibly a brazier to warm the place."

"I have no orders to provide such things. You have a decent place to sleep. That should be enough."

"I suppose if it were up to you, you'd have me sleep in the stables, or worse." Bridei kept his voice light. Dermot didn't answer, but his expression revealed his agreement.

"Have you a particular dislike of bards?" Bridei asked. "Or are you wary of me simply because I'm a visitor?"

Dermot's blue-gray eyes focused on him coldly. "'Tis said you beguiled everyone at Cahermara with your tales and songs. You'll find that our tribe isn't as soft and easily led as those fools."

"Speaking of tales," Bridei said, "when I was at Cahermara, they told me how your king, Tiernan O'Bannon, burned the old rath to the ground and killed Queen Dessia's family. But there are always two sides to every tale. I wonder if O'Bannon was provoked in some way. Or if the feud between your tribes goes back to previous generations."

"Of course it does," Dermot answered hotly. "Our people were here long before the Fionnlairaos. Then they came and stole our lands!"

"How long ago did this happen?"

Dermot frowned. "I don't know. Too many generations to count."

"Is that why your people appear to have mostly dark coloring, while the Fionnlairaos have reddish hair?"

"Aye. We're two different peoples."

"There must been some intermingling of your tribes over the years."

"Some. But that doesn't mean it's right."

"You think your tribes should remain separate?"

"Aye. We're nothing like the Fionnlairaos. They're sly and cunning and not to be trusted."

"But it appears you live much the same as they do," Bridei said, gesturing. "Your houses, clothing and the way you wear your hair is almost the same."

"That doesn't change what's inside people. We're very different." Dermot folded his arms across his chest. "I have no use for the Fionnlairaos. If it were up to me I would have burned Cahermara a second time and killed everyone of them I could get my hands on."

"Even Queen Dessia?"

Dermot's eyes gleamed with hatred. "Especially her. I can't understand what Tiernan thinks he's doing. This plan of his is witless."

"What plan is that?"

Dermot hesitated, as if deciding whether he dare answer. He tightened his lips, then responded. "He plans to wed with her, the fool!" The next moment he glanced around, as if worrying someone might have heard him.

"Well, it seems like a sensible plan to me," Bridei said. "By making her his wife, the conflict between your two tribes will be ended. Then you'll both able to use your resources to become more prosperous instead wasting them fighting each other."

Dermot's face flushed a vivid hue. "What about all the people who died at the hands of the Fionnlairaos? Who will avenge their deaths?"

"Did someone in your family die at the hands of the Fionnlairaos?"

"Aye. My father was killed by Queen Dessia's father."

"And you've nursed a grudge ever since?"

"It's not a grudge. It's my duty to avenge him!"

"Are you the eldest son?"

Dermot nodded.

"What do you think the chieftain should do with Queen Dessia?"

"Kill her, of course! Spill her traitorous blood. She's the last of the line. Then we can begin anew."

Interesting, thought Bridei. "Are there others at Dun Cullan who feel as you do?" he asked.

"Of course. There are many who of us who lost family members at the hands of the Fionnlairaos."

"But O'Bannon won't listen to you? Is that it?"

Dermot nodded. "He fears if he kills Queen Dessia, her people will want revenge and keep fighting us."

"Isn't that likely true?"

"I suppose so."

"It seems to me that if O'Bannon weds Queen Dessia and ends the conflict between your tribes, everyone will benefit."

"It doesn't matter. I'm honor bound to avenge my father."

"If you feel that way, perhaps you should take matters into your hands," Bridei suggested. "Perhaps you'll have to kill Queen Dessia on your own and thwart O'Bannon's plan."

Bridei watched Dermot carefully. When the warrior's gaze shifted briefly, he knew a sense of triumph. For a split second, Dermot had glanced toward the back of the hillfort, suggesting Dessia was being held somewhere near there.

"I can't do that," Dermot finally answered. "I can't go against the chieftain's wishes. I have a duty to him as well."

"Then I guess you'll have to make the best of what happens. Of course, there's always the possibility Lady Dessia will refuse to wed O'Bannon."

"Oh, she'll agree, eventually." Dermot's voice was grim.

"What does he mean to do? Starve her into submission?"

"If necessary."

"She might choose to die rather than give in to him. Has Dermot considered that?"

"Why would she do something so foolish?"

Bridei shrugged. "Just as you are unwilling to give up your hatred toward the Fionnlairaos, she may well be unwilling to let go of her animosity towards O'Bannon. She might choose to die rather than submit to him."

"She's a woman. She'll weaken in the end." Dermot's gaze fixed on Bridei. "You seem to know a great deal about Lady Dessia. But of course you would." Contempt flickered in his eyes. "You've shared her bed."

"Is that what they're saying?"

"Aye."

"Did O'Bannon have a spy at Cahermara? Or, perhaps more than one?" Bridei asked the question casually, but his heart was pounding. As he'd guessed, Dermot's moody nature had worked to his advantage. The man had already told him a great deal.

But Dermot finally seemed to realize what he was doing. "Of course he had spies," he answered. "But who they are is none of your business."

"Fair enough," said Bridei. "As for my relationship with Lady Dessia, bear in mind that it's my business to please the ruler who employs me. I wouldn't last long as a traveling bard if I didn't know how to ingratiate myself with my patrons."

"Is that why you bedded her?"

"It's as good a reason as any. Then again, she's not bad to look at."

Dermot made a face. "If you like wenches that are the same size as a man, with cat-green eyes and a haughty, disdainful manner."

Bridei raised his brows. This man's grudge against Dessia appeared to go deeper than simple vengeance. "I like all kinds of women," he answered, grinning at Dermot. "I'm not generally particular."

"Fond of Lady Dessia, are you?"

Bridei shrugged. "Now that she can no longer be of benefit to me, I care little for her circumstances. When dealing with women, I always put my own interests first."

"What about when you're dealing with men?" Dermot asked.

Bridei laughed. "Aye, when dealing with men, I also put my own interests first."

Dermot gave him a dark look. "So, you have no loyalty to anyone?"

"I have loyalty to my family and tribe back in Britain, of course. But since they're not here, I don't see why I shouldn't make decisions based on what will benefit *me* the most."

Dermot gave Bridei a canny look. "At least a man knows where he stands with you."

"Aye. And I'm more than willing to return favors done for me. If you were to put in a good word with Dermot as far as having me stay here for a time, I might be able to make it worth your while."

"How?" Dermot asked.

"That's for you to decide. Bear in mind, as an outsider, I might be able to do something that your relationship to O'Bannon wouldn't allow you to do. For example, if I were given the opportunity to visit Queen—Lady Dessia, and something were to happen to her, it couldn't be linked to you."

"Are you offering what I think you are?" Dermot asked, sounding surprised.

"Perhaps. I would, of course, expect to be compensated for anything I did. And I would need a means of getting away from this place before what I'd done was discovered."

Dermot nodded slowly. Bridei watched him, thinking how easy most people were to manipulate. "But if I'm going to be of any use to you," he added, "you must make certain that O'Bannon lets me stay awhile."

"How will I do that?" Dermot asked.

"Convince O'Bannon to let me perform at the meal tonight. I'm very good at what I do. I'll make certain O'Bannon won't be able to send me away for awhile."

Dermot looked at him. His expression was wary and suspicious, but also intrigued. Bridei flashed him an easy smile, then went into the guest house.

Chapter 18

Bridei glanced around the crowded feasthall. The cavernous room was smoky and close, the scent of the turf fire mingling with the odors of damp wool, sweat and cooking food. The people were dressed in plaid garments, many woven in a similar pattern: blue and green with a few thin bands of red. As they found their places at the plank tables, their faces shone with expectation and excitement. Dermot had obviously done his part and spread word that a bard was going to perform.

Bridei was elated. The first part of his plan was falling into place. He would sing for awhile, then set aside his harp and begin a long story. After a time, he would claim he was tired and his voice failing. Desperate to know how the tale ended, the people would demand he return the next night to finish it. O'Bannon would be forced to allow Bridei to remain there for several nights.

Bridei had given a lot of thought to what story he would tell and decided on the tale of King Arthur. The life of the former high king of Britain was a dramatic one, with plenty of twists and turns. Tonight, he would describe Arthur's humble beginnings. In subsequent nights he would detail his exceptional rise to power, the battles he fought, the passion he aroused in his followers and finally, his tragic end. The story lent itself well to the sort of exaggeration and embellishment that would hold his audience's interest. There were those who said Arthur was fast becoming a legend even before his defeat at Camboglanna. Bridei meant to develop that legend even further, to transform a mortal king into an almost godlike hero.

Inspired and confident, Bridei struck the first chord on his harp and began singing. It was a ballad in his native tongue, which meant his audience wouldn't understand the words, but only experience the emotion. He knew they would grow restless soon, but he wanted to start off with something simple so he wouldn't have to concentrate.

As he sang, he sized up the crowd. Although his conversation with Dermot had given him an obvious plan, he wasn't comfortable with it. He might able to use the pretext of killing Dessia to get in to see her, but it wouldn't go very far in setting her free. It seemed better to stick to his original idea of bribing someone to help him get Dessia out of the hillfort. Such a scheme appeared much less risky as it didn't involve double-crossing his accomplice. Dermot was a man of strong passions, and wouldn't be pleased to have his plan to murder Dessia thwarted. O'Bannon made a formidable enough opponent; Bridei didn't need a vengeance-crazed warrior after him as well.

Scrutinizing the people gathered in the hall, Bridei noted once again the contrasts between them and Dessia's subjects. At Cahermara, most people were tall and long-limbed and almost all of them had at least a tinge of red in their hair. This tribe ran to short and stocky, with brown and black tresses predominating.

Finishing the first song, he began another. This was in the Irish tongue, and people began to take more interest, the crowd quieting so they could hear the words. The next song was a tune he'd learned since arriving in Ireland. As he'd hoped, people responded by mouthing the words along with him. Good, he thought as glanced around and saw he had the crowd's attention. Now he must stop singing and still manage to keep them interested. As he played the final chord of the melody, he sent a silent prayer to the goddess Rhiannon, asking her for aid.

Finishing the song, he set his harp in his lap and cleared his throat. "My apologies. I'm recovering from a slight ague I caught while imprisoned at Cahermara and my voice isn't as strong as it usually is." He raised his brows meaningfully. "The Lady Dessia is a harsh critic. If she doesn't like what you play, her response is quick and certain." Hearing twitters of laughter, he continued, "Although now it seems the proud wench is experiencing some ill favor of her own." He quirked his mouth into what he intended as a bitter, satisfied smile. Then he added, "Since my voice isn't strong enough to keep singing all night, I'll tell you a tale instead."

After taking a deep breath, he plunged in: "It's a long tale, and to be told properly, I must start at the beginning. Although it's a story of glory and greatness, it begins in very humble and human fashion...

* * *

A long time later, Bridei paused and took a drink from the cup of ale beside him. Finishing it, he spoke in faint tones. "My apologies, but it seems my voice is failing. I guess I'll have to finish the story tomorrow night. That is, if Lord O'Bannon allows me to remain here." He gave the chieftain a questioning look.

There were exclamations of dismay from the crowd, while others muttered things like: "He can't stop now." "Oh, no! He must tell us the rest of it."

O'Bannon fixed Bridei with a hard expression, and Bridei sought to appear genuinely wan and weary. As O'Bannon continued to glare at him, Bridei found himself holding his breath. It was clear the chieftain knew he was deliberately stringing along the audience. Would O'Bannon's anger at being manipulated override his desire to keep his people content?

The chieftain smiled sourly. "You're a sly, cunning sort, Bridei ap Maelgwn, and I don't usually tolerate such men around me. But you're also a fine bard, and it's obvious my people desire to hear the end of your tale. For their sake, I'll let you stay one more night."

The emphasis O'Bannon put on "one more night" made it clear that Bridei would be expected to finish his tale within that time period. But he felt confident he could delay his departure even longer. There was much left to tell about Arthur's story, and if he continued to embellish it, finishing tomorrow would require he continue long into the night. Too long for people who had to get up and go about their usual duties the next day.

Keeping with his claim of being tired, Bridei sluggishly got to his feet and made his way through the crowd. Some of the older children try to stop him and have him tell them more about Arthur, but their mothers drew them away. He was alone as he left the hall, or at least he thought he was. As he reached the guesthouse, Dermot slipped out of the shadows to confront him. "I did as you asked," he said. "Now you're in my debt."

"Aye, that's true," Bridei answered agreeably. "But whatever you want in payment, can't it wait until tomorrow?"

"I suppose it can," Dermot responded. "But come tomorrow, you must do as I say."

"And what is it that you intend me to do?"

"Kill Queen Dessia," Dermot said in a voice harsh with loathing.

"And how am I supposed to do that when I don't even know where she is?"

"I will take you to her when the time comes."

"And how will I kill her?" Bridei asked. "I'm no warrior, and she'll be suspicious and wary. It might be difficult for me to overpower her, even if I had a weapon."

Dermot snorted contemptuously. "I've considered that. Clearly, we must use a more subtle means of ending her life. To that end, I've obtained some poison. I'll put it in some wine. You'll take it to her and pretend to share it with her. But of course, you must not drink any."

"What makes you think she will trust me enough to accept the wine, even if I pretend to drink it? The lady and I didn't part on the best of terms. I doubt she'll accept any gifts from me, no matter what the circumstances."

"You convinced her to let you share her bed. I feel certain you can manage this."

Bridei pretended to nod resignedly. In fact, he was pleased with Dermot's plan. It would be easy for him to fail to kill Dessia, yet still appear to have tried to do so. "What sort of poison is it?" he asked. "Does it contort the limbs and make the victim foam at the mouth?"

"I don't know what it will do," Dermot responded. "I didn't ask about that when I got it from Emer."

"Who is Emer?"

"A wisewoman. Although she's very young, she knows all about herbs and potions."

"Was she in the hall tonight?" Bridei asked.

Dermot shook his head. "The little rat-faced wench knows better than to show her face in the hillfort."

Bridei was taken aback by Dermot's cruel description. If other people at Dun Cullan had the same attitude toward the young woman, she couldn't be happy living here, which meant she might be a useful ally. Perhaps he should seek her out on the morrow. For now, he needed to know more of Dermot's plan.

"I'm curious," he said. "Once I've administered the poison to Dessia, how long do you think it will be before her death is discovered? Someone must take her food and water every day. They'll certainly notice if she's succumbed. They'll tell O'Bannon, and he'll be furious. Even if no one knows I've visited Dessia, I'll be under suspicion. I'm a stranger at Dun Cullan and I've made it clear I bear her a bitter grudge. If I leave as soon as I've made certain Dessia is dead, I'll have at best a day's start. If O'Bannon decides to track me down, it will be relatively easy for him to find me and vent his rage on me over the loss of his prize. I may be in your debt, and I may want Dessia dead, but I'm not willing to throw my life away. If I agree to your plan to poison Dessia, you must come up with a scheme that allows me to get away safely."

"You've already agreed to do this!" Dermot said hotly. "Now you're trying to back out!" He took a threatening step toward Bridei. "It's too late for you to change your mind. If you don't do as I say, I'll go to O'Bannon and tell him of the plot and claim it's all your plan. If it comes down to your word against mine, who do you think he'll believe?"

"He'll believe you, of course," Bridei answered calmly. "But I think I can convince him you also had some part in the scheme. I'll make him doubt your loyalty from now on. Is that what you want?"

Although Bridei couldn't see Dermot clearly, he had a strong sense he was glaring furiously at him. Bridei's muscles grew taut with tension, but he stood his ground. He didn't think Dermot was enough of a hothead to attack him.

"You're a sly, slippery one, aren't you?" Dermot sneered.

"I don't see why looking after my own skin is something to be ashamed of. Although I bear no love for Lady Dessia, that doesn't mean I despise her enough to imperil my own life in order to end hers. If you want me to help you, you'll have to come up with some means of assuring my escape. You'll also have to tell me those means in advance."

"Very well. I'll think of some way to give you time to escape. But you'd better not fail me, or there'll be one less bard in Ireland," Dermot said in a voice edged with menace.

"I'm very weary," said Bridei. "I would ask your leave to seek my bed."

"Until tomorrow," Dermot growled. "The day that Lady Dessia dies."

Despite the comforts of the guest house, Bridei slept poorly that night. It wasn't so much that he feared Dermot, but the strain of this deception. It wasn't easy to pretend to hate the woman he loved. "Ah, Dessia, you will forgive me, won't you?" he whispered into the darkness. "If I get you free of this mess, you'll have no reason to complain of anything I did to bring about your escape."

He slept for a time, then toward dawn, woke and instantly knew an aching sense of loss. Although he'd only slept with Dessia one night, now every morning he felt a deep yearning to find her beside him. *Soon*, he thought as he rose and dressed. *Soon I'll hold my beloved in my arms once again.*

After dressing, he left the guest house and went immediately to the kitchen. The cook and serving maids were startled to see him, but he soon put them at ease. Long ago, he'd learned that treating servants and underlings with a bit of kindness and consideration was usually all that was needed to win their undying loyalty. To that end, he complimented the cook on the excellent food of the night before and commiserated with her on how difficult it must be to serve so many people on such short notice.

She, in turn, told him that although she hadn't had the chance to hear the tale he'd told, she'd caught a bit of his singing and enjoyed it immensely. He then offered to sing a song for her. He chose a light, playful song about a man trying to seduce a maid by offering her all sorts of silly inducements to get her to share his bed. It was a bit crude and bawdy, but he knew from experience that such frank humor was unlikely to offend those of lower status.

As he'd anticipated, the cook and serving maids were soon laughing with delight, their normally blank, dull expressions transformed. As he gazed upon them, it seemed to Bridei that even the plainest woman could appear lovely if she were happy and enjoying herself.

He finished the song, and after eating the steaming oat bannock the cook gave him, inquired as to where he could find the so-called "rat faced" Emer.

The cook, who was called Maeve, looked askance at him. "Whatever would you want with *her*?"

Bridei shrugged. "I heard she was a wisewoman, and since I'm having trouble getting over this ague I acquired on the journey here, I thought she might be able to give me a tinsane that would ease my sore throat."

"For a man with a sore throat, you sang well enough just now," Maeve said.

"It's not bad in the morning," Bridei responded. "But as the day wears on, it gets dry and scratchy. Since the chieftain expects me to finish my tale this night, I thought I should try to heal up as much as possible."

"Aye, Emer might be able to come up with something that would help you," one of the serving girls said. "She does know a lot about herbs."

"I get the sense that Emer isn't well-liked," said Bridei. "Why is that?"

The women all looked at each other. It was Maeve who spoke, "Emer has a great sense of her own importance. Which is strange, given how incompetent she's shown herself to be when faced with a real challenge. I might recommend her to help ease a sore throat, but I wouldn't send anyone I cared about to her if their life were really at risk."

"Why not? What makes you think she's incompetent?"

The four women looked at each other, as if debating whether to respond. Again, Maeve broke the silence. "She let Lord O'Bannon's wife die when she was in travail. The other midwife said it need not happened, that Emer was to blame for Lady O'Bannon's death."

Bridei frowned at this. "Surely you know that childbirth is always risky, and sometimes even the most skilled of midwives can do nothing to save a woman. How do you know the other midwife wasn't merely saying this to better her own reputation?"

"Because the other midwife is Emer's own mother, and I don't think she would say such a thing unless it were true," Maeve responded.

"So, Lord O'Bannon's wife died in childbirth? Did this happen recently?"

"Aye, only last summer," said Maeve.

How convenient for O'Bannon, mused Bridei. With his wife dead, he would be free to take another one. And according to his plan, this next one would be Dessia, who brought with her a rich dowry of land with access to the sea. Bridei couldn't help wondering if O'Bannon had somehow arranged for his wife to die... perhaps by bribing Emer to do something to end the woman's life as she labored. It was a rather horrifying idea, and bespoke an utterly ruthless and determined nature. But then O'Bannon had already shown himself to be that sort of man.

Bridei smiled at Maeve and the other women cheerfully. "Perhaps this Emer bungled that poor woman's treatment, but I'll wager she can make a simple tinsane. Tell me where I can find her, so I can get this business over with. Perhaps once I'm treated, I can come back and have another bannock and perhaps sing another song."

"Emer no longer lives in the hillfort," Maeve said. "After what happened, she's no longer welcome here. She moved to a tumbled-down hut a short distance into the forest."

"I'll be off then," Bridei said. "But I promise to back before you get too busy preparing the evening meal."

"Aye, see that you do come back," Maeve answered, her gray eyes sparkling. "I'll have some sort of treat waiting for you. Do you favor something sweet or something hearty?"

"Oh, sweet, I think," Bridei answered. Although he wasn't particularly fond of honeycakes or spiced fruits, they were dishes that were easy to prepare.

He made his way to the gate by a circuitous route, first visiting the midden and then looping around the back of the hillfort and moving along the timber wall past the smithy and stables. When he reached the entrance to the hillfort, he was relieved to find the gate open. At least he wouldn't have to call up to the guard and explain his business in leaving. Now the only concern was that Dermot might be the guard in the watchtower. But he walked down the worn trackway without incident, then circled around the hillfort and headed toward the forested area beyond.

On the way he saw several horses grazing and admired the grace and beauty of the beasts. One mare in particular caught his eye. She had the fine small head, arched neck and elegant lines similar to some of the desert horses he'd seen at the famed horsemarket in Narbonne. Her coat was a pale silvery color with darker gray markings on her legs and head. Based on what Dermot had told him about the Fionnlairaos, it was possible they'd brought the ancestors of this mare when they came to Ireland. How long ago had it been? Dessia had always made it seem her family had held their lands for generations. Was it really possible that these two tribes—one that had already been living here and one that arrived more recently—had intermingled so little in all those years? Or, was it more likely that it had been it had been only a generation or two since Dessia's family arrived?

How quickly Ireland beguiled and seduced those who came here, Bridei thought. After all, he'd been here for only two waning and waxings of the moon and he was already ready to make his home here. But it wasn't simply the place that enchanted him; it was Dessia. Wherever she was, he wanted to be there. She'd become like the moon and sun to him, the center of his world.

A pang of anxiety went through him at the thought of how much he still had to do in order to free her and escape this place. Spying a pathway leading into the woods, he took it, moving with urgency. He hadn't gone far when he came upon a tumbled-down dwelling. Nearby was a stone hearth with the flames banked low and hanging over it, a small iron cauldron. Bridei went to the cauldron and bent over to sniff the contents. The acrid odor that filled his nostrils didn't come from food, but some sort of herbal potion. Straightening, he went to the door of the hovel and called out. "Emer? Are you here, Emer?" Seconds later, a woman pushed aside the hide door covering and regarded him with narrow golden brown eyes. Her small features scrunched up into an expression of hostility. "What do you want?"

"I have a bit of the ague, and I heard you were a healer."

Emer—for surely that was who it was—made a sound of disgust. "I *was* a healer. Now I'm an outcast."

"But that's not really your fault, is it?"

The young woman came out of the dwelling and stood with her hands on her hips, glaring at him. "What do you mean? Who have you been talking to?" She gestured. "What are you doing here?"

Bridei fixed her with an easy smile. "I'm a bard, visiting Dun Cullan. I have a scratchy throat, which makes it difficult for me to perform. Someone suggested you might be able to help me."

"Who?" Emer demanded.

"Dermot."

Her eyes widened in shock. Then a look of intense suspicion again clouded her face. Bridei decided she wouldn't be bad looking if she would only smile. Her nose was pointed, aye, and her lower jaw a bit small, but she hardly looked like a rat. Indeed, with her red-gold hair, ruddy complexion and light brown eyes, she actually reminded him much more of a fox.

"Dermot sent you?" she asked in a disbelieving voice. Then she shook his head. "Nay, he didn't. He doesn't like me, and besides..." Her voice trailed off, and she looked uneasy.

"Besides, you've just given him some poison to kill the captive, Lady Dessia. Isn't that right?"

Emer took a step backwards. Fearing she would bolt, Bridei grabbed her arm. "Aye. Dermot told me everything. That's because I'm the man who's supposed to give the poison to her."

"You? Why? What is he paying you?"

"Enough to get me safely to Ath Cliath. At least, that's what I've let him think. The fact is, I don't intend to kill Lady Dessia, but rather, set her free." He was taking a risk in being honest with this woman, but he was confident he could convince her to help him. She clearly bore no love for Dermot. Indeed, he suspected she deeply resented almost everyone at Dun Cullan. Which meant she had plenty of reasons to undermine O'Bannon's scheme.

"Free her?" Emer asked blankly. "Why would you want to do that?"

"Because what O'Bannon's doing isn't right. Lady Dessia has done nothing to him, other than reclaim the lands he stole from her father. I've served as a bard in her household for nearly two months, and found her to be a just, kind and generous ruler. I admire her devotion to her family heritage and to her people. My sense of right and wrong compels me to try and help her." *That and my passionate love for her,* Bridei thought, although he knew better to speak of this to another woman, especially an unhappy one.

"You'll never be able to do it," Emer said. "She's locked away deep in some underground chamber at the back of the hillfort. There's no way you'll ever be able to free her. O'Bannon's warriors may not love him, but they're loyal."

"All of them?" Bridei asked. "What about Dermot? He's willing to ignore his chieftain's wishes in order to get revenge. If one man is willing to betray his lord, I'll wager there are others."

"But even if you get her out of the hillfort, you'll never get away. O'Bannon will pursue you. He won't stop until his horse falls dead beneath him," she said emphatically.

"I know the man is utterly ruthless. I suppose that's why he made certain his wife died in childbirth. Then he was free to wed Lady Dessia and claim her lands that way."

Emer's jaw dropped open and she gaped at him. "How . . .? Who told you? Even that pig Dermot doesn't know."

"It wasn't hard to guess," Bridei answered. "Dermot told me there was no reason for O'Bannon's wife to die, and yet she did. I immediately suspected O'Bannon had arranged her death so he would be free to wed Dessia. What did he do? Pay you to give his wife something? A poison perhaps? Or maybe something to lengthen her labor so she died of exhaustion?"

The tawny freckles stood out starkly against Emer's suddenly pale face. She let out a sigh. "It wasn't supposed to end that way. I thought at least the babe would survive. I never guessed they would both perish."

Bridei patted her arm. "Many babes die at birth. That part might not be your fault."

She jerked away from him, her golden eyes wild. "None of it's my fault! I didn't know what Lord O'Bannon intended until it was too late. He told me that a visiting Druid said to make certain the babe was born on a certain day. That being born at that time would ensure the child was a great warrior. So, when his wife went into labor too soon, I gave her an herb that eases the contractions of the womb. I never realized it would kill her!"

"How did it kill her? What happened after you gave her the medicine?"

"As it was supposed to, it slowed her contractions. But it didn't stop them. She was in travail for two days. I guess the ordeal weakened her. On the second night, when nothing seemed to be happening, I left her and went to my bed. The chieftain woke me, appearing very distraught. He said his wife was dead. He demanded I cut her open and get the babe out." She shuddered. "I felt terrible cutting into her flesh when her body was still warm with life. The babe also felt warm. But it never drew a breath."

"You weren't there when the woman died?"

"Nay."

"So, you don't know exactly how her life ended, if she stopped breathing or cried out, or anything like that?"

"Nay. But she must have given some sign. O'Bannon knew she'd expired and fetched me immediately."

"It seems to me you have little to feel guilty for," said Bridei. "Even if the herb you gave her slowed the contractions, I doubt the effect would have lasted two days. And, as you've said, I see no reason it should have caused her death. I think it's likely that O'Bannon did something to cause her death and then put the blame on you."

"What could he have done?"

Bridei shrugged. "Poisoned her. Smothered her. Then he came and got you, hoping to get the babe out before it died. Or, he might not have cared if the babe perished. By forcing you to cut the infant out of his wife's body, he distracted you and kept you from looking too closely at the corpse. He might have been trying to hide the evidence of how he killed her."

Emer stared at him, her expression horrified. "That is..."

"Disgusting? Cruel? Aye, but do you doubt O'Bannon capable of such things? I don't. Tell me, why did he marry this woman? Did she bring him a dowry of wealth or land? Or was it a love match?"

Emer raised her brows. "A love match? Certainly not. He cared little for Morrin, that I could see. And, aye, her father did pay a significant dowry when they were wed."

Bridei nodded. "You see my point, don't you? It's unlikely you caused this woman's death, yet O'Bannon set it up so you would take the blame."

Emer's face flushed with anger. "And his plan worked. Everyone scorns me. Even my own mother. I'm forced to live here by myself, begging scraps of food from the kitchen at Dun Cullan." She pointed to the nearby cauldron.

"I doubt there's anything I can do to restore your place in O'Bannon's household," said Bridei. "But I might be able to give you an opportunity to get revenge on the chieftain and also get away from here and start a new life."

Emer drew back. "Why would you do this?"

"Because I think you can help me. O'Bannon is holding Lady Dessia prisoner somewhere at Dun Cullan. I intend to free her. To do that, I need to devise some sort of distraction so I get her away from the hillfort."

"I can't help you," Emer answered flatly.

"But you haven't heard my plan."

"It doesn't matter." Emer shook her head, looking obstinate.

"You might consider that if you help me, you would be denying Tiernan O'Bannon what he desires most. It seems like a fitting revenge against the man who wronged you."

Emer frowned at him. "It's all very easy for you to speak of these things. If your plan succeeds, you'll be far away from here. I'll be left to face O'Bannon's wrath. While my life is grim, I'm not yet so miserable I'm willing to throw it away to get revenge."

"There's no reason you couldn't come with Dessia and me. Then you would be able to start over in a new place. You have knowledge of herbs and medicines, as well as midwifery. Most tribes would welcome someone with those skills."

Emer seemed to be thinking it over. Then she glanced at him, her expression bleak. Gone was the shrewish, argumentative woman. Emer looked like a lost, lonely child. "But if I go someplace else, I'll be all alone!"

Bridei spoke soothingly. "All the better to begin again. To start over in a new place with a new life. I believe you can do it. Look at how you've managed here, on your own. Many women wouldn't be able to do that. If cast out of their homes, they would simply go off and die. But you're strong, and so you've made the best of your lot and tried to improve it." He gestured to the dilapidated hut, parts of which had been recently repaired. "You're no ordinary woman, Emer. You have courage and strength, as well as valuable knowledge of herbs and healing. In a new place, where no one knows about your past, you could start over again and earn yourself a position of respect and honor."

Emer crossed her arms and glared at him. "And all I have to do to make these wonderful things happen is help you, is that it?"

"Oh, there's more to it than that. If you go to a new place, you'll have to prove yourself. But I'm confident you can do it."

"What makes you think I'm capable of such things? You hardly know me."

"I've traveled far and wide in this world, everywhere from Gaul in the east to Catraith in the north and all over Britain. I've learned to size up people very quickly, otherwise I'd never have survived. It's obvious to me you have a fierce spirit and a strong will. Most people possessed of those qualities will eventually prosper."

Emer nodded, and he could see she was starting to believe what he was telling her. "What will I have to do?" she asked. "How do you want me to aid you?"

"I'm not sure yet how we'll manage things. For now, I want you to come back with me to Dun Cullan."

The life seemed to drain out of Emer's amber eyes. "They'll shun me."

"And you will hold your head high and ignore them, because you know that you did nothing wrong. If anyone asks what you're doing there, I'll tell them that you gave me tinsane for my sore throat and out of gratitude, I've asked you to come to the hillfort to hear me perform."

"Very well," Emer said. "I'll do it. Bards are always respected and honored. If you invite me to the hillfort, everyone will have to accept it. If nothing else, I'll get a decent meal. I can endure their scorn for a night if I can fill my belly properly."

Bridei gave her a warm, encouraging smile. Things were beginning to fall into place. Now he had a real ally at Dun Cullan. One who wanted to thwart O'Bannon's treacherous plans as much as he did.

Chapter 19

Bridei waited for Emer to get her cloak, then they set off for the hillfort. As soon as they entered the gate, Dermot approached them. "Why have you brought her here?" he demanded.

"Emer gave me a tinsane for my throat," Bridei responded. "In payment, I asked her to come and listen to my tale tonight."

Dermot gave Emer a hostile look. "You may come back tonight. But for now, you must leave."

Bridei reached out and put his arm around Emer protectively. "Nay. She's my guest for the whole day. That's what I promised her."

"You have no right to offer such a thing. 'Twill be the chieftain who decides whether she's allowed to stay."

Bridei could feel Emer's confidence wavering. Fearing she would flee, he said, "I'll have Emer stay in the guesthouse until this evening. No one need know she's here until I'm ready to perform after the evening meal."

Dermot regarded Emer as if she were some sort of loathsome insect. "The guest house is far too good for the likes of her."

"That may be," Bridei answered briskly, "but under the circumstances, it's the most reasonable plan. I'll go and get her situated, then seek you out. I believe we still have some important matters to discuss."

Dermot waved them away. "I'll wait here for you."

Bridei shook his head. "I don't think this is the place to discuss what's between us. Perhaps we should meet somewhere closer to our... objective." He gave Dermot a knowing look.

Dermot nodded grudgingly. "Very well. I'll meet you at the midden."

Ah, Bridei thought. *Dessia is being kept somewhere near the midden.*

Bridei led Emer toward the guest house. As soon as they were out of earshot of Dermot, she said venomously, "You see how they treat me? I would like to poison all of them. And I know just the means to do it."

Bridei spoke sharply. "That would be evil, and you know it. You should save your wrath for the man who turned these people against you. Help me and you will have your revenge against O'Bannon. Then you can move on and do something worthwhile with the rest of your life, rather than wallowing in bitterness."

"I can't help being bitter. I've lost everything, and it's all because of the chieftain."

"Nay. You haven't lost everything. You still have your pride and your healing abilities. Use them wisely and you may yet regain all the rest."

They reached the guest house. Bridei held the door for her. Inside, Emer sat down on the bed and stroked the rich fur coverlet. "So, this is the guest house. I've never been inside before."

"Well, today it's yours," said Bridei. "I'll fetch you some food, and then you can lie down and rest if you wish."

Leaving her, Bridei hurried to the kitchen. Maeve was waiting for him with more bannocks, butter and a crock of apples and dried berries stewed with honey. Bridei expressed his gratitude and told her he was taking the food back to the guesthouse. Maeve pressed a full wineskin into his hand and with a blatantly seductive look, asked if there were anything else he might require of her. Guessing what she offered, Bridei gently declined, saying he must save his energies for his performance that night.

When he returned to the guest house, Emer was delighted with the food and immediately began eating. Bridei hurried to the midden and found Dermot pacing impatiently.

"You took long enough," he said.

Bridei shrugged. "I'm here now. So, tell me your plan. When do you want me to give the poison to Lady Dessia? And how do you intend to make certain I'll be able to get away afterwards?"

"Tonight, after your performance, you'll go to her and give her the poison. Then you'll pretend to go to bed. Instead, you'll leave the hillfort and meet me at the edge of the forest. I'll have O'Bannon's fastest horse waiting for you. If you ride all night and the next day, you should be able to get well away before O'Bannon discovers Lady Dessia is dead."

"Surely someone will take her food in the morning. As soon as they realize she's dead, they'll go to O'Bannon."

"I've taken care of that," Dermot said.

"How?" Bridei asked.

"I'm going to make certain Druim doesn't feel well tomorrow. He's the one who usually takes food to the prisoner. If he's too ill to do so, I doubt any one else will check on her. By the time they think of it, you'll be far away."

Bridei raised his brows. "How will you make certain Druim is too ill to perform his usual duties? Do you mean to poison him as well?"

"I'm only giving him a sleeping potion. He won't be harmed by it."

"And you think it will last until I've had a least a day's start?"

"That's what Aine, Emer's mother, has promised."

Bridei regarded Dermot skeptically. He felt certain Dermot was using him. As soon as Dessia was dead, Dermot probably planned to kill him as well. Bridei said, "For your plan to work, I must see her now, then take her the poison tonight."

Dermot's eyes narrowed. "Why? What purpose will seeing her now serve?"

Bridei rolled his eyes, pretending exasperation. "You don't really think that if I suddenly show up tonight with a wineskin, Lady Dessia will drink a drop of it? Nay, I must win her confidence back before your plan will work. I need to see her now, and have a little time to smooth things over with her or she'll never trust me enough to take even a swallow."

Dermot frowned, and Bridei could see him working things over in his mind. "It's risky," he finally said. "No one is supposed to go near the place where Lady Dessia is being kept. If the chieftain discovers I took you there, he'll be very angry."

"Then he must not find out," Bridei said. He motioned. "I don't see anyone around. Why not take me there right now?"

Dermot continued to eye him suspiciously. Then he seemed to make up his mind. "This way," he said, "but we must be quick."

He led Bridei around a storage building. Behind it was a thorn bush. Dermot pointed to the back of the bush. Bridei slipped into the small space and saw a small door set in the ground. He raised the door and saw steps leading downward. His heart began to race with anticipation as he carefully made his way down the steps. He reached another level. Although it was very dark, he could see there was opening in the floor, faintly illuminated from below. Crouching down, he slid the wicker covering away from the opening and gazed down into a small chamber, illuminated by a candle burning on a table. "Dessia?" he called with his heart in his throat. He heard rustling noises, and then she was there beneath him, gazing up with wide, incredulous eyes.

"Bridei." She spoke his name in a voice of awe and desperation.

"Aye," he answered thickly. "It's me. I'm here."

"Oh, Bridei." The emotion in her voice filled him with aching love. "How did you find me?"

"It's a long tale, and one I haven't time to tell you now. How did they get you down there? Did they use a ladder?"

"Nay. They simply lowered me down."

"I would give anything to hold you in my arms, *cariad*. But now is not the time. How are you? Are you well? O'Bannon hasn't..." Bridei hesitated, unable to say the word.

"Nay, he hasn't touched me. But he means to force me to wed him." Her voice shook.

"I know. I suspected as much. Don't worry. I have a plan to free you."

"How?"

"I don't know all the details. But if a young woman comes for you tonight, know that she's helping me and you must do whatever she says."

"A woman? Who? Surely not Aife."

"Nay. Aife is still back at Cahermara."

"And she's safe?"

"Aye."

"And everyone else in the hillfort—they are safe as well?"

"Aye," Bridei repeated. Now was not the time to tell her that her people had fled the hillfort.

"Bridei!" Dermot's harsh half-whisper echoed down the passageway.

"Aye!" Bridei called up. "I'll be there in a moment."

"Hurry!" Dermot responded.

"Who is that?" asked Dessia.

"Dermot. He's not to be trusted, although he brought me here. If Dermot comes for you, you must resist with all your might." Bridei sighed heavily, feeling as if he were being torn in two. How could he leave Dessia like this? What if his plan failed? What if he never saw her again?

"Bridei!" Dermot called again. He sounded on the edge of panic.

"I have to go," Bridei said. "But know this: I love you, and intend to free you." On impulse, he stuck his arm down into the opening. Dessia reached up and entwined her fingers with his.

"Bridei," she whispered. "I love you. I'm so sorry I ever doubted you. I should never have put you in the souterrain. If I'd trusted you, none of this would ever have happened."

"Oh, aye, it would have. O'Bannon was very determined, and he had someone at Cahermara who helped him. Indeed, if you hadn't put me in the souterrain, I would probably be dead. If O'Bannon had come for you while I was around, I would have given up my life defending you."

"Oh, Bridei." He could see the tears glistening on her cheeks. How he longed to hold her and kiss them away. But he had to hurry or Dermot would become suspicious.

"Fare thee well, *cariad*," he whispered. Then he released her fingers and drew back from the opening. A moment later, he climbed the steep, narrow stairs to where Dermot waited.

* * *

Was it a dream? Could it really be true that Bridei had come for her? Dessia held her fingers to her lips and savored the memory of Bridei's touch. He'd promised to free her. But how? There were so many questions she should have asked; now it was too late. She'd been so stunned and excited to see him, all her wits seemed to have fled.

Her first thought had been that her people had attacked Dun Cullan and taken control of the hillfort. But if that were true, Bridei wouldn't have appeared so rushed and desperate. O'Bannon must still be in control, curse the man. Yet, all was not lost. Bridei had a plan to free her.

But how could he possibly do so? He was but one man, surrounded dozens of warriors. But Bridei was resourceful, and he also seemed to be favored by the gods. She must have faith in him; she must not give up hope.

Dear Bridei. He hadn't died in the souterrain as she'd feared. Nor had he run away and left her. He'd come for her and meant to free her. She took a deep breath, trying to calm herself. "You have to trust him," she spoke aloud. "You have to be strong. You must do it for his sake. And for your own."

* * *

"I've found out where Dessia is being held, and I have a plan to free her," Bridei announced as soon as he was alone with Emer in the guesthouse. As Emer gazed at him skeptically, he continued, "Tonight, while I'm performing, you will leave the hall. You will head toward the gate, as if you are going back to the forest. But instead of going out the gate, you will circle around to the back of the hillfort. Near the midden, there's an old thorn bush. Behind it is a door. The door leads down some steps to another level, and lower still is the prison where O'Bannon has secured Dessia.

"I'll leave a rope behind the thorn bush near the door. I want you to tie one end of the rope to the thorn bush, then enter the underground chamber and throw the other end down to Dessia, so she can climb out of her prison. Then the two of you will secure the door as it was and take the rope and hide it behind a workshop or storage building. Then you'll give Dessia your cloak. Pretending to be you, she'll leave the hillfort and go to your dwelling in the woods.

"After you've freed Dessia," Bridei continued, "you will return to the hall, where I will still be performing. When I'm finished, we'll both leave the hillfort. I'll say I'm escorting you home, but of course, I have no intention of coming back to Dun Cullan. The last part is especially tricky, as Dermot expects me to go to Dessia tonight and give her some poisoned wine. But I have a plan to get Dermot out of the way. I've become friendly with the cook, Maeve, and I'm going to have her put something in his food. It won't kill him, but it will make him too ill to do very much for the rest of the night. By the time he recovers, you, I and Dessia will all be far away."

"Where will we go?" Emer asked.

"There's a forest near Cahermara that's protected by a magical spell. We'll stay there for a while, long enough for O'Bannon to think we've fled the area."

"And then?"

Bridei hesitated. He hoped that once Dessia was free, her people would regain their courage and rejoin her at Cahermara. The hillfort was well enough fortified that Dessia's warriors should be able to defend it. But he wasn't certain Dessia's people would rally around her. Their confidence in her "magic" was badly shaken, and it might not be easy to convince them to fight for her.

But Dessia's problems weren't Emer's concern. He said, "As soon as it's safe to travel, I'll take you to Ath Cliath. It's a large settlement. Someone there is bound to need the services of a skilled healer."

"You expect me to live in a place where I know no one?" Emer asked, her eyes wide and anxious.

"I know it's frightening to think of beginning a new life in an unknown place. But it's the only way you'll ever have a chance at happiness. Besides," he soothed, "I'll stay with you for a time and help you."

Even as he said this, Bridei wondered how he could bear to leave

Dessia for so long. But perhaps such a journey wouldn't be necessary. He might be able convince Dessia to make a place for Emer in her household. But he didn't want to mention this idea until he was certain Dessia would agree.

"Can you remember everything I've told you about my plan?" he asked.

Emer nodded. "Although I'm not certain it will work. What if the guard at the gate stops Lady Dessia as she's leaving? How will she convince him that she's me? Even if she gets away, the guard will think it very strange if he sees me leaving a second time."

"Don't worry about how Dessia will get away. As you may have heard, she's a sorceress. She'll find a way to fool the guard."

Emer's expression grew scornful. "If she's a sorceress, how did O'Bannon manage to abduct her? And why doesn't she free herself rather than having us put our own lives at risk?"

Bridei struggled to control his impatience. "What do you expect her to do? Shapechange into a bird and fly out of her prison? She possesses special abilities, have no doubt of that. But for her powerful magic to work, she requires certain materials to cast a spell, and she's unlikely to possess those things in the prison where she's being kept. As for how she was abducted, her spell of protection worked to guard Cahermara from attack for many years. Unfortunately, it was not proof against treachery from within her household."

"Oh, you mean Beatha," Emer said. "She was the one who arranged to let O'Bannon into the hillfort."

"Beatha? She betrayed Dessia?"

"Aye," Emer responded. "I'm certain she was the one."

Bridei was shocked. He thought of the beautiful cloak the young widow had given him. He'd never questioned the reason for her generosity; now it seemed he should have.

"Where is she now?" he asked.

"I'm not certain," Emer answered. "I know she came here afterwards, thinking O'Bannon would welcome her. She was wrong. The chieftain was very harsh with her. He told her he didn't want a traitorous bitch like her in his household."

"You observed this yourself?"

"Nay. My mother told me about it. She was trying to convince me to leave this place, and mentioned what had happened to Beatha as proof that O'Bannon would never forgive me for what I'd done to his wife."

"How did Beatha come in contact with O'Bannon?"

Emer shrugged. "She has family who live between the Fionnlairaos territory and ours. Perhaps she met him there and that's when they arranged things."

Or, perhaps her family carried a message to her when they came to hear him perform, Bridei thought with a stab of regret. Dessia had resisted the idea of inviting everyone to Cahermara for a celebration. He'd pushed her to agree, and inadvertently given O'Bannon the opportunity to find a way into Cahermara and abduct her.

Yet O'Bannon was not as clever as Bridei had once thought. Having used Beatha and Emer to gain his ends, the chieftain then rejected them. O'Bannon must think that as women they were too unimportant to worry about. It was a foolish outlook, and a mistake Bridei intended to use to his advantage.

"Do have any other questions?" he asked Emer.

"I'm certain I will," she responded. "But I can't think of any of them right now."

"Then I'm going to see to the other details of my plan." Bridei drew near to Emer. "I think you are very brave to help me, Emer. I won't forget what you've done, and neither will Dessia. We'll make certain you're rewarded."

Emer's eyes narrowed and she pursed her mouth sourly. "Of course, you make promises to me now, since you're trying to convince me. That doesn't mean I'll ever be repaid."

"Listen to me," Bridei said sternly. "Lady Dessia is a woman of honor, and she has always rewarded those loyal to her. I vow upon my life, she won't forget how you've helped her."

Having reassured Emer, Bridei left the guest house and started toward the kitchen. He had much to do in the next few hours if he was to honor his promise to Dessia. "Be with me now, Lady Rhiannon," he whispered under his breath, "Grant me good fortune as you have so many times before."

* * *

Bridei watched the crowd gather in O'Bannon's hall and tried to calm himself. A flock of tiny swallows seemed to be swooping and dipping inside his belly. He kept thinking about everything that could go wrong with his plan. Emer might decide not to help them, out of fear of O'Bannon. She might be observed and stopped before she was able to free Dessia. The guards at the gate might prevent Dessia from leaving. Dermot might not fall ill from the tainted food Maeve had prepared for him. Or, Dermot might sense something was amiss and refuse to eat it. The guard at the gate could recall that a woman he thought was Emer had left earlier in the evening and become suspicious when she saw her leaving with Bridei.

Bridei took a deep breath. He'd done all he could. Now Dessia's fate—and the fate of Emer and himself as well—was in the hands of the Goddess.

Despite his reassurances to himself, Bridei couldn't eat. Instead, he took out his harp and began to tune it, holding it to his ear as he plucked the strings, so the noise in the hall didn't interfere. He'd decided he would do as he did last night and sing a few songs before he began the tale, then drag out the story until it was very late. He needed to give Emer as much time as possible to get Dessia away.

As Bridei tuned the harp, he glanced over to where Dermot sat next to the other warriors near the hearth. Dermot appeared nervous, as well he might. given his own plan. Was he too nervous to eat? Again, Bridei fought back the waves of dread that seemed to clutch his belly, and began to strum the harp. The crowd quieted. Bridei began to sing.

Chapter 20

As he had the night before, Bridei chose a lively tune to begin his performance. He followed it with another rousing song that got them clapping. As he played and sang, Bridei kept an eye on Dermot to see if he was eating. Maeve had promised to lace Dermot's food with an herb that would cause violent stomach cramps. Bridei worried the warrior would taste the herb and not eat enough for it to have an effect. Getting Dermot of the way was crucial.

With effort, Bridei forced his gaze away and told himself he must trust in the Goddess. He wouldn't think about all the things that could go wrong; instead he would concentrate on making his performance so enthralling no one would want to leave the hall.

Finishing the second song, he began another. Although many people were clearly enjoying the music, others seemed to be growing restless. When he paused at the end of the song, someone called out, "The tale! Tell us the rest of the tale!"

Bridei smiled and inclined his head. Setting aside his harp, he began. He told the tale of Arthur's adult life, embellishing as he went along, making a legend out of the high king's accomplishments. All the while, Bridei kept an eye on Dermot. For a long time nothing happened, then all at once the warrior grew pale and began to shift uneasily in his seat. When he got up abruptly and left the hall, Bridei knew this was his chance. He let his voice fade and grow hoarse. Casting a regretful glance around the hall, he said, "There's more to Arthur's tale, but I'm afraid my throat is sore and I'm not able to continue. Perhaps Lord O'Bannon will allow me to stay another night so I can finish." He inclined his head to the chieftain.

Conflicting emotions warred on O'Bannon's face. It was clear a part of him wanted to chastise Bridei for not finishing as he'd promised. But it was also obvious he'd enjoyed the tale as much as anyone and was eager for the rest of it. "One more night, I'll grant you," he finally said. "But no more."

Bridei put his harp into the leather bag he carried it in, then stood. Although he wanted to leave immediately and find Emer, he forced himself to be patient and respond cordially to the people who came up to speak to him. *Behave as you usually would,* he told himself. *Don't let anyone guess you're anxious to leave.*

The questions people had for him seemed to drag on. Then all at once, he looked up and saw Emer. She gave a slight nod, and his heart leapt in his chest. He smiled at those gathered around and said, "If you will forgive me, I promised to escort Emer home."

As the warmth vanished from people's faces. Bridei felt pity for Emer. No wonder she was so eager to leave this place. The people here seemed to despise her. Pretending not to notice the change in mood, Bridei bid everyone goodnight. Then he went to where Emer waited. "All is well?" he murmured under his breath.

"Aye. So far," she responded.

They left the hall and started toward the gate. "Have you seen Dermot?" Bridei asked, again in a near whisper.

"Aye. He was headed toward the midden when I saw him. Clutching his belly, he was." Bridei saw the flash of Emer's teeth as she smiled. He had to repress a guffaw himself. Maeve had done exactly as he'd asked and gotten Dermot out of the way.

But there was one more trial ahead of them. They had to get safely out of the hillfort.

The gate was closed, which Bridei had expected this time of night. But it made things trickier as they would have to get the guard to open it. "Hullo," he called up to the gatehouse. "Can you come down here and help me open the gate?"

They could hear the guard coming down the ladder. "O'Bannon said nothing about anyone leaving this night," he grumbled. Reaching the ground, he grabbed one of the torches from its bracket and held it up. "What's this? The bard? And you..." The guard drew in his breath as he recognized Emer.

"Now you can understand why we're leaving," Bridei responded in crisp tones. "O'Bannon allowed Emer to listen to my performance, but now he wants her gone."

The guard's gaze veered back to Bridei. "What's your part in this?"

"I said I would escort her home. I have no reason to dislike her. Whatever happened between her and O'Bannon is no concern of mine."

"She let the lord's wife die, is what happened. Or, perhaps I should say she killed her."

"Many women perish in childbirth," Bridei responded. "I doubt it was her fault." He motioned. "If you want her gone, then open the gate."

"And what of you? Why are you going with her?"

"She gave me a tinsane for my throat. As payment, I said I would make certain nothing happened to her during her visit to Dun Cullan."

"As soon as I see the back of her, she'll be safe enough. There's no reason for you to escort her home."

"I gave Emer my word, and I mean to keep it. I don't see what concern it is of yours if I escort the lady home."

"Something might happen to you, is all. Then we'd never hear the rest of your tale."

Bridei smiled and made a casual gesture. "I'm not as helpless as I appear. I have a knife with me. I think it would suffice against most threats."

Would this guard ever let them pass? Bridei felt his stomach squeeze with anxiety. It worried him that the guard had taken so much notice of them leaving. Now, when Bridei didn't return, the man might think something had happened to him and raise the alarm. He had to prevent this. All at once it came to him. He leaned near to the guard and whispered, "The truth is, the woman has promised to make it worth my while if I see her home. It's likely I won't be back until morning... if you understand my meaning."

The guard drew back, appearing startled. *"Her?* I can't believe it. When I left the hall to begin guard duty, half the women there looked to be yours for the asking."

Bridei shrugged. "Every man has his own taste, and I happen to favor redheads."

The guard gaped openly at Emer, then shook his head. "Your taste in women is very strange, bard. But do what you will." He went to open the gate.

As soon as they were through it, Emer muttered. "Did you have to make me look like a slut?"

"Well, I had to give some reason why I wouldn't be returning to the hillfort this night. Besides, if all goes as planned, you'll never have to see him again."

"Aye, I suppose that's true," Emer said. "If we get away, that is."

"I mean to do my best," Bridei said. "Come now, we must hurry. I want to be far from here by daylight."

Bridei was ready to run all the way to forest, but in deference to Emer, he kept to a fast walk. "So, all went well in freeing her?" he asked as they hurried along.

"Aye. The rope was where you said it would be, and she climbed out easily. I presume she made it through the gate, although I didn't stay to see."

"She must have left early enough that there was a different guard at the gate than the one we spoke to. That was a stroke of good fortune."

"I was a bit worried when I saw how much taller she is than I am," Emer said. "But she must have gotten out. If she'd been discovered, we would have known it."

"Aye," Bridei agreed. He imagined one of the warriors dragging Dessia into the hall and explaining she'd tried to get out of the hillfort by pretending to be Emer. If that had happened, he felt certain he and Emer would now both be dead. *Thank you, Great Queen Rhiannon. I'll never forget what you've done for me.*

He quickened his pace, and Emer hurried after him. At last they reached the woods. As they entered the darkened forest, Bridei called out, "Dessia? Are you here?"

For a few terrible seconds, there was no answer. Then he heard rustling noises and Dessia called out, "Aye. I am here."

Bridei rushed to her and pulled her into his arms. "Ah, *cariad,*" he sighed. "So long I have waited for this."

"Oh, aye," she murmured, nuzzling her face against his. "I thought I would never see you again."

They stood entwined for a few moments, and Bridei savored the almost unbearable joy and relief of holding her close. Nothing felt better than this, to feel her next to him.

"Shouldn't we leave now?" Emer asked in an anxious voice. "What if they come after us?"

"Emer is right," Bridei said, gently disengaging himself from Dessia. "If we're going to get away, we have to hurry." He grabbed Dessia's hand and started out of the forest.

"Where are we going?" Dessia asked.

"To get horses."

"What of me?" Emer asked in a shrill voice.

Bridei grabbed her arm with his free hand. "You're coming with us, as I promised."

This was dream, thought Dessia as she raced along beside Bridei. She'd begun to think she would die in that awful place. But there were still many challenges ahead of them. They had to get back to Cahermara before O'Bannon discovered they were missing. Then they had to deal with his inevitable attack. Although she'd fought in many skirmishes, she'd never defended a hillfort.

It was a clear night, with a half moon and myriad stars. She was impressed that Bridei seem to know exactly where he was going. He led them to stone enclosure, then opened the wooden gate and went inside. Dessia heard Bridei whistle softly. A short while later, to Dessia's amazement, he came out of the pen leading a horse. "We'll have to ride bareback," he said. "I was able to sneak bridles out of the stables, but I knew I'd never manage saddles."

Dessia nodded wordlessly. He'd seemingly thought of everything.

"That's Cahir," Emer said in awed tones. "Tiernan's stallion."

"Aye," Bridei responded. "Having him with us will make it easy to get one of the mares."

"But how did you get him to come to you?" Emer asked. "Everyone I know is afraid of him."

"I spent a lot of time with horses when I was a slave," Bridei answered. "I learned how to talk to them."

Dessia was also stunned. She'd never guessed Bridei had these sorts of skills.

"Come on," Bridei said. "We need to get one of the mares and be off."

They went to a different pasture where the other horses were kept. "Here," Bridei said, holding out Cahir's reins to Dessia.

Gazing at the large, strong animal, she suddenly felt afraid. "It's been years and years since I've ridden," she said.

"It will come back to you," he said. "Besides you aren't going to ride this animal, merely hold the reins while I fetch a mare for you."

Swallowing hard, Dessia took the reins. Bridei disappeared into the shadowy darkness. They heard his soft whistle. "It's like magic," Emer said.

Dessia nodded. She'd acquired a reputation as sorceress, but it was

Bridei who could do extraordinary things. The stallion whickered behind Dessia. A short while later, Bridei appeared leading a light-colored horse. As the two horses greeted each other, Bridei said, "Come here, Dessia. I'll help you mount."

"What about the stallion?"

"Drop the reins. He'll stay here with the mare." Dessia did as Bridei asked. He moved behind her and boosted her onto the mare's back. Handing her the reins, he said, "Just hold them loosely. The mare should follow the stallion without you having to guide her."

Dessia nodded wordlessly. Her whole body felt taut. When she'd ridden horses as a girl, it had never seemed like such a long way to the ground.

"Relax," Bridei said. "You're making the mare nervous."

Dessia willed her stiff muscles to ease.

"What of me?" Emer asked.

"You'll ride with me," Bridei said. "Come on. I'll help you up."

"I don't know if I can do it!" Emer's voice was squeaky with fright.

"Of course you can," Bridei reassured her. "I'll be right behind you." He boosted Emer up, then mounted behind her. "See," he said. "Nothing to it."

Dessia wished fervently that she was the one riding in front of Bridei, feeling his strong arms around her. She told herself not to be such a little mouse. This was much better than being imprisoned in an underground chamber. Bridei clicked his tongue and the stallion started off. As he'd predicted, Dessia's mount followed easily.

Bridei guided the stallion back to the forest, then skirted the edge of the woods. He kept the animal to a walk at first, then when they reached open country, urged the stallion into a trot. Dessia's horse followed. Bouncing along on the animal's back, Dessia at first felt sick with dread. Then, gradually, as she realized she hadn't fallen off, her panic began to ease.

I'm free, she thought. *And I'm riding, something I haven't done in years.* Exhilaration began to replace her dread. She started to get comfortable on the horse, to relax and let her body merge with the animal's. At last, she had the courage to urge the mare next to Bridei's mount. "How long before they come after us?" she asked.

"With luck, they won't discover you're missing until late tomorrow. That is, if Dermot has done what he said and given Druim something to sicken him."

"Why would Dermot do that?" Dessia asked.

"It's part of his scheme. His plan was to have me take you some poisoned wine. Then he was going to murder me, and tell O'Bannon he'd caught me in the act of poisoning you. He wanted to make certain Druim didn't discover what had happened."

"Why did he think you would want to kill me?" Dessia asked.

"I told him how you'd imprisoned me."

"Oh, Bridei, I'm so sorry. I shouldn't have done that. I should have trusted you."

"It worked out well enough. As I told you before, if I'd been free at the time you were abducted, I'd have probably done something rash and gotten myself killed, just as Keenan did."

"Poor Keenan," Dessia said sadly.

"Aye. Although I never much liked the man, I didn't wish him dead."

Having an experienced warrior like Keenan around would have been very helpful in regaining Cahermara, Dessia thought. But she didn't express her thoughts. She didn't want Bridei to think she didn't trust him to protect her. After all, he'd rescued her when she'd thought her circumstances utterly hopeless.

"Poor Aife," said Dessia. "I'm certain she's heartbroken.'

"Aye. She is that."

"I can imagine what she's going through," she added. "If anything happened to you, I don't know how I would go on."

"I'm certain you'd manage." Bridei spoke in a strangely jesting tone. Dessia was confused. She was trying to tell him how much she loved him and he was making light of it. Why? Was it because he didn't want to discuss such things in front of Emer?

Dessia regarded the young woman with narrowed eyes. What was Emer to Bridei? She'd obviously been his accomplice in arranging her escape. What exactly had Bridei done to gain her cooperation?

Stop it, you fool, she told herself. *Bridei risked his life for you; there's no reason for you to be jealous.*

"Emer," she called out. "I haven't thanked you for helping Bridei rescue me."

"I would do nearly anything to spite that worm, Tiernan O'Bannon."

"Why? What did he do to you?"

Dessia listened in amazement as Emer told what O'Bannon had done. When the young woman got to the part where O'Bannon told her to cut the babe out of his recently dead wife, Dessia's stomach squeezed with revulsion. She'd known her enemy was ruthless, but not to this extent. "And you think O'Bannon deliberately caused his wife's death?" she asked in horror.

"Bridei does," Emer responded.

"I do," Bridei said. "I think once he came up with this plan to abduct you, he knew he had to get Morrin out of the way. Women die in childbirth all the time. There was no reason anyone would question what had happened."

"Except that he made it look as if it were my fault, and caused everyone at Dun Cullan to despise me!" Emer broke in fiercely.

Dessia nodded, turning things over in her mind. It was cunning scheme. O'Bannon's wife dies and Emer takes the blame. Then the widowed chieftain is free to take another wife. "The part I don't understand," she said, "is why after all these years, he decided to abduct me."

"It's hard to say what gave him the idea," Bridei answered. "Perhaps he thought of this plan long ago, then had to wait until he had an accomplice at Cahermara to help him carry it out."

"Aye, the accomplice," Dessia said. "Do you know who it was?"

"Emer said it was Beatha," Bridei answered.

"Nay, that's not possible!" Dessia exclaimed. "She had no reason to do such a thing."

"Aye, she did," Bridei said. "Her husband died defending you. Then when she thinks there's a new man in her life, you take him from her as well."

"I don't understand. What do you mean?"

"It appears she was infatuated with me," said Bridei. "While I only had eyes for you."

"But why would she think she had a chance with you?" Dessia was more puzzled than ever.

"It happens all the time," Bridei said. "It's one of the hazards of my trade. If I sing a love song, half the woman in the room think I'm singing to them. Or, at least they hope I am."

Beatha had hated her enough to betray her to O'Bannon. The thought shocked Dessia. "I scarcely even noticed Beatha," she mused. "Yet she nearly cost me everything."

"That's often the way it is," said Bridei.

"Think of all the time I wasted mistrusting you," Dessia said ruefully.

"I could scarce blame you under the circumstances. I appeared out of nowhere, acting cocky and arrogant. Why should you trust me?"

Again, Dessia thought Bridei's response sounded odd. Then she guessed what he was trying to tell her: *You ignored Beatha and thought her unimportant, and she ended up nearly destroying you. Don't overlook Emer. We might need her.*

"You are very clever to figure all this out," Dessia said to Emer. "Few women your age are so shrewd."

"I've had to be clever," Emer answered in bitter tones. "I have nothing else to rely on. Certainly not my looks."

"What's wrong with the way you look?" asked Dessia.

"I'm too thin. My teeth too prominent. My nose too sharp. And I have this wretched red hair."

"What's wrong with red hair?" Dessia asked.

"Everyone knows it's bad luck to have red hair."

"If that's true, then almost everyone I know is cursed," said Dessia, laughing.

"Perhaps they are. Perhaps that's why the rest of your family were killed long ago and why one of your own people turned against you and betrayed you to O'Bannon."

Dessia suddenly felt cold. She'd been jesting, but Emer had answered seriously. What if the young woman's words were true? What if she was cursed?

"What nonsense," said Bridei. "My mother has red hair, as do three of my siblings, and none of them have experienced any great misfortune in their lives. You've been taught to despise your red hair because it makes you look different. But among some tribes, it's very common. It seems to me that it's your 'difference' that caused your misfortune, rather than the color of your hair."

Bridei's calm explanation reassured Dessia. When she'd first met him, she'd thought him flippant and shallow. But he'd shown himself to be thoughtful and wise, brave and strong. He'd managed to rescue her against enormous odds. *She loved him so much.*

"How long will we have to ride like this?" Emer asked.

"It's still a good distance to the Forest of Mist," responded Bridei.

"Why are we going there?" Dessia asked. "Why not Cahermara?"

"I'm not certain we'll be safe at Cahermara."

"The wall is almost finished, thanks to you and the other workers," she said. "With it in place, I feel certain we can hold off O'Bannon's forces, at least for a time. We have to make a stand against him now. Even if I die fighting him, we have to finish this. Otherwise I'll have to live in fear the rest of my life, dreading what he will do."

Bridei pulled the stallion to a halt. Dessia's mount stopped beside him. Dessia experienced a sudden flare of dread as he spoke in soft, gentle tones: "I would agree with you, except for one thing... You have no warriors, Dessia. They've all left Cahermara."

"What do you mean—left?" She couldn't understand what he was saying.

"After you were abducted, people were afraid. All these years they believed they were protected by a magical spell. But then you were gone, and they felt vulnerable and afraid. So, they left the hillfort and went back to their families, if they had any. Otherwise, they scattered among the hills and forests."

Dessia found herself gaping in shock. "How could they betray me like that?" she whispered.

"They haven't betrayed you. Once they know you're free, they'll return to Cahermara, I feel certain. But for now, the hillfort is nearly deserted and it isn't safe to go back there. That's why I think we should go to the Forest of Mist."

She hadn't expected this. The realization of how alone she was struck her like a blow. The next moment she brushed aside her fear. She wasn't alone. Bridei was with her.

Chapter 21

They rode all night. As dawn broke, the bare trees of the Forest of Mist loomed ahead of them. "I've never approached the forest from this direction," said Dessia. "We need to find a place where we can enter."

Bridei watched as Dessia gingerly slid off the mare's back. She stretched to loosen her muscles, then led the mare toward the trees.

Even in winter, the dense oak and elm trees and holly and hawthorn bushes created a nearly impenetrable barrier. Bridei followed on the stallion as Dessia and the mare walked along the edge of the woodland, searching for an opening in the underbrush. As time passed, he grew anxious. What if the forest wouldn't let them pass?

At last she called out, "Here!"

Bridei rode closer. "I'll try to follow you on the horse. That way we won't have to wake Emer until we've reached the lake." He motioned with his head to Emer, who'd fallen asleep leaning against him.

Dessia led the mare into the forest. Bridei attempted to follow, but as soon as he reached the edge of the woods, the vegetation closed up in front of him. "Dessia!" he called.

"What's wrong?"

"The forest won't let me enter."

Dessia returned with the mare, the forest opening up for her. She gazed at him in dismay. "I don't understand. The forest has always permitted you to pass."

"Perhaps Emer is the problem."

"Aye. That might be it. What are we going to do?"

"Perhaps she could stay at Cahermara with Aife and Doona. Nay. That won't work. While O'Bannon isn't likely to hurt Aife and Doona, if he found Emer there, he would certainly kill her."

"I have an idea," said Dessia. "We could have Aife take Emer to stay with her family. They live some distance away. Far enough that Emer should be safe from O'Bannon."

Bridei wasn't entirely pleased with this plan. It meant they would have to go to Cahermara, something he'd sought to avoid. Seeing the abandoned hillfort would break Dessia heart. And, having returned to her home, she might insist on staying there, rather than seeking sanctuary in the Forest of Mist. But there seemed no other answer.

Dessia mounted the mare and they started around to the other side of the woodland. As the stone walls of Cahermara came in view, Bridei watched Dessia anxiously. "We can't stay here long," he said.

They rode through the open gate. Bridei halted the stallion and called out, "Aife? Are you here?" When Aife didn't appear, he shouted Doona's name. Again, there was no response. "Perhaps they're in the kitchen area," he suggested. "That's where I found Doona last time."

Dessia nodded and dismounted. Leaving the mare with her reins dangling down, she set off toward the hall.

Bridei's tension built. If everything went as planned, O'Bannon wouldn't know Dessia had escaped until much later that day. But something could always go wrong. They had to get to the safety of the Forest of Mist as soon as possible.

Time dragged on and his insides churned with worry. He reached back with his free hand and gently shook Emer. "Wake up, Emer."

"What? What is it?" she mumbled, sitting up.

"We're at Cahermara." He disengaged himself from her grip and slid off the horse, then reached up for her. As soon as she was down, she grabbed for him. "Oh!" she cried. "My legs won't seem to hold me!"

Bridei steadied her, then drew away.

Emer looked around. "Why have you brought me to this place? I thought we were going to some sort of enchanted forest."

"Our plans have changed. We've decided you'll be safer away from here. One of Dessia's people is going to take you to the farm where her family lives."

"A farm?" Emer frowned. "Who will protect me there?"

"You won't need protection. O'Bannon won't go searching you out in the countryside. He'll assume you're with Dessia and me, and when he can't find us, he'll give up and go back to Dun Cullan."

"I thought you were going to take me to Ath Cliath." Emer's frown deepened and her voice rose. "You said you'd find me a place as a healer there."

"Plans have changed. We can't leave for Ath Cliath for several days at least, until O'Bannon has given up looking for us. In the meantime, Dessia and I can take shelter in the Forest of Mist, but the wildwood won't let you enter."

"You're lying!" Emer's amber eyes flashed. "You only want to be rid of me! I knew I shouldn't have trusted you! I should never have helped you free that haughty bitch! She's the reason you won't let me go with you!"

Bridei was at his wit's end. He didn't know how to explain things so Emer would be satisfied. Maybe they would have to take her back to the forest so she could see for herself that the dense woodland wouldn't let her pass.

He glanced toward the hall, hoping to see Dessia returning. When he didn't, he decided he would have to seek her out. He led the stallion over the gatetower and secured the reins to a post, then motioned to Emer. "Come on."

"Where are we going?"

"To find Dessia."

Emer set her feet and crossed her arms over her chest. "I'm not going. I'm tired of you always worrying for her. What about your promises to me?"

"Stay here, then." Bridei started walking toward the hall.

Emer hurried to catch up with him. "I don't want to be alone!"

Bridei gritted his teeth. The sooner they were rid of this troublesome woman, the better.

They found Dessia in the kitchen with Aife and Doona. Dessia's and Aife's eyes were red; it was clear they'd been weeping. "Did you tell Aife of our plan?" Bridei asked Dessia.

"Nay. We were discussing other things." Dessia looked at him, her expression resolute. "There's no reason to go back to the forest. We'll stay here and bar the gates. Even if O'Bannon comes with a whole army of warriors, they won't be able to get in."

Bridei shook his head. "They could burn down the wooden gate and get in that way. Or attack from the north where the stone wall is only partially finished. With only five of us, we could never hope to defend this place by ourselves."

"Then we'll go and search out some of my warriors. Now that I'm free, I'm certain they'll overcome their fear and fight for me. It wouldn't take that many men to fend off an attack. "

"We can do that later, after O'Bannon has been here looking for you," Bridei said desperately. "For now, there's only the five of us, and it isn't safe to stay here, or go searching the countryside for your men."

"But what if he takes over the hillfort while we're gone?" Dessia persisted. "Then it will be much more difficult to reclaim."

Bridei drew near to her and stroked her arm soothingly. "I'm afraid we'll have to take that chance. For now, we must concentrate on keeping you safe. If you fall into O'Bannon's hands again, he'll likely kill you."

He watched Dessia's face. She must feel as if she were on the verge of losing everything she'd fought so hard for. While he sympathized with her distress, he wasn't about to relent. "Dessia," he said, "I went to a great deal of trouble to free you. I'm not going to risk losing you again. We have to stay in the forest, at least for a time."

Dessia let out an agonized sigh.

Motioning to Emer, Bridei said, "Aife, this is Emer. She can't stay in the forest with us because the woods won't let her pass. Would you be willing to take her to your family's farm? I'm certain O'Bannon won't pursue her there. Once he sees our tracks leading into the woods, he'll assume she's with us."

Aife shrugged listlessly. "I have nothing better to do."

"I won't go there." Emer raised her small chin stubbornly. "You can't make me."

"Very well." Bridei met her gaze with a determined look of his own. "But since you can't enter the forest, you'll have to stay here. And I'm fairly certain O'Bannon will search this place thoroughly. Those are your choices: You can either go with Aife or you can remain here and hope that O'Bannon doesn't find you."

"That's not fair!" Emer exclaimed. "You're so concerned for Dessia's welfare, but refuse to think of mine."

Bridei gritted his teeth. He was sick to death of arguing with this woman.

Doona spoke, her voice cold. "Dessia is our queen, Emer. The future of our whole tribe depends upon her. I agree with Bridei. She must seek refuge in the forest, at least for now." She looked at Dessia and her voice softened. "Please milady, listen to him. He loves you. His only concern is that no harm comes to you."

Dessia let out another sigh, then she met Bridei's gaze. "You've risked a great deal for me. I owe you a debt for my very life. I will do as you say."

"Come on, Emer," Aife said resignedly. "I'll get my things and we'll set out."

Emer looked as if she were going to argue some more. Then she shot a glance at Doona. Seeing the cook's forbidding look, she said, "Very well, I'll go with Aife. But I won't forget your promise, Bridei. I'll expect you to take me to Ath Cliath find me a place as a healer. If you don't, I'll make certain you pay."

Aife hugged Dessia and Bridei, then left the kitchen. Emer trailed after her.

"We must also leave. I want to get to the forest before dark," said Bridei. "But first, we need supplies. "What's left that you can spare, Doona?"

* * *

As they rode out of Cahermara a short time later, Bridei said, "Don't worry, *cariad*. We'll come back. The gods favor you. They intend for you to rule these lands."

Dessia repressed a sigh, hoping his words were true. It seemed wrong to leave the hillfort behind. And yet, she couldn't help recalling the night O'Bannon had burned the old rath. She hadn't wanted to leave her family, yet she'd known they were beyond hope. The only choice she could make was to save her own life. As she'd trusted the spirit cat to lead her to safety, now she must trust Bridei.

It began to rain. Bridei pulled up the hood of his cloak, and Dessia did the same. Her body felt stiff and wooden. Part of it was her fatigue. But there was also a terrible emptiness inside her, a sense of defeat. As much as she loved Bridei, even his tender concern couldn't banish the ache inside her. Until she reclaimed Cahermara and her kingdom, she feared she'd never feel whole again.

At last the winter bare branches of the Forest of Mist appeared out of the gloom. Bridei headed for the pathway they'd always taken before. Finding it, he dismounted. Dessia did likewise. She waited until she saw him lead the stallion into the woods. The magical realm had accepted him. It seemed a sign she must trust him. As they walked along, rain continued to fall. Dessia's cloak grew sodden and heavy with moisture. Bare gray branches surrounded them, their starkness broken only by gleaming dark patches of rowan and thorn bushes. Dessia had the sense that forest was in mourning for her lost kingdom along with her. As it was winter in her heart, so it was cold and desolate in this place.

They reached the place where the mist usually came, but nothing happened. Farther on, Dessia caught sight of the lake through the trees. Bridei led the stallion down to the water's edge to let the animal drink. Dessia followed with the mare.

"Should we look in the water today?" he asked.

Dessia shook her head. "I'm afraid of what I might see."

Bridei came to her and put his arms around her. "Come, *cariad*. Let's find a dry place to sleep."

Dessia nodded. She was so tired, her head felt as if it was stuffed with unspun wool.

* * *

Bridei gazed up at the overcast sky and wondered why he remained awake. With his cloak spread over the pile of leaves and grass, the make-shift bed wasn't that uncomfortable. Dessia had fallen asleep almost instantly, but slumber eluded him. He felt as if he'd forgotten something, something important.

Disengaging himself from Dessia, he got to his feet. He glanced down at her and felt a lingering anxiety. She looked so pale. He wanted desperately to keep her safe, but how was he to do so? At least here in the forest, she would be protected for a time. But after that . . .

His thoughts made him restless, and he decided to walk down to the lake. Maybe if he looked in the water he'd see something that would reassure him. On the other hand, as Dessia had said, he might see something he didn't want to see.

His heartbeat quickened as approached the water and gazed into the glassy still depths. Although the woods around him remained winter bare, in the lake he saw a forest bedecked in the bright green of summer. It made him think of the tales he'd heard of the magical kingdom beneath the water where the Fair Folk lived. The Irish called the place Tir 'd Og, the land of youth, while in his homeland it was known as Awan. It was said to always be summer there.

As he continued to stare into the water, he heard laughter. A moment later, he saw someone running through the trees in the lake. He could catch quick glimpses of them: Two children—or at least they were the size of children. They both had red hair, and the ruddy hue contrasted strikingly with the green of their surroundings as they raced to and fro among the trees. Who were they? Children of the Fair Folk?

The image faded. Bridei waited for a time, but nothing else appeared. Finally, he made his way back to where Dessia lay and settled himself beside her.

* * *

When next he woke, Dessia was gone. He sat up and called out for her. When she didn't answer, the familiar dread afflicted him. He got to his feet, feeling disoriented. It was still overcast but the light seemed different. His instincts told him it was morning, which meant they'd slept through the whole day and night. Then he heard a strange sound, like someone gagging. He followed the sound and discovered Dessia, bent over, retching. He started toward her, but she waved him away. After a moment, she straightened and wiped her mouth.

"What is it?" he asked.

She shook her head. "It started a couple of days ago. I thought my stomach ailed because I was so distraught about being imprisoned. But now that I'm free, I don't understand why it's still happening."

"You haven't eaten anything in a long while. Perhaps that's why you're ill."

"That's the problem. I've already eaten, but I couldn't keep it down."

Bridei looked at Dessia closely. Had she contracted some illness during her imprisonment? "Have you any other signs of sickness?"

"Nay. Really, Bridei, you must stop worrying for me. And you should eat. Just because my stomach ails doesn't mean you should go hungry."

Still watching her with concern, Bridei went to fetch the food Doona had given them. He unwrapped the bundle and ate one of the bannocks and a little of the cheese. Rewrapping the remainder of the food, he returned it to their pack. While he was doing so, he found the wineskin the cook had also sent with them. He unstoppered the skin and took a few swallows, then carried it over to Dessia, who was washing in the lake. "Feeling better?" he asked her.

She stood and nodded, then took the wineskin from him and drank. Bridei watched her, marveling at every detail of her exquisite face. Her eyes, like shimmering foliage in the bottom of a cool, still pool. The elegant cast of her auburn brows and the curve of her cheek. The rich splendor of her full lips. The faint amber freckles on her nose and cheeks, barely visible now that it was winter. She was wearing a plain green wool gown. It was soiled and rumpled, but still set off the moon cool pallor of her skin and russet hue of her hair. Yet, it concealed her other dazzling charms beneath it.

All at once, he was aroused. It seemed too much to hope for that she would be interested in lovemaking, especially after being sick. But he couldn't help but say, "For the first time in weeks, we're alone, Dessia. Perhaps we should make the most of it."

She looked at him in surprise, but then, to his amazement, her expression turned seductive. "Aye. Perhaps we should," she said. "Although I want to finish washing first."

Feeling almost dazed, Bridei returned to their makeshift bed and began to remove his clothing. He could scarcely believe his good fortune; he was finally alone with Dessia and she wanted him. A short while later, he saw her walking towards him, completely naked. His breath caught. She was so womanly. A goddess. "You're magnificent," he breathed.

Her lips curved enticingly. "I feel the same for you. You're so beautiful."

He laughed. "That's not what you're supposed to say to a man."

"Why not? It's true."

He reached out and traced the line of her cheek with his fingers. "I'm not nearly as beautiful as you are."

She mimicked his motion. "Ah, but you are... at least to me. I've never met a man so handsome."

"You've never left this small corner of Ireland, so you're hardly in a position to judge. I, however, have been to many, many places. So, when I say you are the most comely woman I've ever seen, it truly means something."

"You don't think I'm too tall? Too muscular and long-limbed for a woman? What about my awful freckles? And my red hair? Emer said it meant I was cursed."

He put his hands on her glorious full breasts and began to make slow circles around her nipples. "Perhaps some men might find you intimidating. But, to me, you look exactly as a queen should look. You've had to fight in battles and endure hardship to become who you are. You couldn't have done that if you were some frail, dainty maid." She gave a soft of moan of pleasure as he continued, "I find your freckles enchanting. As for your red hair... I think that's what makes you so fiery and passionate in bed. I'm hardly going to complain about such an attribute."

Dessia closed her eyes and gave into the delicious sensations Bridei's touch aroused. It was remarkable how much her mood had changed since the day before. When she'd come to this place, she'd felt despairing and empty. Sleeping for so long had restored her. Or perhaps the enchantment of the woods had banished her misery. Her resentment of Bridei had also faded, and as soon as her stomach had settled, she'd found herself suddenly eager for lovemaking.

Mmmmm. His fingers were magic. No wonder he could play the harp so skillfully. She half-smiled to herself as he continued to stroke her breasts. They felt heavy and throbbing. Incredibly sensitive. Her nipples were taut, aching peaks. She needed... wanted... He seemed to have guessed her thoughts, for the next moment he replaced his beguiling fingers with his mouth. He suckled her, his lips and tongue inflaming, teasing. She could hardly remain still. Arching her back, she offered herself to him. Wanting more... more... .

He switched to her other breast, his hand gently cupping her flesh, while his mouth sucked greedily. She felt as if he dragged her toward some precipice, and she half feared going over it and being utterly lost. But she also wanted, yearned for the release. The tension built inside her, squeezing deep in the core of her body. At last she surrendered, crying out. She seemed to dissolve. Her being shook with ecstasy. She was blind with sensation. Drowning in dazzling, shimmering, molten... fire.

Her whole body felt limp and boneless. Her knees, weak. Vaguely, she was aware of Bridei picking her up and carrying her. By the time she thought to protest that she was too heavy, he'd reached the bed he'd made and gently lay her down. She gazed up at him in wonder. "That was ..." she shook her head, overwhelmed.

He smiled down at her, his violet blue eyes glistening. "Aye. It was."

All he'd done was touch and mouth her breasts and yet somehow he'd made her reach her peak. As she recalled how she'd lost control, she felt vaguely embarrassed. She'd let him do everything for her and hadn't even thought about him. She sat up. "That was selfish of me. To let you pleasure me like that and give no thought to your own satisfaction."

"You think *that* didn't satisfy me?" He gazed at her, eyebrows raised. "I enjoyed every moment of it. I've never had a woman so responsive. So passionate. You were breathtaking."

"But what of your own..." She knew it was important for a man to spill his seed. Indeed, she had overheard men complain how uncomfortable it was if they didn't get release.

He laughed. "I'm in no hurry. That's the disadvantage of being male. A man can only peak once, at least within a certain time." He grinned at her. "It's quite unfair. As a woman, you can make love all night and peak over and over again. I must rest each time."

She gazed at him skeptically. "I couldn't do that all night long. 'Twas too intense. Too overwhelming."

"Does that mean you wish to sleep for awhile?"

"That would hardly be fair of me. To allow you to pleasure me, and leave you dissatisfied."

"I'm not dissatisfied. I told you how much I enjoyed it."

"Aye. But I can see you're still aroused."

Feeling her gaze on his groin, Bridei stood up. He'd intended to be the most considerate of lovers and let her rest. But if she were going to stare at his cock like that... "If you're going to rest, you must do so now." He grimaced as his voice came out harsher than he intended. Then he saw the bold, teasing look on her face and knew she did indeed understand what he was going through.

"I could rest," she said. "Or I could do things to you."

"What sort of things?" His voice was choked; his breathing harsh.

"I could touch you. May I?"

He nodded, wondering if he'd be able to bear it. Only a green boy spilled his seed at the mere touch of woman. But right now, he had about that much control.

She stood up facing him and began caressing his face, delicately tracing the shape of his mouth and then his jaw line. His heart thudding heavily as he watched her. Her expression was so intent. Her eyes, a smoky, mysterious green.

"Your mother must be beautiful," she said.

He gave a strangled laugh. "Why are you discussing my mother? Do you seek to take the edge off my lust?"

"Nay. I was thinking that your beauty must come from your mother."

"I suppose. Although she's hardly my concern at this moment."

"What is your concern?"

My hard, throbbing cock. That's all of can think of. I want you to touch it. But I can wait. I will wait.

When he didn't answer her, she began to fondle and stroke his neck, and then ran her hands down his chest. He took deep, even breaths, trying to ease the nearly unbearable tension building in his groin.

"Are you enjoying this?" he murmured.

"Oh, aye," she answered as she glided her fingers along his ribs and then down his back. "From the first time I saw you, I've wanted to do this."

"Truly?"

She nodded. "You're the first man I've ever wanted to touch. The first man to make me understand why a man might want to... do things to a woman."

"Ah..." He let out a groan, then regained control. "What sort of things do you want to do to me?"

"This." She drew close to him and slid her hands down to his buttocks, stroking and squeezing him there, cupping his flesh in her long, elegant fingers.

"By the gods," he gasped.

"Every part of you is fascinating to me. I've never had a chance to do this with a man before."

"Hmmm." He could no longer speak. The sheer eroticism of her touch was driving him to madness.

"You're so different than me. Your body is much harder than mine. And hairier."

"Aye, I am harder," he ground out. "Especially in one certain area."

"Oh." She widened her eyes in mock innocence. "I can't think what you mean."

He could take no more. Grabbing her tormenting, teasing fingers, he placed them on his cock. "Here. This is where I'm especially hard."

"Aye." Her voice was a husky whisper. "You're like a steel blade, but overlaid with soft, silky flesh."

Her touch was much too gentle. He felt he would burst apart at any moment. He pulled her hand away.

"What's wrong?" she asked, looking confused.

"Someday I'll teach how to pleasure me like that. But at this moment, all your caressing and fondling makes me want only one thing—to be sheathed in your sweet, silken flesh."

She nodded. "Aye. It makes me want that, too."

"I warn you, I doubt I can be gentle. I'm too aroused."

"I don't want you to be gentle."

Looking into her eyes, he believed her. She was no fragile, delicate maid, but a strong, capable warrior woman. Even so, he wanted to make certain she was ready.

She lay down on the makeshift bed. He knelt near her feet, then grasped her thighs and slid them apart. Eyes closed, she gave a soft moan of anticipation. Leaning down, he placed his mouth on the delicate petal-like flesh of her womanhood. She gave a shriek of delight. He held her thighs and suckled and kissed and licked until she was moaning wildly. Then he raised himself over her and thrust deep.

She'd thought she could feel no more pleasure than what he'd given her earlier. But this time her peak came in deep, heaving waves, submerging her in a torrent of vivid, blinding sensation. Yet even as she slowly glided down, he thrust deeper and her body responded, the delicious tension building once again. Higher and higher she soared until she crashed in a glorious, swirling, starlit release.

Chapter 22

Bridei reached his peak, his body exploding with vivid, overwhelming sensation. He collapsed on Dessia and buried his face in the heavy silk of her hair. A few moments later, as he raised himself off of her, he realized they were surrounded by vivid green vegetation. "Dessia. Look," he whispered.

She opened her eyes and gazed up at him with a lazy smile. Then she looked around and realized what had happened. "How . . .?" She sat up, appearing as stunned as he was. Then she burst out laughing. "I knew your lovemaking was magical, but I never dreamed you could do this."

"'Twas not me," he said. "It must be the Goddess."

She stroked his hair, her eyes glowing. "You're like Belenos, god of sun and fire. With your passion, you've brought summer to this place."

"I don't know how it happened, but I wish to thank whatever force or being transformed this place." He lay back down again, and Dessia nestled against his chest. The lassitude of utter satisfaction crept over him.

He fell asleep and dreamed of summer. The sun was high in the sky, the air warm and fragrant with growing things. After a time, he woke and realized it was night. He found Dessia's cloak and draped it over them. When he woke again, it was growing light. He stood and stretched, then went off to relieve himself.

Dessia was still asleep when he returned. He'd covered her up to keep her warm, but as she'd slept, the cloak had fallen away. The sight of her nakedness aroused him, and he wondered whether he could coax her into making love again. He sprawled down beside her and began to play with her breasts. As he fondled one of her nipples, he noticed her breasts seemed more voluptuous than he remembered, the nipples a deeper rose. Perhaps it was this place, he mused. As the landscape ripened into the abundance of summer, perhaps it had affected them as well, heightening his virility and her womanliness. His hand stilled as he had another thought. Perhaps the change in Dessia appearance wasn't caused by magic, but by something simpler and more mundane. What if she were pregnant?

He gazed at her, his thoughts racing. Everything fit together: her ailing stomach, her fatigue, her fuller breasts. Even her amazing responsiveness.

Dessia stirred and opened her eyes. "Hmmm. I had such a beautiful dream." She reached out, grasped his hand and brought it to her breast. "Keep touching me," she said.

Bridei's arousal, so intense a few moments before, had ebbed. Dessia must have sensed something was wrong for she let go of his hand and said, "I guess that was part of my dream."

"Nay. It wasn't a dream... it's merely that..." He must find out if his suspicions were true. Touching her hair, he said, "Dessia. I must ask you something. Have you had your courses since the night we lay together?"

"My courses?" She shook her head. "I was worried they'd come when I was imprisoned, and I dreaded having to ask Druim for some cloths. But nothing happened, and I decided my distress had kept me from bleeding."

"Before we made love—how long had it been since your last one?"

Dessia shrugged. "I don't know. Perhaps a fortnight or a little less."

Bridei felt breathless. A wise woman had once told him that if he wished to avoid impregnating a woman, he should be careful to only sleep with her while she was having her courses, or the first few days afterwards. By the time a week had passed, the likelihood she would conceive became substantial.

"What's wrong?" Dessia asked. "Why are you looking at me like that?"

He took a deep breath, wondering if saying it aloud would make it more real. "It's early yet. But even so, I'm fairly certain you're pregnant."

She stared at him. "Why do you think this?"

"You have all the signs."

"What do you mean?"

"Your ailing belly." Bridei gestured. "Your breasts seem fuller, and I suspect they're tender as well. Perhaps that's even why they're so sensitive."

Her eyes widened, then she grabbed her gown, stood and pulled it over her head. She began to pace beside him. "Oh! How could I be such a fool? I never thought..."

He got to his feet and took her arm. "I'm sorry, Dessia. It's my fault. There are ways to prevent pregnancy. I failed to use any of them."

She looked at him glumly. "What do you mean? What could we have done?"

"I usually carry sheathes made from animal gut, but they're back in Britain with my harp and other possessions. And there's another simpler method. A man can withdraw before he reaches his peak and thus avoid spilling his seed inside the woman. That's what I should have done with you, but..." He smiled ruefully. "I was far too carried away to think of such things."

"We both were. But... oh, my... I never thought... never even considered this." She drew away and began to pace again.

His heart went out to her. Motherhood altered any woman's life. But for a queen, especially one facing her current situation, it must seem overwhelming.

"I'm sorry," he said again. "I had the knowledge to prevent this and I failed to use it."

Her voice was anguished. "You can't take all the blame. I know how babes are conceived. 'Twas witless of me to not consider the possibility."

"But you were a virgin and unused to worrying about such things. As experienced as I am, I should have known better."

She stopped pacing and looked at him, her expression uncertain. "Do you regret it so much?"

He hesitated a moment, then caught her hand, brought it to his lips and kissed her fingers. "If I'm to have a child, you're the woman I would wish to be its mother. I didn't plan this, but I can't truly regret it either."

She nodded, her eyes a misty green. "I feel the same, but...oh..." Her expression turned anxious again. He knew exactly what she was thinking. The idea that she was carrying his child filled him with wonder and excitement, but also, terror. He hardly knew how he was going to protect *her*, let alone a child. "It does complicate things," he agreed. "Even before this happened, I worried for you. But now..." He gave her a weak smile. "Now I'm paralyzed with dread for you."

Seeing the dazed expression on Bridei's face, Dessia wanted to tell him that this changed nothing, that she could still do everything she always had. But she knew it wasn't true. She was now responsible for another life besides her own. The idea stunned her.

Bridei pulled her into his arms. "Don't worry. I'll find a way to keep you safe." His tender concern touched her, yet failed to ease her anxiety. She hadn't felt this vulnerable and afraid since she was a child. He stroked her hair. "There's no other solution. We'll have to go somewhere else, at least until you have the babe."

"Where? Ath Cliath?"

"It would be far too easy for O'Bannon to pursue us there. Nay, I think we must travel to a place where he couldn't follow, even if he wished to do so."

"Where are you thinking of?"

"We'll hire a boat in Ath Cliath to take us to my father's household in Gwynedd."

Dessia drew away from him. "But I thought... you've always spoken so coldly of your father. Are you certain we'd be welcome there?"

The familiar haunted look darkened his features. "*I* may not be welcome there, but he won't turn *you* away. Even if he should wish to do so, my mother wouldn't let him."

He took her hands in his. "You'll be safe there, I promise. My mother is skilled in the healing arts and knows all about having babies. And no one will attack my father's fortress, I can assure you of that."

"But what about Cahermara? What about my people? I can't abandon them!" As the implications of what he suggested sank in, she felt a growing anguish. She'd fought so hard, struggled for so long and come so close to realizing her dream. Now it was all crumbling before her eyes.

"There's no reason you couldn't come back here someday and reclaim your kingdom."

"How long is 'someday'? How long do you think my people will wait for me? They've left Cahermara and scattered to the hills. Even if I began tomorrow to try and coax them back, it would be difficult. But if I wait..." she hesitated. "We're probably talking at least a year, and likely longer. By then they'll have forgotten me."

"I don't believe that. They rallied behind you all those years ago, when you were still a child. Now you're a woman grown and a proven warrior. They won't forget you. I don't believe that for a moment."

Dessia looked down at her body. Except for her slightly swollen breasts, she looked no different. Her stomach was still flat. Her muscles strong. It would be months before it was obvious she was pregnant, and even longer before she grew so big and ungainly that she couldn't fight. "Nay," she said, "I won't go to Gwynedd. Not yet. I still have some time to gather together my people and make a stand against O'Bannon."

"It's not safe. What if O'Bannon captures you and discovers you're pregnant? He'll kill you and our child."

Dessia raised her chin stubbornly. "Then he mustn't capture me. I have to succeed in this. If I don't, I won't want to live anyway."

"And what of our child? Do you think you have the right to choose whether it lives or dies?"

He looked angry, which she wasn't used to. A flare of resentment rose inside her. She faced him stubbornly. "For now, the babe is part of my body and couldn't survive without me. That gives me the right to make decisions regarding its future."

His eyes flashed. "It's my child as well as yours. I won't let you throw its life away!"

"You think that's what I'm doing? You have so little faith in me that you're convinced I'm doomed to failure?" As her anger and frustration increased, she suddenly felt dizzy and nauseated. She moved away from him, leaned over and began to retch.

There was nothing in her stomach to bring up. She finally straightened and wiped her mouth. Her eyes filled with tears. How could she have let this happen? She'd given in to one night of passion. Now all her dreams were shattered. She felt the tears course down her cheeks.

Bridei touched her shoulder. "You should eat something. I'll fetch the food."

She turned to look at him. How did he always seem to know what she needed? "Have you ever been in this situation before?" she asked.

He raised his brows. "You mean..." His gaze went to her belly.

She nodded.

"I've never gotten a woman with child before, at least not that I know of. But I have five younger brothers and sisters, and in addition to my mother, I've been around a number of pregnant women in my life." He grinned. "I've even bedded a few."

"You mean... they were carrying other man's child, and you...?"

He shrugged. "Sometimes the father wasn't around. Other times... well, some men are put off by the changes in a woman's body."

"But it doesn't bother you?"

"Nay."

She sighed. "I suppose that's good. At least I know you'll still want to bed me."

"Aye. Indeed, when you are feeling better..." He let his voice trail off.

He'd never put his trews back on, and she could see he was aroused. A half dozen emotions washed over her: Desire. Need. Longing. She also felt helpless. And resentful and angry that he could make her feel like this. But her strongest emotion was contempt of herself for being so weak. If Bridei wasn't so blindingly handsome, she would never have given in and found herself in this predicament. Despair overwhelmed her, banishing every other feeling.

Seeing the look on her face, Bridei's arousal vanished. She blamed him. He could see it in her eyes. His dismay was replaced by anger. He wasn't pleased about their situation either. But he'd put aside his own feelings to reassure her. To let her know he loved her and would do whatever he could to protect her and the baby. He was even willing to take her back to his homeland and face his father's hostility and disdain in order to keep her safe. But all she could think of was that he'd robbed her of her dream.

He inhaled slowly, thinking what a lackwit he'd been. He'd broken all his own rules and let her get close to him. Let her steal his heart. He'd done everything he could for her, including saving her from O'Bannon. And she responded like *this*. By the gods... the expression on her face.... It was obvious she loathed him.

His insides seemed to grow cold. He'd wondered if bedding a queen would be different than it was with other women. Now he knew. A queen's heart belonged to her land and her people. No matter what he did, Dessia would never love him the way he loved her.

He fought to recover his composure. It wasn't the end of the world if she didn't love him. It really changed nothing. He would still do whatever he could to protect her... and his child. Even if she were willing to throw her own life away, he wasn't going to let her risk the life of the babe she carried.

Looking at Dessia, he felt miserable. Then he remembered the babe and set his jaw. This time he wasn't going to run away from trouble, but face it squarely and do what needed to be done... no matter what it cost him.

* * *

Dessia sat on her cloak beside the lake and stared morosely at the still, glassy water. Always before she'd thought of the Forest of Mist as a place of refuge. Now it felt little different than the underground cell where O'Bannon had imprisoned her. This time, it was Bridei who stood guard. He might claim to know all about pregnant women, but his attitude toward her was infuriating. Treating her like some frail, fragile thing! She wasn't allowed to search out berries and nuts to supplement their food supply, but had to wait for him to fetch them for her. He also insisted she eat several times a day. When that didn't help her nausea and she went off into the trees to be sick, he insisted on coming with her. Then when she was finished being ill, he would lead her back to the bed of grass and bracken and have her lie down.

His attitude toward her was endlessly patient and considerate, and it was driving her to madness. She didn't want him to tenderly stroke her back and wipe her brow; she wanted him to kiss her passionately and make love to her. Was he so repulsed by her condition that he no longer desired her? Or, was it something else? Beneath his solicitousness she sensed simmering anger and stubborn determination. The change in him worried her. But not as much as the change in herself. She was so tired; she wanted to sleep all the time. It drove her to madness. Instead of hiding here in the Forest of Mist, she should be rounding up her warriors so they could make a stand at Cahermara!

But Bridei would never consider such a thing, and the sad truth was that most of the time she didn't have the energy to argue with him, let alone act upon her desire to do something to regain her lands. What was happening to her? How could the tiny babe growing inside her have changed her so much? She touched her belly thoughtfully. There was no way to tell a babe was growing there; she couldn't even feel it yet. Bridei had explained that the quickening—when she felt the babe move—wouldn't happen for a couple more months. That gave her some time, although it was rapidly slipping away. She needed to get started in gathering together her warriors.

Filled with sudden resolve, she got to her feet. She wasn't going to argue with Bridei about leaving the forest. Nay, she was simply going to do it. Now, while he was away.

She found her cloak, then fetched the bridle from the branch where Bridei had hung it. The mare was grazing by the lake. Dessia approached her cautiously and was relieved when the horse allowed her to put on the bridle. She led the mare over to a fallen tree and climbed on the animal's back. The familiar nausea assaulted her, and she wondered if she should take some food from their store. But that would take time, and she needed to get away before Bridei returned.

She shook off the weakness and rode in the opposite direction from the one Bridei had taken to go foraging for food. As she recalled, this pathway led to edge of the forest that was farthest from Cahermara. If

O'Bannon were waiting for her, he would likely be on the other side of the woodland.

Despite this, she knew a growing dread as she guided the horse along the pathway. Once she left the protection of the forest, she would be very vulnerable. She didn't even have a dagger or eating knife to defend herself.

As she rode along, she debated what she should do first. Return to Cahermara and try to find a weapon? Or set off for Comlyn's farm? He lived fairly close to the northern edge of the Forest of Mist, and he'd always been one of her staunchest supporters. He would help her, she knew it. And it would be safer to go to him than back to the hillfort, where she might encounter O'Bannon and his men.

Having made up her mind, Dessia urged the horse faster. As she rode along, she thought about what she would say if she encountered Bridei. She would tell him she'd grown restless. Or, perhaps explain that she trying to get used to riding so it wouldn't be so difficult for her when they set out for Ath Cliath.

At the thought, she set her jaw. She wasn't going to Ath Cliath; she was staying here, where she belonged.

* * *

Dessia drew the mare to halt and looked around, puzzled. Could she have taken the wrong path? The Forest of Mist wasn't that big; by now she should be clear of the trees. What was happening? It almost seemed as if the forest didn't want her to leave.

Frustrated, she turned the horse and started back the way she'd come. In no time at all, she found herself at the lake. *Nay,* she thought, *I won't give up.* Clucking her tongue, she guided the horse in the other direction.

* * *

Bridei hurried down the forest pathway, worrying that he'd been away from Dessia too long. He couldn't explain what he feared would happen to her. But ever since he'd found out she carried his child, he'd spent most of his time sick with worry.

Finally, he reached the lake and saw Dessia crouched down by the water, gazing into it intently. "What do you see?" he asked as he drew near. When she didn't look up or answer him, he said, "Dessia?"

She got to her feet, her mouth set in a grim line. "Nothing. I saw nothing. I've been staring at the water for what seems like hours and no vision appeared." She made an angry gesture. "You look. This place seems to favor you."

Bridei approached the water and crouched down. As he stared into the dark depths, his muscles tightened with dread. Although he wasn't much concerned about his own future, he didn't think he would be able to bear it if he saw a vision suggesting something was going to happen to Dessia or the babe.

He looked and looked, straining until his eyes watered. Nothing happened. Not even a ripple disturbed the mirror-like surface of the lake. He stood up, uncertain whether he felt relief or distress. It was probably best if he didn't know the future. But doubts still gnawed at him. Was he doing the right thing in taking Dessia away from here?

"What did you see?" Dessia asked impatiently.

He turned to look at her. What if he told her he'd had a vision of O'Bannon and his men taking control Cahermara? Would she finally give up this foolish plan of hers? Nay, he couldn't lie. Doing such a thing might anger the Goddess. And without the Great Queen Rhiannon's aid, he felt certain he'd never get Dessia to safety.

"It was the same as for you. I saw nothing."

The magic hadn't worked for him either, Dessia thought with relief. She'd been very afraid the lake would reveal something to Bridei, after denying her. Then she would feel even more miserable. As it was, she felt utterly despairing. She'd had the perfect opportunity to get away and start gathering together her warriors, but the forest had refused to let her leave. Every path she took seemed to go in circles. She'd tried three different routes and always ended up back at the lake. But she wasn't going to give up. The next day, when Bridei went looking for food, she would try again.

She suddenly realized Bridei was loaded down with bundles. "Where did you get those things?" she asked.

"Cahermara."

She was startled. "You went to back to Cahermara? I thought you said it wasn't safe to leave the forest."

He put down his bundles. From one of the smaller ones, he drew out a bannock and handed it to her. Her mouth watered as she inhaled the delicious scent. The wheatcake was freshly made. "From Doona?" she asked.

"Aye." His voice changed, becoming gentle. "I thought we needed some supplies. We must leave for Ath Cliath. Now, while O'Bannon isn't around."

Nay! Dessia wanted to shout. *I'm not going! I won't forsake my duty here!* But in her heart, she knew she had no choice. She looked away from him, trying to hide her resentment. If only she hadn't given in and made love with him. Yet, it wasn't fair to blame him. She'd been as out of control as he was. Tears filled her eyes. Why couldn't she be a normal woman and give into her desires without losing everything?

Shaking off the mood, she asked, "When will we leave?"

"As soon as you've eaten."

She nodded glumly and took a bite of the bannock.

Chapter 23

Bridei glanced at Dessia riding beside him and wondered if it would be like this all the way to Ath Cliath. If they would ride along silently, as distant from each other as if one of them was on the other side of the Irish Sea. The bitterness rose up inside him, reminding him that he'd finally fallen in love, but it was with a woman who would never love him back. It didn't matter, he told himself. What was done was done and he must see it through. He would get to Dessia to safety, even if it cost him every shred of her regard.

* * *

She couldn't bear this, Dessia thought with a stab of anguish as they rode along. It was bad enough that she was leaving behind everything she'd worked so hard for. But to feel Bridei's anger, his coldness, was equally wrenching. She knew she'd hurt him. He felt she cared more for her kingdom and her goals than she did for him and their babe. But it wasn't true. If it were, she'd have found a way to stay at Cahermara.

She knew she must heed the clear message the forest had given her. She was meant to stay with Bridei. Her destiny was with him. But, oh, it was horrible to leave her home. She felt as if her heart had been torn out. How was she to endure it?

They'd been traveling for two days already. When they stopped, she was so weary, she fell into an exhausted sleep immediately after eating. Although Bridei lay near her, wrapped in his cloak, Dessia could feel the distance between them. In the morning, they set out as soon as they'd broken their fast.

She repressed a sigh. Bridei had said it would take them many days to ride to Ath Cliath. She couldn't stand this grim silence the whole way. While she wasn't yet willing to speak of the rift between them, she must at least get him to converse with her. Perhaps she could ask him to tell her a story. He'd mentioned the long tale of Arthur ap Uther he'd told at O'Bannon's settlement while he waited for an opportunity to free her. If he'd been able to fill up several nights with the tale, it would go a long way towards passing the time on this journey.

She cleared her throat and said, "You've mentioned King Arthur several times. I'd like to know more about him."

Bridei looked at her in surprise. Then he nodded and began.

Although Dessia had come upon this idea out of sheer desperation, as he told the story, she found herself caught up in it. Unlike most *filidh* she'd heard, Bridei didn't simply give dry accounts of alliances and battles. Instead, he made Arthur come alive, and seem as real to her as if she'd truly met the man.

He began with Arthur's remarkable birth, and all the elements of lust, destiny and magic, which were a part of it. After describing Arthur's childhood, Bridei told about how Arthur came up with the plan of bringing the warring British tribes together to fight the Saxons. Dessia felt a surge of empathy for Arthur. He'd loved his homeland fiercely and done everything in his power to protect it against the invaders. But when Bridei related how Arthur had sought to convince chieftains who'd been enemies for generations that they should become allies in the war against the invaders, her enthusiasm for Arthur began to wane. That would be like asking her to put aside her differences with Tiernan O'Bannon and fight beside him. Her whole being rebelled at the thought. Even losing her lands seemed better than that!

Her distress over this part of the tale distracted her, and it wasn't until some time later that she really began to pay attention again. Now Bridei was explaining how Arthur had wed a northern chieftain's daughter because she brought him a dowry of warriors. But what started out as a marriage of convenience had eventually become a lovematch, Bridei added. The only thing marring it was that the woman, called Guinevere, was apparently barren. It was a great blow to Arthur that he couldn't sire an heir, but he refused to blame Guinevere. There were even tales he suggested she lie with one of his warriors and try to beget a child, a child who he would claim as his own son.

This part of the tale shocked Dessia. She couldn't imagine a man deliberately asking the woman she loved to lie with another man. Nor could she imagine any man claiming a child he knew wasn't his own. She couldn't help blurting out, "Why would Arthur do such a thing? It makes no sense."

"It made sense to Arthur," Bridei answered. "For you see, he cared more for his goal of preserving Britain than he did for his own pride. He felt if Guinevere had a son he could claim as his heir, it would give his people hope for the future and keep his dream alive."

"A son?" said Dessia. "What if Guinevere gave birth to a daughter?"

"Although I have no doubt Arthur would have loved her well, a girl child would never have served his plans. The British tribes aren't like those here in Ireland. They would never have accepted a woman as a leader."

"Why not?"

"It's the influence of the Romans, I suppose. Before they came to Britain, there was a tradition of powerful queens. Indeed, a woman named Boudica once led a huge army against the Romans. But after the Romans came to power, women ceased to train as warriors, and because of that, they were no longer seen as viable leaders."

His words outraged Dessia, but she realized Bridei wasn't describing his own feelings, but those of his countrymen. She had to admit Bridei had never exhibited anything but admiration for her abilities. She said, "The idea that a woman can't rule as well as a man is absurd. But I have to wonder why you don't share the belief. I've never felt you considered me unfit as a leader. *At least until now, when I am pregnant with your child,* she added in her thoughts.

"I suppose it doesn't bother me because I have no aspirations to possess that kind of power for myself," answered Bridei. "I'm content to be a bard and let others—male or female—fight the wars. Yet, I like to think that as a performer and storyteller I have a kind of power in my own right. I'm able to influence the men who make the decisions and wield the weapons—not always, but sometimes."

Aye, you have influenced me, Dessia thought. *You've stolen my heart away.*

A tremor of emotion went through her as she considered the truth of this. What she felt for Bridei was too powerful to be denied. She'd sought to hate him, but always failed.

Bridei continued the tale, saying, "The story grows sad now. For unbeknownst to Arthur, he had an heir all along. When he was very young and living at the court of Uther, he became close with a young woman named Morguese. Arthur knew she was kin of Uther, although he didn't realize she was his daughter. Nor did he know, at that time, that Uther was his father.

"Some people say that Morguese knew Arthur was her half-brother and she deliberately seduced him so she would have a hold over the future high king. I don't believe that. I know Morguese, indeed I once knew her quite well. It's true she's manipulative and calculating, but I think that came later, when she was married off to much older man and sent away to the far north. When she and Arthur knew each other—and loved each other—I think her affection for him was genuine. And innocent. They were drawn to each other because they shared similar traits from their sire. Like Uther, they were both passionate and driven. Arthur's passion led him to greatness; Morgeuse's to despair.

"Perhaps that was because she was a woman and, therefore, could have no say in her destiny. Perhaps that's what turned Morgeuse against Arthur," he continued. "At any rate, she channeled all her frustrated ambition into the son she bore him, named Mordred. All that attention seemed to warp Mordred, made him shortsighted and foolish, yet cunning. But Arthur made mistakes as well. He never recognized Mordred's abilities, nor gave the youth the love he craved. And so, the son who Arthur so longed for became the instrument of his death."

"What?" Dessia found herself exclaiming. "I thought you said Arthur died in a battle with the Saxons."

"He did. But it was Mordred's hand that slew him. For Mordred had chosen to fight on the side of the enemy. It was a great humiliation to Arthur. He could win thousands to his cause, but couldn't convince his own son to fight at his side."

"That's outrageous!" exclaimed Dessia. This twist of the tale struck her as very far-fetched. And yet, the rest of it had the distinctive ring of truth.

"Sons and fathers don't always see eye-to-eye." Bridei responded, a hint of wryness in his tone. "I'm living proof of that."

Dessia recalled all he'd told her about his father, the great Dragon of the Island. There was much bitterness there. And yet, despite his estrangement from his sire, Bridei was willing to return home, because he believed she would be safe and cared for there. Thinking of it, Dessia's anger weakened further. Bridei was willing to sacrifice a great deal for her sake. He'd already risked his life on her behalf. And he'd done so before he'd known she was carrying his child. It was unfair of her to think of him as selfish and uncaring. To blame him for her losing control over her lands. That was O'Bannon's doing.

All at once, she felt a deep urge to have Bridei hold her in his arms. To soothe her and love her and call her *cariad*. But, she didn't think he was ready for that. Some of the things she'd said to him had hurt him deeply. She must give him time to heal. He also needed to feel they were safe from O'Bannon. Although they'd left her enemy's territory far behind, she knew Bridei worried their enemy would follow them. Perhaps when they reached Ath Cliath, Bridei would relax and she would have an opportunity to tell him what he meant to her.

* * *

Bridei pulled the stallion to a halt and inhaled deeply. "I can smell the sea. We must be close to Ath Cliath." He glanced over at Dessia. She appeared deep in thought, as she'd been on much of the journey. He wondered what she was thinking, if her anger over leaving Cahermara had begun to ease. His own bitterness had certainly ebbed. Although he might regret falling in love, there was nothing he could do to change it. He cared for Dessia and the babe she carried more than he did for his own life, and that was the way it was.

Gradually, the oak and elm forest they were riding through thinned, and they could see a river ahead. Observing dozens of buildings on their side of the water and many more across the waterway, Bridei's heartbeat quickened. This was surely Ath Cliath. Now all they had to do was find someone to take them across the Irish Sea and Dessia would finally be safe.

"How many people live in Ath Cliath?" Dessia asked as they approached.

"I would guess several hundred," he answered.

"So many." She shook her head. He could tell she was amazed. For someone who'd never visited any sort of large settlement, it must seem overwhelming.

"Not all these buildings are dwellings," he told her. "Some of them are probably workshops where they make jewelry, metalware and other valuable items. Or storehouses, where they store trade goods. And up there..." He pointed to the timber-walled palisade built on a hill above the river. "That must be the fortress of the chieftain who rules this place."

They rode near a group of roundhouses and a man came out of one of the dwellings and hurried toward them. He was bowlegged, with thinning brown hair. "Welcome," the man called. "I'm certain you're hungry and thirsty after your journey. My wife, Catrina, was just cooking some oatcakes. Let me see to your horses, while you go inside and eat." He gestured to the roundhouse.

Something about the man's enthusiastic welcome made Bridei uncomfortable. "Thank you for your offer," he said, "but we want to cross the river before we stop." Bridei nodded to the man, then turned the stallion toward the ford.

"It won't be low tide until tomorrow," the man called. "You might as well eat while you're waiting."

"Why didn't you stop? asked Dessia when they'd traveled a little farther.

"All I have to pay for the food is gold, and I don't think oatcakes are worth that much."

Dessia gave him a surprised look. "Gold? Where did you get gold?"

Bridei wondered if she would be angry at him for cutting up the torc. Surely she would see he'd had no choice. He met her gaze. "I thought I might need some wealth to bribe someone at Dun Cullan to help me in freeing you. When I mentioned this to Aife, she told me about a stash of valuables buried near the wall at Cahermara. We found it and dug it up. I cut up one of the torcs and had Aife sew the pieces into my tunic."

"The treasure," said Dessia. "What did you do with the rest of it?"

"We reburied it," he added. "The gold from the one torc should be enough to buy us passage across the sea several times over. All the pieces in the cache were enormous. I can't imagine anyone actually wearing them. Do you know where the treasure came from? Who made it?"

"As I recall, one of my father's bondsmen uncovered the box when he was plowing on his farm," Dessia said thoughtfully. "This was long ago, well before I was born. The man gave the treasure to my father, and he buried it near the wall of the old hillfort. There were stories that the things must have come from the Tuatha de Danann, that they were fairy gold. I think that's why my father reburied it. He thought keeping it inside the hillfort would bring us favor with the ancient race. After O'Bannon's attack, I wondered if perhaps my family's bad fortune meant the Tuatha de Danann were angry. But over time, as things improved, I forgot about the cache. Yet, I must have mentioned it to Aife at some point."

"Aye. She remembered it. But she didn't know it was reputed to be fairy gold. If she had, she'd never have told me where to find it. When we dug it up and saw how huge and strange the pieces were, Aife insisted they must belong to the Tuatha de Danann. She was afraid we'd be cursed if we didn't put things back. But at the time, I was so concerned about how I would free you I couldn't worry about fairy curses."

"Don't you believe in such things?" Dessia asked.

Bridei shook his head. "I believe in the forces of the land and the gods that control such things. But as for a magical fairy race ... it seems very unlikely to me. Still, I don't understand who could have made such things. The pieces are too large to be worn by normal people. Perhaps they were made by the Firbolgs, the race of giants that used to live in Ireland."

"You believe in giants, then?" Dessia asked playfully. "But not fairies?"

Bridei shrugged. "I suppose so. There are men, like my father and brother Rhun, who are uncommonly tall. Maybe there was a whole race like that at one time. But enough talk of magical beings. We need to cross the river."

They reached the ford. While the man they'd met had insisted the tide was rising, it was actually going out, revealing the latticework of wood that had been laid across the river to facilitate crossing. Bridei could see why this place was called Ath Cliath, "ford of hurdles."

"We'll have to dismount and walk across," he said. "Our horses aren't going to be comfortable walking on such an uneven surface. Besides, their weight might damage the latticework."

They waited until the tide had ebbed some more, then dismounted and started across. Reaching the other side, they led the horses down the pathway along the river. A woman came toward them with a toddler on one hip and a pottery jar in her other hand. Bridei nodded to her. "Greetings, milady. We're travelers. Can you tell me what chieftain or king rules this place?"

"His name is Conla."

"Does he live in the rath above the river?" asked Bridei.

"Aye."

"And is he there now?"

"Aye."

"What about a place to keep our horses?"

"There's a stable that direction."

"Thank you," said Bridei.

"She didn't ask your name or where you were from," Dessia said as soon as they were out of earshot of the woman.

"I'm sure they're used to travelers around here. They probably think nothing of it."

"That seems so odd. To meet someone and not even exchange names or mention what tribe you're from," mused Dessia.

"Aye. I suppose it does to you. But in trading settlements, your name and what tribe you come from is usually much less important than how much wealth you carry with you."

"Are you going to use the gold to pay for our stay?" asked Dessia.

"Not if I can help it," responded Bridei. "My plan is to go to the king and offer to perform for him in exchange for lodging for a night. But first, we must get the horses settled."

"I hate to leave them." Dessia reached to stroke the mare's neck. "Their coloring makes me think they might even be of the bloodline of the horses O'Bannon stole from my father."

"Unfortunately, we can't take them with us across the sea," said Bridei. "Although it's possible we could arrange to come back for them."

"You think we could do that?" asked Dessia. The thought of someday returning to Cahermara on the beautiful mare filled her with excitement.

Bridei smiled at her, his blue eyes bright with warmth for the first time in nearly a sennight. "I'll do my best."

A lump formed in Dessia's throat. It had been unfair of her to blame Bridei for having to leave Cahermara. He hadn't planned to get her with child. And she must remember that if he hadn't rescued her from O'Bannon, she'd have no hope of ever reclaiming her heritage. She owed him so much. When they finally had a chance to be alone in a proper bedchamber, she intended to show him how grateful she was.

They reached the stables, which was a large timber building. A small, dark-eyed man came out to greet them. Bridei nodded to him. "We'd like have our horses cared for, perhaps for an extended period of time."

The man scrutinized the two animals. He looked back at Bridei, his eyes narrowed in speculation. "How will you pay? Do you carry coin or trade goods?"

"Alas, we have neither. But I'm a trained *filidh*. I was hoping I might perform for King Conla and he would pay you."

"A bard, you say. Where's your harp?"

Bridei motioned in the direction of the sea. "I had a very rough crossing. Most of our possessions were lost overboard. While I was grieved to lose my harp, at least I escaped with my life."

Dessia gazed in puzzlement at Bridei, wondering what he was up to. Then she told herself to relax. Bridei knew what he was about. Then she thought about what he'd just said. Her workmen had made him another harp, but he'd had to leave that one behind at Dun Cullen. He'd given up so much for her.

Bridei continued, "If there's a harp in the settlement, perhaps I could borrow it for my performance. Otherwise, I'm perfectly able to sing without accompaniment. Or, I could tell tales. The last place I visited, the people particularly enjoyed the story of Arthur, King of the Britons."

"Arthur. Aye. I've heard of him," the man responded.

"I used to be Arthur's bard," Bridei said. "So, the tales I tell of him are based on fact... mostly, that is." He smiled enigmatically.

The man glared at him. "You're surely lying now. Arthur's bard was the silver-tongued Bridei ap Maelgwn."

"Aye. That's my name."

"You couldn't be him," the man insisted. "The bard of the great King Arthur has to be a far older man."

Bridei grinned. "I started young."

"Prove it," said the man.

Bridei began to sing. To Dessia, it was pure enchantment. All Bridei had to do was open his mouth and the music poured out, rich, beautiful and vibrant. The man's eyes widened and he smiled. Although he was obviously convinced of Bridei's identity, he said nothing, clearly wanting Bridei to finish the song.

As the last notes died away, Bridei gazed at the man questioningly. The man nodded. "I believe you now. You're welcome to keep your horses here as long as you wish. Finian and Sorley will care for them." He gestured toward to youths who'd appeared not long after Bridei started singing. The two young men kept their gazes fixed on Bridei, regarding him with awe. The stablemaster snapped his fingers. "Stop gaping and see to your work!" he called to the youths.

Bridei turned to the stallion and began unfastening the bundles containing the few supplies they'd brought.

"Here now," the man said. "Let me do that."

Bridei stood back, and the man quickly undid the leather thongs holding their packs on the horses.

"We need to find someone to take us across the sea to Britain," said Bridei.

"You'll be wanting Ronat then," the man answered. "He's my cousin and a skilled sailor. Ask for him down by river where they keep the boats."

Bridei discussed their plans to go to Gwynedd while Dessia patted the mare, saying goodbye.

After the stablemaster left, Bridei came up next to her. "Now that I've convinced Eachan I'm a famous bard, I'm confident he'll take good care of the horses until we return." He grinned at her, and she smiled back. *Oh, aye, as soon as they were alone, she would make Bridei understand she appreciated everything he'd done for her.*

"Before we go to the king's rath, we should probably wash," suggested Bridei.

"Aye. That would be wise," agreed Dessia. "While you can easily prove you're a bard with your singing skill, in my current bedraggled state, no one would ever guess I was once queen of a substantial territory."

Bridei's deep blue eyes focused on her intently. "No matter what happens, you'll always be a queen to me. And I mean to make certain you once again reign as queen of the Fionnlairaos."

Dessia felt herself melting. This was bliss, to have him look at her like that.

His expression turned regretful. "It grows late, and I'd rather not arrive at the rath after the gates have closed."

Dessia nodded, recalling what was still ahead of them.

They asked another woman they met the direction of the nearest cistern, then found it and washed at the large stone basin. After splashing his face and drying on his undertunic, Bridei touched his jaw and said, "I'd like to shave. I wonder if there are any barbers here."

"Why don't you wear a beard, like most men?" asked Dessia, also drying off.

"When my beard first grew in, I was living in Gaul, where the old Roman ways are still strong and most men shave their faces. Then when I returned to Britain and grew a beard, I found it itchy and uncomfortable. I've shaved regularly ever since, at least when I've had access to a knife sharp enough to do the job." He shrugged. "I suppose I like that it makes me look different than most men."

"It makes you look younger, which would seem to be a disadvantage for a bard. You heard what the stablemaster said."

"And you saw how I silenced him. I'm confident enough in my abilities that I don't need to look like a sage old master." He cocked his head. "Although I didn't succeed when I first sang for you. Despite my best efforts to impress you with my skill, you set me to breaking rocks."

Dessia felt her face flush. "I don't know what I was thinking. Although I was enthralled by your singing, I resisted. I suppose I knew if I ever gave in to your charm I would succumb completely."

Bridei motioned in the direction of the hillfort and they started walking. "I understand why you resisted me. You were thinking of your people and your kingdom rather than giving in to your own inclinations. Back then, you never considered what *you* wanted. All your decisions were made on the basis of what was best for the Fionnlairaos."

"And now it seems as if I've forgotten them."

"Just remember, if you die, the legacy of the Fionnlairaos vanishes into the mists of time. You're their only hope, and you must do what is necessary to preserve your life, and also the life you carry within you." He nodded to her still-flat belly. "This child represents the future, and you must do what you can to protect and nurture it."

The next moment, he added, "We should hurry. It's always troublesome to gain entrance to a fortress after the gates have closed for the night."

ChApTER 24

They walked swiftly, not speaking, and finally reached the gate of the rath. Although it stood open, an armed warrior immediately stepped in their pathway. "State your business."

"I'm a traveling bard," Bridei responded. "Let me in and I'll entertain your household for the evening in exchange for a place to sleep."

"Where's your harp?" the man asked.

"Alas, I was forced to leave it behind. But if your master would be willing to let me borrow one, I would gladly sing for him."

Dessia watched the man wearily, wondering if Bridei would once again be forced to prove he was a bard. But the man moved aside so they could enter, then summoned a young boy and said, "Take them to the king."

The boy took them to a large round structure. Although the hall was built of timber with a thatched roof, the lintel over the wide doorway was of stone and had images of various gods and heroes etched into it. The boy escorted them inside, where Dessia saw more evidence of wealth. The timbers supports of the hall were carved with intricate swirling designs and painted bright colors, and vivid weavings covered the walls. A group of men were gathered around the fire. Dessia regarded them warily, wondering which one was Conla.

Bridei bowed. "I'm Bridei ap Maelgwn, a bard from Britain. I would be pleased to offer my humble skills to entertain you for the evening, in exchange for a place to stay and something to eat." In response to Bridei's words, several of the men turned to look at a squat, swarthy fellow in their midst. He looked very foreign, and Dessia could scarce believe he was the ruler of this place. But when he opened his mouth, his Irish was clear and easy to understand: "What's a British bard doing traveling in Ireland? And who is the young woman with you?"

Bridei reached out and pulled Dessia close. "I'm afraid we're leaving behind a rather awkward situation. I was performing in the household of a chieftain named Tiernan O'Bannon when I became enamored of his daughter." He looked fondly at Dessia, and his hand stroked hers reassuringly. "When O'Bannon discovered us in a compromising situation, he became enraged. I offered to wed his daughter and even pay a substantial dowry. He refused and threw me into an underground chamber. With the aid of some of the chieftain's retainers, I was able to escape with my paramour and come to this place. As you can see, Lady Dessia is of an age to make her own choices, and she has chosen to come with me. We hope to get passage to Britain as soon as possible. My father, Maelgwn the Great, is a powerful chieftain there."

Dessia's heart was thundering in her chest. Would these men believe Bridei's explanation?

"It's a charming tale," responded Conla, his face expressionless. "Worthy of a bard. And you are a bard. I can tell from the smooth tone of your voice and the way you phrase things that you're used to spinning tales. I'm inclined to believe at least part of your story. I've met Maelgwn the Great. While you're not a giant of a man like he is, you do bear some resemblance."

"You've met my father?" Although Bridei's voice was easy, Dessia was standing close enough to feel him tense.

"Aye." Conla's teeth glinted in the dark of his beard as he smiled in a way that was both ironic and vaguely sinister. "Although not under the most pleasant of circumstances."

Bridei nodded, but didn't press the man for more information. Recalling that Bridei had told her the Irish often raided the coastlines of Gwynedd, Dessia could guess how Conla might have encountered his father.

"So," said Bridei. "Now that you've learned how we've come to be here, are you willing to give us food and shelter for the night?"

Conla nodded. "For the price of a few songs, you and Lady Dessia may join us."

The other men made room for them, and Dessia and Bridei sat down near Conla. Servants brought roast pork, hot savory bannocks and wine.

As they ate, Bridei and Conla discussed where Bridei might find a boat to take them across the sea to Gwynedd. Once that matter was out of the way, they talked about trading. Conla told them he had once been a slaver, raiding the coasts of Britain and then taking his captives back to Ireland to sell. But raiding was dangerous work, he said, and after a nearly fatal encounter with a certain Cymry chieftain—he grinned at Bridei as he said this—he decided to find a different means of making a living.

He'd become a trader, and later, when he'd grown tired of traveling, settled in Ath Cliath. Because of its natural harbor and its location, the site was an ideal trading center. He'd built the hillfort, which was called Rath Conla, and he was now known as the "king" of Ath Cliath, mainly because he had the resources to defend the settlement.

Bridei mentioned the traders who'd been at Cahermara only a few weeks before, and asked if they'd come to Ath Cliath. Conla's expression grew grim. "I know the men you speak of, and I'm afraid I have bad news of them. About a fortnight ago, their currach went down in a fierce winter storm just north of here. Presumably, everyone on board perished."

"Their boat went down?" Bridei repeated, looking stunned. "How can you be certain it was them?"

Conla shook his head. "The wreckage of their vessel washed ashore, and among the items found lashed to the hull was some jewelry they'd purchased here. The pieces were made by Branach Ui Diarach, the finest metalsmith in Ath Cliath. I would know his work anywhere."

"Isn't it possible they sold the items to another trader, and it was their boat that went down?" asked Bridei.

"Why would they sell the jewelry to another trader?" asked Conla. "Besides, there are only so many large currachs that sail these waters." His expression grew thoughtful. "Who are these men to you, that you appear so distressed by news of their deaths?"

Bridei looked at Dessia, then shook his head. "If things had gone as I intended, I would have likely been in that currach when it set sail from here."

All at once, Dessia understood. Bridei had told her he'd intended to meet up with the traders after they left Cahermara. Because she'd misunderstood Bridei's conversation with Penrick and Rinc and had him imprisoned, he hadn't be able to meet them. It now appeared her mistrust of Bridei—which she'd regretted so bitterly these past few weeks—had actually saved his life.

"Ah," said Conla. "It's often strange how the gods arrange things, isn't it? It would seem that Mercury was protecting you and kept you from a watery grave."

"Mercury?" Bridei responded. "It's been years since I heard that name."

"Your race would know him as Llud or Llew, but I grew up with the god Mercury, so that's the name I invoke him by."

"Clearly, you weren't born in Ireland," said Bridei.

"Nay. I'm from Constantinople, on the dark sea."

"That's a very long way away. How did you ever end up in Ireland?"

Conla grinned, strong, healthy teeth glinting in his beard. "My family was poor in all but children. As the youngest, I was sold into slavery to pay their debts."

"Having been a slave, I would think you would loathe the practice," said Bridei.

Conla shrugged. "My own experience wasn't so harsh. I served a wealthy merchant who was fond of me and treated me well. Indeed, I was like a son to him in some ways. He taught me his business; it was from him that I learned how to bargain and trade."

"How did you go from slave to merchant?" asked Dessia.

"My owner and his family all perished in a fire. I took what wealth of his that I could salvage and set out for Aquileia, which is a large trading center similar to Narbonne. It was there I learned about the slave trade. It has its risks and dangers, certainly, but to a young, adventurous man, it seemed an easy life. Most coastal settlements are easy picking. The men are usually off fishing and the women and children put up little defense. Unless there's a strong chieftain in the area, such as your father, we seldom encountered much resistance. Although some say slaves are too much trouble, because they have to be fed as well as carefully guarded, for a time I thought I'd found the perfect way to earn my fortune."

Dessia could control herself no longer. This man seemed to have no feeling for the humans who'd made him wealthy, viewing them as if they were cattle or other livestock. "Did you never feel pity for those poor unfortunates you captured and enslaved?" she asked. "Never think of the terror and degradation they had to endure because of you?"

Conla shrugged. "Some men mistreat their slaves, but most do not. They're too valuable to abuse. And you must consider the grim life most of these poor wretches would have had if they'd stayed with their families. A good share of the children would have starved or died of disease before even reaching adulthood. At least as slaves they had enough to eat and proper clothing."

"But they're not free," persisted Dessia. "You escaped servitude as soon as you were able. Surely you can understand how miserable it is to always be at the mercy of another."

"Oh, I understand," said Conla. "I understand very well. That's why I've made the decisions I've made in my life." His smile was fierce. "'Twas no accident that my owner and his family died in a fire."

Dessia felt a sudden chill. For all his friendly demeanor, Conla was a very ruthless man. She and Bridei would do well to remember that.

Bridei sat back from the table and said, "If you wish me to perform for you, I'd better do so now. With my belly full of hearty food and excellent wine, I'm likely to fall asleep at any moment."

Conla also pushed back from the table. With his big belly and languid manner, he reminded Dessia of a plump, well-satisfied cat. And like a cat, she guessed he could turn into a deadly predator in a heartbeat. "It's time for you to earn your supper, master bard," said Conla. "Will you sing us a song, or tell us a tale?"

"A song, I think," said Bridei. "Although I'd like to have a harp for accompaniment." He gestured. "Surely in a settlement of this size, someone has a harp I could borrow."

Conla nodded. "I'll send a servant to search the storehouse."

As they waited for a harp, servants brought stewed apples with cinnamon and more wine. Once again, Dessia was impressed by the quality and quantity of food. Even when her father was at the height of his wealth and power, their household had only eaten this well on very special occasions. That Conla could afford to dine like this at an ordinary meal bespoke exceptional resources.

At last the servant returned with a cloth-covered bundle. Bridei removed the cloth to reveal an elegant harp. Unlike the simple, boxy instrument Dessia's men had made, this harp was triangular. Delicately made and adorned with jewels and gold, it looked more like a work of art than a musical instrument. Bridei regarded the harp with a reverent expression, then ran his fingers along the strings. A sweet, crystalline sound echoed through the hall.

Bridei played a soft, sad melody and began to sing. It wasn't a song Dessia was familiar with, and she couldn't understand the words since they appeared to be in Bridei's native tongue. She glanced at Conla, wondering at his reaction. To her surprise, the fierce chieftain had closed his eyes and was listening with a rapt expression on his face. The tension eased from her body. Part of Bridei's magic was that he seemed to know exactly what sort of song would please his listeners. He was like a sorcerer choosing the perfect spell to cast.

She allowed herself to relax and let the music carry her away. Perhaps it was because she couldn't understand the words, or because this harp had such heartbreakingly lovely tone. Whatever it was, the music seemed to reach inside of her and touch her deepest, most vulnerable self. The melody soared and built. Bridei's fingers flew over the strings and his voice rose, deep and throbbing. Finally, the song ended, the last few notes trickling away like drops of water raining down upon moonlit pool.

Dessia took a deep breath. She wanted to tell Bridei how wonderfully he'd sang, but she was unable to speak. The knot of emotion in her chest paralyzed her. *This is what it it's like to be spellbound*, she thought.

When she finally recovered herself and glanced at Conla, she was stunned to see tears glistening on his broad face. He swiped at his eyes and said in a choked voice, "You're very good, Bridei ap Maelgwn. A master. So, good that I'm loathe to let you leave. What say you? Rather than risking a treacherous winter crossing of the Irish Sea, you could stay here and dwell in comfort."

"Your offer is very tempting," said Bridei, "but I'm afraid we must decline. Although O'Bannon could do little if he pursued us here, I'd rather not take the chance. As secure as this settlement is, I suspect my lady wouldn't feel safe here. Better that we should leave Ireland for now."

Conla looked at Dessia. "I would hate to think you doubt my ability to protect you. This O'Bannon is but a minor chieftain. He could scarce think to challenge me."

Although his expression was neutral, Dessia sensed warning in his eyes. Her heart pounded as she wondered how to answer. Bridei broke in swiftly, "Of course she doesn't doubt you. But you must understand..." He leaned near to Conla. "Milady is with child. Because of that circumstance, she would feel more comfortable in a household where she has family around. My mother is a skilled midwife and could attend the birth."

Conla's dark eyes probed Dessia, making her uneasy. He turned to Bridei. "The birth of the babe—if there is one—will not happen soon. You could stay here until spring, when travel is less perilous, and still reach your homeland before Lady Dessia's time of travail. For that matter, we have several midwives here Ath Cliath." He looked at Dessia again. "I'm certain Lady Dessia will find the accommodations here very comfortable and secure. There's no good reason you shouldn't remain in my household for a time."

"You're right, of course," Bridei responded.

Dessia went rigid. The thought of being trapped in Conla's household made her almost as panicked as when Tiernan O'Bannon took her captive. But, clearly, she couldn't reveal her feelings to Conla. He might take offense, and then there was no telling what he would do.

Bridei and Conla discussed the song he'd sung. Then Bridei asked some questions about the harp—where it was from and who might have made it. Dessia listened impatiently. All she wanted to do was get out of this place. At last, Conla called for a servant to take them to a bedchamber. As Bridei carefully set the harp on the table, Conla said, "Why don't you keep it, as my payment to you for your performance this night."

"I hardly think one song merits such largess," responded Bridei.

"I'm a wealthy man," said Conla. "If you choose to remain here as my bard, you might be surprised what riches you could acquire."

Bridei bowed to Conla, then covered the harp with the cloth bag and cradled it in his arms.

He and Dessia followed the servant to a corridor that ran along the back of the hall. Walking along it, they passed several elaborately carved oak doors. The servant stopped in front of one of them and bowed. "Your sleeping chambers, master bard."

Bridei opened the door and gestured for Dessia to enter. Stepping into the chamber, she glanced around, staring in awe. The good-sized room was furnished with every luxury Dessia had ever encountered, as well as some she'd never see before. There was a large bed with a fur coverlet and a thick crimson rug on the floor. Fine woven fabrics covered the walls. On a table by the bed sat a massive beeswax candle in an elaborate silver holder, as well as a gold ewer and two glass beakers. And to make certain of their comfort, there was a dog-shaped brass brazier near the bed, the glowing coals in the beast's mouth sending delicious warmth into the room.

"It's... incredible," Dessia said as Bridei closed the door. She went to the table and examined one of the shimmering glass beakers, then turned to face Bridei. "I've only encountered glass once before, when the traders brought a set of drinking cups packed in a box of straw. They didn't even take them out to show me, knowing I would never purchase such impractical and extravagant goods."

"Aye, Conla is wealthy," said Bridei. "I'm sure if we stayed here, we would experience every comfort his wealth can buy."

Dessia drew near and gazed at him pleadingly. "But I don't want to stay here. Conla frightens me."

Bridei nodded. "He frightens me as well. If I agree to be his bard, he'll quickly come to see me as one of his possessions. He'll think he owns me."

"We have to find a way to leave," said Dessia.

"I know. And we must do so tonight."

"Tonight?"

"Aye. I know you must be very weary, but that's what Conla's counting on. He won't set a guard on us tonight. But after this... he might. "

Dessia sighed. Every muscle in her body ached. She was so fatigued she felt as if she could fall asleep standing up. Regretfully, she glanced at the bed. Then she straightened her spine and faced Bridei resolutely. "I'm willing to do whatever is necessary to make certain we don't get trapped here."

"The trick will be to get out of the hillfort without arousing suspicion. We'll have to leave separately and each of us give our own reason for departing." He rubbed his stubbled jaw, looking thoughtful. Glancing at Dessia, he said, "I know what we can do."

"What's your plan?"

"I'll tell the guard at the gate you aren't feeling well and I'm going to one of the local healers to fetch a tinsane to settle your stomach. Then, a short while later, you'll go to the gate and ask to be let out. You'll say you're feeling better and don't want me to go to the trouble of fetching the medicine tonight. Tell the guard you hope to catch up with me before I go all the way to the healer's house."

"I'll do my best," Dessia said. She raised her gaze to Bridei's, "But I do worry the guard will think it too dangerous for me to be outside the hillfort alone at night, and insist I stay here until you return."

Bridei nodded. "It might be a problem. But I can think of no better plan." He motioned. "If you succeed in getting out, meet me at the bottom of the hill, in front of the metalsmith's shop we passed. If you don't come after a candle hour or so, I'll assume you weren't allowed to leave the hillfort. I'll come back and pretend I've fetched the tinsane. That way we won't arouse Conla's suspicions, and we might be able to get away another time." He gave her a tender look, then leaned down and kissed her. "'Twill be all right, I promise," he said. "The Goddess has gotten us this far. I don't believe she'll forsake us now."

Dessia tried to smile hopefully, but her insides were clenched with worry.

After Bridei left, time seemed to pass with painful slowness. Dessia paced back and forth on the thick, soft rug, worried that if she so much as sat down, she would fall asleep. After awhile, she went to the table and picked up the harp. Removing the covering, she stared at the instrument. It was the most beautiful object she'd ever seen. As dazzlingly exquisite as a piece of fine jewelry, but so much larger and more complex. And then there was the sound it made. She strummed her fingers along the strings and was startled by the pure, lovely tone that issued forth. Even her clumsy, unskilled fingers could evoke beauty from this instrument. "Bridei deserves a harp this fine," she said aloud. "Some day I intend to buy him one."

She replaced the covering, then began to pace again. When she was convinced enough time had passed, she put on her cloak and crept out of the bedchamber. All seemed quiet, and as she moved stealthily along the corridor, she met no one. Bridei had told her there would be a door at the end of the corridor leading to the outside. She found the door and slipped out into the night.

She made her way to the gate by the light from the half-moon. There she paused, gathering her nerve. Finally, she called up to the gatehouse, "Hullo! I need the gate opened!"

There was the sound of footsteps as the guard descended the stairs. He approached her, wearing a look of puzzlement. "Lady Dessia. I didn't expect to see you up from your bed. The bard said you were ailing. He went to fetch you something for your stomach."

"I know. I hope to catch him before he's gone all the way to the healer's. I'm feeling much better." She smiled what she hoped was a sheepish, apologetic smile. "Bridei is too good to me. He indulges my every whim. But I regret sending him out so late. I don't want him to waste his time searching for medicine I no longer need. I thought I would go after him."

The guard stepped nearer, as if he meant to bar her way. "I'm not certain I should let you leave. For a man to be out in the settlement at night is one thing, but it might be hazardous for a woman."

"Oh, I'm certain I would be safe," Dessia responded. "We're guests of Lord Conla and he has a very formidable reputation. I can't believe anyone would risk angering him by harming anyone under his protection."

"That's likely true."

The man was wavering. Dessia knew she must not let up. "Please let me leave... for Bridei's sake. The sooner I find him, the sooner he can return to the hillfort and to his bed. Conla wouldn't want Bridei catch an ague from the cool night air. Then he wouldn't be able to sing and your master would be deprived of his artistry."

The man nodded. "Lord Conla was most impressed with the young bard's skills and hopes to hear him sing every night. In light of that, perhaps I should let you go. But hurry, and bring him back as soon as you can. Now that you remind me of my lord's interest in the bard, I see I should never have let him leave at all."

The guard opened the gate for her, and Dessia hurried out. Her heart was pounding and her skin sticky with sweat. It had been a very unnerving to spin lie after lie, but somehow she'd managed it. Now, she must find Bridei and hope they could escape Ath Cliath before morning.

* * *

Bridei shifted back and forth and rubbed his hands together in an effort to stay warm and to deal with his growing agitation. *Where was she? Was she having trouble getting through the gate?*

He'd no sooner had the thought when he saw a cloaked figure hurrying toward him. Rushing to meet Dessia, he pulled her into his arms. "*Cariad,*" he murmured in relief. "I was worried you wouldn't be able to get away."

"It wasn't easy," she responded after kissing him. "I had to argue with the guard. I finally convinced him to let me fetch you. Which means he expects us back soon. We don't have much time."

Bridei nodded.

Although the moonlight illuminated the many buildings around them, it was difficult to see where they were going. Dessia followed after Bridei, wondering how he knew where to go. "How will we find our way?" she asked breathlessly.

"It's easy. If you want a boat, you must head toward the water."

Even as he answered, Dessia realized she could hear the lap of waves. The next moment she smelled the odor of fish and garbage. The people of the settlement probably discarded their waste in the river, depending on the current to wash it away.

At last they reached an open area.. Dessia could make out the glint of water and along the bank, several boats. There were some daub and wattle dwellings nearby. Bridei raced to the nearest one and rapped sharply on the wooden door frame. "Ronat!" he called out. "I'm looking for Ronat!"

They could hear noises from inside the roundhouse. After a time the door covering was pulled aside and a sleepy woman's voice said, "Ronat's house is the last one up the hill."

"Thank you," Bridei responded.

They hurried up the slope. Reaching another roundhouse, Bridei called out for Ronat. This time it was a man who came to the door. "What do you want?" he asked, his voice thick with sleep.

"We need you to take us across the sea to Britain," Bridei responded. "We must set out tonight."

"Tonight?" The man snorted. "You must be mad."

"Not mad. Desperate. Don't worry. I'll make it worth your while. I have near five hundred drachmas worth of gold sewed inside my tunic."

"Five hundred?" Ronat sounded incredulous. "Where did you get such wealth?"

"I'm a bard, and I had a patron who was willing to pay dearly for me to entertain him."

"Who was your patron? There's no chieftain in Ireland with such resources, unless perhaps the high king."

"Nay. It was a man in Gaul. A merchant named Atharaxis."

Ronat grunted. "I've never heard of him. But I know there are men in the markets there who are rich beyond imagining. Come in, then, and let me see the gold."

"There isn't time. We must leave now."

"Why? Who are you trying to get away from?"

"Conla," Bridei answered. "He wants me to stay in his household and be his personal bard. But I have no desire to settle here. I'm trying to get back to my father's household in Gwynedd."

"Who's your father?"

"Maelgwn the Great."

"You claim kinship with the Dragon?"

"Aye."

Ronat grunted again. Then he said, "Give me a moment. I'll have to dress and grab a few provisions." The flap door fell back into place.

"He's going to help us!" Dessia said excitedly.

Bridei released his breath in a sigh. "Aye. I think so."

A few moments later, Ronat pushed through the doorway carrying a torch. He handed the torch to Bridei, then went back in and returned with two heavy leather bags. Now that they could finally get a good look at Ronat, Dessia was surprised to discover he barely reached to Bridei's shoulder. Even so, the seaman appeared wiry and strong.

Ronat motioned to Dessia. "You said nothing about passengers."

Bridei moved nearer to Dessia. "This is my lady wife, Dessia."

"I don't usually allow women in my boat," said Ronat. "But with the sum you're paying me, I guess I can forgo my usual precautions."

"I know some seamen think women bring bad luck." responded Bridei. "But I can assure you, my wife has only brought me good fortune so far." He smiled at her reassuringly. Dessia smiled back, although she still felt irritated by Ronat's attitude toward women.

Ronat led them down the hill. Halfway to where the boats were kept, he stopped at another roundhouse. He banged on the doorframe and called out, "Ollam! Wake up, Ollam."

He turned to Bridei. "My son. I'll need his help. Unless you want to take turns rowing all the way across."

"Whatever will get us there the fastest," Bridei responded.

Ollam came to the door and Ronat gave him terse instructions. A few moments later, he came out of the dwelling. He was the same size of his father. Ronat motioned and they all followed him to the boats.

Dessia expected he would take them to one of the larger vessels, but Ronat picked out one of the smaller ones. As Bridei helped Ronat and Ollam launch the boat into the water, Dessia felt a sudden surge of panic. The boat seemed so tiny compared to the vast, wild sea.

Bridei reached for her hand, clearly intending to help her into the vessel. Dessia took an involuntary step back. "Are you certain... it's... safe?" she asked.

Bridei glanced in the direction of the boat and nodded. "As safe as any means of crossing. Now we just have to pray to the gods for good weather."

Dessia's stomach clenched with another wave of dread. "I've never been on a boat before."

Bridei pulled her close. "Don't worry, sweeting. We'll make it. We've come this far, haven't we?"

Dessia nodded, trying to swallow her fear. She let Bridei lead her down to the water. He picked her up and waded out to the boat, where Ronat and Ollam helped her climb in. Dessia stood frozen for a moment, feeling the boat sway beneath her.

"Sit," Ronat ordered.

Bridei climbed in the boat. Dessia gestured to his soaking trews. "You're going to freeze."

He shook his head. "In short while, I vow I'll be too ill to care if I'm cold."

"What do you mean?"

"I'm afraid you're about to discover one of my most embarrassing frailties. I suffer terrible seasickness."

Chapter 25

The sky was lightening in the east as Ronat and Ollam rowed the boat toward the sea. When they reached the river mouth, the two seamen pulled in the oars and raised the sail. Dessia watched, amazed by the balance and agility of the two men as they maneuvered in the swaying leather and wicker craft. They seemed to be able to adjust to every pitch and toss of the boat. The boat's movement made her faintly queasy. As for Bridei—a quick glance revealed his face had turned the same grayish white as the sail. He was slumped against the side of the boat, eyes closed, jaw clenched, looking like a man being tortured.

She sat up and inhaled deeply, which seemed to ease her nausea. The air was fresh and invigorating and she was relieved they were finally on their way. The wind caught the sail and the boat moved in a swift, straight course. She watched as the sun began to come up. In moments the sky was radiant with shades of pink and lavender, and the waves gilded a gleaming gold.

As the boat picked up speed, she knew a surge of excitement. Then she turned and looked back at the shores of Ireland, receding in the distance. "I'll come back," she whispered. "Someday I'll return and claim what is mine."

As she was making her vow, Ronat leaned near. "I guess Bridei was right. The gods appear to favor you."

"You mean, otherwise I'd be sick?" Dessia asked.

"Aye," said Ronat. "Or we might have encountered fog, a storm, or unpredictable winds. 'Tis a gorgeous day. We couldn't ask for better sailing weather."

"How long of a journey is it?"

"'Twill take us all day, and that's if the wind holds." He pointed. "See? That's where we're headed." Dessia strained her eyes to make out the blue-gray blur in the distance. "The first land we'll encounter is Mona, the sacred isle. Our destination is Deganwy, east of Mona on the northern coast of Gwynedd. That's the stronghold of Maelgwn the Great."

Hearing Bridei's father's name, Dessia felt a twinge of apprehension. "I know they call him the Dragon of the Island. Is he truly that formidable?"

Ronat shrugged. "Many of the traders I've carried across like him well enough. He has the resources to buy luxury goods and is willing to do so. Now, if you're planning to raid, that's another matter. He's killed more than a few slavers in his day, which is why the people living on the coast revere him."

How ironic it was, Dessia thought. Maelgwn the Great had freed his people from the threat of enslavement, yet his own son had ended up in servitude. She glanced over at Bridei. His eyes were closed and he appeared to be asleep.

* * *

"Wake up, Bridei!" Bridei roused to the sound of Dessia's excited voice. He sat up slowly, startled to realize he'd actually slept.

"Ronat says this place is called Mona," she said. "We're going to spend the night here, as it's getting too dark to continue on."

Bridei watched the approaching shoreline, barely visible in the fading light. Ynys Mon, the sacred isle. The ancestors of his people had once considered the island sacred to the old gods. There were still traces of their worship: an ancient burial mound, some standing stones, a lake from which fishermen still pulled weapons and jewelry, offerings made to the deities many years ago. Now, rich grainfields covered much of the island, the source of most of the wheat that fed the Cymry.

Ronat and Ollam had lowered the sail and were rowing hard toward a broad, sandy beach. On the high hill beyond the beach, Bridei could see the glow of torches from the watchtower. As the lights glinted in the purple twilight, he wondered if he knew any of the men garrisoned at the small fort located there. One of them might be looking out at the sea even now, watching their approach.

As they neared the beach, Ronat and Ollam drew in the oars, jumped in the water and guided the boat toward shore. Bridei stretched his stiff limbs and climbed out to help drag the currach onto the beach. When it was grounded, he turned to aid Dessia, but she was already scrambling out of the boat.

The next moment they heard hoof beats and saw a half dozen mounted warriors riding down the hillside carrying torches. As Bridei watched them approach, his stomach clenched with warning. He reminded himself that these men were his people; he and Dessia should have nothing to fear from them.

The horsemen halted a few paces away and the lead man called out, "Where do you hail from and what's your business here?"

Bridei hesitated, still not quite prepared to confront his past. But he had to say something. "We're from Ireland," he called out. He motioned to Dessia. "This is Queen Dessia of the Fionnlairaos. Her lands have been overrun by her enemies and she seeks refuge here in the lands of Maelgwn the Great."

As the band of horsemen drew nearer, Bridei shifted uneasily. There'd always been tension between his people and the Irish. Would these men perceive anyone from Ireland as an enemy?

The warrior who'd hailed them spoke. "The woman may be Irish, but I doubt you are. Tell us your name and what you want."

"I speak Cymry because I was raised here," Bridei answered. "But that was a long time ago. I'm a bard, and I've traveled many places, most recently Ireland."

"A bard? What's your name?"

He was going to have to reveal himself sometime. Still, when he answered, he couldn't quite get his father's name out. "I'm Bridei... Bridei the... Silver-tongued."

To his surprise, the man laughed. "Is that all the better you can do at making up a name?" He dismounted and approached Bridei, holding the torch. The flare of light made it difficult to see the man's face, but he obviously got a good look at Bridei. "I can see you're far too young to be bard," the man said. "Tell the truth now. Why are you here?"

Bridei felt Dessia make a move toward him. He motioned for her to stay back. Then he began to sing. It was a song about King Arthur. He'd composed it several years ago, before Arthur was high king. It told of Arthur's bravery, his ability to inspire his men and how he'd routed the Saxons in those first few battles. As Bridei sang, he wondered if he'd made a mistake. While this piece would clearly demonstrate his abilities, there was no telling what these men would think of the subject of the song. Men either seemed to love Arthur or hate him, and there was no way of knowing which viewpoint these men held.

When he finished, he was greeted by silence. Then, all at once, the man let out a bark of laughter. "I don't believe it." He turned and gestured for the other men to dismount and come near. As they gathered round, the man pointed at Bridei and said, "Look at him. Even with a beard, he's the very image of the Lady Rhiannon." The man turned to the other men. "It's Bridei ap Maelgwn. Can't you see it?"

A second man, much bigger and bulkier than the first, moved nearer to Bridei. "By the White Christ, I think you're right." The man held out his hand. "It's Eleri. I taught you swordplay when you were a boy. Or, at least I tried to. You never had much interest in such things."

Bridei felt as if the ground beneath him was shifting, like a sand dune giving way before the pounding sea. He reached out and grasped the man's hand, feeling the tough calloused skin and iron-like grip. "Eleri," he said faintly as he released him. "Your father and mine have been together since they were boys."

"Until recently, that is. Balyn died last winter."

Bridei's sense of unreality increased. Balyn couldn't be dead. He was like one of the hills surrounding them—massive, immoveable, eternal. If Balyn could die, that meant anyone could... even his father.

"Why didn't you tell us who you were in the beginning?" asked the first man. His tone had changed dramatically, from threatening to jovial.

Bridei shook his head, almost dizzy with shock. "I don't know. It's been so long. I thought maybe you wouldn't believe me."

"I'm Senewyr, by the way. My father was Gavran. You might recall him as well." The man grasped Bridei's hand firmly.

"Gavran. Then you must have red hair underneath that leather helmet."

Senewyr laughed. "Aye, you're right, although it's streaked with silver now. You've been away a long time, Bridei."

"Aye. Going on ten years."

"And you come back a bard. Who would have guessed it," said Senewyr. "You always hated learning your lessons from Father Islwyn."

"Singing and telling stories is different from learning to cipher Latin." Bridei could hardly believe he was having this conversation. It was too strange, as if he'd fallen asleep for ten years and woken up to find everything changed... and yet somehow the same.

"You've won quite a name for yourself," said Eleri. "Bard to the High King. Said to be as gifted as Talisen and Aneirin."

Bridei felt himself bristle. He didn't like being compared to those old men. They told stories and strummed their harps in accompaniment. They might be poets, but they didn't really sing or compose songs. Songs that lingered on the mind. Songs that made people laugh and weep.

"Bridei." Dessia came to stand beside him. With a start, Bridei realized he'd almost forgotten she was there. He'd been transported back to the past, to the time before he knew what love was. Or how much it could change a man's life.

He put his arm around her and gently urged her forward. "Senewyr. Eleri. This is Queen Dessia of the Fionnlairaos... my wife." As he said this, Bridei realized he had no right to introduce Dessia this way. They hadn't been formally wed, or even hand fasted. Indeed, he'd never asked her to become his wife.

All of the men bowed. "Welcome to Gwynedd, Queen Dessia," Senewyr said formally. Then his tone became playful. "A queen, Bridei. Who would have thought it. Although you always did have a way with the wenches."

Bridei suppressed a grimace. The conversation was straying too close to memories he'd rather keep in the past. He said briskly, "Although it's certainly a pleasure to see all of you again, we've just made a long journey across the sea and we're tired onto death. Is there somewhere we can eat and spend the night? It need not be extravagant. A roof over our heads, some warm food and a straw pallet would be more than adequate."

"Of course," Senewyr said. "Since there's a lady with you," he nodded to Dessia, "we should probably take you to the guest house at the priory."

"Priory?" Bridei asked.

"Aye. Maelgwn... your father... provided funds for a priory to be built here. A brother named Cybi runs it. Kind of a trouble-maker, he is, but you how your father feels about keeping both sides happy."

Bridei grimaced. He had no desire to have contact with any Christian brothers. He'd watched how they sought to control and manipulate Arthur. Ultimately, they were part of the reason the end had been such a disaster. "We'd rather not stay at a priory," he said. "If you have a stable up at the fort, that would be good enough for us."

"It appears you hold the same opinion of the Christians as your mother," Senewyr said, grinning. "I can understand that. I can scarce tolerate the holy men myself. But there's no need for you to stay in the stables. If you're satisfied with the simple fare we eat and your lady isn't uncomfortable around a bunch of rough soldiers, you can sup with us and bed down in the barracks."

"We'd be pleased to do so," said Bridei. He turned to Ronat and Ollam and told them in Irish, "You're welcome to come up to the fort with us if you wish."

Ronat shook his head. "We'll stay with the boat."

"I'll have them send down some food for you," Bridei told him.

"There's also the matter of payment," responded Ronat. "Unless you have a strong desire to make the rest of the journey by sea, I see no reason why you couldn't travel to Deganwy from here on horseback."

"That's true," Bridei said. He glanced out at the dark roiling sea. Although he'd fared better on this sea journey than most, he had no desire to go any farther by boat. "We'll have to take some sort of craft from Mona to the mainland, but we could make the rest of the way by land."

"I'll have the gold then," Ronat prompted.

Bridei nodded and removed his cloak.

"What are you doing?" Senewyr asked as Bridei began to undo his belt so he could take off his outer tunic.

"The man wants payment for bringing us here, and all the wealth I can carry is sewn into my undertunic."

"I'm certain your father would pay him," Senewyr said. "Tell him all he has to do is come with us to the king's court and he'll be well compensated."

Bridei continued to undress. "This man took some risks to bring us here. I think he should be rewarded now, rather than having to wait for payment." Finally reaching his undertunic, he used his knife to rip out the hem. Sliding out two thumb-size pieces of gold, he held them out to Ronat.

Ronat examined the gold, then grinned at Bridei.

Senewyr whistled. "It looks as if you have done well for yourself, Bridei."

Something prompted Bridei to say, "That's not gold I earned. It's part of Dessia's heritage."

They collected their few possessions from the boat and said farewell to Ronat and Ollam, then walked to where the warriors waited with their horses. One of the men insisted Bridei and Dessia take his mount, saying he could easily walk back.

As they rode along, Dessia said in a mock-chiding voice, "You made me think there was some reason for you to dread going home. Yet everyone appears pleased to see you."

"So far, that is," responded Bridei.

"You still think your father is angry with you?"

Bridei shrugged. "I don't know. When we last spoke, he told me to get out of his sight and never come back."

"He's had a long time to get over whatever it was you did to upset him so much."

Bridei didn't say anything, and as the moments passed, he felt the silence stretch out between them. Dessia wasn't going to ask him, but the question must be on her mind. Perhaps she respected his privacy, or maybe she was afraid to find out what terrible thing he'd done to earn his father's animosity.

Bridei chewed his lip as he rode. He wanted to tell her, truly he did. But he dreaded what she would think of him. What he'd done was awful, he knew that now. But hadn't he paid for it many times over? Bitter memories filled his mind. Memories he'd hoped to keep buried. He sighed heavily. Maybe this was the real reason he hadn't wanted to come home. Not because he was afraid of facing his father, but because he was afraid of facing his past, the memory of the selfish, arrogant youth he'd been.

The lights of the fort finally came into view. It was a tiny stronghold; large enough to house a dozen warriors at most. His father's men would take turns being stationed here, serving for a month or so at a time and then going back to Deganwy or one of the other small fortresses Maelgwn had built along the coast. Bridei was a little surprised to find men like Senewyr and Eleri here. Men who had families and strong connections to their lord didn't usually end up in this sort of place. But perhaps they enjoyed taking their turn. It was a pretty area, with fairly mild weather. Not as beautiful as Deganwy, but few places were. Bridei felt a sudden pang of homesickness. It seemed odd to think he would soon be seeing the places where he'd grown up.

The guard in the tower had seen them coming and the gate was open. They rode in and dismounted. Senewyr came over to them. "As I told you, we have no guesthouse here but there's room in the barracks. Or, if you and your lady would like some privacy, there's a small office. We could bring in a brazier and some blankets. Nothing like what you're used to, but perhaps for one night it would suffice."

"After sleeping on the ground for a week and in the boat last night, I vow we'd be content in a cattle byre," responded Bridei.

They followed Senewyr to a small rectangular building. Inside Senewyr set the torch in a bracket on the wall, then used a taper to light some candles. The candlelight revealed a narrow room furnished with several hide-covered stools and a table. "I'll fetch the brazier and some food," said Senewyr.

"I hope you don't mind that I refused Senewyr's offer of a bed in the barracks," Bridei said after Senewyr had left.

"Nay, of course not."

"I was afraid you wouldn't feel comfortable there, especially since you don't speak the language. And I worried the Senwyr would want to know about everything I've been doing the past ten years."

Dessia looked at him. "Despite our warm welcome, you seem unsettled. What is it, Bridei? Everything is going so well, yet you seem tense and anxious." When he didn't respond, Dessia added, "It's your father, isn't it? You're worried how he will react to seeing you again." Her green eyes probed. "What happened between you, Bridei? You've never told me, and yet I can see how it weighs on you."

She'd finally asked the questions he'd feared for so long. He had to answer her, and yet he was afraid. Terrified that when she learned the truth about him, she'd lose all faith in him. That she'd stop loving him.

She struck his shoulder playfully. "Oh, come now. It can't be that bad. You were only a boy. Everyone does foolish things when they're young."

"Aye. I was a child then," he said, his voice tight. "In many ways. The pampered, spoiled king's son."

"So, tell me," she persisted. "I vow I won't think less of you, whatever it was. I love the man you are now; I don't care what you did in the past."

Bridei nodded. He had to tell her. If he didn't, she'd eventually learn the truth from someone at Deganwy. Then it would be his father's side of the story she heard, rather than his. "I was barely fourteen," he said. "Still a child, as you've pointed out. Yet old enough to know better." He clenched his teeth, grimacing. "The awful thing I did was... I raped a woman."

Dessia stared at him. He continued, "I didn't set out to hurt her. I thought she was lovely and desirable. And she seemed to like me well enough. We were alone. One thing led to another. But then she changed her mind... and I... I got angry. So, I pushed her down on the ground and forced her." He glanced at Dessia, terrified at what she might be thinking. "At the time ... it didn't seem to me I'd done anything so evil. I'd thought she wanted it, at least up until the time she tried to push me away. When she complained to my father and he confronted me, I thought the blame was as much hers as mine. It was only later when I..." The words seemed to freeze in his throat. He'd buried the memories so deep. Speaking of them made them real and alive in his mind. He was a boy again, reliving the pain... the humiliation.

He took a deep breath. "When I was a slave, I was forced to submit to the man who bought me. I knew the horror of being forced against my will. I understood then what a terrible thing I'd done."

Dessia was stunned. At one time she would have thought she could never care for a man capable of doing something as vile as rape. But Bridei hadn't really been a man when he'd forced that young woman, and he'd obviously paid bitterly for what he'd done. Most importantly, he changed. The man standing before her wasn't that cold, selfish youth any longer, but a man who'd risked his life for her sake.

She saw him watching her with an anxious expression. He feared she would despise him for what he'd done, as his father had. She said, "It was a long time ago. And I think you clearly learned your lesson."

He nodded. "I can't take back what happened, but I've never forced a woman since. If a woman says no, or even acts reluctant, I leave her be. I know exactly how horrible and degrading it feels to be coerced."

Again, his face spasmed with pain, and Dessia felt a stab of sympathy. "I can scarcely imagine the despair and anger you must have felt when you were a slave. I don't know if I could have endured what you did. When I was in O'Bannon's prison, I thought about what I would do if he tried to rape me. At the time, not knowing I was carrying your babe, I'd made up my mind I'd rather die than submit to him. But you... you didn't die. You survived, and eventually got your revenge. You didn't let what happened crush you. How can you think your father will still be angry with you? He has only to look at you to see a man who endured terrible things and yet triumphed."

"I'm not certain he'll see it that way," said Bridei. "Especially since I'm never going to tell him what happened."

"What do you mean?"

He was on the verge of answering when Senewyr arrived with several other men. They carried blankets, a tray of food, water for washing and a brazier. After the men left, Bridei and Dessia washed, arranged the blankets in a kind of bed near the glowing brazier, then sat down at the table to eat. They quickly consumed the cold roast fowl and bread, washing it done with wine the men had brought.

When they'd finished, Bridei sat back and said, "I'm very tired. I think I'd better lie down before I fall off the stool."

"Lie down if you will," said Dessia, "but I insist you answer my question before you sleep."

"What question is that?"

"You said you're never going to tell your father that you were enslaved. I don't understand that. Why shouldn't he know what his actions cost you?"

Bridei rose. "I never want to speak of that part of life again, especially not with him."

"But if he doesn't know how you suffered, how his actions hurt you, he'll never understand who you are and how much you've changed."

Bridei shrugged. "So be it. I have no desire to have him know what I endured. It's too... humiliating."

"I suppose I can understand that. But it doesn't seem quite right he'll never realize how much his actions hurt you, even if it was unintentional."

"I don't care," said Bridei. "I don't want him to learn that I was a slave, and not only a slave, but a rich merchant's catamite." He grimaced as he used the Latin word for a young male kept for sexual purposes. Dessia wouldn't know the word, but she would guess the meaning.

"Your secret is safe with me," said Dessia, her voice low and gentle.

He turned to her, searching her face in the firelight. "Does knowing these things about me... does it change how you see me?"

"If anything, it makes you all the more dear to me. When you first came to Cahermara, you appeared so confident, so certain you were irresistible. But now that I know you have doubts and fears, and regret things you've done, you seem even more appealing. I know you're a man, not some beautiful god-like creature I must be wary of."

"God-like!" Bridei gave a hoot of laughter. "You thought I was god-like?"

"Well, your appearance at least." She made an embarrassed gesture. "You know all those tales where a god visits a human household to test them, to see if they behave with nobility and honesty? Well, the thought did cross my mind that you might be someone... something like that. You were so beautiful. I'd never seen a man like you, so unscarred... so perfect."

He strode over to her, grasped her hand and brought it to his lips. "When first saw you in the hall at Cahermara, I thought I'd never seen a more magnificent woman. I'd known many beautiful women, but none of them were queens. And none of them looked as if they would be formidable on the battlefield."

"You liked that about me? That I've fought beside warriors? That I've killed men in combat?"

"It's not so much that you did such things, as the reason for it. I was impressed that you believed so powerfully in your dream. That you endured what you did as a girl and went on to reclaim your lands and rebuild Cahermara."

"Which I've since lost," Dessia said bitterly. "I'm not so brave and magnificent now. I'm a queen without subjects or lands."

"Ah, but you'll always be queen to me," Bridei whispered. He pulled her close and kissed her.

The heat built between them until they both drew back. Dessia gazed at him thoughtfully. "You said you were very tired."

"Not *that* tired," he said smiling.

They both hurried to undress. After taking off his cloak, Bridei found himself shivering. "The brazier doesn't help much, does it?"

"Nay."

He gave her a meaningful look. "There's really no need to take everything off."

"I suppose not," she agreed.

Bridei unfastened the tie of his trews and let them drop. When he looked over, Dessia had lain down on the makeshift bed, still wearing her gown. As he drew near, she slowly raised the garment. Bridei's breathing quickened as he gazed at the beautiful image before him: long, creamy-skinned legs, curving hips, the vivid red triangle of maidenhair. Part of him longed to take time to fondle and caress her. To kiss the sweet, tender flesh between her thighs. But at this moment, he felt he would burst if he didn't enter her. Glancing at her flushed face and slitted eyes he guessed she felt much the same.

He positioned himself over her. She slid her legs apart, welcoming him as he thrust deep. "Uhhh," he groaned. "I won't last long."

"There's... really... no need... to last..." she gasped back, then let out a hoarse cry as the passion broke over them, as wild and tumultuous as the churning sea.

ChAPTER 26

As the raft neared the shore, Bridei motioned toward the fortress on the hills above them. "There it is—Deganwy." Dessia stared at the stone walls of the hillfort, glowing pale gold in the fading sunlight, and a wave of relief rushed through her. It had been a long journey here, nearly two days of riding, as well as a boat ride across the straits between Mona and the mainland and now having to cross this river.

Reaching the other side, they climbed off the raft and waited for the other vessel carrying their horses to dock. At last their horses arrived and they were mounted. They followed the winding trackway along the coast—edged with gorse and hawthorn—then made their way up into the hills. Finally, they reached the grassy slopes at the bottom of Deganwy Hill. Gazing up at the massive stone hillfort, Dessia felt a shiver of apprehension. The fortress looked so forbidding, perhaps reflecting the nature of the man who'd built it.

Dismounting, they led the horses up the path that wound around the hillside up to the entrance of the fortress. When they reached the timber gate, it was already closed. Bridei called up to the watchtower. The guard responded, and there was a long exchange.

"What's happening?" Dessia asked Bridei. "Doesn't the guard believe it's really you?"

"I haven't told him who I am," Bridei said. "I merely said I was a traveling bard"

"Why don't you tell them you're Maelgwn's son? Are you still afraid your father won't be glad to see you?"

"It's bound to be a shock to have me come back after all these years. I thought I would wait until they've had a chance to know me before I told them who I really am."

Bridei truly dreaded confronting his father and meant to put it off as long as possible. But Dessia didn't think he'd get away with it. "You don't think they'll recognize you?" she asked. "If Senewyr knew you by torchlight, your own family is bound to guess who you are as soon as they see you."

"Maybe there's a way we can avoid seeing anyone but the guard and a few servants tonight. I'll say I'm very tired and would rather not perform tonight. It's hardly a lie. It's been a very long journey."

Although the idea of going directly to a bedchamber sounded wonderful, Dessia still doubted that Bridei would be able to avoid greeting their host.

They could hear the guard making his way down the ladder from the watchtower. As he reached the bottom, he spoke to someone. A moment later, the wooden gate creaked open, and they rode into the fortress.

Ahead was a sprawling timber structure Dessia guessed must be the hall and the main living quarters. One of the well-armed guards closed the gate behind them. The other spoke to Bridei.

As Dessia drew near, Bridei said in Irish, "I tried to beg off going to the hall tonight, but these men insist we must join the chieftain and his wife for the evening meal."

"They didn't recognize you? she asked.

"Nay. I think the beard helps, not to mention that it's been nearly ten years since I've seen either of them."

"You know these men?" asked Dessia.

"Aye. They're older looking, of course, but still recognizable."

One of the men gestured. Bridei nodded, then said to Dessia, "I guess we can't delay any longer."

Dessia felt a surge of sympathy for Bridei. Grasping his arm, she said. "I'm right beside you."

They started after the younger guard, leaving the older one to climb back up to the gatetower. As they neared the entrance of the feast hall, Dessia's heart began to pound. The cavernous room was full of people eating. A least three dozen adults and another dozen children sat on benches pushed up to the long wooden tables. Glancing beyond them, Dessia saw the banner of a dragon hanging on the far wall, gold emblazoned on dark red. Halting, she gasped aloud.

Bridei leaned near. "What is it? What's wrong?"

"The banner," she said. "I've seen it before... in a vision." She felt a sense of wonder as she recalled how the banner had appeared behind Bridei when he first stood before her in the hall at Cahermara. She laughed weakly. "It must be destiny that I come here."

"Of course it is," said Bridei, smiling. Taking her arm, he led her forward.

At the back of the hall, beneath the banner, was a table on a raised platform. Seated at the table was tallest man Dessia had ever seen. His hair and beard were black streaked with silver. When he raised his gaze to stare at them, she saw he had deep-set blue eyes. Sitting next to Maelgwn was the Lady Rhiannon. She seemed tiny compared to her husband. Her russet hair was also threaded with white, but her face seemed ageless, her features delicate and perfect. After a glance at the visitors, she gestured for a servant. She spoke quietly to the woman, most likely telling her to bring food for the unexpected guests. Then she resumed eating.

Meanwhile, Maelgwn was staring hard at Bridei. The king motioned to the guard who'd escorted them in and spoke in a deep, rumbling voice. The guard answered, looking uneasy. Maelgwn's gaze snapped back to Bridei. Dessia couldn't tell exactly what Bridei said in response, but she knew he hadn't given his name.

The next moment, Lady Rhiannon looked up. She studied Bridei for a moment, then a stunned expression came over her face. She stood, swaying slightly, and said something to her husband. Maelgwn shook his head, his tone short. But Lady Rhiannon clearly knew who was standing before them. Her luminous eyes fixed on Bridei. Her chest heaved slightly. Then she smiled, her lovely face radiant. "Bridei," she said.

Bridei whispered a word that even Dessia could tell was "mother," then made a choked sound—half laugh, half sob. His mother moved with amazing quickness. Two heartbeats and she was off the dais and embracing Bridei. She held him tight for a long while. When she released her son, her face was wet with tears. Bridei's eyes also glistened, although he appeared stunned as much as anything.

Still grasping Bridei's hand, the Lady Rhiannon spoke to the people gathered, clearly announcing who he was. In moments, a petite dark-haired woman and two boys with reddish tresses appeared at her side. Bridei gazed at them in amazement, while they stared back at him. As Lady Rhiannon introduced the three young people to Bridei, it struck Dessia all at once: These were Bridei's siblings, his sister and twin brothers. The young woman had Rhiannon's fine-boned grace, while the two boys were tall and lanky like Maelgwn. But something in all of their smiles reminded Dessia of Bridei... and Lady Rhiannon.

Bridei hugged his sister, then shook the hands of his brothers. The slight awkwardness of their greeting reminded Dessia that these youths would have been little more than babes when Bridei left Deganwy. They could not remember him.

As she was having these thoughts, Dessia looked at Maelgwn, wondering at his reaction. She was startled by the wary, cold expression on his face. Her insides squeezed with dismay. Although she hadn't thought it possible, it appeared Maelgwn hadn't forgiven his son. A fierce anger overtook her. She wished she spoke Cymry. Then she would tell the great king everything Bridei had endured, and chide Maelgwn for his cruelty in sending his young son away to fend for himself!

She glanced at Bridei, her heart going out to him. He'd feared this moment, dreading his father would feel this way. She reached out and touched his arm. As she did so, the Lady Rhiannon's gaze focused on her and the queen smiled. The warmth in her expression soothed Dessia. Perhaps Lady Rhiannon loved her son enough that it wouldn't matter what her husband thought.

Bridei's mind struggled to function. This was so overwhelming. To see Mabon, Gwydion and Elen once again. And his mother, of course. She looked older, but still beautiful. He'd forgotten how she seemed to fill the room with warmth and light. Glancing again at Dessia, his mother said, "Who is this young woman, Bridei? Is this your wife?"

"In a manner of speaking. We haven't hand fasted yet." He couldn't lie to his mother, couldn't pretend he had any right to claim Dessia as his wife.

His mother gazed a Dessia quizzically. "She doesn't speak Cymry?"

"Nay. She's Irish."

"You should introduce me."

His mother's prompt was gentle, but it reminded Bridei of his terrible breach of manners. He'd been so overwhelmed by seeing his mother and brothers and sister again, he'd almost forgotten about Dessia. "Dessia," he said, turning toward her and speaking in Irish. "This is my mother, the Lady Rhiannon. And mother..." He switched to Cymry. "This is Queen Dessia of the Fionnlairaos."

Dessia bowed, which pleased him. He then introduced her to his siblings. Elen made a dainty curtsy, while Mabon and Gwydion bowed low.

His mother continued to smile at Dessia, then she looked at Bridei, her eyes sparkling. "A queen, my son? You always did aim high."

"Aye," he answered. "I wanted the most beautiful woman in the world, and now I've found her. Excepting you, of course, Mother," he added swiftly.

She beamed back at him. Then she perused Dessia. "Aye, she is beautiful. The two of you shall have fine bonny children."

"And sooner than you might expect," Bridei added.

"Ah," said his mother. She looked at Bridei. "Why haven't you wedded her yet?"

"The last few weeks have been very eventful, for both of us. It's quite the tale, but perhaps I should save it for another time."

"*Another time?*" Her brows shot up and she gave his brothers and sister a look of mock horror. "My son returns after nearly ten years and I'm supposed to wait to hear where he's been and what he's been doing for all that time?" Elen giggled, while the twins appeared bewildered.

Bridei leaned near to his mother. "Perhaps you want to hear the tale of my life, but I doubt my father does." Bridei shot at bitter glance at the man who'd sired him. He'd hoped after all these years his father had changed. It appeared he hadn't.

Rhiannon looked at her husband, still seated at the high table, then back at Bridei. "He doesn't like to be surprised. The way you came here... pretending to be a bard... giving a false name. It's upset him and made him suspicious of your motives. But he'll get over it. He loves you. Once the shock wears off, he'll welcome you home as I have. Come." She took his hand. "You and your lady... Come and dine with us." His mother reached out and grasped Dessia's hand in her other one and led them toward the high table.

Bridei shot an uneasy glance at Dessia. She smiled back at him.

In moments, they were seated, Bridei between his mother and Dessia, and Dessia beside his father. Elen, Gwydion and Mabon had gone back to their seats somewhere among the crowd, where presumably they were sitting with youths of their own age.

Bridei could feel his father's gaze on him. He wanted to say something, but the words seemed stuck in his throat. Then a servant placed a hunk of bread and a bowl of pottage in front of him, and he concentrated on eating.

As he ate, he heard Dessia and his father conversing. He'd forgotten, but his father did know some Irish, probably from dealing with traders all these years. But they soon felt silent, and Bridei began to worry that Dessia would be too uncomfortable to eat. His father could be very intimidating. But when he glanced at her, she shot him a quick smile.

"So," his mother said. "Tell me when the babe is due."

"I suppose next summer. It was about a month after the Blood Moon when Dessia conceived."

"You know exactly when?"

"Aye. We were together one time, then separated for almost a month."

His mother stopped eating and gazed at him. "Why were you separated?"

Bridei let out his breath in a sigh. It still pained him to think of Dessia as O'Bannon's prisoner. "A neighboring chieftain kidnapped her. His intent was to imprison her until she agreed to wed him. Then he could claim her lands."

"How did she escape?"

With more than a hint of pride, he answered, "I rescued her... by trickery."

His mother nodded. "And because you tricked this chieftain, you had to flee Ireland?"

"Aye."

"What about her people? Did no one try to help her besides you?"

"It makes me angry to think that they abandoned her, but I suppose I can understand it in some ways. You see, everyone believed Dessia was a sorceress and that she and her lands were protected by magic. When she was kidnapped, their faith in the magic was shattered, and they were too afraid to do anything."

"But your faith remained strong."

Bridei found himself smiling. "It helped that I never believed she was a sorceress in the first place. Oh, there is magic surrounding her, great magic, but it's much more complex than a simple spell. There's a forest near her stronghold that is surely enchanted. The place remains lush and green even in mid-winter. And in the lake there, both of us have seen visions. When I'm in that place, I feel the ancient powers very strongly. For whatever reason, I think those powers want Dessia to survive and prosper, and to rule the surrounding lands."

"And so, you're going back there... someday." His mother's voice was tinged with sadness.

"Aye. After the babe is born. We have to. Dessia belongs to that place and I..." He smiled at his mother. "I belong to her."

His mother sighed. "Ah, my darling, I'd always hoped you'd fall in love. But it's hard to accept I must lose you again, so soon after you've come back."

"We'll stay here until summer at least. Perhaps by then, my father will have thawed enough that he'll speak to me."

His mother shot a look at his father, her expression both loving and sorrowful. "Give him time. As I said, this is rather a shock." She reached out and touched Bridei's arm. "Now, you must tell me everything that's happened since you've left. How you came to be a famed bard, renowned throughout Britain. Rhun told us some, of course. But mostly about what happened in recent years, since you both served King Arthur. I want to know the rest of it."

The ease with which she spoke of Rhun startled him. Had she adjusted to his older brother's death so easily? True, he wasn't her natural son, but she'd always seemed to love him deeply. "Rhun... aye... 'tis sad to think he isn't here to see me finally succumb to love."

"He should be back before the babe is born, at least. He and Eastra visit several times a year, even though they make their home in Londinium now."

Bridei struggled to make sense of what he was hearing. "What do you mean? I thought... the battle of Camboglanna... they said it was a rout. I presumed... I presumed Rhun had been killed along with Arthur."

His mother shook her head. "Nay. Rhun is fine. In fact, he's prospered since the Saxons took control. He's largely responsible for the fact that everything hasn't fallen into complete disorder and confusion in the East. Rhun is able to see both sides and negotiate between the British chieftains and the Saxons."

"Aye, he would be good at that," Bridei said, feeling a sense of wonder... and relief. He'd always cared a great deal for his much older half-brother, although he'd been loathe to admit it, even to himself. Now that he'd found Dessia, it was also easier for him to understand Rhun and why he cared so passionately about things.

"So... you still haven't told me about yourself. Ten years is a long time, my son. You were only a boy when you left here. I still grieve over that, as does your father. He should never have sent you away. Rhun said you always pretend to be carefree and easy-going, but that underneath he sensed you were very bitter and angry, especially at your father. He feared you endured some awful things after you left here, and that's what had made you act like that."

His mother's words struck too close to the truth. He wouldn't distress her by telling her what had happened to him. It was all in the past, anyway. "I suppose there have been times I felt bitter, especially towards my father, but I'm a new man now. Since I met Dessia, I've come to look at things altogether differently." He glanced at Dessia fondly. "She's suffered much more than I have, yet she never lost her courage nor her commitment to her cause. She's a queen, Mother, in every way. Proud, strong and as capable as any man."

"She also appears to love you deeply, which is all that matters to me," said his mother.

"I hope so. For I love *her* with all my being. And I feel certain we are meant to be together. I've felt that way since soon after I met her. Indeed, I've had visions of her and me. I think I must have inherited some of your gifts. I've had several visions in the past few months, all of them involving Dessia. Even more amazing, I was actually able to call down a storm and save myself from being drowned by slavers."

"Slavers?" His mother's eyes widened. "However did you end up in the hands of slavers?"

"As Rhun probably told you, before the battle of Camboglanna, I headed north to the land of your people, the Brigantes. While I was there ..."

He had no trouble telling his mother this part of the tale. It was the earlier part of his life he didn't want to reveal to her. He knew it would grieve her to think he'd suffered such degradation. But the story of his life in Ireland was full of joy and magic. He told her how stunned he'd been when he'd first met Dessia, how impressed he was with her beauty and cool authority.

Then he told his mother about Dessia's life. How she'd survived the attack that killed the rest of her family. How she'd learned to fight and gathered together men still loyal to her father and with their help, reclaimed her family's lands. How she'd rebuilt Cahermara, this time in stone, so it would be easier to defend. He also told about the enchanted forest where she'd taken refuge as a girl and how he'd followed her there soon after arriving at Cahermara. And how when he held her in his arms in that ancient, sacred place, he'd known it was his destiny to fall in love with her.

As he spoke, his mother smiled, and watched him in that tender, knowing way of hers. Just being near her had made him feel better about things, and it shocked him to think he'd let his pride stop him from coming home for all these years. Only someone very foolish would do such a thing. But he'd behaved foolishly for a good share of his life. He could see that now. Being in love had changed him and made him understand what was really important.

He was telling his mother in more detail about how he'd rescued Dessia, when his father interrupted. "Bridei, your lady friend appears tired. I think you should take her to the guest chamber now. You'll have time to talk with your mother tomorrow."

"Aye. Of course." Bridei got to his feet, but before he could reach Dessia, his father had helped her from her chair. Maelgwn bowed to Dessia. "Goodnight, my lady. Sleep well."

She bowed back. Bridei took her arm and started to lead her off the dais. "Goodnight... my son," Maelgwn called out.

An older woman servant led them out of the hall. Bridei struggled to remember the woman's name. Hywel... Hefina... something like that. She was married to one of his father's men. He couldn't remember the man's name either... He was still puzzling on the matter when they reached the guest bedchamber.

As they entered and he glanced around, Dessia said, "Bridei? Bridei, have you been listening to me?"

"Of course." He focused his attention on her.

"Then what did I say just now?"

"Ummm... I don't know."

"Ah, so you weren't listening." She raised her brows. "I suppose I should get used to it. I remember my mother saying that men never listen to women."

"I'm sorry. What *did* you say?"

"I said, I think there's hope your father will warm to you after all."

"Why? What makes you think that?"

"The way he said goodnight to you. The way he looked at you. For a moment, the mask he wears... the fearless visage of the powerful, formidable king..." She raised her eyebrows again in a look of exasperation. "For a moment it slipped away and I swear I saw yearning in his eyes. And perhaps even regret."

Bridei snorted. "I think you've had too much wine and you're imagining things. The only time my father's expression warms is when he looks at my mother. And... my sisters. Although that was years ago. They might have done something to earn his animosity by now."

"Nay. I saw the way he looked at you as we left the hall. He's just too proud to reveal to you what he feels. At least for now. But give him time."

"That's what my mother says."

"Anyway." Dessia turned to look at the room. "I'm so happy to be here, to finally feel safe. And certainly I couldn't ask for a more luxurious place to spend the night." She gazed around the room, astounded by the extravagance of the furnishings. The room was almost as opulent as Conla's guest chamber. Thick colorful rugs covered the floor, and a glowing brazier sent toasty warmth into the room. Dessia gazed longingly at the huge carved wooden bed covered with a beautiful plaid blanket in shades of red and blue. And then she noticed the tapestry hanging above the bed. She drew nearer to examine it, marveling at the forest scene it portrayed. Among the thicket of swirling green threads, she spotted the golden blaze of a small fox, a shy doe hidden behind a thorn bush and a multitude of birds, so detailed that she could almost see their feathers. "It's so... real," she said, "so alive."

"My mother's work," said Bridei

"It must have taken her months, nay years, to create such a thing."

"Perhaps months, aye. But she loves it. She oversees every detail, from the dyeing of the wool to the spinning of the thread, to weaving the background cloth. Then she sits down at her table in her workroom with needle and thread, and creates a world as vivid as any tale I might tell. Indeed, her tapestries are very like tales. You were too probably too distracted in the hall to notice, but there's one on the far wall that tells the story of her and my father's life together. I'll have to show you sometime."

"To someone who can barely wield a needle well enough to hem a gown, her skill is awe-inspiring."

Bridei widened his eyes at her. "You can't sew? I'm horrified. What sort of wife will you make?"

She poked him playfully in the chest. "I can't wield a needle, but I wield a sword well enough. That's a much more valuable skill for a queen than sewing."

"Oh, aye, it is." He grabbed her hand and pulled her to him. "We're even then. My abilities with a sword are limited, which some would say doesn't make me much of a man. But I try to make up for that lack with my other gifts."

"Oh, aye, your other gifts." She pressed herself against him, smiling teasingly. Bridei kissed her deeply, then nuzzled her neck. Dessia felt her body responding. Her nipples tingled and her lower body filled with a melting heat that made her legs weak. She let out a sigh of pleasure, all thoughts of sewing, swordplay and everything else vanishing from her mind. "It's so warm in here," she whispered.

"Aye. Perhaps we should remove our clothing," Bridei responded, his voice husky.

He released her and Dessia hurried to undress. She felt breathless with desire as she stripped off her cloak, then started on her gown, shift, shoes and stockings. In moments she stood naked before him. He'd removed his tunics and shoes and was now unfastening the leather tie holding up his trews. Finally undoing the knot, he let them fall. Dessia let out her breath in anticipation. It had been so very long since she'd seen him completely naked. He was so beautiful. So perfectly, tantalizingly male.

"Do you like what you see?" he whispered.

"Oh, aye," she murmured. "Speaking of gifts," she added in a throaty voice as she stared pointedly at his up-thrust manhood. He smiled one of his beguiling smiles, then approached her and guided her hands to his phallus. Dessia sighed with delight. It felt so wonderful to touch him. To feel silky warm skin overlaying firm, solid flesh. She cupped the soft tip, and a daring thought came to her. It had almost undone her to have him kiss and tongue her nether parts. Why could she not do the same to him?

Kneeling down on the plush rug, she brought his heated flesh to her mouth. She licked the flushed engorged tip. He tasted warm and alive, faintly sweet. Intrigued, she took him in her mouth. Just the tip at first, then, closing her eyes, she drew him deeper. He filled her mouth with a delightful and tantalizing sensuality, and she sucked upon him as if he were a ripe fruit full of juice. Hearing his gasp, she leaned back so only the tip of his manhood was in her mouth, then opened her eyes and gazed up at him. His eyes were closed; his face wore an almost agonized expression. Yet it was not pain he felt, she knew, but pleasure so intense he struggled to endure it.

She swallowed more of him, entranced with her sense of power. Now it he who was in was thrall to her. He who was helpless.

She cupped his ballocks gently and drew as much of him into her mouth as possible, enjoying weight and pressure against sensitive skin. He filled her to bursting, satisfying her in a way she had not known she yearned for. Slowly, she drew back until the tip of his phallus was like a ripe succulent plum between her lips. Opening her mouth wider, she grazed him with her teeth, then sucked hard. She heard him moan. His fingers grasped her hair and he eased her away from him. "By the Goddess, but you torture me!"

"Don't you like it?" she whispered.

"Aye, I like it. If I liked it anymore I'd expire from sheer pleasure!" When she tilted her head and smiled teasingly, he murmured, "Oh, you are a sorceress. And I'm your helpless victim, ensnared in your spell."

Their eyes met. Dessia felt she could drown in the depths of his gaze, like the darkest midnight sky. "I love you," she whispered.

"And I love you, *cariad*."

"Show me. Make love to me." Her voice was pleading. She was wrong; she could never have power over this man. Even when she pleasured *him*, it only inflamed her own desire.

He drew her near and whispered into her hair, "Ah, my darling, I thought you would never ask."

He held her against him, cupping her buttocks, then sliding his fingers down to the wet, aching flesh between her legs. Lightly, he caressed her, until she sighed and shivered and her legs seemed too weak to hold her. As she swayed against him, he wrapped his arms around her torso and lifted her. Still holding her, he carried her over to the bed and sat her down on the edge of the straw mattress. Before she could lie down, he grabbed her splayed thighs and pulled her toward him, impaling her on his engorged cock.

Overcome by the sensation, she let out a half-scream.

"Hush, sweeting," he murmured against her hair. "You don't want anyone to think I'm hurting you."

"Oh... my... ohhhh!" She gave another wordless moan. She felt as if she were being rent asunder. His erection was huge, so deep within her that she felt as if he possessed her very essence. As he began to move, she was carried away on a giant wave of pulsing pleasure until her body surged into an explosive peak.

He held her tight, his sweaty face pressed against her shoulder, his breathing labored. She felt a choking rush of love. He was so dear to her, so precious. This beautiful, glorious and magical bard. Oh, how she loved him.

"I guess you liked that," he said as he caught his breath.

"You could say that," she said with a half laugh. "How many more delightful ways are there for a man and a woman to make love?"

"At least a dozen," he said. "Well, perhaps there's more, but that's all I've tried."

"And how many women have you tried these things with?"

He disengaged himself from her and lay on his back beside her. "There are some things that are better not discussed. Just consider how fortunate you are that I learned so much before I met you."

"That's true, I suppose. But I can't help wondering about all the other women you've pleasured."

He shook his head. "Don't wonder. I may have given other women pleasure, but I never gave any of them my heart. You're the first, and last, woman to ever get this close to me."

"Do you regret it?" she couldn't help asking. "Do you wish you hadn't fallen in love with me?"

"I didn't get to choose. The gods chose for me, when they answered my plea and sent the storm that brought me to the shores of your lands."

"You believe the gods sent you there?"

"Aye. When I first lay eyes upon you, I was beguiled. And then, when I held you in my arms in the Forest of Mist, I knew there could be no other woman for me." He smiled. "I worried when my plea to the gods was answered and the storm came. I thought I might have conjured my own end. And in a way I did. For the storm brought me to you, and in your arms the old Bridei died, to be replaced by a new and different man. One who loves you and would give his life, his heart and his soul for you."

"I suppose I knew you were my destiny the day you walked into the hall at Cahermara," she answered. "For that was the day I had my first Seeing. As I gazed at you, I saw behind you the image of your father's banner. The golden dragon on a background of deep red. And in that instant, I think I knew our futures were entwined."

"Entwined. They definitely are now," Bridei said, gently stroking her faintly swollen belly.

Chapter 27

"My lord Bridei! Are you awake?" Bridei sat up in the luxurious bed. The female voice called out again, "My lord. I'm sorry to wake you. But your father requests your presence in the hall."

"And when the Great Dragon requests something, one must obey," Bridei mumbled grimly as he climbed out of bed.

"What is it?" Dessia asked in a sleepy voice. "Is something wrong?"

"Not a thing, sweeting. Go back to sleep."

No need for her to get up. This was his battle to face. Besides, she must be exhausted after everything she endured yesterday, ending with their passionate lovemaking.

He dressed quickly, splashed his face with water from the ewer on the table, then went out. The maidservant waiting for him was young and sweet-faced, but unfamiliar. He told himself she would have been a small child when he left Deganwy, so there was no reason he would recognize her. She smiled at him tentatively and gestured. "This way, my lord."

As he'd guessed she would, she led him to his father's office—the Dragon's Lair, he'd heard it called. He'd been there before, of course, as a child. Back then he hadn't been afraid of his father. Now he was. He couldn't explain why. Perhaps because falling in love with Dessia had forced him to face what he felt rather than burying it away. There was a part of him that wanted his father's regard. A part of him that yearned for his father's love.

But he wouldn't die if he didn't get it, he told himself. He still had Dessia, and that was what mattered. With that thought to fortify him, he entered the office.

The place hadn't changed much after all these years. On one wall were shelves with manuscripts. On the other side, a parchment map of Gwynedd was pinned to the timber supports. His father sat at a table by the window. He turned to look at Bridei, his expression unreadable. As the moments passed, Bridei observed the small changes in his father, the evidence of ten years passing. To his surprise, the awareness of his father's aging distressed him. He didn't want to think of his father as mortal. He'd always seemed so formidable, so powerful. He was the Dragon, a beast found only in stories.

"You're much changed," his father said. "Taller than I expected. You must have grown two hand spans since you left here."

"Aye. I was a puny child. Perhaps that's why I was always so arrogant and difficult. I felt I had to do something to gain attention. How else was I to compete with my great, tall brother Rhun?"

"Was that it, then?" Maelgwn rose from his chair and approached Bridei. Bridei saw how slowly he moved, the toll a lifetime of riding and fighting had taken on his body. "You did those things to gain attention? To compete with Rhun?"

"I suppose so," Bridei answered. He wondered if his father was doing this intentionally, standing over him, trying to intimidate him with his height. Then he had the sudden awareness that his father had drawn near so he could see him clearly. There was a vague filminess in Maelgwn's blue-gray eyes, suggesting his sight was no longer sharp.

His father sighed heavily. "Your mother told me that. I should have listened. But I didn't... I don't know why."

He turned toward the window, shaking his head. Then he faced Bridei again. "Nay, I do know, although I've never admitted it to anyone, never said it aloud. You see, there were things about you that reminded me of my sister, Esylt. You have her coloring, and the kind of charm, the allure, that she did. When you hurt that girl, I was afraid you had her cruel nature, too." He sighed and shook his head again. "Esylt was cold and manipulative, cared for nothing but her own self. I feared you were the same, and so... I sent you away."

He turned and walked back to the table, fidgeting with a manuscript there. "I convinced myself that you'd done something only a man can do—raping a woman—and so that meant you were a man. But you weren't a man. You were a boy. A child. To send you away was..." He sighed again, "... unforgivable."

Bridei felt his throat grow tight. His father was doing what he'd never imagined he'd do. Maelgwn the Great was saying he'd made a mistake.

"By the time we had any more news of you, it seemed you'd managed well enough." his father continued. "You were a bard. Chieftains and kings paid you to perform for them. You were as successful and admired for what you did as any man in Britain. I thought then that I'd been wrong in every way. Wrong to think you were like Esylt. And wrong to despise myself for casting a boy out into the world alone. I wanted you to come home, but I was too proud to beg you to do so. I thought your love of your mother would eventually bring you back. And seeing how missing you wore on her, I started to resent you and mistrust you all over again."

He shrugged abruptly. "And then Rhun encountered you and brought news of you home, and still you didn't come. I began to wonder at the character of a man who would make his beloved mother suffer for the sake of his own pride."

A sudden desperation and despair came over Bridei. "You might have asked me to come home," he said tautly. "You might have sent word with Rhun that I was welcome. But you never did."

His father let out a long, drawn-out breath. "So your mother always said. She never blamed you for not coming home. She said I was the parent and therefore, it was my responsibility to repair the breach. But I couldn't see it." He took another deep breath, almost like a sob. "I was wrong, my son. I was wrong."

Bridei nodded stiffly. He didn't know what else to do. Although he wanted to embrace his father, that seemed too strange.

"Anyway. You're here at last. And you have a beautiful woman with you. And not just any beautiful woman, your mother tells me, but a queen." His father smiled suddenly. Bridei was relieved to see he had all his teeth. That was a sign of good health; he might live many more years.

"Aye, she is a queen," Bridei responded. "And as proud and strong and capable as any ruler. Alas, at this moment, she is exiled from her lands and her people." Quickly, he told his father the tale of her capture by O'Bannon, how he'd helped her escape and how they'd returned to Cahermara to find it deserted. "She would have begun gathering together her warriors to again take control of her stronghold, except we discovered she was with child. Knowing that, we thought it too dangerous to stay there, and I decided to bring her here until the child was born. As soon as she recovers, she plans to return and reclaim her lands."

Maelgwn went back to his chair. Sitting down, he said, "You'll forgive me if I seem overwhelmed, but this is a lot to take in."

"Aye. I suppose it is. In a matter of moments, you must deal with things I came to terms with over a span of months."

"When will the babe be born?"

"Near Beltaine, I think."

At that moment a young woman with reddish brown hair came rushing in. Seeing Bridei, she halted and took a step back. "Oh," she said, her blue eyes wide with surprise.

"What do you want, Anwyl?" asked Maelgwn.

Anwyl's gaze shot to her father. "I didn't realize you had a guest."

There was a hint of defiance in her tone, and when Maelgwn answered, he sounded provoked, "Regardless of whether I had a guest or not, you might have knocked."

"Sorry, Papa." Anwyl's mouth quirked as she spoke, making her apology seem almost contemptuous.

"Well, Anwyl." Bridei approached her. "You've certainly grown up to be a beauty."

She immediately tensed, reminding Bridei of a cat ready to spring. There was no doubt his oldest sister was a handful. Even the mighty Dragon would be hard put to tame her.

"Who is this?" Anwyl asked. She gave Bridei a wary look.

"If you'd come home to dinner last night you would know who our guest is," her father answered irritably.

"I was riding and lost track of time."

"Riding? Alone?" Maelgwn scowled. "I've warned you many times that it isn't safe. You should take one of the grooms at least."

"Why isn't it safe? The raiders haven't come around for years, and everyone else I might encounter is far too afraid of you to harm a hair on my head."

There was such arrogance in her manner; it reminded Bridei of himself at that age. Although she was far older than he'd been when he left Deganwy. She must be close to eighteen winters by now. Fairly old to remain unwed, especially for a princess.

"It's not safe to ride alone," Maelgwn responded. "Even if you were male, it would be risky."

"Mother goes walking in the forest alone," she said pertly.

Maelgwn sighed, and Bridei could tell this conversation had taken place many times before and his father was weary of it.

"You still haven't told me who this man is," Anwyl said with a coquettish toss of her head. When she smiled, Bridei saw she still had the dimple on her cheek he remembered from when she was little. "Is he another prince you fancy wedding me to? He's handsome enough, although I don't doubt I could beat him at swordplay."

Bridei choked on a laugh. His sister felt free to behave with a boldness that would have caused his father to thrash him.

Glancing at Maelgwn, he saw his father's face had turned an alarming hue of red.

"Nay, he's not a potential suitor!" Maelgwn exploded. "Thank the gods for that! Indeed, I no longer invite marriageable men to visit our household for fear of how you will shame me!"

"So, who is he?" Anwyl asked, studying Bridei. "There's something familiar about him, although I can't place what it is."

"I'm your brother," Bridei said, laughing. He reached out and pulled a lock of her ruddy hair, the way he used to tweak her braids. "It's Bridei, Anwyl."

She stared at him, and Bridei noted that her eyes were a stormy gray blue, like their father's. "Bridei," she said almost tenderly. The next minute, she looked furious. "How dare you stay away so long! Rhun told us you were in Britain years ago. He came home, but you never did. How could you do that to Mama? You broke her heart! And mine as well. The younger ones don't really remember you, but I do. Oh, how could you do it? How could you leave us?"

Her response was so extreme that Bridei put his hands up reflexively. "I'm sorry, Anwyl. I didn't know it mattered so much. You have three other brothers, after all."

The anger seemed to leave her. "It's not the same," she whispered. "They're nothing like you."

Bridei felt a sudden warmth wash over him. He'd never realized his sister cared so much for him. "Well, I'm back now," he said. "And I plan to stay awhile. I've brought a woman with me, a woman I intend to wed. And she's going to have a baby, so you will be an aunt. I'm certain that will please you."

"I'm already an aunt. Rhun has a baby boy."

"I didn't know that. But I've scarce had time to find out all the news. We only arrived last night."

"Who is this woman you intend to wed?" asked Anwyl.

"She's a queen," said Bridei proudly. "Queen of the Fionnlairaos. And she's nearly as bold and fearless as you are, so I think you'll like her.

Indeed, I should go and fetch her now." He nodded to his father. "We'll meet you in the hall. I'm certain Dessia will be eager to break her fast. Although she's over the worst of being sick in the morning, she still needs to eat frequently."

"The hall, aye," his father said. "We'll gather there and you can tell all of us what you've been doing for the past ten years."

* * *

Dessia watched Bridei bathe in the wooden tub in the guest bedchamber. She'd already had a chance to wash. Now she sat on a stool, carefully combing out her wet hair.

"You should have a maid do that," said Bridei.

"Rhiannon sent a girl to help me, but I sent her away. I wanted to be alone with you."

Bridei stopped washing and looked at her pointedly. "We don't have much time, my love. If you want to make the most of it, you'd best get over here."

"*That's* not why I wanted to be alone with you," Dessia answered. "I wanted to find out how things went with your father."

Bridei hesitated, trying to decide how to answer. Finally, he said, "He apologized, if you can believe that. Said he should never have sent me away. I almost got the sense that he'd missed me and was glad I'd come back."

"I'm sure he does," Dessia said. "I'm so glad you've mended the rift between you. He's not a young man any more. You don't know how long he'll be around."

"You're suggesting the great Dragon is mortal?"

"Of course, he's mortal. We all are."

"Why so melancholy, sweeting?" Bridei asked.

She shook her head. "I suppose it has to do with carrying a babe. It reminds me how precious life is. And, I have to say, coming here and meeting your family, it makes me feel sad. You've lost a lot of time that you could have had with them. But at least you're able to be with them now. My family is lost to me forever. It's a wound that never seems to heal."

"I'm your family now," said Bridei softly. "The babe and I."

Dessia got up and took Bridei a drying cloth. He stood and wrapped it around himself. As soon as he was out of the tub, he pulled her close. "My darling," he whispered. "I love you."

"I love you, too," she whispered back.

Epilogue

"Bridei, stop pacing!"

"I can't help it, Mother. I'm beside myself with worry." Bridei gestured toward the closed door of the bedchamber.

"Perhaps you should go in and see her," Rhiannon suggested. "Perhaps that would ease your mind."

Bridei froze. "That's allowed? I thought men were forbidden from being part of these things."

Rhiannon smiled. "It's not the usual way. But your father was there for your birth. Anyway, I wasn't suggesting you stay. I just thought if you saw her now, when she's uncomfortable but not miserable, it might make you feel better."

"If only you hadn't told me there are two babes. You know such births are risky."

His mother drew near and squeezed his shoulder soothingly. "I thought you should be prepared. If it's any comfort, remember that I bore twins and all was well."

"But you —" Bridei took an anguished breath. "You're special... blessed of the Goddess. No one ever believed She would take you."

"Your father certainly feared for my life when you were born. That's why he ended up in the bedchamber. He said couldn't stand around waiting helplessly."

"Were you afraid?" Bridei asked. "Did you think you would die?"

"Nay. I never did. I'd been through so much by then." A faint sadness crossed her face. Then she smiled at him, that radiant lovely smile that always eased his heart. "I shouldn't tell you this. It's probably best if you do suffer and worry, much as your wife has to suffer. But... I've seen a vision of your children, Bridei. I think the Seeing was of the two she's carrying now. But even if it isn't, even if they both perish, it means I'm certain Dessia will give you two children at some point in the future. I've seen them. A boy and a girl."

"With red hair?" Bridei asked. He gripped his mother's arm tightly. "Did the children you saw have red hair?"

"Aye."

He let out his breath. "I've seen them, too, when I was in the Forest of Mist." He shook his head in amazement. "Should I tell Dessia?"

She smiled at him. "Just reassure her that all will be well. That's all she needs to know for now. She has a long night ahead of her." Easing from his grasp, his mother headed toward the bedchamber door.

* * *

Bridei held the side of the large currach and looked out at the vast stretch of gray blue waves disappearing into the horizon. "I can't believe I'm doing this," he said. "There was a time when I vowed I'd never set foot in a boat ever again."

"Your last crossing wasn't so bad, was it?" Dessia rocked back and forth as she spoke, moving in the age-old dance meant to soothe the two babies she carried, one in each arm.

Bridei took one of the infants from her, snuggling his son against his chest. "Nay, it wasn't so bad, because I slept most of the crossing. I doubt I'll be able to do that this time." He looked down at his solemn-eyed son and smiled. "You won't let me sleep, Darragh, will you? You haven't done so the last few nights, so I doubt this day will be any different."

"They're teething," Dessia said. "Not a good time for this, perhaps, but I didn't want to wait any longer. We were fortunate last time, but everyone says winter crossings can be dangerous."

Bridei nodded. His heart wrenched whenever he thought of the potential dangers ahead of them. Bridei felt sure Dessia's people would rally around her as soon as they had news of her return, but they might still have to fight a few battles to retake Cahermara and gain control of her family's lands. But it would be much easier to do these things with the aid of the warband Maelgwn had lent them. Two score of Cymry warriors massed on the beach behind them, saying their goodbyes to their families. This time it wouldn't be one boat that crossed the Irish Sea, but more than a dozen.

Bridei's heart squeezed as he thought about how generous his father had been, offering them not only men but horses. Farther down the beach, two of Maelgwn's most experienced men were trying to coax a mist-colored stallion and mare into a huge currach. They were the beginning of the herd of horses that Bridei hoped would one day graze the rich green hills around Cahermara. Someday in the future, the Fionnlairaos would once again stand for "the tribe of the white horse".

Darragh began to fuss, and Bridei stroked his little round head, covered with only a few sparse reddish gold curls. Then he turned to look at Dessia. Since becoming a mother she seemed even more beautiful. His heart squeezed with love as he looked at her, and at his rosy-cheeked daughter, Angharad, cradled in her arms. "We're going back, Dessia," he said. "Back to reclaim your kingdom."

She drew near and embraced him. "My heart may belong to Ireland, Bridei. But my soul is yours."

The End

Dear Readers,

In 1991, soon after starting work at a public library, I decided to write a historical romance. In choosing my time period, I considered my favorite historical novels: the Merlin series by Mary Stewart (*The Crystal Cave*, *The Hollow Hills*, etc.), *Sword at Sunset* by Rosemary Sutcliffe, *Here Be Dragons* by Sharon Kay Penman. They were all set at least partially in Wales, and two of the stories take place in the time of King Arthur.

I went to the Wyoming State Library, which back then had a good British history and literature collection, and began my research. Everything I read reinforced my fascination with this era. And then, in some obscure dusty tome discussing the historical evidence for King Arthur, I read about a monk named Gildas, who had written a manuscript in the early 6th century called *On the Conquest and Ruin of Britain*. The manuscript was not a historical account of the era, but a heated condemnation of five kings, who Gildas blamed for pretty much everything wrong in his time period. Chief among them was Maelgwn, king of Gwynedd, who Gildas refers to as "o, thou dragon of the island." Gildas account of Maelgwn was pretty venomous, but his words also revealed a larger-than-life and intriguingly complex man. I instantly knew I'd found my hero, and inspired by these historical tidbits, I began writing.

The "dark ages" are called that for a good reason, as very little is known about this time period. The few literate individuals in this era, like Gildas, had very definite agendas and didn't write much of anything meaningful to a modern historian, let alone a novelist. But as much as I struggled to get the details and history right, I had no problem with my characters. From the moment I imagined them, Maelgwn and Aurora were real and alive to me, and their story carried me away to an enthralling world of love, hatred, sex and violence.

Having visited this vibrant, passionate world, I found I didn't want to leave it. And so one book evolved into two. Then I realized I had to tell Rhun's story...and then Bridei's. As I wrote the ending chapters of *The Dragon Bard*, Anwyl appeared: fiery, stubborn and rebellious, and I knew this daughter of Maelgwn would have to have a book as well. So the story of the Dragon of the Island doesn't end with this book, but continues on, likely as long as I have the energy and imagination to keep writing.

Happy reading,

Mary Gillgannon

CDARY GILLGANNON

Mary Gillgannon writes romance novels set in the dark ages, medieval and English Regency time periods and fantasy and historical novels with Celtic influences. Her print books have been published in Russia, China, the Netherlands and Germany. Raised in the Midwest, she now lives in Cheyenne, Wyoming where she works full-time at the Laramie County Library.

She is married and has two grown children. When not working or writing she enjoys gardening, traveling and reading, of course! She always enjoys hearing from readers. You can write her at P.O. Box 2052, Cheyenne, WY 82003, or contact her through her website: http://marygillgannon.com

www.ingramcontent.com/pod-product-compliance
Lightning Source LLC
Chambersburg PA
CBHW020916200626
46814CB00001BA/363